For Dominique

THE HYPNOTIST

Enjoy!

Gordon Snider

The Hypnotist

Helm Publishing

For information address:
Helm Publishing
P.O. Box 9691
Treasure Island FL 33706

www.publishersdrive.com

ISBN 978-0-9841397-3-6

Printed in the United States of America

CHAPTER ONE

Marta Baldwin had always believed she could tell a lot about people by looking at their hands. Not that she believed in reading palms. Lifelines and fortune-telling did not suit her practical nature. No, it was the texture of the skin that interested her and how the fingers flowed and expressed themselves. Were they bold? Were they elegant, calloused or tanned? Or, as in the case of the hands she was studying now, were they merely soft and insipid?

The hands belonged to Angela Cummings, a woman who represented everything Marta found displeasing about San Francisco's nouveau riche society. In her opinion, Angela was vapid and boring, with little intellect or curiosity beyond choosing a gown for her next formal ball or dinner party. Occasionally, Angela liked to go, in her words, "south of Market Street" in the guise of doing social work. It was something many of society's elite did. Their contributions of time and money were welcome, of course, but Marta couldn't help wondering if their participation was worth the effort.

Angela was a perfect case in point. She looked as if she had been interrupted on her way to tea. Her hair had been fussed over until its red highlights glistened in the sun. She wore a full-length, silk dress, the back of which protruded outward in a series of cascading folds that reflected the very latest in ladies' fashions, and she held a matching parasol in her bejeweled hand. Her nails had been carefully manicured, yet her hands had no grace. The one holding the parasol clung to it as if she feared a sudden wind might whisk it away, while the free one fluttered about her body like an intoxicated butterfly.

In contrast to Angela's attire, Marta prided herself on wearing practical clothes: trousers instead of dresses, comfortable shoes and wool blouses that could stand the rigors of her daily forays into the warrens of tiny shacks in the Mission District. Marta could have used a manicure herself, she admitted grudgingly, but there was no time. Besides, she got her hands dirty when she worked and she needed to keep her nails short so they wouldn't break off.

Marta shifted her weight from one foot to the other, anxious to get started on her day's busy schedule. She was on her way that morning to visit two families on the verge of becoming destitute. They were families who needed practical advice on how to manage meager incomes earned from toiling long hours in a weaver's mill, not pleasantries and a few coins that would last less than a day if their husbands got hold of them. For Marta, the shanty town "south of Market Street" was her life's work. For someone like Angela, poverty was little more than a way to pass the day before dressing for dinner and sharing stories with friends about the deplorable conditions of the poor.

As Marta observed Angela, she couldn't help thinking about the words of a notorious critic who had described San Francisco's turn-of-the-century rich as "mediocre people with too much money to spend and too much time on their hands, who dressed in peacock fashion so as to show themselves to their best advantage." Marta thought the description suited Angela perfectly. Of course, Angela *was* married to one of the richest men in the city, a young railroad mogul named Herbert Cummings whose father had been instrumental in bringing those gleaming rails west, but that did not impress Marta. She knew it was her husband's inherited wealth that gave Angela entry into San Francisco's upper echelons of society, not her own money or talents.

After what seemed an interminable length of time, Marta finally bid Angela a good day and hurried on her way. She never walked anywhere slowly, but her crisp strides that morning told the world she was out of sorts and that her head was blazing with displeasure. Normally, the trolley cars clanging their way along Market Street would have brightened her mood, but not today, nor did the paper boys hawking their morning editions in their sing-song voices.

Marta knew Angela was the cause of her ill temper. It wasn't so much Angela's cavalier attitude or impractical clothes that had riled her. It was the name Angela had used to address her. Angela had called her Matilda, and while Matilda might be her given name, Marta hated it. The Cummings woman probably did not know this, but Marta was rankled nonetheless. So, there she was charging along the uneven sidewalks, muttering to herself and knowing she was acting the complete fool. Why, she wondered, did she let that silly woman aggravate her so?

Marta was so lost in her thoughts, her eyes fixed on avoiding the street's potholes and other imperfections and her feet moving as rapidly as her five-foot-two body would permit, that she hardly noticed the wild-looking, angular man approaching from the opposite direction until he blocked her way. He had halted in the middle of the pavement, forcing Marta to do the same. She found herself looking at a willowy figure that reminded her of a birch tree swaying in the blustery winds that regularly blew off the bay. His unkempt hair and patchy beard had the look of someone who had tried to trim them too quickly with nervous hands. He wore an ill-fitting, black coat that was too tight to be buttoned in front and an amber ring that flashed brilliantly when he waved his hand in front of her face.

She instantly noted how the hand's bony fingers splayed outward in a fashion that made the hand appear tormented and she wanted

3

to look away. But she couldn't take her eyes off of the ring. It flashed and danced before her with a mesmerizing guile that held her spellbound. It was only when the man began jabbering at her in a language she did not recognize that she managed to look up. She was immediately absorbed by the most intense, stark pair of eyes she had ever seen. They never wavered or blinked, and they bore into hers with such force that Marta felt heat building behind her pupils, a heat that burned her skull.

An incredible wave of euphoria swept over her. She became aware of images she had never seen before, but felt certain were lost memories from her youth. One image, a smiling woman, streaked across the horizon of her thoughts with the radiance of a shooting star. Somehow, Marta knew it was her mother, but that was impossible. Her mother had died giving birth to her, something that had always pressed on her conscience with the weight of a great stone. Marta had seen a picture of her mother; her father had always kept it on the mantle when he was still alive. The image she saw now did not match the one in the photo, yet Marta realized the beaming face could be no other and the woman was telling Marta that everything was all right, that it wasn't her fault her mother had died. Marta instantly raised her hand to her neck and fingered the pendant hanging there. It had been her mother's and Marta had worn it ever since her father had given it to her when she was a small child. Not only was it a remembrance of the mother she had never known, it was also a reminder of how quickly the ill winds of fate can change one's fortunes.

Marta was vaguely aware that the strange man standing before her was somehow manipulating her thoughts, and that her mind no longer responded to her will, but she didn't mind. The feelings spawned by the stranger were so enthralling she was ready to follow wherever he would have her go, an idea she found both captivating and frightening. Clearly, the man's powers were extraordinary. They made her shiver with anticipation and fear at the same time.

Slowly, Marta's brain grew darker and a feeling of claustrophobia engulfed her. It was as if her mind had become trapped inside a cavernous space filled with glacier-cold temperatures that pressed in on her from all sides and sucked her beneath her consciousness. There didn't seem to be any air to breathe. It was similar to a feeling she had once experienced as a child playing at the beach when an unexpected wave had crashed over her head and sent her tumbling beneath the surf. She felt as though she was plummeting now and found herself holding her breath and flailing her arms in a desperate effort to return to the surface of her mind.

Even as she struggled, Marta understood that she was still standing on the pavement, unmoving, but that knowledge didn't help. Something was pushing her under the cold waves washing through her mind. She felt certain if she didn't regain control of her senses she would drown. Her lungs were already burning from holding her breath so long.

She was being swept along quickly now in the currents racing inside her brain. Her mind grew numb and she stopped flailing her arms as resignation set in. She no longer had the will to resist the forces pressing against her. The lack of oxygen was causing her mind to shut down. Time for her seemed to end.

This is what it is like to die, she thought. *In a few moments death will overtake me, and I will drown in an ice-cold world without air.* In fact, Marta could already *see* death's long arms snaking towards her with irresistible promises of warmth and comfort. Before death's arms could envelope her, however, a survival instinct took hold and pulled her free from the surging currents. She shook her head to clear her mind. Her will grew stronger as she focused her thoughts on defeating the forces trying to submerge her. Slowly, her will to live surmounted her sense of helplessness and she swam back to the surface of her consciousness. Just when she believed she could hold her breath no longer, just when she was certain that every last drop of oxygen had expired from her lungs, she broke through the barrier that had held her captive and gulped the deliciously sweet air waiting for her there.

Marta shivered uncontrollably as she tried to grasp what had just happened. The world spun around her with the recklessness of a child's toy top launched by a piece of string. Her body shook so hard she couldn't maintain her balance and she staggered to a nearby wall for support. Gradually, her world stopped spinning and her breathing returned to normal.

Marta became aware of passing people gawking at her. One man offered assistance but she waved him off. She kept her eyes focused on the pavement until her shivering body quieted, then steeled herself and looked up, only to discover that the man blocking her path was gone. *What an odd fellow he had been*, she thought, *with his gangling legs and waving arms*. He had spoken to her, but in a language that sounded like gibberish. Just the thought of the man's blazing eyes made her shiver again. Their power to control her had been absolute. But it was the tortured-looking hand that stood out most clearly in her mind. It had been an unnatural hand, one that should have frightened her, yet it hadn't. Because of the amber ring, she decided, the ring whose light danced with the brilliance of liquid gold. It had so beguiled her that nothing else mattered.

How long had she been standing there in her stupor? It seemed an hour or more had flown by, yet when she consulted her timepiece, she was shocked to see less than five minutes had passed. The strange man had disappeared like a wisp of morning fog chased by the sun. Had he been real, or just a brief moment of insanity? The entire episode had been so dream-like she might have imagined it, except for those hypnotic eyes. When she remembered how they had held hers in their viselike grip, how they had torn her gaze away from the ring and almost melted her will to live, she knew the man had been all too real.

A shudder rippled through her as she thought about it. She had never experienced the raw fear of dying like that before. Instinctively, she knew that, on some level, it had been a near-death experience. She had almost passed on to another world but whether physical or spiritual she couldn't tell. One thing was certain. The experience had left her too shaken to continue her work that day. Her mind still spun with trauma and her lungs still burned with memories of frozen wastelands without air. All she wanted to do was retreat to the sanctuary of her home and lie down awhile. She scolded herself for acting like one of those silly society women having an attack of the vapors, but it couldn't be helped. Her encounter had sapped her strength to the point of fainting, and that she refused to do.

Marta turned around and headed back to the small office she maintained near the Mission District. She would have to ask her assistant, Missy, to carry on for the day and to reset her schedule for tomorrow, something she had never done before. It grated on her to abandon her commitments, even for a day, but the strange encounter still left her shaking whenever she remembered it. There was little choice but to reschedule. It was either that or leave her charges to the likes of Angela Cummings. That was not something she was prepared to do.

The office was a thimble-sized space barely large enough to house a desk and filing cabinet, but it gave her Pacific Aid Society the physical presence needed to serve those less fortunate souls who eked out livings making shirts for a dollar a dozen or cigars for five dollars a week. Marta couldn't help shaking her head when she thought about the plight of those she helped. Many families had to survive on fourteen dollars a week or less and that was where Marta's services were truly needed. Other social organizations ran soup kitchens and taught simple trades, such as sewing, at local churches or other public facilities, but Marta visited the tenements on a daily basis and helped families learn how to budget their meager earnings. She also delivered basic staples, such as coal for cooking and winter heat and potatoes, but it was learning to budget their money that she felt did the most good. It was possible to cover the basics such as food, rent, lighting and heat, all for the meager earnings these people received if the wife could only control the purse strings and keep her husband's hands out of the money jar. Marta tried to sit down with husband and wife together, but she usually found it more practical to put the money in the hands of the woman. She had found from experience that men often faced temptations, such as drink and opium. Those two vices could quickly undermine the best of plans.

Marta paid for all the expenses of her Pacific Aid Society out of her own pocket, including the office rent and a small salary for Missy. She was able to do that thanks to a monthly income from her father's estate. The amount was not large by society's standards, but it was enough to support her causes and to meet her personal needs, which were fairly simple compared to the Angela Cummings in the world.

When she entered the office, she found Missy gone on some errand, so she left a note and hurried to Gough Street where she caught a street car to Pacific Heights, a fashionable neighborhood with fanciful Victorian houses that rubbed elbows with the less embellished Edwardian architecture of nearby Cow Hollow. She had always loved her two-story home with its gabled roof and tall windows, but lately she had found her anxiety rising whenever she returned there. Her father had left her and her older brother, Samuel, a reasonable inheritance when he had passed away five years before. He had earned a small fortune in the 1850s selling supplies to those seeking their fortunes in the Klondike gold rush and then investing the money in a successful shipping business.

As the older brother, Samuel had taken charge of the family business and finances, an arrangement Marta found increasingly uncomfortable. Samuel had never shown more than a passing interest in their father's affairs and his unpredictable behavior seemed ill-suited to managing anything more complex than a newsboy's stand. She feared his inattention to the business would have disastrous consequences, but shipping was a man's world and every time she tried to put her nose in the company's books she was rebuffed.

Like her comparison to Angela, there was a great divide between the lifestyles of Marta and her brother. She had dedicated herself to helping the poor while Samuel spent much of his time drinking and socializing with his friends, fellow well-to-do young men who lacked the money to belong to the highest echelons of society, but who still craved to be counted among the wealthy and spent money accordingly. She did not care about his nightly sojourns so long as there was enough money to cover their home and living expenses.

Whether it was nine dollars a week or nine hundred, it didn't matter. The principle remained the same. If income did not match expenses, it was only a matter of time before the money ran out.

Samuel promised to review the status of two missing shipments, but Marta found him still lounging in his bathrobe, coffee cup in hand, when she entered the house. Despite her confused state of mind, her teeth clamped shut in anger. The night before, she had heard him banging around the house long past midnight. Now, he sat in a stuffed, living room chair with one leg draped over an arm. He yawned and stretched with the contentment of a large cat. Marta wondered anew at how two such different siblings could emerge from the same parents.

"You were out late last night," she said matter-of-factly. Normally, Marta would have spoken more sharply, but her combative forces had been drained by the harrowing incident that morning. She could only look at her brother in disbelief. When he gave her an insolent glare, she grasped the tiny amulet that hung from her neck and began rubbing it, something she often did when she was upset with him.

"I was at my club," he responded with a huff, "although I don't know what business that is of yours." He shifted uncomfortably in his chair and sipped his coffee to disguise his annoyance.

It had always seemed to Marta that her brother had benefited in ways that detracted from her own life. He enjoyed the privileges of manhood, while she struggled to overcome the handicaps of being a woman. She did not even have the right to vote, another cause to which she had dedicated herself. He had commandeered every bit of the height she lacked, and at six feet he made quite a comparison to her small stature. Even her brother's pale skin, blue eyes and blond hair contrasted sharply with her olive complexion, black hair and sapphire eyes, which she was certain had been inherited from her great-grandfather's Italian wife. She had once seen a small, painted portrait of her great-grandmother and knew at once the source of her curious traits, which had lain dormant for two generations before erupting in all their gypsy glory in Marta.

It wasn't her inherited features that bothered her now, however.

9

It was the spectacle of a lazy brother who would expect her to wait on him like royalty. But when she thought about those fierce eyes that had so nearly captured her in their web, her anger dissipated and she gave her brother a quick smile.

He raised his eyebrows at her unexpected warmth and his defiant expression dissolved into one of curiosity. "You're home. How come?" A note of uncertainty crept into his voice. They both knew she should be at her office or visiting one of the thousands of tiny wooden houses crammed into the back streets south of Market Street.

"I had a rather terrifying run-in just now with a man on the street." The brisk walk had produced a thin film of sweat on Marta's forehead. She wiped her brow with a small handkerchief she kept in the pocket of her trousers. The strange eyes she had just encountered haunted her memory and she trembled.

"Terrifying, how?" Samuel swung his leg off the arm of his chair and shifted his weight forward.

Marta was pleased to hear a small measure of concern in his voice. He might not be the ideal sibling, but his instincts as an older, protective brother reassured her.

"It's hard to describe. I'd never seen the man before, and believe me, I would remember him if I had. He was very strange. Had an ill-kept look about him that reminded me of an unmade bed. Rumpled clothes that didn't fit. Unwashed. That sort of thing."

"Sounds like your typical vagabond to me." Samuel had never cared for Marta's work and the hint of disdain that now slid into his voice irritated her. She ignored it, however, and continued.

"He had the oddest eyes I have ever seen. They seemed to bore right through me. Oh, and he wore a large, amber ring on his right hand, which he kept waving in front of me while he muttered words I couldn't understand. I . . . I was completely under his spell," she stammered, "but when I returned to my senses, he was gone."

Samuel chuckled and began inspecting his finger nails, an annoying habit he often displayed when he was bored with a topic. "Sounds like one of your female fainting spells to me. Don't tell me you're going to start acting like those silly society women over at the Emanuel Sisterhood. They are always near fainting over their encounters in the shanty towns where you work. I thought you disliked being associated with their sort."

Marta felt the heat rising in her face. She bristled at her brother's unsubtle hint that she was nothing more than a member of the weaker sex, but his reference to the Emanuel Sisterhood galled her even more. That was where Angela Cummings spent her time and it was precisely the kind of frivolous organization that Marta disliked.

"Well, thank you for your *understanding*." She emphasized the last word to be sure her brother caught the irony in her voice. "It's nice to know I can depend on you for support." With that, she whirled around and left the room, but her anger could not deflect her continued feelings of unease. Whatever that odd man had wanted, she sensed he had failed to achieve it. She made a mental note to watch out for him when she made her rounds.

CHAPTER TWO

During the next few days, Marta kept a sharp eye out for the stranger who had accosted her, but when he failed to reappear, she slowly pushed the bizarre incident into the recesses of her mind. It was nearly springtime, a time of year that always enthralled her with its promise of fresh flowers and warmer days, a time when she felt her energy and excitement rising. Things always seemed more optimistic in springtime.

One particular morning gleamed with the brilliance of polished brass. There was no sign of the rain clouds or fog that so often settled over the city. The cheerful day buoyed Marta's spirits to the point of exuberance and reminded her of all the reasons she loved living in San Francisco. Life there bustled with an energy and hopefulness rarely found in other cities. The place had a gold rush feel about it. It was a noisy city filled with a maelstrom of life. People were more independent in thought than their eastern brethren. There was a rush to invent things. Fads became fashions. Theater and cultural development were embraced. The city was growing so rapidly and was already the ninth most populous in the country. Not bad for a place located in the cradle of the western frontier.

One of Marta's favorite pastimes was watching the cable cars clanging their way along Market Street and climbing the steep grades to the surrounding hilltops. Sometimes, she paid the five cent fare simply to ride up the hills. She enjoyed watching the grip man hammering his foot gong and throwing back the large lever that engaged the cable. Many of the cars began their run from the new Ferry Building by the bay, which was easily identified by the clock tower that rose into the sky with the majesty of London's famous Big Ben. Unlike London, however, the Ferry Building was surrounded by busy wharves where eager hands unloaded everything from coal and lumber to elegant, finished goods from the five-mast schooners, brigs, sloops and other ships arriving daily from ports of call around the world.

Horse drawn carriages and wagons still offered the most practical way to move about, although the horses were becoming increasingly spooked by the new automobiles sputtering and backfiring along the boulevards. Flat tires and breakdowns were a common occurrence with these newly-invented machines. The standing bet was trying to guess how many times the driver would have to make a repair during a day's outing. Still, they were becoming more prevalent and Marta knew the auto was here to stay.

Even the layout of San Francisco's busy streets stamped the city with its own unique flair. The streets south of Market Street, where Marta spent much of her time working, formed orderly rows of perpendicular avenues, similar to those found in any other city, but the streets on the north side veered off at forty-five degree angles which created pie-shaped wedges of property wherever they intersected Market Street. Life was also divided by Market Street. To the north lay the hilltop mansions of the Stanfords, Crockers, Floods, Hopkins and, of course, Cummings. The south side was inhabited by people of moderate incomes, as well as by the poorer districts with which Marta was so familiar.

It took only a brief ride up Market Street on the cable car to see the city's vigor. The street teemed with men in suits and top hats, women in long dresses, wagons and carriages, the occasional rider on horseback, newsboys waving their papers, and the new automobiles which delighted in seeing how close they could come to the cable cars without hitting them as they swooped across the tracks.

The city's growing wealth was evident as well, although many easterners still viewed San Francisco as nothing more than an outpost in the middle of the Wild West. New hotels, such as the New California on Bush Street, the Occidental on Montgomery Street, and the Grand and Palace hotels on Market Street, greeted visitors with brilliant chandeliers and posh interiors. French restaurants like Marchand's and Maison Tortoni served frogs legs and other delicacies for as little as fifty cents. There was also Zinkand's, a German restaurant that was a favorite with the after-theater supper crowd as well as Italian, Turkish and Mexican establishments. New office buildings sprouted up with the persistence of uncut weeds. No better example could be found than at the corners of Third, Kearny and Geary Streets, where the red sandstone and brick Chronicle building, the Spanish-style Examiner and the fifteen-story Call building, capped by a dome, all competed for news readers and advertisers for their respective papers.

The stores on Kearny Street displayed the newest fashions in silk dresses, coats, hats and decorating items, but Marta had little interest in them. She left those establishments to Angela and her friends. The bookstores, antique furniture stores and photography shops on Post Street were more to her liking. She especially enjoyed the artistry that was now possible with a camera and often spent time gazing at the miraculous, black-and-white images.

In the midst of all these sights and sounds stood Chinatown, a place so draped in mystery, few white people dared to venture there. Those who did described a world so ancient in its culture, it was nearly impossible to fathom how such a place could exist in the middle of a modern city. Marta had heard about the powerful

Six Companies with colorful names like Hip Kat, Hop Wo and Sam Yup that ran the enclave as if it were a territory in China. More frightening were the infamous tongs, organized gangs that terrorized the Chinese people. They ran the opium dens and imported slaves, called "sing song" girls, to work as prostitutes. When feuds erupted, they hired hatchet men to settle them. It was claimed a hatchet man could be hired to kill someone for as little as forty cents.

And, of course, there were San Francisco's crown jewels, its noble hilltops, which rose majestically above the city. No other feature was as charming or dramatic. The hills were so steep it was said that "a dime dropped on the crest of California Street would gather enough speed to kill a horse on Market Street, unless it hit a Chinaman on Grant Avenue." Nob Hill was the most famous of these breathtaking retreats, due to its palatial residences, but the surrounding hills were equally colorful. There was, for example, Russian Hill, known as the haunt for artists and writers and Marta's favorite, Telegraph Hill, which could only be scaled on foot. Its panoramic views of the city, shorelines, and mountain ranges beyond the bay made the climb rewarding beyond imagination.

Marta wished she had the time to climb Telegraph Hill that morning but her schedule would not permit it so she headed for her small office instead. Missy was already busy preparing the day's schedule and greeted Marta with her Scottish brogue. Missy's musical accent delighted Marta and she never grew tired of listening to the way Missy shortened some words and lengthened others. "Doing" would be shortened to "doin'," for example, while "person" would be stretched into "perrson."

"It's about tyme you got here," Missy said with a quick smile that scattered her freckles and let Marta know she was glad to see her. "I think you're goin' to be busy todye."

Missy was an abandoned girl Marta had hired two years earlier more from pity than need, but it had proven to be a wise decision. Now seventeen, Missy doted on Marta with the loyalty of a younger sister and ran the office with an exuberant energy that not only kept things humming smoothly but gave Marta more time to spend working with families in their homes. Missy had arrived alone from Scotland. Her father was supposed to be waiting for her when she landed, but he failed to show and Missy found herself lost in a city a hundred times larger than her small village back home. She was lured by a man promising her work as an entertainer, but she quickly discovered the only entertaining she was expected to do was on her back in one of the local brothels south of Market Street. She managed to escape before being put to work by hiding in a basket filled with dirty laundry in the back of a wagon. Then she began roaming the streets in search of lodgings and food. Without money, all she could hope for were handouts at places like the Emmanuel Sisterhood. Marta found her sleeping in a filthy hovel without water or heat on the edges of the Mission District.

Eventually, they had located Missy's father, drunk and uncooperative, in one of the many dimly lit bars along the waterfront docks in an area known as the Barbary Coast. Marta had seen his kind enough times to know he could never take responsibility for his daughter. He only worked when he needed. There were plenty of jobs along the docks to keep him employed, but the money soon disappeared in the drafts of beer and glasses of whiskey he poured down his throat. The night they found him in a bar called The Bohemian, he was so bleary-eyed it took a great deal of shouting over the din of the place before he understood Missy was his daughter. A moment of recognition eventually flared in his eyes, but it died quickly as he returned to his drink. Missy left the bar in tears and never tried to contact him again. Marta became her family and found a room for her to rent in the Mission district.

In the two years she had worked for Marta, Missy was transformed from a slovenly waif with rawboned cheeks into a perky young woman whose red hair tumbled in natural curls about her winsome face. She was just slightly taller than Marta and exhibited the same feisty disposition as her employer. The two made quite a pair when they ventured forth together. There was a tough, inner strength in Missy that Marta particularly admired. She knew that particular strength had saved Missy from the brothel and helped her survive until Marta found her. Only five years older, Marta *did* feel like an older sister, a role she very much enjoyed, given the lack of either a mother or female sibling in her life.

"There's a bit of news that's botherin' me." Missy gathered her freckles in her furrowed brow as she spoke. "The McClain family you've been helpin' says their daughter's gone missin'. Been four days now without a word. Some say there's a demon what's taken her. A demon that haunts the Mission District."

"Oh, Missy, that's just an old wives' tale." Marta waved her hand dismissively as she spoke. Missy may have blossomed into an intelligent young woman, but Marta knew she was still naïve enough to swallow the silly stories often passed around in the tenements. Like Missy, many of these people came from the old country and brought their folklore with them. "I'm sure there's a rational explanation. She probably ran off somewhere." It was not uncommon for older children from poor families to strike out on their own, but even as Marta suggested this possibility, she wondered if it was likely. The girl had always seemed sensible. Not the kind to just leave without telling her parents.

"Beggin' your pardon, but I don' think so," Missy responded as if reading Marta's thoughts. "There's people who've seen the demon in broad daylight. He bewitches you, then spirits you away so you're never seen again."

Marta had only been half listening as she looked at her appointment calendar, but something in Missy's reply caught her attention. She straightened and looked at her companion more closely. Missy was busy studying her feet, which she often did when Marta disagreed with her.

Marta knew how hard it was for Missy to assert herself, despite her feisty personality, and she softened her tone of voice. "How do you mean, bewitches? What happens?"

"I don' know exactly. Some say he has magical hands that can cast spells. That sort of thing. All I know is the McClain's girl hasn't been seen for some tyme, now, and people say she's gone for good." Missy kept her eyes cast towards the floor as she spoke, aware of Marta's skepticism.

But Marta was listening intently, now. Images of waving hands and an amber ring flashed before her. Even as memories, the images had the power to cloud her mind, and she found herself inhaling as much air as she could, fearful that at any moment she would be drawn back into the cavernous world where she had been so nearly trapped. Was it possible there was some connection between the man who had accosted her on the street and the demon described by Missy? *Surely not*, she thought. Yet, she couldn't deny the magical hands that had so bewitched her. Marta shivered involuntarily as she considered the similarities between her experience and the story told by Missy. "Does this demon of yours wear an amber ring?" she asked almost tentatively.

"I don' know about a ring, but some claim the eyes of the devil can be seen flashin' from his hand. They know it's the devil because it's such an unnatural light."

More shivers slithered down Marta's spine. She had to rub her hands together to keep them from shaking. There could be no doubt that someone very real was out there roaming the streets. She had faced him and barely escaped. Was he the demon of whom Missy spoke? Was such a thing possible? Her first instinct was to call the police, but she knew that would be futile. Children approaching adulthood went missing all of the time in the tenements and stories about demons would only elicit chuckles and admonishments not to listen to fairytales. Like her, the police would consider it nothing more than a silly superstition.

Marta no longer doubted Missy's story, however. She had seen the demon with her own eyes and she knew something was out there, something very evil.

CHAPTER THREE

My name is Harold Prigg. I wake every day to that name, just as I do now, and am reminded of its power to ruin lives. It is an abominable name, one that attracted school bullies and made girls giggle when I was young. As I lie in my bed, I remember how the bullies chased me and threw stones and how the girls smirked at me from behind their books. I should have had a sanctuary at home but it was as empty of understanding as the schoolyard. If I came home crying, my father belt-whipped me for acting like a baby. If I whimpered to dear old mum, she stared cross-eyed at me as if I was crazy. But she was the crazy one, not me.

Cooking odors tease my nose. The odors fill my drowsy mind with long-ago images of mum and I turn in my bed. What adventures we had, mum and I! She would take off with me to nearby towns where we would hole up in hotels until her money ran out. At those times we lived like fugitives. I found the experiences exhilarating. And all the while she stormed and screamed at me about what a horrible man my father was. She shouted until spittle flew from her mouth and her rage exhausted her. Then she sat on the bed shaking uncontrollably and muttering to herself. I agreed with her about my father and grew to hate him, not so much because of mum's violent words as for those whippings. Something else happened during those flights from home, something both frightening and wonderful. Voices began speaking to me inside my head. At first, I wondered if I was as crazy as my mum. The voices were mild in the beginning, but they became stronger as my anger towards my father grew. At times, they left me shaking and muttering to myself, just like mum.

Other voices are assailing me now, the chirping, high-pitched voices of my Chinese neighbors, who are chattering in rapid-fire exchanges outside my door. They remind me of squealing mice and I slowly move my head to one side half-expecting to see the furry animals that often visit at night. They like the straw that escapes from my mattress and they leave droppings behind to let me know they have visited. None are evident this morning, however, and my eyes continue their slow progress around the room. Dirty clothes are strewn across the dusty, straw-littered floor. Other than my bed, which is pressed against the wall, the only other objects are a round wooden table cluttered with yesterday's dishes, a chair squeezed into one corner beside a grimy sink, a toilet and a wooden chest that holds my few belongings. The bed is too short for my lanky body but I don't mind. I always sleep with my legs pulled to my stomach, a position I have assumed each night since I was a boy.

That's because I outgrew my bed at a young age. But height had its advantages. I soon grew taller than the bullies and when I turned on them and raised my fists they fled as bullies always do when faced with uncertain odds. The bullies outran me, just as I had them. Fear is a wonderful motivator. Father, on the other hand, had been weakened by a bout of flu that killed a great many people. He could not outrun me. When the voices riled me, I whipped him with a tree branch.

Ah, and then there were the girls. I had gained more than height, you see. I had also gained a special talent, one I first learned about at a circus sideshow where I saw a man hypnotize people from the audience. The performance mesmerized me. I had already developed a glare that warned the boys and scared the girls and when I approached the hypnotist after his performance, he was intrigued by me. I spent every available moment with him until the circus left town. By then, I had learned what he could teach me, and I felt no need to follow.

The voices continued to clamor in my head until I decided to test my new powers on my worst tormentor, a girl named Shirley who I had come to despise with a particular vehemence. One day, I cornered her alone on a dirt road behind the school and willed her into a trance. Her initial anger at my rude behavior melted away and, to my amazement, her shoulders sagged as she stood there waiting for me to do with her what I wanted. I won't bother with what happened that day except to say that I knew I had found my calling.

I soon learned the boys were a different matter, however. They grew muscular with broad shoulders and brawny arms, while I remained as thin as a fishing pole. It was not long before they stopped running away from me and gave chase once more. To my chagrin, I quickly discovered that my hypnotic powers had less effect on them. When I did succeed in hypnotizing a boy, it took so much energy I was left weakened to the point of exhaustion, and my failures often led to blackened eyes and bloodied noses. So, I avoided the boys and stalked the girls.

It did not take long, of course, for word to spread about my strange behavior, and I knew it was time to move on. Mum was institutionalized by then and school no longer mattered. So, I beat my father once more and left home for good.

Years have passed since then, lonely years that carried me from city to city until I ended up here, a place where my special talents are appreciated and rewarded. The thought of reward reminds me that this morning I am *not* alone. A companion has been added to my kingdom . . . a girl in her teens with a black beauty mark in her right eye. My gaze quickly swings to the foot of the bed where she lies curled up, her wrists and legs bound so that she cannot stand on her own. A dirty cloth covers her mouth to keep her from crying out, although it did not prevent her from whimpering during the night. She is positioned on her left side just like me, with her legs pulled up to her stomach and her chin tucked against her chest. Her brown, woolen dress is hiked above her knees, revealing sturdy legs discolored by several bruises. I can tell from the way her regular breathing disturbs the dust on the wooden floor that she is sleeping.

It is time to stretch my bony legs and try to push away the curtains of sleep that overwhelm me at the onset of winter and cling to me until the early days of spring. I raise my head, inch by inch, until my slumbering body is bent at enough of an angle for me to swing my feet to the floor and achieve an upright position on the edge of my bed. The motion is violent enough to jar my sensitive vision and I quickly press my long fingers to my temples and close my eyes. I know it is useless to attempt any further movement for awhile.

Time passes. I have no idea how long I sit this way. Time is irrelevant in the morning, especially when I have gone hunting the day before. March is very early for me to venture outside my room and it takes all my energy to do so. But now that the days are getting warmer, my employers expect me to resume my work.

Many years ago, I realized that winter had the effect of a sleeping potion on me. Once the days grew shorter and colder, there was nothing to do but find a quiet place, a sanctuary, where I could hide from the world until the days grew longer again. I used to berate myself for my weakness, much like my father had berated me with his belt, and I did everything I could think of to fight off the veils of sleep that blanketed my mind. Until I remembered the bears. I had learned about bears in school, about how their bodies shut down in winter, just as mine did, and how they hid away in caves where they slept until spring. My mind and body do not shut down so completely, but they do slow to the point where I can hardly function and have to sleep for days.

Now that I understand the cycle, I plan for winter just like a bear.

I store canned foods, extra clothing and extra eating utensils, because it is nearly impossible for me to perform such simple tasks as buying food or washing a dish or spoon. Then, I hide away until spring. I hibernate.

Two years ago I arrived in Chinatown and my whole world changed. Here, people bring me fresh food and tend to my needs in exchange for my unusual services. I am currently employed by the Mock Chin Tong, one of the ruthless gangs that keep a stranglehold on Chinatown's numerous opium dens and brothels. The tongs share my services, rotating me from gang to gang to avoid conflicts among them. They give me this place to stay, a single room hidden away in Ross Alley where the surrounding buildings are pressed so tightly together, the sun only shines between them for a few hours each day. Each morning, a pudgy woman with shiny, black hair pulled into a knot behind her head brings me food, consisting of rice or noodles, and sausage, fish, or pork, and removes my dirty plates. Once a week, she washes my clothes. When I feel other needs rising, a girl with a painted, rice-powdered face visits me. I never use the girls I bring to the tongs. They have made it clear that I must not touch my victims.

I can feel warm air struggling to reach me in my windowless abode. I slowly take my hands away from my face and open a small slit in my eyes. Once again, I become conscious of the singsong voices of my neighbors as they go about their morning chores. The cooking aromas I smelled before tell me rice is steaming in pots, along with fish, bamboo shoots and bitter melons for soups. I have dwelled in Chinatown long enough to be used to the flavors and smells of the place, but I have never adjusted fully to the cacophony of voices and clanging cooking utensils that endlessly elbow their way through the warren of narrow alleyways from dawn until night. The noise often stirs a cauldron of pain inside my head, but it is a small price to pay for my sanctuary. No one ever bothers me here. No one glares at me or steps across the street to avoid me. My neighbors go about their business as though I am not there, which suits me perfectly. I am as invisible to them as they are to me. Besides, I am used to living alone, in a world without the warmth of hands on my body or smiles on my skin. It is better to remain invisible.

My only meaningful contact is with the tong bosses. To them, I deliver young women like the girl at the foot of my bed, not an easy task. It takes a great deal of energy for me to venture into the streets and capture the right girl, especially in early springtime or late fall when I am not at full strength. She must be young enough to appeal to the older men who will become her customers and from a poor enough family that the police will not be too concerned about her fate. And, like my current prize, she must be white. There are a few white prostitutes working voluntarily in Chinatown, but they are hardened women who have nothing to offer the leaders of the powerful tongs. The tongs want unworldly women who will only yield to their clients' whims after protestations and tears. Of course, they are drugged before they actually begin their work. Not heavily, but just enough to mute their cries and lower their resistance. The most prized, like the one I am about to deliver this morning, are the virgins. These never fail to please my employers, due to the high prices they can charge the first customers.

The girl by my bed stirs and slowly lifts her head. Her fearful eyes scurry around the room in an effort to understand where she is and what has happened to her. There is a black mark in one of her eyes. Will my bosses consider it a flaw? I think not, for she is young and well-proportioned. She will please the tongs' customers. The girl tries to cry out but can produce nothing more than a gurgle through the cloth in her mouth. Not that it matters. Her voice would be drowned in the sea of voices that awakened me and no one would pay her any attention. My neighbors understand that I work for the tongs. They would not dare to intervene.

After awhile, the clients will tire of this girl and demand new blood. By then, she will be too addicted to her diet of drugs to protest, and she will be sold to a brothel in Sacramento or another inland city. I care little for her fate. My interest is in the hunt which can be beset with challenges. I never know exactly how my quarry will respond to my magic. Some melt at once, others resist for awhile. And more than once, I have been accosted by a male companion of the woman I am stalking. When that happens, I abandon the hunt and walk away.

At first, the tongs pressured me to work year 'round, but when they realized I could not function during the winter months, they left me alone. Now, the cherry blossoms have announced an early spring and I am expected to make up for lost time.

My first victim should have been delivered days ago, but things went terribly wrong. I selected an ideal candidate, high-spirited and young. When I hypnotized her, however, a power I had never faced before blocked my thoughts and forced my eyes to lose focus. The woman had slipped deep within my spell, but when the visual link between us was broken, her strong will asserted itself and she escaped my control, leaving me no choice but to abandon my efforts and flee.

Nothing like that had ever happened before. The unexpected development stoked the fires of self-recrimination within me. The voices inside my head mocked me for my stupidity at selecting such a strong-willed woman before I was fully recovered from my winter ordeal. Early spring has always frustrated me. I want to move about normally, but my body is still drowsy and unresponsive. My reactions remain slow and my balance unsteady.

Yet, even as I reprimanded myself, I realized it was not her will or my reduced strength that allowed her to escape. Something intervened to block my powers, something I have never encountered and do not understand. Its power was equal to my own, and that worries me greatly. Whatever it was, I shall not rest until I learn its source.

Even worse, the Mock Chin Tong bosses were anticipating my delivery. I had never before failed them. They do not understand failure and they do not accept excuses. So I was forced to venture out again without rest, which was a chancy prospect. This time of year I need several days to recover my strength and balance after one of my forays, but I had to forgo my normal rest and strike again. Fortunately, I found the young woman who now lies captive on the floor of my room. Her resistance was weak, and no one interfered.

At last I struggle to my feet and put on a shirt and trousers. The girl squirms to be free as I lift her from the floor and release the rope that binds her feet. I keep her wrists bound in front of her, however, and hold her close as we emerge from my eight foot by 10 foot room into the busy alleyway. Almond-eyed men shuffle past us in black trousers and jackets. Bowler hats sit atop their heads and braided queues dangle down their backs. Women with their hair tied in knots bend to their morning chores. Their bound feet, black pantaloons and gowns look so natural to me now that I hardly give them a passing glance. And, as always, they ignore me. We are all invisible.

The wealthier men and women own shops or trade in the goods suited to Chinese tastes, such as hogs, eels, octopi and roast ducks. They belong to one of the tong societies for protection and pay any amount demanded of them without question. Fear dominates their relationships with the tongs. This fear is reinforced by the hatchet men who work for the tong bosses. They terrorize the people and keep them under the tongs' hardened fists. At first, I found it strange that Chinatown's citizens would not complain to the police, but I soon learned that the Chinese would never consider seeking help from outside their community. Back home in China they faced warlords and bandits who placed similar demands on them and corrupt officials who always demanded high bribes before considering their cases. They are used to the kind of treatment they receive at the hands of the hatchet men and they distrust officials too much to consider appealing to the white man's system of justice. It is their stoic nature to accept their fate and so they swallow the hatchet men's insults without protest. It is better to settle disputes out of court and accept the tongs' heavy-handed justice than to risk complete ruin or death.

The plight is even worse for the poorer inhabitants such as the coolies who are easily spotted by their straw sandals and rough-hewn clothing. One passes me now with two buckets balanced on a long pole braced across his shoulders. He cannot afford the tongs' protection and is totally at the mercy of the bullying hatchet men.

Some might argue that such a violent system has no place in a modern world, but there it is. It gives me no concern for I am as invisible to the hatchet men as I am to the others. There are two reasons for this. First, I am white. The tongs are careful to confine their acts of violence to their own kind. The police know what goes on here but as long as it does not affect them they look the other way. The second reason is the precious cargo I am about to deliver. I bring the tongs something they could not obtain otherwise: young white women for their brothels. My offerings are worth more than gold. No hatchet man would dare to touch me so long as I remain in the tongs' good graces.

The girl has begun to whimper through the folds of her gag and to struggle in my grasp but I maintain my tight grip on her arm and walk her towards the Mock Chin Tong's gathering place at the rear of a restaurant in Church Alley. Her breathing is coming in rapid puffs which betray her fear. She beseeches passersby with her eyes for help but they look away. They know she is meant for the tongs and that makes her as invisible as me. When I have had enough of her antics, I yank her to me, close the fingers of my free hand around her throat and tell her to be quiet. She flinches under my hot breath and hunches her shoulders in a futile effort to shrink away from me. I permit myself a tiny smile of satisfaction as I watch her. She might have been easy to hypnotize, but she will struggle against her captors. They will like that and it will enhance my standing in the eyes of the tongs, something I badly need after my recent failure with that other woman.

It is important that I come to them in triumph. I must never show fear or uncertainty to these ruthless men. If they ever doubt my powers, they will devour me.

CHAPTER FOUR

Marta was still trying to digest Missy's story about a diabolical man with magic hands who kidnapped young women in the Mission District when a fresh rumor sent new shockwaves through her. Herbert Cunningham had left his wife, Angela, and was now being seen at social events with a younger woman who had arrived from Europe a few months earlier. She was a countess and her popularity was rising in society with the brilliance of a comet, while Angela's star was sinking just as quickly into oblivion. Angela had not been seen in public since the separation and there were rumors she would be left nearly penniless once the divorce was finalized. The reason was simple. Prior to their marriage, Herbert Cunningham had a contract prepared and signed by his wife-to-be stating that she had no claim to any of his property or income outside of the marriage. In effect, should they divorce, Angela would receive nothing from the Cunningham estate.

Marta's initial reaction to the news had been a satisfied smirk and nod of her head as she sat in her office balancing the ledgers for the previous month. It was just deserts, she told herself, for such an insufferable woman. The prospect of no longer running into Angela in the tenements gave her a flush of pleasure but that thought was quickly followed by shards of guilt that pierced her conscience. She knew the fate of a woman like Angela when she lost her bread-winning husband. Bleak prospects awaited her as she descended almost overnight from pretentious wealth to near poverty. Even if a stipend was provided for her, it would not be enough to support her in the manner to which she was accustomed, and she would disappear from the social pages of the city's newspapers.

As Marta leaned back in her chair and tapped her pencil on the desk, she contemplated Angela's future. She would likely join other abandoned women whose soft hands had never done anything more than pick up a writing pen or play a piano, women who quickly became outcasts among their fashionable friends. Her companions at the Emmanuel Sisterhood, for example, would offer Angela a few empty words of sympathy before turning away, and with no formal education or training, there would be few job opportunities available. Angela's education would likely have included the piano, oil painting and a sufficient knowledge of French or Italian to make conversation, but she would know none of those subjects well enough to teach them to others.

When she found an entry Missy had placed in the wrong column Marta grimaced and corrected it with a sigh. Missy was just becoming familiar with bookkeeping and Marta knew she had to be patient. Like any skill, bookkeeping took time to learn. This realization returned her thoughts to Angela. Marta was certain Angela wouldn't know bookkeeping.

There were low-skilled jobs for women at places like the Mint or the newspapers but those attracted far more applicants than openings and many of the applicants had practical experience. Even housework would be hard to find, because those who could afford hired help already knew the limits of women from the better social classes. That left labor intensive jobs, such as sewing, where Angela would have to make button holes for fifty cents a dozen and compete with the low wages of Chinese labor. Her earnings to start would not surpass seven dollars per week. Even a forewoman or department head could only expect to make thirty dollars per week. All-in-all, it was a bleak future for someone used to spending thirty dollars or more on a single dress.

Angela's plight reminded Marta of her own concerns. She angrily closed the ledger, causing several papers on her desk to scatter. Samuel still had not located those missing shipments and she wasn't convinced he had even tried to find them. When she asked about them, she was told to mind her own business. Just the thought of her brother's cavalier attitude made her temples pound with frustration. She could feel her father's estate slipping through their fingers, along with her own prospects. If her brother did not pay more attention to the business and less to gambling, whoring and drinking with his friends, she feared the day would come when she, too, would have to seek employment at the Mint. And while her skills might be more practical than Angela's, she did not relish the idea of becoming a member of the poorer classes she now helped.

Well, there was no time to worry about that now. As soon as Missy arrived, they were going to visit the McClain family in hopes they could learn more about what had happened to the missing daughter. Marta also wanted to learn as much as possible about the frightening man who had confronted her. She still shivered whenever she remembered his flashing amber ring and fierce, penetrating gaze.

* * *

Their mission took them deep into the shanty-town tenements where streets were filled with such deep potholes even a horse and wagon had to think twice about traversing the area and where children squealed as they played in fetid water that leaked from poorly maintained sewer lines. The water's putrid odor mixed with the smell of cooked cabbage and baked bread to create an odd mixture of pleasing and acrid smells that both sweetened Marta's mouth and soured her tongue. Rat infested buildings and tumble down shanties bordered the worn out streets. Boarding houses mingled with junk shops, whiskey mills and houses of ill repute, and the air was thick with smoke spewing from hundreds of nearby factories and foundries. It wasn't the end of the earth, but it was the closest thing to Hell San Francisco had to offer.

Street numbers were not reliable in that portion of the tenements, but Missy was familiar with the area from the bleak days when she had survived on those very streets. Marta had not visited the McClains and was not certain how to find them. She had hesitated to ask Missy's help, but Missy had readily agreed despite her dark memories of the area. As they walked deeper into the slums, however, her discomfort became more and more evident. She cast furtive glances around her. Her normal, sunny disposition was obscured by a cloud of apprehension. She stayed as close to Marta as seemed proper. Marta put an arm around her companion's shoulders to tell her she understood and was pleased to see Missy respond with a weak smile.

"The McClains should be down two more blocks on the right," Missy said as she fidgeted with her hands and glanced around as she spoke. They hurried the two blocks and stopped in front of a shrunken wooden shanty that leaned so far to the left it would have fallen over if it were not propped up on either side by two equally frail houses. All three were pressed so tightly together they seemed to meld into one. Whatever paint had once brightened the door had long since peeled away, leaving raw planks of wood braced by iron hinges. The rapid chatter of children's voices escaped through the cracks in the door, indicating the family was home.

Marta knocked and waited. The voices hushed to whispers, but no one answered her knock. She knew many of the people living in this part of town were newly-arrived from other countries and suspicious of strangers. And now that a daughter was missing, she could imagine the fear slinking through the neighborhood.

"Mrs. McClain, it's Marta Baldwin from the Pacific Aid Society. I'm here with Missy. Can we come in please?" A moment's silence was followed by scrambling feet and more whispers. Then the door swung open to reveal a slightly stooped woman with a worn face defined by fallen cheeks and heavy crevices. It was a face that had been pillaged by a life filled with too many worries and too little money. Two smaller heads with wide, brown eyes peered around her frayed dress. She pushed the children away and opened the door wider.

"Com'in, if you want." The twang in her voice suggested the family had resettled from somewhere in the south, Tennessee or Kentucky if Marta remembered correctly.

They stepped into a dusky room permeated by stale cooking odors. Enough bunk beds were stacked against the far wall to sleep at least six children, but only two girls, roughly five and seven years old, were home now. They ran to their beds and sat with bare feet dangling while they stared at the strangers, their curious expressions highlighted by dark, brown hair that tumbled to their shoulders. A larger bed curtained off by a threadbare blanket stood near a door that Marta guessed led to a kitchen. She pictured a room furnished with a coal-fired cooking stove and sink and some kind of rough-hewn, wood table surrounded by mismatched chairs. It was the typical home of a downtrodden family trying to make do on less than fourteen dollars a week, but it was reasonably swept and cleared of clutter and the girls had freshly scrubbed faces. Marta had seen far worse.

Mrs. McClain fussed with the loose strands of her hair and looked at them both with quick, nervous eyes that said she was uncertain what to do. There was no place to sit other than the beds and it was obvious she hesitated to invite them into the adjoining room. Marta knew such an invitation should include an offer of tea or coffee along with a biscuit, none of which the woman could afford to share. Marta decided to conduct their interview standing where they were.

"We are worried about your daughter and hoped you might know something more about her disappearance. Maybe a word from a neighbor or a new rumor, perhaps." Marta reached out and touched the woman's sleeve to express her concern. The fabric's heavy texture had the feeling of rough woodchips on her fingertips.

The wrinkles and lines on the woman's face twisted into a look of grim despair. "Nothin' to know. She's just gone."

"Have the police told you anything? Are they looking for a man who can cast spells with his hands?" Marta suspected this would be a difficult concept for the woman to grasp, but she felt compelled to ask. "Someone like a magician?"

"No police been 'round here. You're the only ones." Her thin lips quivered as she mulled what Marta had said. "Some says a man took her. An evil man. I don't know." Tension mingled with the cooking odors in the room as the woman resumed fiddling with her hair and then forced her trembling hands to her sides. The moisture in her pale eyes told Marta there was nothing more to be said. It was time to leave. As Marta had feared, the police were not very keen on chasing a fairytale story told by illiterate people in the shantytowns south of Market Street. Their attention was focused on the other side of the city where those with money and power resided. It was obvious that Mrs. McClain could expect little help from that quarter.

Once they had expressed their regrets and departed, Marta thought about trying to convince Mrs. McClain to go with her to the police station to file a report, but she knew it would do no good. Mrs. McClain had no evidence of wrong-doing and the report would only be filed away.

"Missy, why don't you return to the office? There're a couple families I should call on while I'm here." Marta saw at once the disappointment etched in her helper's freckled face at this suggestion and quickly changed her mind. Missy was eager to do more than office work and had learned a great deal during their two years together. It was probably time to give her some added responsibility. If she did put Missy in the field, it would mean hiring an additional staff member to mind the office and that would take money from her pocket. She sighed and glanced at her protégé. Missy had been a Godsend, and if it meant tightening her own budget to keep her happy, it would be money well spent.

"Better still, why don't you come with me? There's nothing at the office that can't wait an hour or two." Marta smiled and nodded in the direction away from the office.

Missy's face brightened. "I'd be most pleased to join you."

They called on two families who had recently lost their husbands and were desperately trying to figure out a way to survive. In the first instance, the man had succumbed to alcohol and disappeared into the labyrinth of bars and bordellos along the Barbary Coast. The second husband had died in an accident working those same waterfront docks. The latter family had been given a few dollars by the shipping company, but Marta knew from her own family's business that there was no insurance or other safety net for the workers. The hardships from such losses fell heavily on the families and Marta experienced a sharp twinge of guilt when she thought about it.

Marta and Missy had finished their calls and were walking back to the office when they turned a corner and saw the gangly man everyone was talking about. Marta nearly stumbled at the sight of him and instinctively reached for her amulet. He stood less than a hundred feet away waving his arms and jabbering in that strange language which had so beguiled her. A young woman stood before him entranced and unmoving. Marta quivered at the sight. Even from where she stood, she felt the cavernous world opening in the woman's mind and the numbing cold drowning her thoughts.

Missy shrank back and cried out with fear, catching the attention of two women who were passing. They both looked over but quickly averted their eyes and hurried away. No one dared to look at the man, let alone confront him.

A flash of anger shoved aside Marta's initial fear at seeing him again. She thought about the McClain woman's lost daughter and the other young women, girls really, who had vanished. Marta clenched her hands when she remembered her own helplessness and how close she had come to succumbing to a similar fate. Something inside her refused to let this malignant man succeed again, even if it meant putting herself at risk.

"Stop that," she shouted as she started across the street towards the assailant. "Get away from that girl." Startled, the man swung his head towards Marta. A sharp look of anger narrowed his gaunt features, but was quickly replaced by surprise and recognition. The man remembered her! He stood there a moment, apparently uncertain what to do while Marta advanced on him shaking her fist. "Leave that girl alone. You're not going to harm anyone today."

Marta's heart was racing so fast, she could hardly catch a breath, and her mind was swirling from the winds of doubt storming inside her head. Why she had decided to confront this man she could not say, and she had no idea what she would do when she reached him. The realization that she might be putting herself in danger nearly caused her to falter, but she refused to let her fears control her. No matter what happened, she was determined to stop the vile man from striking again. To her relief, she saw him take a step backwards and look wildly between her and his intended victim. It was the first sign of weakness she had seen in him and it bolstered her courage. The girl continued to stand unmoving, but Marta ignored her. All of her attention was focused on the man who had so nearly drawn her into the depths of Hell. A fresh burst of anger reinforced her determination, even though her mouth was as dry as sand. She felt him glaring at her, but she refused to look into his eyes. That, she knew, would be fatal. She concentrated on his chest, instead, and raised her fists, ready to pummel him

To her surprise, he suddenly wheeled around and sprinted away, his feet flying down the street at such odd angles to his body he reminded Marta of an old rag doll whose legs were falling off. She stopped and pressed her hand to her heaving chest as she watched him turn a corner and disappear. The reality of what had just happened sank in, and her body shook so hard, she collapsed on the curb.

Missy ran over and knelt beside her. "That was a terribly brave thing you did. Are you no worse for it?" Marta answered by throwing her arms around Missy and holding her as tightly as she could. Once she had caught her breath, she looked around for the man's intended victim, but the girl had disappeared as quickly as her assailant. Marta knew from her own experience that she would be terrified by what had happened, and Marta wished she could comfort her. She had never seen the girl before, however, and had no idea where she lived.

Marta needed to come to terms with her own feelings but had no idea how she felt about what had just happened. It seemed foolhardy in retrospect, but she'd had no choice. She also knew that while the danger may have momentarily passed, it wasn't gone. It had retreated to a place she dared not follow, but it would return. She would have to find some way to deal with it when it did. Otherwise, she feared the day would come when she would sink beyond hope in those cold caverns in her mind and, like the McClain's daughter, never be seen again.

CHAPTER FIVE

Following her second harrowing encounter with the strange man haunting the tenements, Marta was uncertain what to do. Going to the police seemed the obvious choice, but what could she tell them? That she had seen a man waving his hands and talking to a girl on the street? That she herself had slipped into a state of mind where she believed she was drowning in cold air? Neither story would make sense to them, but she had to do something.

So she marched into the nearest police station with a determined stride and asked for the officer in charge of missing persons. She was directed down a corridor that reeked of stale cigars to a tiny office where a man sat behind a desk poring over reports. When he glanced up at Marta, annoyance scoured his face, which was magnified by a slight cleft in his upper lip. His short neck nearly disappeared into his heavy shoulders. He had a lumbering look about him and Marta sensed by the way his body tensed when he looked at her that a layer of violence lurked just below the surface.

He quickly assessed her with a hard stare and gestured to a

wooden chair in front of the desk. From the disinterested way he looked at her it was apparent he didn't consider her worth much of his time. Marta glanced down at her work shirt and pants and knew he thought she had come from the tenements. Her back stiffened at his presumptive attitude but she sat down on the edge of the chair without comment.

"You missin' somebody?" he asked without preamble in a raspy voice. Men's voices could be heard passing in the corridor outside. One burst with laughter at another's comment and Marta suddenly wished she had taken the time to put on a dress before coming here. She knew her work attire put her at a disadvantage.

"Girls have been disappearing from the tenements," she responded at last. "I believe they are being kidnapped."

The officer's chair groaned under his weight as he leaned back in it. He laid his hands flat on the desk and narrowed his eyes. "Girls go missin' all the time from the tenements. They take off with boyfriends or go looking for work. That don't call for a charge of kidnapping."

Marta leaned forward with a sense of urgency. "It's more than that. There's a strange man prowling the streets. I saw him trying to lure a girl to go with him and I had a run-in with him myself. He nearly bewitched me."

The officer smirked at her word choice and she immediately regretted using it. She didn't know how to describe the effect the man had on his intended victims without sounding like an uneducated woman telling wives' tales.

"Look," she continued more forcefully, "I'm not just some silly woman spreading rumors. I know my clothes don't reflect the latest in ladies' fashion, but I do come from Pacific Heights. I run an aid society to help the poor, which is why I'm not wearing a dress and why I was in the tenements."

The officer sat forward and toyed with the papers before him. Marta knew the last thing he wanted was another report on his desk and she feared she would be turned away. He finally pushed a form across the desk to her, however.

"Here, fill this out. I'll keep it active for a few weeks. See what turns up."

* * *

Marta left the police station with an empty feeling in her stomach. She knew the officer had not taken her story seriously and had only requested her report to be rid of her. It was the reaction she had expected, but she still felt frustrated. She stood on the pavement and watched the trolley cars clanging by while she decided what to do next. If the police were not involved, she had to find some other way to proceed. Her first thought was to learn more about the kind of spell the man was inflicting on his victims. For that, she needed advice from someone who was experienced in such things. Her immediate thought was of her brother, Samuel. Not that she expected him to have the answers, but he might know someone who did. *Yes* she thought *she would begin with her brother*. She turned and headed towards home.

Samuel was gone when Marta entered the house. Her heart sank. She knew better than to expect him before dinner, if he returned at all. Half of the time, he ate out with his friends without bothering to notify her. She was little more than a servant in his eyes, one who should have his meals ready whether he wanted them or not. They'd had a maid and cook at one time, but Marta had let them go when she saw how far over budget their expenses were going. Not that Samuel cared for budgets or paid attention to them. He left that to Marta but made it clear that if she refused to keep a maid or cook on staff then she was expected to fill those roles herself.

Marta accepted her situation with stoicism. It was not easy running her relief agency during the day and taking care of her brother and the house at night, but she was determined to keep things on an even keel. There was some money from the shipping business and the house was without debt. Even if Samuel proved inept at running the company and it had to be sold, they would still have income from the trust and a roof over their heads. Those two thoughts gave her comfort and fortified her resolve.

Her disappointment at not finding Samuel at home did vex her, however. She was still edgy after her latest encounter with that frightening man on the street and she wanted to talk to someone about it. She was vaguely aware of the hypnotic powers some men possessed and she hoped to learn more about them. She remembered as a little girl attending a theater performance where a man had brought people on stage and magically put them under his spell. One had been made to take off his coat and shirt. Another had crawled around on his hands and knees barking like a dog. Even a woman had been enticed onto the stage where she sang a bawdy song off key. What had the magician been called? Marta could not remember, but she was certain the man on the street was doing something similar. Only he was not making his subjects do simple parlor tricks. His manipulations were far more sinister.

To her surprise, she heard the front door open and close with a thud, indicating that her brother had returned. She hurried to the entryway, where she found him shedding his jacket and checking the mail. "You're home early," she acknowledged in a friendly tone. This was one time she didn't want to get into an argument with him.

Samuel eyed her suspiciously as he thumbed through the bills. "As are you. Is dinner ready?"

It was sad how much they argued now. As children growing up, Samuel had looked out for her. He had enjoyed his role as the protective, older brother and she had respected him for it. Without a mother, their father had fulfilled the role of both parents. They had been a close family. That had changed after their father died. Samuel was an adult by then and his placid manner had shifted to a more abrasive one. Marta suspected his friends had something to do with his changed personality. He badly wanted to be seen as a member of their social standing and he was easily influenced by them. The result was an ungrateful brother who spent most of his time at parties and other social gatherings while Marta worried about the practical aspects of running their household and paying the bills.

"I was about to start cooking some lamb chops. Are you staying?" she asked hopefully. She preferred to broach her subject with Samuel after he'd had a chance to relax and have a drink. Not that another drink was really necessary. She suspected he had already had more than one that afternoon at his club.

Samuel nodded and headed for the bar.

Marta waited until they sat down to dinner before asking her question. "Do you remember the time father took us to the theater to watch that man who cast spells on people? They had a name for him. Do you remember what they called him?" She sliced a piece of meat and put it in her mouth.

Samuel leaned back in his chair and thought a moment. "A hypnotist. I believe they called him a hypnotist. It was a funny show." He smiled at the recollection. Marta had to admit that he was quite handsome when he wasn't growling at her about something.

"That's it!" She put down her fork to emphasize her delight. "Yes, I remember, now. A hypnotist is somebody who can get others to do his will."

"Well, I'm not sure he could get people to do things they didn't want to. I think they had to be willing." Samuel pushed a few peas around with his knife. He had hardly touched his food, but Marta could see he was through eating. She wanted to finish their conversation before he escaped into the night.

"I remember a man on his hands and knees barking like a dog. I can't imagine he was willing to do that."

"Maybe not, but I think he had to be willing to be hypnotized. Otherwise, nothing would have happened." He put his hands on the edge of the table, ready to push back his chair.

Marta grabbed his hand. "Before you go, I need to ask you something." She saw the surprise in his face at her forwardness. They rarely touched. "Do you know anybody, at the club perhaps, who knows about hypnotism?"

Samuel looked at her, but said nothing. When she saw him hesitating, she pushed on. "I saw that wild man again today. I think that is what he does -- hypnotizes people. Only he does it against their will. He was hypnotizing a young woman right there on the street, just as he nearly did me. I believe he would have kidnapped her if I had not intervened." She removed her hand from his. "I don't know what he is, but he really scares me. I need to find

41

someone who knows about hypnotism. Can you help me?"

Concern furrowed her brother's brow. "You really think this guy is dangerous?"

She nodded.

"Just stay away from him, then. Don't go 'intervening' as you put it. Let the police handle the matter."

"I've already been to the police but I don't think they took me seriously. Look, the man tried to hypnotize me once and I'm afraid he might try again. He must live near where I work. Otherwise, I wouldn't be hearing stories about him and running into him like this. If I see him again, I don't know what he might do." Her eyes pleaded for understanding.

Samuel thought a moment. "One of the club members did a parlor trick once where he put a waiter to sleep and got him to answer a bunch of embarrassing questions. I'm not sure how much he knows about it, but he might be able to tell you something. His name is Byron Wagner. I don't think you've met him. His family's big in mining operations."

A narrow face with a thin, prominent nose and tousled, brown hair leaped to Marta's mind. Not a particularly handsome face, but one that showed an interest in others. Marta had not met Mr. Wagner, but she remembered seeing him at one of the few dinner parties she had agreed to attend. From what she could recall, he had made a favorable impression. "When can I talk to him?"

Samuel shrugged his shoulders. "Anytime you want, I suppose. He will be at the club tomorrow. Plays chess there in the afternoons."

Samuel's club was for men only and one had to be a member to enter. Its rules were quite strict and its memberships highly sought after. It was not uncommon for a membership to be passed down from father to son like an inheritance. Samuel had assumed his membership in just that fashion from their father. Women were generally forbidden, thus Marta knew her only chance to get in was with her brother. "Can you take me tomorrow?" She saw him hesitate. "Please. I wouldn't ask if it were not so important."

Samuel hesitated a moment longer, then nodded. "Two o'clock.

Be on time."

Marta wanted to throw her arms around him and hug him, but she settled for a smile and a thank you, instead. A hug would have shown too much affection for her obdurate brother.

* * *

Samuel's club sat atop Nob Hill like a fortress castle, with thickset, stone walls that covered half a city block. It looked surprisingly squat compared to the rounded turrets and peaked roofs of the surrounding mansions. The heavily draped windows gave the place a sense of mystery. Marta had arrived early and paced back and forth on the street outside the club's entrance, aware that men were eyeing her as they entered the building. She had yielded to her brother's demand that she wear a dress and squirmed under their frank gazes. All of the men, she noted, were dressed in fine, woolen suits, which were custom tailored to fit their various sizes and shapes. These were very wealthy men, she knew, and she wondered how her brother could afford to maintain his membership there.

Before she had a chance to begin worrying about money, Samuel stepped from a cable car and strode towards her. "I had to get permission to take you inside," he announced irritably by way of greeting. "If Mr. Wagner had not interceded on your behalf, we would have had to make other arrangements."

Her brother's abrasive words lashed Marta's pride and she had to bite back angry words of her own about women's rights and pompous men. Samuel's club represented another example of the things she disliked about San Francisco society. Not only were women excluded but these men had the power to destroy careers and reputations on a whim. She was entering the lion's den, but since she needed help, there was no better place to look for it than among such men. So, instead of offering a tart reply, she smiled sweetly and thanked her brother for his efforts.

A butler waited to take their coats when they entered. Marta noted how he averted his eyes from hers and lifted his chin in a subtle gesture that said he, too, resented her presence there. She was dumbfounded by his haughtiness. He was, after all, only a servant, but it seemed his surroundings had shaped his behavior to mirror his employers'. Marta ignored him and followed Samuel through a large, square room covered by a thick, grey carpet and filled with heavy, leather chairs and coffee tables inlaid with intricate wood patterns. Several men sat reading newspapers or talking quietly over brandies. Two in particular sank so heavily into the folds of their leather seats, Marta wondered how they would get up again. A layer of cigar smoke wafted across the room as several pairs of eyes stared at her through the haze with frank hostility. Their dismissive attitudes made it abundantly clear how much they disliked her being there. Marta lifted her own chin, mimicking the butler, and marched past them.

Samuel led her through sliding doors to a dark paneled room with marble flooring covered by two immense Persian rugs. More than a dozen men milled about or sat at tables concentrating on game boards. Marta's attention was immediately drawn to the far corner where several men stood watching a chess match. She couldn't make out the face of the man seated with his back to her but she recognized the thin face of the other. The man was thoughtfully smoking a meerschaum pipe while he pondered his next move.

There was a noticeable stir and murmur of clandestine voices when she entered, causing Byron Wagner to lift his head. Irritation spread across his furrowed brow at having his concentration interrupted, but the expression quickly shifted to one of interest when he saw the source of the disturbance. He spoke briefly to a rather odd looking man with wild, sand-colored hair and bushy eyebrows, who nodded and headed her way. "You must be Miss Baldwin," his voice boomed across the room. Marta cringed as all eyes fixed on her. Why did this obnoxious man have to be so loud? "Allow me to introduce my sister, Marta Baldwin," Samuel interjected. For once, Marta appreciated her brother's formal manners, if only because they helped her maintain a sense of respectability in the presence of these men.

"I am grand master Konrad von Reich, visiting from Germany."

The guttural tones imbedded in his heavy accent made it unnecessary for him to announce his country of origin, although his English was quite good. He puffed his chest out as he spoke, telling Marta he was as full of conceit and self-importance as the other men in the room. She had learned chess from her father and understood that grand master was the highest rank one could attain. From the looks of his fine, silk jacket and carefully pressed trousers, she suspected he came from aristocracy. Her suspicions were confirmed when he bowed, took her hand, and kissed it. His unexpected gesture startled her, as did the moist lips on her skin. She withdrew her hand as soon as he released it.

"Please join us." He swept his arm towards the table she had noted when she entered and lightly pressed his warm hand against the small of her back as he guided her through the curious audience. Samuel was left standing, uncertain what to do. After a moment's hesitation, he hastily followed them.

Byron Wagner was absorbed in his game again, so Marta joined the other observers and studied the two men's positions. It took only a few moments for her to see that a pawn sacrifice would allow Wagner to open attacking lanes for his queen backed by his bishop. The combination would be too powerful for his opponent's black pieces to withstand for long.

"What do you think of this game, Miss Baldwin?" the grand master whispered in her ear. His breath was as moist on her neck as his lips had been on her hand. She wanted to move away from him but was confined by the others standing around the table. "Do you know the names of the pieces or how they move?" His tone was light, but she understood the condescending nature of his question. Only men played at his level. Women's minds were considered too delicate for such an intricate game.

Marta furiously rubbed her amulet as she considered her situation. She was there to seek help from Mr. Wagner, but she could not ignore the slight towards women that had just been made by Konrad von Reich. His demeaning question stung her cheeks and goaded her into action.

"Yes, I do Mr. Reich," she responded a little too loudly. "In fact,

I understand well enough to know white already has a winning position." The heat in her voice echoed through the stillness with the force of a cannon shot, causing Byron to look up sharply at her. "I'm sorry," she said, mortified. "I did not mean to be so rude." She felt all of the men's eyes burning her skin, but she kept hers fixed on Byron's, pleading for his understanding. "It will not happen again," she finished lamely.

But Konrad von Reich seized the moment. He was obviously entertained by her remark and, to her dismay, would not let it pass. "A winning position? My, my. And you can discern this in less than a minute?" He turned his attention to Byron. "Forgive me, sir, but I must see how she thinks this is to be done. Is the game of importance, or may we be enlightened by her analysis?"

Byron leaned back in his chair with a slight smile and removed his pipe from his mouth. "It is just a game to pass the time. By all means, let us see what Miss Baldwin has in mind."

Ridicule permeated the room. It rose in waves and crashed against Marta's skull until a great roaring filled her head and her eyes could no longer focus on the table before her. A hot tongue of anger rose in her throat, but it was mixed with trepidation. Had she been wrong in her thinking? Why else would Mr. Reich mock her like that? No, she was certain she was right. Her temples pounded as she continued to stare at the board. God, how she hated these men. Even Byron was watching her with the intense stare of a hawk ready to pounce on his prey. She suddenly wished she had worn trousers instead of the silly dress. Maybe, then, these men would have taken her more seriously.

"Show us your move, Miss Baldwin. Please. We are all eager to see it." Konrad von Reich spoke more gently this time, as if he grasped the embarrassment he had caused her and wanted to make amends.

Marta stared at the white pawn and willed it to move on its own, but it stood its ground, taunting her. Her hand trembled as she reached for it. Doubt overcame her, and she withdrew her hand, bringing a murmur of disapproval from the crowd of men. The hot anger in her throat returned. She'd be darned if she was going to let this group of self-important men intimidate her. Her father had not only taught her chess, he had praised her intelligent mind. She had eventually matched her father's game and had thoroughly whipped her brother anytime he dared to play her. Well, it was time to prove her father right, time to show that women were a match for men.

She reached again, this time quickly and decisively and pushed the pawn. Byron immediately smiled and nodded. "Yes, I think you have it," he said with a note of admiration.

"Indeed, she does," Konrad von Reich responded with a satisfied chuckle. "But it was a rather obvious move, don't you think? And it is one thing to stand back and look at a simple position, but quite another to face someone across the board. How well do you play, Miss Baldwin?"

Marta was trembling from her small triumph, but also from the continued attention being drawn to her. She had come there to learn about hypnotism, not become embroiled in a match of wills with these men. But the challenge Mr. Reich had just thrown at her could not go unanswered. If women were ever going to get the vote and assume greater leadership roles, they must stand up to every challenge. *She* must stand up to his challenge now.

"I can beat any man in this room," she announced sharply. Voices buzzed at her defiant response. She glanced at Byron and saw a look of amusement. *He is just like the others*, she thought.

"Well, perhaps all but one, my dear," Reich responded. "I must withdraw my name from consideration. But what about Mr. Wagner, here? He is the club's best. Surely, he would represent us all."

Marta wanted to protest. What could she hope to achieve by confronting the man whose help she sought? She looked around for Samuel, but he had melted back into the crowd. There would be no support from that quarter. Reich had isolated her and put her in a very unwelcome spotlight, although she supposed she was partly to blame. If she had just kept her mouth shut and played the role expected of her, none of this would be happening. That, however, was not something she was prepared to do.

The man sitting opposite Byron got up and offered his chair with a smirk on his face that told Marta her fate was sealed. There was nothing to do but show these arrogant men that women were just as smart as they were. Marta sat down and looked at Mr. Wagner across the board. She was pleased to find no smirk on his face. Instead, she saw what looked like encouragement and understanding, and that surprised her. No, she decided, it was too much to ask for understanding from this lot. It was enough that he seemed willing to treat her with respect. Mr. Wagner held up two fists. She indicated the right one, which revealed a white pawn. Marta would have the advantage of the first move. The hand revealed more than a pawn, however. The skin's texture was not callused but firm, suggesting a man who was willing to put his hand to useful tasks, rather than expecting servants to wait on his every whim. The thumb nail was slightly chipped, confirming her first impression. But it was the fingers that held her attention. They did not so much reveal the pawn as display it as one would a delicate and valuable object. It was evident that Mr. Wagner respected the chess piece he held, and Marta found this oddly satisfying.

Now was not the time, however, to dwell on such things. Marta's mind was swirling with so many other thoughts it was all she could do to set up her pieces. She had never played in front of an audience like this before. How should she begin? How much risk did she want to take? She recalled what her father had taught her. Opening with the king's pawn would allow for a more predictable game, at least for the first dozen moves. A queen's pawn opening, on the other hand, would signal a willingness to take on more complex positions with greater volatility. The queen's gambit was the preferred opening, but there was a variation of it that created a very fast-paced game. After a moment's reflection, she made her choice. She would test Mr. Wagner's mettle with a variation of the queen's gambit.

Without further thought, she pushed her queen's pawn to the fourth square. He immediately matched her move with his queen's pawn. Just as quickly, Marta pushed her queen's bishop's pawn to the fourth square. That was the standard gambit. If Mr. Wagner took the bishop's pawn, he obtained a small material advantage, but Marta would gain an edge in development. There was, however, an even bolder variation, and when Byron accepted her gambit and took the pawn, she pushed her knight's pawn to the third square, offering Mr. Wagner that pawn as well.

She watched Byron's reaction as she made the move, certain she had caught him by surprise. Unruffled, he leaned back in his chair, relit his pipe, and puffed on it thoughtfully. His cool response fascinated Marta, but not half as much as what he did next. After reflecting on the move, he looked up and nodded to her, indicating his appreciation for her bold strategy. Mr. Wagner's acknowledgement caught her so completely off guard, any residual anger she had felt towards him instantly melted away. He was not treating her like a silly woman who had no business invading his club. Reich and the others were another matter, of course, and she still felt the heat rising in her throat when she pictured them. But Mr. Wagner was different. She could see it in his thoughtful gaze. He was taking her seriously, and he was treating her as an equal!

A pleasant warmth spread through her body. As the game progressed she began to study him as much as she did the board. He had wonderful little habits, such as clamping the stem of his pipe between his teeth while he was thinking and briefly rubbing his hands before making a move. His nose twitched when Marta made an attacking move and he often tapped the piece he was going to move with his long fingers before picking it up. When he did move a piece, his hand flowed sensuously across the board with the light touch of a bird's wing.

She touched her hair absently to see if it was in order, and as soon as she realized what she was doing, the warmth that had spread through her body rose to her cheeks. When Mr. Wagner glanced up and caught her watching him, she looked down at her pieces in confusion. Strange sensations were invading her emotions. Her heart fluttered uncontrollably, and her face grew moist with perspiration, forcing her to take a small handkerchief from a pocket hidden in her dress and damp her brow and cheeks. Worst, of all, the distractions were causing her mind to wander, and she found herself making moves based more on instinct than cool analysis. She scolded herself for acting like a silly fool, but she couldn't help it. She was sliding under a spell, one every bit as powerful as the hypnotist's, and she was having a very hard time understanding why. Nothing like that had ever happened to her before. She prayed the emotions would pass before Mr. Wagner noticed how unsettled she was.

Despite the disarray in her mind, Marta studied the board and realized her rapid development had put her in a winning position. If she sacrificed her bishop, it would expose her opponent's queen. And if he refused to take the sacrifice, she would mate him in three moves. Either way, he had lost the game! The warmth that rose in her now was one of triumph. This was what she had played for, the chance to throw the insults of Reich and the others back in their faces. She could hardly wait to see their expressions when she, a woman, defeated their champion. When she glanced up and saw the concern etched on Reich's face, she knew he saw what she did. He knew the end was near. She gave him a satisfied smile, and he quickly glanced away.

But then a strange thing happened. When she looked back at Mr. Wagner, her feeling of triumph vanished. He was staring at her with his lips slightly parted in the hint of a smile. It was, she saw, a smile of admiration. He was telling her he knew he was beaten, and he was congratulating her! Marta's mind whirled with a flurry of conflicting thoughts and doubts. She was about to embarrass a man whom she realized she admired, and she didn't want to do that. This conclusion only made her head spin faster. What was she thinking? Of course, she had to sacrifice that bishop and win the game. How could she face herself if she didn't? How could she face all those men waiting for her to fail?

Yet try as she might, she could not bring herself to do it. Her hand shook as she reached for the bishop, and she withdrew it to her lap. Silly woman, she scolded! What are you doing? This man is no better than the others. Destroy his ego and be done with it. But he *was* better than the others. She knew this intuitively. And there was more. Losing to her would not destroy his ego, she realized. His look of confidence in the face of losing told her he was a better man than that. He had an inner strength much like hers, not something that could be said for the other men in the room, including her brother!

As quickly as the storm of emotions and thoughts had formed, they subsided, and Marta found she could breathe freely for the first time since entering this citadel of male chauvinism. Her mind was at peace. Her hands stopped shaking. She knew what she would do. She saw it with such clarity she wondered how she could ever have doubted her instincts. She reached out and pushed a pawn.

Only two men in the room knew what she had done. Reich, whose breath whistled through his teeth as he expelled the air he had been holding, and Mr. Wagner, whose intent eyes were framed by a curious frown. They played the game for another half hour, but Marta could see Mr. Wagner's heart was no longer in it, and neither was hers. Whatever happened after that fatal move was anticlimactic, and they both knew it. But there were still important matters at stake, and the room grew heavy with tension as the game progressed. Marta was contesting the club's best player move for move, and she could sense the fear running through the room, fear that Mr. Wagner might lose to a woman. In the end, he kept his pawn advantage from the game's opening and managed to push it down the board for a queen.

Marta's stomach knotted with anguish as she helplessly watched that extra pawn march down the board, and she struggled mightily with the storm of conflicting emotions assaulting her. By failing to exploit her advantage, she had let the man win. It had been a stupid thing to do, and she was miserable for it. Yet, when she looked at Mr. Wagner's face, she saw a sad expression that told her he was not enjoying his pending victory any more than she was, and she could not help showing a tentative smile of gratitude.

When Marta resigned, relief swooped through the room. The men around Mr. Wagner slapped his back and congratulated him for his victory, but he waved them off and announced to the group that his opponent was every bit as good a player as he was, perhaps even better. The warmth of his words comforted Marta, and her tentative smile broadened.

"Is there somewhere we can talk in private?" she asked when the commotion had quieted down.

"Of course. Come with me." He offered his hand to hers, as any gentleman would, but she sensed more than formality in the gesture as she rose from her chair. Her fingers tingled from his gentle yet firm touch. Once standing, she had to force herself to let go.

They entered a smaller sitting room with slip covers over several couches and chairs. "This room is not used much," Mr. Wagner noted as he removed the covers off two chairs. "We can have some privacy here." He indicated a chair for her and sat opposite. They stared at each other while Marta fidgeted with her hands. She sat upright, her back stiff with tension, uncertain how to proceed. Mr. Wagner's silence only exacerbated her unease.

"Tell me, Miss Baldwin, why did you forego the bishop sacrifice?" he suddenly asked.

"Mr. Wagner . . ."

"Please, call me Byron." He leaned back in the chair, much as he had done while they played chess. He retrieved his pipe from his coat pocket where he had placed it when they finished their game, but instead of lighting it, however, he simply held it in his hand and gazed at her.

Marta took a deep breath. "Byron . . . I suppose I could say, 'whatever do you mean,' but it is not in my nature to be coy. I apologize if my behavior was . . . inappropriate." She looked into his soft, grey eyes and her stomach did a flip flop. What was wrong with her? Why did this man make her so nervous?

"Actually, I thought what you did was quite amazing. I know how badly you wanted to win, but you refused to capitalize on your advantage." His eyes danced with pleasure when Marta's face turned red. "And you blush very nicely."

Marta looked down and fumbled with a fold in her dress. "You asked me why, but I cannot tell you. I do not know myself. A silly woman's prerogative, I suppose."

"I doubt that, at least in your case, Miss Baldwin." His face widened into a broader smile, which she found endearing. The smile expanded his narrow face and brought flecks of green to the surface of his grey eyes.

"If I am to address you by your first name, perhaps you should call me Marta," she replied at last.

"Marta. What a charming name. I should be delighted to address you by it from now on." Byron rubbed his hands just as he had done at the chess table and leaned forward. "Now, how can I help you? Samuel said something about hypnotism. Did you want to know how it is done? Or be hypnotized yourself?" He chuckled at this last comment.

Marta smiled and then grew serious. "I may have been hypnotized already, at least partially." She described her fears and feelings of helplessness during her first encounter with the hypnotist and how she fought to regain her self-control. "I really thought I was drowning, even as I stood there on the sidewalk. The whole episode was terrifying," she concluded.

Byron frowned and rubbed his chin with the long fingers of his free hand. It was a simple gesture, but one Marta found charming. Despite her anxieties, she could not help staring at the fingers' elegant movements. When he put the unlit pipe in his mouth and clamped his teeth on the stem, Marta knew it was a signal that he took her story seriously and was all business. She pushed aside her silly distractions and hurried on with her tale.

"There's more," she said quickly. Now that she had his attention, the words gushed from her with the urgency of water escaping a drainage pipe. "There are stories circulating in the tenements of an evil man who causes young women to disappear. Yesterday, I encountered him again. This time he was hypnotizing a girl no more than eighteen right on the street. She looked as helpless as I felt when he confronted me. I believe if I had not chased him away, he would have taken her."

Byron's expression narrowed into a deep frown. "What you have told me is quite disturbing. It sounds as if this man can manipulate others against their will, and I have never heard of that." He paused, deep in thought. "But I don't know much about these things. I was shown by my good friend, Charles, how to hypnotize people, but only as a parlor game. Beyond a few simple tricks, I know nothing. Charles is the one to talk to, but he comes and goes without telling anyone where he is. I will look for him and call you as soon as I hear something."

"Any help would be very much appreciated."

Byron stood. "Let me escort you to the front door. The men here get a bit stuffy about their privacy, and they do not look kindly upon visitors wandering around alone." By visitors, Marta knew he meant women. Her throat grew hot again at the implication. However, when Byron gave her a warm smile, her anger wilted. The smile told her he did not condone such pompous attitudes and it wrapped her in its protective warmth. As they walked through the adjoining rooms, she basked in that warmth and ignored the stares of the other members. Rarely had she felt such pleasure in the company of a man. Her thoughts whirled in turmoil.

Only one thing troubled her, the haunting memory of the man she had faced twice in the streets of the tenements. She feared she had not seen the last of the hypnotist.

CHAPTER SIX

Taunting voices boom in my head as I storm about my room. My rage overflows into the alleyway outside, where the normal dissonance of chattering voices has died to a whisper. My neighbors shrink back from my howls of anger. A primeval force has been unleashed by my fury, and they dare not stand in its way. They abandon their chores and huddle in their houses while I bellow like a wounded bear.

My torment has a face, the face of a woman whose strange powers have twice prevented me from fulfilling my promises to the Mock Chin Tong. What sort of enchantress is this woman who can thwart me like this? She must be a witch. Only a witch has the power to materialize from nowhere, as she did, and stay my hand. How else to explain what she is doing to me?

Even as I rage, I remember the dark, olive skin and coal black hair that first drew me to her. That and the fire in her eyes which struck me with the force of lightning. What a catch she would make! One I would seriously consider keeping for myself, even if it meant risking the wrath of the tongs. To think I had her in my grasp, only to see her escape my trance-inducing charms!

Today, she appeared as a bad dream, shouting at me and raising her fists like a wild mare. I was too stunned to think what to do until she was nearly on top of me. Once again, I sensed her power and knew I could not stop her. In the end, I was forced to abandon my victim and flee.

My room is spinning. My mind is seething. I am boiling with fresh anger and self-loathing. Why has she victimized me so? She is like my father, who whipped me, only she uses magical charms, not a belt. The result is the same. I am the child, once more, frightened and furious at the same time.

My instincts warn me to stay away from this witch, yet, how can I ignore her? I am drawn to her by a magnetic force that is pulling me into her orbit and I know it's only a matter of time until we confront one another again. It is our destiny. My voices continue pounding in my head. They urge me to find her and strike her down, but I am wary. I must take my time and stalk her with all of my cunning and stealth. I must discover the secret to her strength. Learn that and I will find her weakness. Then, I will snuff out the force she uses to deny me and she will be mine.

Dust rises from the floor as I pace the room. Soon the dust invades my nose and makes me sneeze. This is a good thing, for it clears my head and sharpens my thoughts. As badly as I want to capture that witch, I have more pressing matters. When I delivered the girl with the black mark in her eye, the tongs were pleased. But since then, I have failed them again, thanks to that woman's meddling, and the tongs are growing restless. I must make amends. Another failure will bring my downfall. I know it. Another failure and I will no longer be invisible to the hatchet men. Panic seizes my chest at the thought of losing my sanctuary and frustration builds with the fury of a blazing fire inside my head. My throbbing temples are scorched by my fear and anger. I roar again in a futile effort to quiet the battles waging inside of me. I must regain control of myself and bring the tongs what they want. There can be no more missteps, no more blunders.

I must choose my next victim carefully and avoid another public encounter like today's. That means I must find the witch and learn her secret. She dwells somewhere in the tenements. She is not invisible. I will find her.

These thoughts settle my mind, and I stop shouting. The neighbors and merchants interpret the silence as a good sign, a sign that my world has returned to normal. They slowly emerge from their hiding places. In no time at all, their voices are chirping again; the everyday noises that fill the street have resumed.

I hardly hear the clamor. I am still thinking about the woman who has escaped me and how much I will savor trapping and imprisoning her.

* * *

Two days have passed, and I still owe my bosses a fresh catch. I have asked them to be patient awhile longer while I search for the witch who has so tormented me. I roam the streets seeking her spoor. It is not a random search. I have followed a logical course, much like an animal hunting for food. I began where I last saw her, and I range in wider and wider circles around that spot. As always, the shantytown people give me a wide berth. They cross the street to avoid me and throw furtive glances when I pass. Normally, their actions would raise my ire, but not now. My mind is focused on only one thing: tracking down the woman. Nothing will get in my way, not even the tongs. It is the first time I have defied them, and to my surprise, they have relented. It makes me realize how much they need me. It is a glorious realization that has raised my spirits and doubled my resolve.

* * *

It is now the third morning of my search and my patience has been rewarded, for I have found the trail I am seeking. It comes in the form of the redheaded girl who was with the woman when she confronted me on the street. My discovery has sparked a blaze of anticipation. This is the bewitching woman's companion. Follow her, and she will lead me to my quarry.

Clouds have masked the sky with a heavy, dark blanket that threatens rain. The wind rising off the bay chills the air to the point

57

of frost. It is a typical weather pattern for San Francisco: sunny as springtime one day, winter cold the next. I welcome the conditions, however. They are perfect for following someone. People always walk bent over in such weather with their eyes forward and their coat collars pulled about their necks. I have sniffed the air and looked for any signs of danger before falling into step half a block behind the girl. There are none. A wave of euphoria sweeps over me, as it always does when I am stalking my prey. A surge of energy heightens my sense of hearing and smell to the point that I can detect the squealing sounds of rats in the walls of the houses around me and catch the scent of their furry coats. My voices have quieted, for they know I hunt. They never bother me then. Soon, I will have my quarry in sight. Soon, I will ensnare the woman who has bedeviled me. Soon, she will be mine.

The girl walks quickly along the broken sidewalks, watching where she steps and never looking back. My task is almost too easy. I must resist the urge to move closer. It would be foolish to risk detection so near my goal, so I push my hands deeper into my pockets and force myself to maintain a safe distance.

We walk a dozen blocks in this manner, the girl and I, before she halts and unlocks the door to a store front with the words Pacific Aid Society painted on the window. Once inside, she opens the blinds to reveal a small office. No one else is visible through the window, but I am certain the woman I seek will come there. So, I duck into the entryway of an abandoned storefront halfway down the block and wait.

The clouds unleash a driving rain that slants into my hideaway and soaks me to the skin. The rain chills me with stabbing pinpricks of water, but I refuse to move. I am used to discomfort and, like any predator, I never let it get in the way of my hunt. An hour passes before the rain subsides to a steady mist, but there is no sign of the woman. Could I be wrong about the relationship between her and this girl? My instincts tell me no, and my instincts are rarely wrong. I must be patient. I have learned that patience is more often rewarded than not.

There are not many people on the street in this weather. The few who walk past, glance uneasily in my direction but keep moving. They are dressed in rough-hewn clothes with frayed collars that tell me they are no better than I am. More important, they are people who rarely ask questions. No one challenges me or inquires about my business.

The rain finally stops and the clouds slide away to reveal a noonday sun. The wet sidewalks are soon steaming with the vigor of water boiling in a pot, reminding me that I have not eaten since early morning. Fingers of hunger begin to drum on my stomach, but I ignore them just as I did the rain. Hunger will not uproot me from this spot. I will wait here as long as necessary, if it brings me closer to my prize. No sooner have I decided this, than my patience is rewarded. For there she is, hurrying along the street to the very office I have been watching. My instincts were right, after all! Now that she is within reach, a new kind of hunger rises in me, the hunger of the hunter who has found his prey. My body craves to leap from my hiding spot and set upon my victim, to clamp my hands on her dark skin and subdue her. Every fiber in my body aches to possess her. It is all I can do to keep from charging into that office and dragging her back to my room. But I know such a rash confrontation would be foolish. I cannot carry her screaming and struggling through the streets. She must come of her own free will and that she will not do unless she is under my influence. Whatever blocked me from seizing her before would do so again. I dare not try to hypnotize her until I find the key that unlocks her power.

As I struggle with my emotions, a new idea strikes me and my violent urges subside. It is such a delicious idea and so diabolically simple, I cannot help laughing out loud, which causes heads of passersby to turn. I ignore them and smile with satisfaction at my plan. If I cannot have the witch, I will take the companion. The girl is someone she obviously knows well and probably cares about. Capturing her would be sweet revenge for the trouble the witch has caused me, and it would satisfy my bosses. Better still, it will draw my quarry closer to me, for I will be sure she realizes I am the cause of her friend's disappearance. Then, I can lure her to

Chinatown where force can be used to overcome her resistance to my powers. It is a wonderful plan. I can hardly wait to execute it.

For now, however, I must retreat from my hiding place. The women have not left the office and I have stayed as long as I dare. Too many people have noticed me. It is only a matter of time until suspicions are raised and the authorities summoned. My voices whisper to me not to go. They urge me to strike now and take them both, but I know better. I will stay with my plan and return early in the morning for the girl. I will wait for her at the office and hypnotize her there. Taking her from her workplace will be less risky than in the street and the satisfaction of capturing her right under the witch's meddlesome nose will be all the greater. I ignore my voices and depart.

Upon my return to Chinatown, I inform my bosses that I will have a fresh prize for them tomorrow. They nod but say nothing. It is time for me to deliver on my promises.

The next morning I force myself from my bed at dawn and eat a quick meal of rice and fish. My Chinese benefactors consider fish a delicacy and eat it any time of the day. Fish for breakfast is unappealing to me. It tastes sour in my mouth. In any case, I am too excited to care about food. My fingers twitch so much I can barely control my chop sticks. It has been years since I have felt so jittery.

Before joining the tongs, I hypnotized women on the streets of New York, Chicago and other major cities. I wore a cheap suit and talked in the strange language of my voices, much as I do now. Once under my spell, the women gave me whatever I wished . . . cash, jewelry and physical pleasure. I would ask for all their money and then say it was not enough. They would take me to their apartments and empty their hidden treasures in my hands. One of them gave me my amber ring and I quickly discovered its power to catch and hold my victims' attentions.

My nerves never bothered me when I worked, although I did have to worry about the police. Word of my prowess quickly spread, even in larger cities, and I had to keep moving. When I landed in San Francisco, I knew it was the end of the line. I either had to change my methods or find work. That was when I met the tong bosses and my career raced off in a new direction. Capturing women was far more interesting than taking their money and I finally had a safe haven where I could rest without fear of detection. No policeman was going to look for me in the back alleys of Chinatown.

Yet, despite all of my years of experience, this morning I am edgy. My body is tense and my mind doubtful. Of course, there is always a high level of excitement surging through me when I begin a hunt. At such times, I feel like a lion that has smelled fresh meat. But this morning's feelings are different, and I know the reason why. It is because of the woman I have come to think of as a witch. I have never faced an obstacle like her. It has thrown me off balance. I worry she will appear before I am finished and ruin my plan, just as she ruined my hunt a few days ago. That is why I am leaving so early, so I can hypnotize the girl and spirit her away long before the witch arrives. I am not prepared to face her again so soon.

As I expected, the office is closed and the curtains drawn when I arrive. An overcast sky has replaced the storm clouds of yesterday and painted the landscape in charcoal grays. The air retains a sodden odor of laundry not yet hung to dry. The few figures who venture forth look as dreary as the day. Their heads are down. Their hands are buried in their pockets. They walk with quiet feet. There is stillness in the air. For most people, it is an unkind morning, but it is a perfect day for me. I embrace it.

To be safe, however, I do not loiter near the office. There is no need to chance the one pair of curious eyes who might blunder upon me. Instead, I wander the side streets and picture in my mind the redheaded girl I am about to capture. I recall her curly hair, the way it bounced as I followed her the day before. She is a young woman full of zest and life. The tong bosses will be very pleased. After walking a few blocks, I veer back to the office, but it remains lifeless. So I wander in a new direction and complete another circuit of city blocks. This time when I return, the drapes are open and a cheery light from the window chases away the morning's gloomy shadows.

Quickly, I look through the window to be sure the girl is alone. My lips turn upward in a cunning smile. There is no sign of the witch. Before I enter, I scour the street in search of inquisitive eyes or busybodies who might try to interfere in my business, but the street is deserted. It is the perfect time to strike. I head for the office without further delay.

The door jars the silence of the street when I fling it open. The girl's head jerks upwards at the unexpected noise. In less than a heart beat, her expression shifts from a questioning frown to the wide-eyed fear of recognition. Frantically, she averts her gaze. I can tell by the way she looks about her that she is searching for something she can use to defend herself. She settles on the two-piece telephone standing on the desk. Her unsteady hands knock papers askew as she reaches for it, all the while keeping her eyes turned away from mine. But it does her no good. Even as she grasps the phone and tries to fling it at me, her attention is caught by the golden light flitting about on the wall in front of her, a reflection cast by sunlight dancing on my ring. She grips the phone until her hand turns white, but she is rooted to her spot.

"Who are you?" she cries in a stricken voice. "What do you want with me?"

I do not answer. Instead, I let my hand float in the room so that the golden light from my amber ring beckons her. Slowly, her body relaxes and she follows the irresistible light back to its source. I continue to wave my hand and the light dances seductively. She is now completely absorbed in its movement. Papers float to the floor, followed by the crash of the phone as she drops it and turns to face me. I speak to her in words even I do not understand. They originate from the voices in my head but I have no idea what they mean. They always pour from me at this stage and their effect is as powerful as a waterfall.

The girl sways to the music of my voice and the beauty of the butterfly light. Then I speak more sharply and she looks into my face. I fix my eyes on hers and snare her gaze in mine. She is under my spell now, in a trance so deep even I am uncertain how long it will last. Perhaps a day, perhaps a night. Long enough for me to lead her back to my room and prepare her for the tongs. When she does awake, she will struggle, but it will be too late, for my melodic words will be replaced by drugs. She will never know the outside world again.

An older man watches from the window next door as I lead the girl from the building and guide her along the street. I do not mind a witness now. He will tell the witch and she will come looking for me, just as I have planned. The girl walks passively at my side, her dulled eyes staring ahead of her into eternity. I have no need to touch my victims. It is a simple matter to control them with my voice.

Morning sunlight has broken through the overcast and shines on our faces, but the girl makes no effort to shade her eyes. She walks obediently at my side along Folsom Street to Third, where we turn left and cross Market Street by Lotta's Fountain, a famous San Francisco landmark. From there it is only a few blocks until we are absorbed by the sing-song world of Chinatown, where I will become invisible, again.

CHAPTER SEVEN

As soon as Marta saw the wide-open door, she knew something was wrong. She raced into the office only to find it lifeless and abandoned. Papers lay scattered across the floor along with the telephone, whose cord had been ripped from its wall socket. Her chest tightened at the thought that some harm might have come to Missy. She frantically looked about her for any clues as to what might have happened. Her first thought was that vandals had broken into the office looking for money, but that didn't explain Missy's absence. Had she struggled with them and run away? If so, why hadn't she returned with the police? It made no sense.

She ran next door to use Mr. Jarvis' telephone to call the police station. Her neighbor was well into his eighties but he still opened his Horse Feed and Saddle Repair shop each morning, just as he had for the past forty years. His hands twitched all the time now, his eyesight was failing and his memory didn't last more than a day or two, but he was remarkably fit for his age. A few loyal customers still patronized his store but most of the time he had little to do.

Marta found him seated in his familiar chair by the window, where he spent hours watching the street. "Mr. Jarvis, may I use your telephone?" She spoke in such haste that the words stumbled over one another. She could see from the worried expression on his face that he was confused. She forced herself to continue more slowly. "I think someone broke into my office. They severed my telephone line and there is no sign of Missy."

Mr. Jarvis scratched his neck with the back of his trembling fingers and frowned in thought. "Let me think, now. I believe I saw Missy this morning." His watery eyes shifted from Marta to the street as he spoke, as if he was looking for someone. His expression brightened and he returned his attention to her. "I did see her, by golly. She was walking down the street with an older fellow. I think it must have been her father. He was talking to her sort of familiar like and she was nodding her head."

That was hardly the answer Marta had expected. Why would her drunken father come looking for Missy and why would she leave with him like that? An emergency, perhaps, but what? Confusion swirled in her mind. Something had clearly upset Missy. The strewn papers and damaged telephone attested to that. Yet, according to Mr. Jarvis, she had left quietly. Marta's instincts told her to call the police, but she didn't know what to tell them. That her assistant had had a fit of anger and left with her father?

The disarray in her office made no sense and try as she might, she could not find an explanation for it. She sighed and looked out the window. There was nothing for it but to go looking for the father and that meant plunging into San Francisco's infamous Barbary Coast along the city's waterfront. It was the only place he was likely to be.

* * *

Marta began her search near the Ferry Building and worked her way towards Fisherman's Warf. A chilly breeze chafed her face and sharpened the briny odors of salt water rippling in the bay. As she walked, she buttoned her jacket and hunched her shoulders in an effort to ward off the cold. Sailors called to her from doorways inviting her inside the grimy bars lining the docks. A red-faced worker leered at her with his one good eye and rubbed his private parts to show her his interest. She turned her head away from him and hurried on. Rats scurried for cover from the feet of drunken men stumbling from one establishment to the next. One sailor emerged from a bar holding a beer mug in one hand and carrying a buxom woman over his shoulder. The woman brayed with laughter as she allowed herself to be jounced along the dust-laden, wooden walkway to another dimly lit grogshop, where they disappeared inside.

At each bar, Marta had to force herself to overcome the stench of urine and spilled beer as she plunged inside in search of Missy or her father. All of her inquiries went for naught. No one had heard of Missy and those who knew her father said they had not seen him in awhile. When she asked what they meant by awhile--a day, a week, or longer--they guffawed and shrugged their shoulders. Days on a calendar had little importance along the waterfront. She had nearly decided to abandon her search when she entered a particularly shabby place where two black men sat strumming on a banjo and guitar and singing bawdy songs.

The bartender turned out to be a woman of such grand proportions that Marta feared she might be smothered if she stood too close. "Old McCallen? Sure, I seen 'im this marnin'." The woman's heavily painted mouth parted in a mean grin that revealed several missing teeth. "Too damned broke to buy his own ale. Went next door to the Pelican's Pail with some sharpy what offered him a drink. Ain't seen 'im since. Probably still thar."

Marta rushed next door and peered into the room's dim light. Her heart hammered in rhythm to the banjo music still audible from next door as she looked about frantically for Missy, but she was not among the handful of solitary customers who sat scattered throughout the room. Marta had not seen the father since Missy first joined her, but a man sitting alone in the gloom at the far end of the bar caught her attention. He had a peculiar way of angling his head to one side as he squinted in her direction. It was a familiar gesture and it told Marta she had found Missy's father.

About the only words she could have used to describe him were weather beaten. He reminded her of the tattered sails and splintered hull of a shipwrecked schooner cast upon some rocky shore. Pasty skin and sunken eyes created a ghoulish image that had so little in common with the man she had previously met that she feared it wasn't him after all. But once she introduced herself, he nodded and asked about his daughter.

"You haven't seen her, then?" She found it difficult to hide her disappointment.

"Not since you took'er from me." The words dribbled from his misshapen mouth without rancor. His hands shook as he leaned on the counter. His body shuddered involuntarily. Marta had seen those signs many times in the houses she visited. They were the manifestations of a man who badly needed his next drink and didn't care how he got it. Marta's hands trembled as well, but for a very different reason. Whatever happened to Missy, Marta was convinced she had not left the office with this man.

Missy's father stretched his vowels in the same tuneful manner as his daughter. It reminded Marta so much of her friend that tears gathered in the corner of each eye. The father was quick to note the anguish on her face and like any good drunk, instantly tried to turn it to his advantage. "Gimme a drink for me troubles." He reached out and grasped her arm as he spoke. Marta recoiled as one would when unexpectedly brushing a spider's web. She immediately regretted her reaction. He was simply a harmless old man who lived inside a bottle.

"Give him whatever he's drinking," she told the barman.

"Rum," he clarified.

"A glass of rum then." She paid for the drink and hurried from the place. The salt air smelled pure and sweet after the rank odors inside the bar, but once Marta was back on the street, depression sank into her thoughts. Mr. Jarvis hadn't seen Missy with her father. She had wasted half a day looking for them and now she was back to square one and was not any closer to solving the mystery of the disheveled office. According to Mr. Jarvis, Missy had left of her own free will, yet it was apparent some sort of struggle had taken place.

As she stood there staring at a street littered with broken glass and dried vomit, a frightening idea wormed its way into her thoughts. At first, she pushed it aside as too diabolical to consider, but the idea was not so easily discarded. It took root in her mind and filled her with dread. What if the man Mr. Jarvis had seen was the hypnotist? The idea sent a wintry chill scudding through her body. It was the only explanation that made any sense. Missy would have been terrified of him and would have tried to resist, which maybe accounted for the mess in the office. Once he began his hypnotic ritual, however, Missy would have become docile and compliant. Marta recalled how close *she* had come to succumbing to the man's will. If he had succeeded in putting Missy into such a trance, Marta had no doubt that she would have done his bidding.

Frightful images of her friend being whisked away raced through her mind. Was such a thing possible? Would he have dared enter the office like that? An excruciating ache deep inside of her told Marta the answer was yes. But where had he taken Missy? And why? Marta guessed he lived somewhere in the tenement district. That was where he had always been seen and where Marta had encountered him.

Again, she considered calling the police, but she realized how futile that would be. What could she say to them? That her office employee had been seen by Mr. Jarvis leaving with a man of her own free will, a man he believed was her father? Their reaction would be quite predictable. Other than the scattered papers in her office and the telephone, there was no evidence of any violence or other misdeed. There were only rumors of a fiendish man who preyed on unsuspecting women.

Another idea crept into her mind, one even more sinister than the first. On two occasions she had confronted the man she now called the hypnotist and both times she had resisted his powers. What if he had followed her back to the office and, in a fit of anger, taken Missy? The possibility that she might be responsible for Missy's misfortune struck Marta with chilling force. If she was somehow responsible for her friend's disappearance, she would never forgive herself.

She had to find Missy and free her from that horrible man's clutches. But where should she begin? The tenements were a maze of narrow streets and back alleys. Even if he did live there, it would be an impossible task to search such a convoluted area alone. If he lived elsewhere, there was a city as large as an ocean in which he could lose himself.

Marta's shoulders sagged under the weight of her helplessness as she trudged back to her office. Her gaze darted continuously up and down the streets in hopes her tormentor would appear, but all she saw were the weary faces of the poor going about their dismal lives. They looked as hopeless as she felt and the sight of them deepened her dismay.

Marta had been in such a rush when she left to search for Missy she had failed to lock the office door. To her surprise she saw a woman waiting inside when she returned. The person seated so primly beside her desk was none other than Angela Cummings. Marta took a quick breath to overcome her shock before entering.

"Angela, what are you doing here?" Exasperation tinged Marta's words, but when she saw the anguished look on the woman's face, a spark of guilt chided her for being so unkind. She knew Angela was going through an awful experience and even though she still wore one of those silly dresses, it had a crumpled look that suggested it had been worn more often than it should without cleaning.

The woman nearly leaped to her feet. She managed a weak smile, but her lips trembled and her jaw worked back and forth in the manner of a horse chewing on its reins. Worry lines flowed from pockets beneath her eyes; her cheeks had the gaunt look of someone who had lost her most precious possessions. She had aged ten years since they last met on the street. Angela's sudden plunge from the ranks of society had obviously taken a great toll on her.

"I . . . I wanted to ask a favor." Angela straightened herself as if to declare that she wasn't there to beg, but from the way she twisted the handkerchief in her hands, it was clear she was having a hard time finding the courage to say her piece.

"Yes, Angela, what is it?" Marta asked in a softer tone. She offered the chair Angela had used while waiting and the woman quickly sat down again.

"I have nowhere to go," she said with simple candor, "and nothing much to do, really, since . . . since my life changed." She stood up again before Marta could reply. "I have a little money," she added quickly, "and lodgings. But it will not last long if I don't find employment and there is little that I can do well." Another pause and a deep breath punctuated the air between them. A tear escaped Angela's bravado and trickled down one of the lines in her cheek. She swiped it away with her handkerchief and pressed on. "The thing is, I *do* know something about working with . . . with the poor, which I guess includes me now, and I really do like helping them. I know you believe I was just being a bubble head about it, but I did try to make a difference."

Angela raised her chin to signal that her self-respect was returning. "And I thought of you, because your work really does have a positive effect on the people who live in the tenements. I admire what you do and I hope I can help."

Thoughts swirled through Marta's mind with the capriciousness of an unexpected snow flurry. Missy's face surfaced, swooshed away and reappeared. Marta desperately wanted to search for her, but she didn't know where to begin. And here was Angela, looking for a handout. No, that was unfair. She seemed sincere about working. Perhaps Marta had misjudged her. Another face unexpectedly appeared: Byron Wagner's. Why hadn't she thought of him before? It was Angela's association with society that reminded her of him. Byron had offered to find his friend, Charles, who knew about hypnotism. Maybe his friend could help her find Missy. It was the slimmest of hopes, but it was all she had, and it buoyed her spirits.

She had to see Byron at once, but not before resolving what to do about Angela. She needed someone to watch the office while she looked for Missy and Angela did have some experience working in the tenements. She wouldn't be the worst choice to help until

Missy returned. And hiring Angela would help the poor woman rebuild her self-worth.

There was only one thing that troubled Marta. If the hypnotist had taken Missy, what was to prevent him from taking Angela? It wouldn't be fair to bring her on board, at least not without warning her first. Marta turned her attention back to the woman standing expectantly before her.

"Missy has disappeared, Angela. I think she might have been kidnapped right from this office. If you work here, you must keep the door locked at all times and only open it for women or couples who have an appointment. Under no circumstance are you to open it for a man who is alone. Is that understood?"

Color rose in Angela's cheeks and her face visibly brightened. "Do you mean you will hire me?"

"While Missy is gone, yes. I will need someone to run the office and answer the phone and I guess you are as well suited as anyone. As long as I can depend on you, I'm willing to give it a try."

Angela's eyes welled up with tears. She threw her arms around Marta and hugged her so tightly Marta felt her lungs would burst. The warmth of Angela's body surprised her. She detected the pleasant odor of rose water on her skin and a faint fragrance of perfume. How much longer could Angela afford such items she wondered? The salary Marta paid Missy sure wouldn't keep her in those luxuries. While she did say she had a little money, Marta suspected it wasn't much. It wouldn't last long if she failed to live within her means.

Marta sighed and looked around the forlorn room. It had been so cozy before, but with Missy gone, it had lost its sparkle. Well, there was no time for lamenting. She had to give Angela enough direction to get her started, then contact Byron and continue looking for her lost friend.

* * *

Somewhere in the back of Missy's dreams she heard women singing, but their songs did not carry a tune. Nor did they remind her of the songs she learned as a child. They were filled with discordant notes and were sung in sharp voices with little harmony.

Other noises, clanging sounds that made her think of metal pots tumbling down a flight of stairs, also interrupted her sleep. She remembered the sound because she had once rolled two pots down a staircase as a child in Scotland. Her mother had scolded her for it. For a moment, she wondered if she *was* in Scotland, although it didn't seem likely, given the rude voices and noises she heard. They sounded nothing like the Scotland she remembered. Her side was sore. She realized it was because she was lying on a hard wooden floor instead of a soft bed. This made no sense to her. She tried to sit up but something held her hands behind her and prevented her from rising. A feeling of panic churned her stomach. What was wrong with her? Why couldn't she get up and go to her bed? Her mind was in such a fog that she could not comprehend what was happening. At last, she managed to open her eyes and was greeted by an un-swept floor covered by a layer of dust and bits of straw. The far wall was bruised to the color of black welts from some violence visited upon it. Nothing she saw reminded her of home or the room where she lived.

Missy was about to cry out when she realized a cloth had been bound in her mouth. Someone had gagged her! She tried to shift her position, but it did little good. The hard floor pained her side relentlessly. Just when it seemed she could stand it no longer, a tall figure appeared in her field of vision and reached down to lift her up. Her hands were still bound behind her but with his help she was able to sit up and look about her. The first thing she saw was the intense gaze of the man standing over her. Her heart filled with giddy relief. It was the wonderful man who had brought her here. Now that she could look into those deep set eyes, all was well again. The pain disappeared from her side and her fear vanished.

Despite her happiness, however, she couldn't blot out the images of the man entering the office where she worked and taking her away. Something about her situation wasn't right. If the man was her friend, why was she bound and gagged, and if he was her captor, why did her skin tingle with warmth at the sight of him? He *had* confronted her and brought her here, yet she remembered coming willingly. The circumstances were too confusing for her to understand. Besides, when she looked into his eyes she no longer cared how she came to be here. Her whole body glowed under his gaze. She surrendered her thoughts to his. He made her blissfully happy. That was all that mattered.

His thin hands untied the rope around her ankles, lifted her to her feet and held her upright until she regained some balance on her unsteady legs. He stroked her hair while his voice mumbled soothing words she could not understand. But understanding his words was not important. It was enough to hear his voice and to know he cared. The panic that had seized her when she first awoke was gone. She was ready to follow him anywhere.

They emerged into the heavy shadows of an alleyway. She understood at once the source of the strange, singing voices she had heard. She was surrounded by Chinese men and women chattering away like songbirds in their cages. Although she had never been there, she realized she was in Chinatown. She shivered with delight at the strange scenes she saw as she walked along the narrow street in her companion's strong grip. Her pleasant interlude was interrupted, however, by a rogue thought that broke through the surface of her reverie. She had no business in Chinatown. It was a fearful place filled with unfamiliar faces. It was a place where people became lost and fell down the stairway to Hell, just like those tumbling cooking pots. She should be at work, not here. Yet, she found the cooking odors of fish and pork and rice exotic and felt no fear. She was in the safe embrace of the man who accompanied her. He would protect her from the evil that lurked in the shadows.

They entered a restaurant where three unsavory men with hardened faces and dulled expressions leaned against a wall. She felt their sinister eyes pricking her skin and she turned her face away from them. A few solitary men sat at small, round tables shoveling rice into their mouths with chopsticks. They sat on wooden chairs with no backs and leaned on their arms while they ate. Silk art hung on the walls and mahogany screens divided the room into discreet sections.

Missy saw smoke hanging in the air from a smaller room in the back where a man in a yellow silk shirt and black trousers sat at an intricately carved mahogany desk. Her companion directed her towards the room and when she entered she saw two more men who reminded her of the ones outside. They were seated on a low couch, smoking. Two young Chinese women with rice-powdered faces and bright lipstick sat on a facing couch. Their parted legs revealed no undergarments under their opened robes. Shocked, Missy quickly looked away. Her prudish behavior prompted the women to laugh in sing-song voices that hurt her ears. She wished her companion had not brought her here. There was evil in this place. She began to worry that he might not protect her from it.

The Chinaman rose from behind his desk and approached her. He spoke to her companion in English but the brazen women's sing-song voices still echoed in her head and prevented her from understanding what he said. From the way the Chinaman's eyes raked her body, however, she was pretty sure he was discussing her. She wanted to look away but her companion held her chin so she was forced to return the Chinaman's frank gaze. The man smiled at her, revealing tobacco stained teeth. All at once, his hands brushed her chest and his fingers swiftly released the buttons on her dress! She wanted to protest, but he gave her such a fierce look she dared not speak. She looked to her companion for help and immediately became lost in his fathomless eyes. She had no idea what to do, but his gaze reassured her. As long as he stood by her she could endure anything, even the embarrassment of exposure to this vile man. She stood like a stone statue while her dress slipped to the floor and her undergarments were removed.

Missy had always been a good girl, a church-going girl, even when she was surviving on San Francisco's streets before Marta rescued her. She had declined the boys' kisses and resisted their temptations. The idea of undressing in front of these men was horrific to her, yet she stood in the chilled air unmoving and let the Chinaman's fingers rove her body. When she closed her eyes, she imagined slimy eels slithering across her breasts and down her back. She had always detested eels. The thought of them on her body made her squirm. It took all of her self-control to resist the desire to scream and run from the room. Only her companion's presence held her there. When the Chinaman was done, a robe was thrown over her making her look no different than the painted women on the couch. She trembled as the men on the opposite couch openly stared at her. The Chinaman who had undressed her gave a curt command, and one of the men stood up. He grasped her arm and began to lead her away. Missy looked wildly over her shoulder at her companion, waiting for him to rescue her, but he remained beside the Chinaman. A wave of hysteria rose in her throat, nearly gagging her. He was abandoning her! She would never see him again. That realization filled her with dread. She tried to scream but no sound escaped her lips. Her mind had become paralyzed with a fear that slithered through her brain like the eels. Wherever she was going, it was beyond the frontiers of her world. She was at sea, traveling to a new world, just as when she came to America. And as before, no one would be there to welcome her or to rescue her from her plight.

Her new escort took her out a back door and down a filthy alley that was no wider than the two of them. Missy still couldn't understand why her companion had forsaken her. She stumbled on the uneven pathway and would have fallen but for her escort's painful grip on her arm. The alley smelled of rotted food and stagnant water. Refuse was strewn about in haphazard piles. Any individuals they encountered hurried out of the way and kept their eyes downcast. Their fear was as palpable as hers. Suddenly, her escort turned into an even narrower alley and pushed her through a doorway into a dingy room where several Chinese women in skimpy lingerie lounged idly on chairs or couches. Missy peered into the smoky gloom with a new sense of dread, for she knew all too well what awaited her here. She had been in the very same situation shortly after her arrival in San Francisco, when she had been taken to a brothel to "entertain men." The idea that she faced the same fate for a second time was too much for her and she collapsed on the dirty floor. The room filled with mocking laughter. Her life had come full circle. This time she would not escape her fate.

CHAPTER EIGHT

Marta had visited a few of the mansions along Van Ness Avenue with her father when she was young, but none as palatial as Byron Wagner's. Three balconies framed green-shuttered windows on the upper floors. Below, shaded verandas with white wicker chairs were sequestered behind palm trees and great oaks. One look told Marta the imposing residence held no less than thirty rooms. As she walked up the tree-lined walkway and rang the bell, she wondered how many people could be housed and fed by just this one house. Hundreds, she guessed. It was just the kind of blatant display of wealth that raised her temper and made her head ache.

The butler who answered the door pursed his lips in a subtle expression of disapproval as he appraised her plain, cotton clothing. Marta knew from his haughty attitude that he thought she was someone's maidservant and should be calling at the back door. When she identified herself, however, his expression flattened into a mask of indifference. He stood back and held the door open, indicating that she should come in. The interior was no less enchanting than the house's exterior. A two-story, marble entryway larger than her own living room surrounded a winding staircase that seemed to float in the radiant light pouring into the vast room from a series of the high-arching windows on either side of the doorway. Green plants in over-sized, clay pots and large paintings on the far walls softened the room's brilliant glare.

Marta was led to a drawing room with two couches and cushioned chairs grouped around a glass coffee table. The stitched, satin fabrics that covered the furniture were as elegant as the clothing worn by 'society' women. A grand piano stood at the far end of the room. China teacups and a silver teapot sat on a side board. She lowered herself delicately on the edge of one couch, her back rigid with tension, and gazed at the paintings hanging on the walls.

The butler left to advise Byron of Marta's arrival. She had called him from home and he had urged her to come at once. The concern in his voice had warmed and calmed her, but now, as she sat in his grand mansion, her indignation at the spoils of the rich boiled to the surface. She had to remind herself that this man had offered to help her. Still, it galled her to think of how much good this wealth could do for the poor families she saw every day. She sighed. It wasn't Byron's fault she supposed. She knew he had inherited a great deal of money and business interests from his father. So, in a way, he was no different from her and her brother. He had just inherited a great deal more.

A voice coughed politely and she turned to find Byron standing behind her in the doorway. How wonderful he looked in his smoking jacket and trousers! It was his warm smile, however, that enchanted her. All of her feelings of indignation at his grand home were shunted aside and replaced by the joy of seeing him again. She smiled and stood up, suddenly uncertain what to do. When she first met him at his club, she had found herself flustered and afraid if she spoke that she would become tongue-tied. It was no different now. Her chest thrummed as though a humming bird had become trapped inside of her and her mouth was as dry as desert sand.

"It is good to see you again, Miss Bald . . . excuse me, Marta."

He joined her and motioned for her to sit down again. Marta leaned back into the folds of the couch. To her surprise, she felt more comfortable now that Byron was present, although the humming bird had not stopped buzzing in her chest. It was disquieting to admit the range of emotions she felt around this man.

Byron sat opposite her. "Would you care for tea?" He indicated the teacups she had noted before.

She shook her head no and smoothed her dress with her hands while she gathered her thoughts. "Thank you for seeing me on such short notice, Byron. As I told you, my helper and companion is missing and I am quite beside myself with worry. I hoped your friend might be able to help, although I'm not sure how. It's just that you said he knows about hypnotism and I believe that is what happened to Missy. I believe the man I spoke of before has taken her."

Marta felt tears welling in her eyes and tried desperately to stop them. She didn't want to appear the foolish, weak woman now. Not in front of Byron. But the tears would not cooperate and were soon streaming down her face. Byron immediately took a clean handkerchief from his pocket and handed it to her. She smiled her thanks and wiped her face. The embroidered, silk cloth felt soothing on her cheeks. She squared her shoulders and calmed herself. "Do I make any sense?" she asked plaintively.

"Yes indeed." Byron rubbed his hands and took his pipe from his coat pocket. She waited for him to clamp it between his teeth, but he merely held it. "In fact, I have just located Charles and was about to go fetch him when you called. He may very well know of this man, or where to find someone like him."

Marta's spirits rose at Byron's encouraging words. "Can we go to him now?" she asked anxiously.

Byron frowned and leaned back in his chair. "I would advise you not to. He's in a rather nasty place, one not fit for ladies. You are welcome to wait here," he added quickly when he saw the disappointment on her face.

"Where is he?"

"Chinatown. He has an appetite for opium, I'm afraid, and often frequents the opium dens found there. The establishment he prefers is called Blind Annie's Cellar. I plan to go find him and fetch him back here."

Chinatown! The name raised chilling images of dark alleys, fallen women and nefarious men. Marta had heard terrifying stories about thugs and murderers and Chinese women sold into slavery. The idea of going there sent icicles of fear and excitement darting through her. It was the last place she wanted to visit, but she knew somehow that she must if she were to find Missy. There could well be a connection between Missy and that Chinese enclave. Where else would the hypnotist take his captured women? It was the one place where he could hide them from prying eyes and inquisitive neighbors. But for what purpose? Slavery? Prostitution? The thought of such fates appalled her. Would that have been her fate if she had succumbed to his charms? Could it be Missy's?

"I want to go with you, Byron. I must." She mustered her courage and looked him in the eye to show her determination not to be left behind. She had to see this place for herself.

Byron's frown deepened to one of concern. She could see by the way he shifted his weight and looked away from her that he was struggling with her request. When he clamped his teeth on his pipe, she knew he had made up his mind. "I have never been there myself, Marta, but I hear it's not a pretty place. However, I'm told it's safe enough in the daytime and we will be accompanied by a police officer. If it's your wish to join me, I suppose there is no harm in it."

Marta beamed him a smile and was pleased to see his face brighten as well. He looked rather handsome when he smiled. This realization brought a flood of warmth to her face and she quickly looked away. She was still confounded by her reactions to the man and had no idea how to deal with them. Her greatest fear was making a fool of herself since Byron Wagner moved in different circles than hers. She did not expect him to show her any interest beyond her problem.

"Then it's decided," he said and rubbed his hands once more.

"Let me call my carriage."

Fifteen minutes later they were on the outskirts of Chinatown. They had arrived there in grand style. Byron's carriage was appointed with leather seats and a family crest on the doors. Its springs were so pliant Marta barely felt the bumps in the uneven pavement. People stared at them as they passed as if they were royalty, which in a way she supposed they were. Well, not her, but certainly Byron. Yet when she observed him, she saw a man who seemed unaffected by his wealth. He wore a simple jacket and tie. His hair was just as tousled as the day she faced him at the club and from the way he fiddled with his pipe, she had the distinct feeling he was ill at ease with all of the attention. In fact, he acted a little shy, a characteristic she found quite endearing.

The brief excursion had been surprisingly uplifting. Marta was amazed at how enjoyable it was to ride in such a fine vehicle, although she knew much of the pleasure came from the company seated across from her. Still, she saw how easily one could become accustomed to such luxury and this insight surprised her. Not that she had any need to worry about falling into such a trap. She would never possess that kind of money, and if Samuel were not more responsible, she might end up with none at all.

"We will go on foot from here. The police captain who works this precinct will guide us." Byron's announcement interrupted her thoughts and she looked up, startled that they had arrived so quickly. No sooner had he helped her down then a man in a black suit with a handlebar mustache approached them.

"Afternoon, Mr. Wagner," he said with a tip of his bowler hat. His eyes swung to Marta. "Didn't know you were bringing a lass. Might be better if you wait here, miss."

"Captain O'Connor, meet Marta Baldwin. Don't worry about her. She has more backbone than most men I know."

Marta blushed openly at Byron's compliment. "Pleased to meet you," she said. The officer's confident demeanor impressed her. Here was a man who got things done, she realized. Here was an officer to whom she could turn if the police at the station failed to find the hypnotist. She would keep him in mind.

The captain gave her a frank appraisal. "We don't get many women coming down here, but the place is safe enough during the day. Just don't come wandering around here after dark. It's a bit different then." With that, he led the way as they started their adventurous journey into Chinatown.

At first, they entered broader streets congested with throngs of people. The men wore black jackets, trousers and bowler hats and shuffled along in thick-soled shoes. By contrast, the women wore pantaloons beneath black gowns, large jade earrings and high rocker shoes. Gold clasps held the women's hair in neat buns at the back of their heads, but Marta was amazed to see pigtails dangling from under the men's hats. Curiosity at the presence of three "foreigners" was evident in quick glances. If Marta stared directly at someone, either man or woman, they instantly looked away. A small girl with silver bracelets on her ankles held the hand of her mother as they passed. She peeked out from under her mother's arm with a tentative smile. A withered, old man leaned on a cane and peered out from under a black skull cap at the three of them. Everywhere she looked, she saw scenes she had never witnessed before.

Shops offered everything from dried lizards to opium pipes. An endless selection of restaurants crowded the busy sidewalks. Sing-song voices filled the air, which was thick with smoke from dozens of chimneys and braziers. The smoke cast an eerie fog that dimmed the light and heightened the quarter's sense of mystery.

The thick air mingled with the odors of plucked poultry, pickled herrings, fresh fish, tubs of snails and roasted ducks packed in ice or glazed with a salty wax. Eels, sharks, octopi, lotus roots and melons poured from the shops onto the streets. Whole hogs could be seen roasting in steaming barbeque pits. Strings of pork and slender sausages dangled from doorways and windows. Eggs sat suspended in wire baskets affixed to the walls. Men passed her with baskets swinging from the ends of poles braced across their shoulders. The baskets were filled with vegetables and exotic foods with which she was unfamiliar.

They passed Chinese temples, called joss houses, decked with balconies, enormous lanterns and brilliantly painted woodwork. The captain explained that the local people fulfilled their spiritual needs there. A pungent wisp of burning incense curled about Marta's nose from each one they passed.

Captain O'Conner walked ahead of her and Byron with the confidence of a wayfarer who had traveled these roads many times before. Soon, they abandoned the busy streets for a maze of narrow alleyways where the buildings were made of wood and brick walls. Second stories often hung out over their heads. The overhangs crowded the narrow space above them and blocked the light. Tiny windows looked out on filthy streets and standing water. At one point, they came upon a small group of hard-looking men heading their way, but the men turned down a side alley when they caught sight of Captain O'Connor.

"Hatchet men," he said matter-of-factly. "As soon kill you as look at you, but they follow the orders of their tong bosses. The tongs don't want trouble with the law, so they stay clear of white folks and me."

Marta had gotten a good look at their grim expressions. Her heart beat faster at the possibility of coming face-to-face with one of those murderous men.

The clustered streets twisted and turned until Marta became hopelessly lost, but it was clear the captain knew where he was going. She was thankful Byron had brought him along. They entered an alley full of cats and refuse that was so foul smelling that Marta had to press the handkerchief Byron had given her to her nose. They walked single file now with the captain in front and Byron at the rear. Chinese lettering on wooden signs announced numerous opium dens and brothels. Sparsely clad Chinese girls beckoned them from dimly lit doorways. It was a slimy world where people easily lost their way, both in a physical and a spiritual sense. Marta shuddered to think that Missy might have been brought here.

"Almost there," the captain announced. He turned a corner and stopped in front of a door with a sign in both Chinese lettering and English, which read: Blind Annie's Cellar. To Marta's shock, the woman who stood in the doorway was white. She was an evil-looking woman with dull eyes, pallid skin and a fleshy face that had lost its beauty years before.

"That one survives by offering herself to any man who will give her enough change for her next bowl of opium," O'Connor commented as they entered.

The air inside was oppressive from the stupefying smoke of opium pipes. Double-tiered wooden bunks covered with thin mats lined the walls. Each bed had an opium lamp and pipe by its side, and four were occupied by men in various stages of drug induced stupors. Two Chinese men lay on their sides in the full effects of an opium trance, their eyes half-closed and their bodies so still that Marta wondered if they had died. The other two were Caucasian. One took a long puff and then let the pipe tumble from his limp hand. His head fell backward as he, too, entered the dreamland of the opium smoker. The fourth propped himself on his elbow while he cooked a lump of the drug and packed it into the bowl of his pipe.

Smoke from the pipes curled around the lamps, reducing the already feeble light to a yellow glow that made the sultry atmosphere even more depressing. Despite the gloom, Marta saw that the floor had not been swept and that the ceiling and walls were blackened by soot. The men on the beds might be in their own paradise, but the room in which they dreamed was only one step removed from Hell.

Byron walked over to the man cooking his drug and spoke to him in a low voice. Marta could see from the man's languid movements that he had maybe already consumed a pipe full, but he appeared alert enough to recognize his friend. Byron helped him to his feet and guided him back to the doorway where Marta and the captain waited.

"This is Charles. He's a bit fuzzy, I'm afraid, but luckily we found him before he went completely under. We will take him back to my place and let him sleep off the opium for a little while." Despite his lethargic condition, Charles' blond hair was neatly combed and his clothes crisply ironed. Unlike Byron's narrow face and prominent nose, the man's features were broad and ruggedly handsome. With his looks and money, Marta wondered why he needed such an insidious drug to cope with his world. She was particularly struck by his blue eyes which shone through his glazed expression with the radiance of a mid-day sky.

The captain and Byron propped Charles between them and set off for the carriage with Marta close behind. She was relieved when they emerged from the dire alleyways and rejoined the lively crowds on the main street, yet she also experienced a twinge of regret at departing. She hated to think she might be leaving Missy behind. Marta had only gotten a glimpse of Chinatown's sinister underbelly, but it was enough to convince her Missy would not survive there for long and, as badly as she wanted to flee the place, she would have gladly turned around and plunged back into its murky depths if she thought she could locate her friend.

Once Charles was safely aboard the carriage, Marta addressed the captain. "My assistant, Missy McCallen, has disappeared. I believe she's been kidnapped and I fear she might have been brought here." She gestured towards Chinatown.

"That's not likely," he replied with an edge of skepticism in his voice. "There's an unwritten law that white folk aren't to be mistreated here. The tongs are careful not to violate that agreement." He teased his mustache with one hand as he spoke.

"But there's a man who is hypnotizing young women from the tenements. I believe he's the one who has Missy." Marta forced down a note of irritation that rose in her voice. She couldn't afford to alienate this officer if she expected his help.

"Sounds like the tenements are the place to look, then," he concluded. "Have you filed a police report?"

"About the hypnotist, yes, but not about Missy. She just disappeared today." Marta knew her worries probably sounded trivial. "My office door was wide open when I arrived this morning and things were a mess," she hastily added. "I'm certain something is wrong."

The captain rubbed his forehead in thought. "Better give it a day or two. If she doesn't show up by then, go back and file a new report. My bet is she'll return with some explanation."

Marta had hoped he would take some immediate action, but she had to admit there was little to go on. Her fears were mostly driven by instinct. She heaved a sigh of frustration but said nothing further. Police wanted facts, not women's intuition.

Captain O'Connor bid them goodbye and Byron directed his driver to take them home. Marta couldn't help contrasting the differences between the netherworld of opium dens, thieves and murderers she had just visited and the world of carriages clip-clopping along sunlit avenues to homes the size of ships. It was as if she had just visited a foreign country. In a way, she supposed she had, for there had been nothing familiar about Chinatown.

CHAPTER NINE

Marta returned to Byron's drawing room and waited while he arranged for Charles to lie down in one of the house's many guestrooms. Her pulse rate still raced a bit from her brief venture into Chinatown. As she paced the room to calm herself, she took a closer look at the paintings on the walls. Several, she realized, were by famous masters and very valuable. In fact, everywhere she looked, she saw the bounteous treasures of wealth, from the gold clock on the mantel above the fireplace and the crystal chandeliers to the heavy curtains and plush Persian carpets covering the polished, wood floor.

Yet, despite all their money, she knew San Francisco's rich faced a dilemma. They could create their exclusive clubs, hold their fabulous balls, build mansions to rival England's castles, wear diamonds the size of small planets and ride in private carriages and railway cars, but all their glamour and ostentatious displays of money could not buy them what they most coveted: acceptance into New York society. No amount of diamonds or old master's paintings could get them admitted to the Astors' ballroom. To the old money in the East, San Francisco was little more than a Wild West mining town with no cultural background. Their favorite joke was that the San Francisco Art Association sued for damages when the copy of Venus de Milo it ordered arrived without arms.

There was only one thing that could buy the West respectability. Titles. Even the most impoverished Bavarian Prince was invited to the grand social events of New York, while San Francisco's elite were ignored. But San Francisco's upper class had found a solution to their problem. Europe was awash in penniless royalty who were ready and willing to marry for money and San Francisco's wealthy families could offer them millions. The result was a shopping spree by Americans for titled countesses, princes, dukes and barons throughout the capitals of Europe. Marta had found the entire charade absurd, but wedding bells were now ringing all over Europe as San Francisco's society breathed a collective sigh of relief.

When she thought about it, Marta realized it was probably the reason Herbert Cummings had chosen Angela. He intended to marry the countess he was wooing and buy his own title.

Marta's musings were interrupted when Byron returned to the room. She couldn't help wondering if *he* was window shopping for a countess or princess.

"I think an hour or two's rest will put Charles on his feet again," he announced. "You are welcome to wait here. Or you can go home and return later, if you prefer." Byron's formal manner framed his polite offer in a way that left Marta uncertain what to do. She preferred to stay but feared Byron's invitation was really a subtle suggestion for her to leave. An awkward silence hung between them. Once again, confusion reined in her mind. Byron seemed warm and heedful of others, but he was also one of the city's wealthiest young men and he moved in circles Marta did not. Nor did she care to, not with people who were only interested in themselves and their fortunes and Byron was one of them. Yet, every time she saw him, she was drawn into his orbit as readily as a planet revolving around the sun. As always, her conflicting emotions left her disoriented.

"You are welcome to stay, if you wish," Byron said as he offered a tentative smile.

Marta suddenly realized he was acting as awkwardly as she. His timid invitation warmed her heart and whisked her uncertainties away. "You suggested tea when I came earlier. Does the offer still stand?" She glanced at the side board. The cups and teapot were gone.

"Being brewed as we speak. Henry will bring it shortly." Byron gestured to a couch. After Marta sat down, he plopped into a facing chair with an air of relief, crossed his legs in a most informal manner and produced his pipe from a shirt pocket. "I hope you do not consider me ill-mannered, Marta, but I find your company relaxing. If I behave boorishly, please tell me at once."

Marta was so startled by Byron's unexpected comment that it took a moment to regain her voice. "My goodness, Byron, I would never presume to do any such thing, but thank you for asking." Was he just being polite, she wondered, or did he truly feel at ease with her? For her part, she was as tense as a rabbit caught in the shadow of a circling hawk. All of her earlier anxieties returned pell-mell. She found herself so short of breath that she had to close her eyes a moment to compose herself. What was it about this man that vexed her so? She was beginning to act and feel like a silly school girl again. She didn't like the sensation at all.

"Are you all right? You look a little pale. I hope what you saw in Chinatown was not too distressing." Byron uncrossed his legs and leaned forward anxiously as he spoke.

His protective behavior embarrassed Marta. Did he think she was so weak she might faint? She quickly stiffened her back and lifted her head to show that she was fine. However, Byron's comment was a welcome diversion. Whatever was happening to her, she was more than willing to blame it on their excursion into Chinatown. "Yes, it was a rather forbidding place, wasn't it? Not unlike the tenements I visit everyday, although they are not half as grim as those back alleys we saw." To Marta's relief, Byron relaxed and leaned back in his chair. The moment of crisis had passed, and she had regained control of her senses. Nonetheless, it was time to change the subject. "How do you manage to live in such a big house without a family?" She hoped she was not being too forward, but she was quite curious to know how one coped in such a massive place.

"Yes, it is a bit too grand isn't it?" Byron chuckled and stopped a moment to light his pipe. "Frankly, I would be happy to sell the place. It's much too ostentatious for me, but I must think of my brothers and sisters. As the oldest son, I inherited the house, but I don't really consider it mine. My siblings are well-settled with excellent incomes from the estate. However, should anything go wrong, I think it is important to keep this place to fall back on." He smiled and swept the room with his hand. "So here I am, trapped in my luxurious dungeon, trying to think of things to keep Henry, the cooks and the maids busy. I'm sure you noticed Henry is quite proper. I'm afraid there are times when he is at his wits end with me. But we manage to rattle around the place without causing much ado about nothing." A glint of humor glimmered in his eye. "I believe I just quoted from Shakespeare, did I not?"

"Yes, the title to one of his plays." Marta let her shoulders relax in the pillows of the couch as she inspected her host more closely. She was thoroughly enjoying Byron's conversation. Rather than boorish, she found his manner intriguing, even charming in its self-effacing way. She never would have guessed someone with his wealth could be so genuine about himself. He was nothing like the others she had met. The more he talked the more engrossed she became. It was as if he was hypnotizing her with his words, just as the hypnotist had nearly done with his eyes.

Henry brought the tea which he served in such a stiff manner, Marta couldn't resist glancing at Bryon with amusement. He winked at her and thanked his servant. "Go see how Charles is progressing, will you Henry? If he's awake, ask him to join us here."

As they sipped their tea, Byron grew more serious. "That is a fine thing you do, helping the poor. I expect you are making a genuine difference to those people. And the way you have befriended Missy is quite admirable. I'm sure she is a fine young woman. We shall do all we can to find her."

Byron's unexpected words of praise and support nearly shattered the calm demeanor Marta had tried so hard to maintain since their return from Chinatown. She quickly reached for her handkerchief to dab at the corners of her eyes. She didn't know whether her reaction was caused by his kind words or her worry about Missy. It didn't matter. The concern in Byron's voice gave her hope and that was something she badly needed at the moment. Before she could reply, Henry returned with the young man on whom she was pinning her hopes.

Byron rose at once to greet him. "And here is Charles, our resident expert on all things occult. Charles, I would like you to meet Miss Baldwin."

The man who stood before her looked much more promising than the one they had retrieved from Chinatown. His previous dull expression and sluggish behavior had been replaced by a livelier step and clearer eyes, although the confusion on his face told her he was still surfacing from his drug-induced state. He reminded her of the men she so often saw in the tenements when they sobered up after a drinking spree. They were like newborns starting life afresh, uncertain where they were or what to do.

"Please, call me Marta," she offered to break the silence.

Charles scratched his head and looked inquiringly at her and Byron. "Why am I here?" he asked.

"We need your help, Charles," Byron replied. "As I said, you are expert in things occult, including hypnotism. There is reason to believe someone is going around hypnotizing people against their will. Miss Baldwin . . . Marta . . . had a chance encounter with the man and now she fears he has taken her helper." He gestured to the chair next to his. "It's an amazing story. Sit down and listen while I pour you some tea."

Marta described the man's mesmerizing gaze and flashing ring, her trance-like state and her near-drowning experience. Then she told of coming across him in the street hypnotizing a young woman and how she had chased him away. Charles listened intently, but his eyes kept sliding down her face to her neck in a most impolite manner that she found discomforting. Nervously, she grasped the amulet hanging from the leather strap around her neck and rubbed it.

After she finished her story, Charles suddenly stood up and stepped towards her. His unexpected action startled her and she instinctively shrank back into the cushions of the couch.

Unperturbed, he reached down and lifted the charm from her chest.

"May I?" Without waiting for an answer, he turned the ornament over and studied it carefully, then abruptly released it and returned to his seat. "Where did you get that amulet?" He continued to stare at it as he spoke.

Marta could not imagine why Charles was so fascinated by such a simple piece of jewelry and thought, perhaps, it had something to do with the drugs he had so recently taken. His aggressive behavior shook her and she instinctively touched the amulet with nervous fingers while she struggled to regain her mental equilibrium. She glanced at Byron, who seemed as puzzled as she at Charles' unseemly interest.

"From my father," she replied at last. "He brought it back from a trip to the Orient. Why are you so interested in it?" Her voice held a tinge of indignation.

"My apologies for being so forward," Charles apologized. He rubbed his face and shook his head. "I've still got a few cobwebs in me. It's just that I've only seen one of those once before. I believe it explains why you escaped your hypnotic spell."

"Seen what before?" she asked as much in alarm as curiosity. Her hand returned to her throat as though she were about to be attacked.

"An *omamori*. That's what you are wearing. It's a Japanese relic that dates back centuries. The one you're wearing is probably over a hundred years old."

"Just what is an omamori," Byron interjected, "and what does it have to do with hypnotism?"

"It's a religious amulet that protects its owner from danger. It's supposed to have spiritual powers that can block treacherous forces meant to hurt the person wearing it." Charles' hands moved restlessly about his face, rubbing his nose, stroking his chin and pressing his forehead. He constantly shifted in his chair. Marta wondered if he was always so restless, or if it was from the residual effects of the opium. She had seen drunks behave similarly when deprived of their whiskey.

"From what you've told me," Charles continued, "this hypnotist is a very powerful and dangerous man. I have rarely heard of anyone who can hypnotize someone against their will, yet this man seems able to do it whenever he chooses. You were very fortunate. Your omamori prevented him from gaining complete control over you, although he nearly succeeded despite your protective charm."

"But why did he come to my office and take Missy?" she asked plaintively. "Was he looking for me?"

Charles abruptly stood up and began pacing around his chair, his head lowered in thought. Marta wished he would sit down; his nervous energy made her jittery. He stopped just as suddenly and looked at her with a worried expression that sent shivers through her. "No, he would realize something was protecting you and would stay away. But he may have been angry that you escaped him. Worse yet, you stopped him from hypnotizing someone else. My guess is, if he took your friend, it was a form of revenge."

Revenge. The word hung in the room with deadly menace. Was it possible Missy's fate had been decided by such a vindictive whim? The awful truth of what Charles implied quickly sank in. If the hypnotist took Missy to avenge her, then Marta was responsible for her companion's plight. If anything happened to Missy, it would be Marta's fault. An agonizing knot of anguish flared in her throat. It took all of her willpower to swallow the knot and stop herself from crying out in sorrow.

"That doesn't make Missy's disappearance your fault, Marta," Byron said softly. He had read her mind. If Charles had not been standing there, she would have walked over and poured herself into his arms. She needed physical comfort in a way she never had before, at least not since her father died. She sat there, instead, and tried to quell the emotions running riot through her.

Charles grasped the magnitude of what he had said and his fidgety behavior subsided. "Byron's right. This man is pure evil. It would be impossible to second guess his reasons or motives. The important thing is to find him. He's going to stand out wherever he goes. He can't hide from everyone. People have seen him and he has to take these girls someplace. My guess is Chinatown. I'll make some inquiries. There're people I know who can help."

Marta grabbed hold of Charles' words and hung onto them for dear life. They were all the hope she had. She desperately needed to believe in them.

CHAPTER TEN

I am gun powder waiting to be struck by a match. I am nitroglycerin sweating in the sun. I am a volcano near to bursting with fire. My pent-up anger is close to boiling over and the voices in my head mock me for my impotence. I press my hands over my ears in a futile attempt to silence them and pace my room, but it does not help.

My world is coming undone.

Oh, my bosses are pleased enough with my most recent conquest. The red-haired girl will bring them a handsome income; they are already taking bids for her. The date for her first customer has been set three days hence, but the bosses are in no hurry. The bidding continues to rise.

Inquiries are being made about her, however, and about me. It is because of that woman, whose strange powers bedevil me at every turn. She has even had the nerve to enter Chinatown. News of outsiders travels quickly here, especially when they leave the main streets. I could not believe it when I heard that a dark-haired woman had ventured into the narrow lanes that spread in spider web fashion throughout my lair. Surely, I thought, it couldn't be her, but when I sped down the alleys and clambered over the rooftops to see for myself, there she was! I hid where I could watch undetected. Oh, how I chaffed to get my hands on her. Oh, how I wanted to curl my fingers around her neck. At one point, I could have reached out and touched her hair!

My arms ached to grab a handful of that dark hair and pull her to me, but she wasn't alone. A male companion and a police captain accompanied her. I shook with frustration and fury at the sight of them. I wanted to charge into their path and turn the full force of my gaze upon them, but that would have been folly. My powers were not strong enough to entrance two men and the witch had already proven she could thwart my commands. So I was reduced to watching them as they entered Blind Annie's Cellar and emerged with a man they called Charles.

* * *

It is a day later, but my heart still thunders inside of me. I cannot stop my mind from racing through yesterday's memories. I cannot prevent myself from thinking about how close I was to the witch who now bedevils my life.

The tongs have heard of yesterday's invasion and they are not amused. They are particularly upset about the police captain snooping through their neighborhoods. They know the police are undermanned here. The few who venture into Chinatown do little more than walk the main streets. The police captain is a different breed, however. He is bolder, one of the few who dares venture into the alleyways that lead to the opium dens, like Blind Annie's Cellar. I fear the tongs will blame me for this development once they learn of the connection between the woman and the red-haired girl.

To make matters worse, the man called Charles has returned to ask questions about the red-haired girl, and about me. As a customer of the opium dens, he knows people who will talk to him. This makes the tongs most uneasy. Imprisoning white girls, even if they are from the poor neighborhoods, must be done with great discretion. The girls I bring are solely for the pleasure of rich Chinese men and are carefully guarded from prying eyes. The tongs do not want too bright a lantern shone on them. It seems I have become such a lantern.

I can feel the walls of my room closing upon me and I must escape. So I abandon my room and hurry through the narrow streets, where familiar cooking odors and sing-song voices fill my senses. How comforting such smells and sounds have become to me! They bring me the peace I never knew as a child. They have become my home, my family. My heart rate slows to normal. My feet abandon their frenzied efforts to flee my doubts and fears.

As I walk, my random thoughts begin to crystallize. First, I must rid Chinatown of the man called Charles. He poses too much of a threat to the tongs and to myself. He cannot be allowed to wander the streets and ask his questions. Second, I must enslave the witch. She will be my finest prize, one that will bring me great rewards and pleasures. To succeed, however, I must overcome the force she possesses that clouds my eyes and causes drums to beat inside my head.

So, I must keep my distance and follow the woman discreetly as she goes about her day. Such energy she possesses! I want to feel that energy coursing through my own body. I want to be free of my endless cycles of winters and summers. Once she is mine, I will feed upon her strength and use it to escape my winter cave.

* * *

She has hired another red-haired woman, but this one is older and not so interesting. I do not think my bosses will want her. *I* do not want her, but I hope to use her somehow. Since I cannot hypnotize the witch, I must find a way to lure her to me. If I threaten those around her, perhaps I can entice her to enter my lair again, only this time without an army of protectors. Then, I need not worry about her ability to resist my powers. I will take her by force and discover the source of her resistance. Then, I will put her under my spell. She will not escape. She will be mine. My voices like my plan and chant their approval.

I have shifted tactics and have begun to stalk the new, red-haired woman through the streets of the tenements. She is not as slim as the girls I normally seek and her feet do not dance along the sidewalk. She is not a woman who would please my bosses and I do not intend to capture her. I shall be content to catch and release her, to muddle her brain and send her back to the woman who torments me. It will tell her I am near and she will come looking for me and the red-haired girl. Then, I shall trap her in my web.

The sky has become overcast and smells of rain. Moisture permeates the heavy air. I regret not bringing a coat. Two little girls kick a ball against a wall down the street and shriek with laughter. Their voices screech in my ears, but I cannot leave my post. The new woman has entered a house not much bigger than my room in Chinatown. I wait for her nearby. When she comes out, I will begin the execution of my plan. In the meantime, I watch the noisy girls and think about hypnotizing them. They are too young for the tongs, but I would be happy to have them entertain me for awhile. It is an idle thought, not one I will act upon, but it makes the time pass and gives me the satisfaction of knowing I could take my revenge for their clamorous behavior anytime I want. The idea brings a smile to my face as I press myself deeper into the shadows of the doorway where I wait.

* * *

Marta had already noticed Angela Cummings' fair complexion under her strawberry red hair, the kind of complexion that was rarely, if ever, exposed to the sun. Even masked by makeup, her face possessed a porcelain quality that reminded Marta of a ceramic sculpture. But the first time Angela took off her jacket and revealed her bare arms, Marta was amazed at the silky white texture of her skin. It had an unblemished finish to it that turned brilliantly luminous in the light.

"Angela, why do you hide such beautiful skin under all those yards of fabric? It is one of your best features."

"Oh, my skin. It never did have much pigment in it. My husband didn't like me exposing myself. So I always covered up." Angela responded in quick, clipped sentences while she looked critically at her arms. "Now I'm free to do what I want. But my skin is starting to sag. Soon, nobody will want to look at me, anyway." She sighed with resignation. "Life isn't fair."

Marta put one hand on her hip and wiped her brow with the other. They had been clearing out old files all morning, which proved to be warm, dusty work, the kind of work that produced a fine film of sweat on one's body and caused fits of sneezing. It had been two days since her meeting with Charles and, as time passed, she became more fearful that Missy was either dead or taken to a place where she would never be heard from again.

Marta had returned to the police station as advised by the captain and filled out a fresh report on Missy. Once again, the officer in charge of missing persons accepted it, but Marta feared that as soon as she left, it was filed away with the first report and ignored. She had nothing new to offer in the way of evidence to support her concerns, and the policeman made it clear by his detached expression that he had other priorities.

To Marta's relief, Angela had pitched in with unexpected zeal. Marta had to admit it was nice having her there. She desperately needed the company in Missy's absence, and Angela had turned out to be a very down-to-earth person.

Angela's psyche, however, was painfully frail from the shock of her separation and impending divorce. Her husband, Herbert, was seen everywhere with the young woman he had begun wooing even before the breakup of Angela's marriage. It was scandalous behavior, but being a wealthy man, he could get away with it, while Angela took the brunt of the snobbish remarks and gossip. Not only had Angela lost all of her social standing and money, it was rumored she had been seen scrubbing floors and washing laundry. That was untrue, of course, but it further damaged the few crumbs of pride she had left. She was convinced no man would ever look at her again now that she was damaged goods and getting older.

The first time Angela expressed her self-doubts, Marta had

snapped at her with irritation to get some backbone, but she immediately regretted it when she saw the wounded look on Angela's face. Marta had spent the past two days bolstering Angela's self-esteem and giving her the courage to face things as they were. When she looked critically at Angela, she had to admit the woman's stocky build and fleshy arms were not her best features, but her hair still shone with naturally brilliant highlights and her skin was radiant.

"Angela, I don't know how you can talk like that. Of course men will look at you. You are quite beautiful."

Angela smiled weakly, but Marta could see it was useless talking that way. She decided it was time to change topics. "Look, I have shown you how I work. With your previous experience you seem capable of doing more than watching the office. A lot needs to be done and I may have to be away from the office more than I want to for the next few days. I think it is time you went into the field and worked directly with the families."

As soon as she made the suggestion, Marta saw Angela's face light up like sunlight breaking through a cloud bank.

* * *

Angela felt good about herself, better than she had in a long time. When she thought about it, she hadn't enjoyed such peace of mind since her marriage to Herbert. What a whirlwind romance that had been, one that had made her young heart giddy with joy. Not that Herbert was all that handsome. It had been his money and social status that so enamored her. She realized that now. He was actually a rather cold, distant person, who had little regard for her feelings or needs. Their love making, for example, had been very functional. He would climb on top of her when he was in the mood, and slide off as soon as they were finished. It wasn't very erotic. Even on their wedding night, there had been more panting than fireworks. She had hidden her disappointments, however, and embraced her charming new life, one filled with glamorous balls and dinner parties. She had enjoyed buying all the new dresses and jewelry she wanted. What woman wouldn't find pleasure in such things? Still, her life had been an empty shell and she had paid a heavy price for her indulgences.

When Herbert discarded her, it seemed as if her life had ended. She considered ways to snuff it out. If she had not been such a coward, she would have done so, but the truth was, she could not stomach the prospect of giving Herbert the satisfaction. And she feared death's dark arms too much to pull the trigger of a gun or swallow a poisonous pill.

Then she was struck by an idea. Why not do social work? It would be respectable and would restore her standing somewhat in the community. She knew such employment would not pay much, but it would be a big step towards rebuilding her confidence and her life. She had enjoyed volunteering at the Sisterhood, but she knew they wouldn't take her back. Not after she had fallen from the upper rungs of their social ladder. Then, when she remembered Marta Baldwin, a beam of hope streaked across her bleak horizon. Why not offer herself to Marta's Pacific Aid Society? She had always admired the vibrant young woman, even though she knew the feeling was not reciprocated. She'd had to muster all of her courage to seek Marta's help, but she had been richly rewarded. Working for Marta validated her reason to exist. It was a validation built on a much firmer premise than money or social status. It was built on helping others, something she had not really understood before. Angela had unearthed another person within herself and she reveled in her discovery.

Of course, her good luck had been based on the misfortunes of Marta's other employee, Missy, and Angela was distressed by that. She didn't wish ill of Missy, even though she knew her return would end Angela's employment. The push and pull of her feelings left her confused. On the one hand, she prayed that Missy was okay and would come back safely; on the other, she hoped Missy's return could be delayed until Angela had time to settle into her new life.

Those conflicting emotions were buzzing around inside her head as she left the immigrant family she had been advising and started down the street. Absorbed in her thoughts, she paid no attention to the man approaching her, but when he abruptly stopped and flashed his ring, she became intrigued. The dancing golden light from the ring enthralled her. It was so beautiful to watch! She would have looked at it for hours if the man had not spoken to her. She could make no sense of his words, but she looked into the brilliance of his unblinking eyes and became enveloped in their warmth. The eyes drew her into a whirl of spinning light and sent her plunging over the edge of a crater into a vast labyrinth of turbulent air. As she tumbled in space, all she could think about was the dancing light and the vivid eyes. She felt as though she was swimming in those eyes, even as she kept falling deeper and deeper into the labyrinth. When she looked down, she couldn't see a bottom and she thought she would keep descending into the void forever.

Angela awoke with a start and discovered she was standing on the sidewalk at the very spot where she had first seen the dancing light. Bewildered, she looked around for the man who had spoken to her, but he was nowhere to be seen. She rubbed her arms and wondered if she had been dreaming. What a strange experience it had been! She would have sworn she had fallen from a great height, yet nothing had happened. When she looked down the street, however, she noticed shadows stretching across the pavement, which made no sense. She had finished her house call at one in the afternoon, yet when she consulted her time piece, she discovered it was ten past three. More than two hours of her life had disappeared!

Angela knew she was in trouble. Marta had an appointment and expected her by one-thirty. She had specifically asked Angela not to be late. How could she explain the lapse in time? The answer was simple. She couldn't. She could only hope Marta would give her another chance. Frightened, she hurried down the street in the direction of the office.

A locked door with a note fixed to the window greeted Angela when she arrived. To her relief, the note did not sound angry. If anything, it was apologetic for locking up before she returned. Angela had no key. Marta had made it clear she wasn't ready to give her one until Angela proved herself reliable. Today's incident wouldn't help. Angela berated herself for being so late, but she still couldn't explain what had happened. It was as if her mind had become lost in a fog and robbed of time. She sighed and turned to leave. There was nothing more to be done today except trudge back to her rented room and face a lonely evening by herself. Grey clouds of depression descended on her and chased away her earlier happiness.

* * *

Marta's displeasure over Angela's failure to return on time was tempered by worry. She couldn't help thinking about what had happened to Missy. Surely the hypnotist had not struck again! She had only employed Angela for a few days, but she could already see the promise in her. She worked hard and she had a good head for business. More important, she understood what was expected of her, and with her experience at the Sisterhood, needed little training.

Now, she was late, which gave Marta little choice but to leave the office unattended, something she hated to do. There were other matters, however, that caused her greater concern. Yesterday, she had overheard her brother talking on the telephone to someone who was obviously a creditor. From what she could understand, there were financial problems with the shipping business, just as she had feared. Samuel asked the caller for more time, which could only mean he had fallen behind in the company's debt obligations. From the pained look on his face, she guessed the requested extension had been denied. An appointment was set at the house for the following afternoon at 2:00 p.m.

Marta said nothing to Samuel about what she had heard, but she feared the worst and was anxious with worry, leading to a sleepless night. When Angela failed to return, she had no choice but to leave. She had to attend that meeting and find out what was going on.

She waited until a few minutes past two before entering the house. When she did, she heard voices in the den and entered to find Samuel deeply engrossed in a conversation with two men who had the stuffy, unyielding look of bankers. Both wore vested suits and sported neatly trimmed beards that were greyer than brown and black. The hands of both men rested on ample stomachs. They reminded Marta of twin doorstops and she nearly smiled in spite of herself.

Samuel leaped to his feet when he spotted her standing there. "Marta . . . what are you doing here? I thought you were at work." He shoved his fingers through his hair the way he had as a boy whenever he was in trouble. His eyes darted between her and the two men, and his lower lip quivered. She had never seen him so nervous. She took that as a very bad sign. Whatever was being discussed did not bode well for her or her brother.

"I am well aware that you are meeting to discuss the business, brother, and I think I should be here, don't you?" Her voice sounded harsher than she had intended, but she couldn't help herself. She recalled all the times she had admonished Samuel to put his back into the business and keep it solvent, if not growing. Now, her own lips trembled, but with rage, not nerves. She looked at the two men who sat, unperturbed, in their chairs watching the events unfolding between her and Samuel. They no longer looked like bookends. They looked like cats observing a mouse. Her stomach twisted so violently at the sight of their watchful expressions, she had to suppress a sudden urge to be sick.

"So, tell me brother, how much trouble are we in?" Marta stood in the middle of the room and swung her gaze between her brother and his visitors. Samuel's face was twisted with anguish. The men, on the other hand, looked alert, as predators do before they pounce. A weighty silence hung in the air. Only the tick tock of the grandfather clock in the hallway disturbed the gloom that had settled over the room. Something was terribly wrong. Marta already knew that, but she worried the trouble might run deeper than she originally feared.

One of the men put his hands on the arms of his chair and pushed himself upright. "I assume you are Miss Baldwin?" She nodded. "I am Joseph Caldwell of Corchran Bank and Trust. This is my partner, James Matteson. Please, sit down and join us." He motioned to a chair.

Marta's sense of foreboding was spreading through her nervous system like a wildfire. Her heart hammered so hard she found it difficult to think and her hands were suddenly moist with perspiration. She feared if she didn't sit down, she would collapse right there in the middle of the room.

"Thank you Mr. Caldwell," she said as calmly as she could. She sat down stiffly and looked at both men. Her brother had begun pacing behind the couch, which succeeded in agitating her even more. "Please tell me what is wrong."

Mr. Caldwell remained standing in deference to Samuel, but now focused his attention on Marta. "We are not here about the shipping company, Miss Baldwin. That is handled by another bank, although from what Samuel has told us, it seems to be in some financial difficulty." He paused and stroked his beard with his fingertips while he pondered his words. "It is your house we are here to discuss. The loan Mr. Baldwin took against the property has come due, and no payment has been forthcoming. We are exploring alternatives to foreclosure, although frankly, we have not yet found one that makes sense."

House? Loan? Foreclosure? The words thundered in her ears. Marta collapsed back into the chair's cushions, thankful she had taken the man's invitation to sit down. She felt as though she had become submerged in a fast moving current and could not breathe. Images of frozen layers of water and the eyes of the hypnotist floated before her. For a moment, she sensed she was drowning again. How could there be a loan against the house? Samuel had never discussed such a thing. *There had to be a mistake*, she thought wildly. *There are other Baldwin families in San Francisco. These men have the wrong house.*

Even as these frantic ideas raced through her mind, she knew they were unrealistic. These well-fed men were not in the habit of making mistakes. They knew Samuel and knew of her. The truth came crashing down with the force of a landslide. For some unknown reason, Samuel had borrowed money and used their home as collateral. He had done it without consulting her. *My God, we are going to lose the house! How could such a thing be possible? No, surely there must be some explanation, some plan to put things right again. But the man who called himself Caldwell had just said they had not found a satisfactory alternative to foreclosure.*

The second man, Mathewson? Matteson? stood up and joined his partner. "Maybe we should leave you folks to discuss things." His voice grunted when he spoke. It sounded like a hog rooting in the earth. Who could trust a man who sounded like that? "Samuel, we will call you in the morning." He raised his hand to stop Samuel when he started towards the door. "No need to bother. We can let ourselves out." *That's right*, she thought, *let yourselves out and never come back.* She looked at her hands and saw they were shaking. Embarrassed, she folded them in her lap.

The two men put on their hats and left. The front door opened and closed softly, and the earlier silence descended more heavily than before. It was a funereal silence, the kind one experienced at mortuaries or cemeteries. It was a silence wrapped in death. Suddenly, death was not so frightening to her after all. Not like losing your house. But it wasn't a house. That was what those vile men had called it. It was a home, and she didn't know where else she could go. Tears streamed down her face. They collected momentarily on her chin then dripped on her hands in her lap. She grabbed the handkerchief from her pocket that Byron had given her and furiously wiped her cheeks. She had no idea why she still carried it. Perhaps because the soft material reminded her of him.

All these random thoughts ricocheted inside her head. *Get a hold of yourself,* she scolded. *Calm down. Nothing can be accomplished if you don't think and act rationally.* She looked at her brother, who now stood behind the sofa with his head in his hands, and knew she would have to be the one to come to grips with their dilemma.

"What have you done?" she asked softly.

His eyes avoided hers as he leaned on the back of the couch for support. When he didn't answer, she pressed on. "What has happened to the company? Why is our home in danger?" Her quiet questions belied the turmoil grinding inside of her, but she refused to give in to her anger or fear. Instinctively, she knew the only way to get straight answers was to calm the emotional storms raging through the room. Samuel's role as head of household was about to end. She knew it and guessed he did, also. It was her strength that would see them through this crisis, but she could do nothing until she knew what was wrong. For that, she needed answers to her questions and she would get nowhere by shouting at her brother or berating him. It dawned on her that her anger was gone. When she looked at his dejected figure, all she felt was pity, but that was another emotion she dared not show. Neither did she reveal anger or pity but just a calming strength wrapped around his fragile state of mind.

"Please," she cajoled him, "tell me."

At last, Samuel stood up and ran his fingers through his hair, but he kept his gaze fixed on the mantel across the room. "The shipping company has been losing too much money," he began in a dull voice, as if reciting a school lesson. "We lost one ship in a storm off England and another to pirates in the Strait of Malacca. Only the Holly Barrett is left. I thought if I could raise fresh capital, I could turn things around, but no one wanted to invest. The banks said there were insufficient assets to provide collateral and my friends just looked the other way. When Corchran Bank and Trust offered a loan using the house as collateral, I took it." He shifted his gaze to hers for a brief moment, revealing bloodshot eyes that were bleary from worry. "It seemed like our only chance."

"Have you done anything to expose the trust money that provides our monthly income?" she asked as calmly as she could.

He looked away again. "The bank cannot get their hands on the principal, but half the income was pledged if needed to help repay the loan."

A sharp knife of fear sliced through Marta's calm. Not only was her home in jeopardy, but so was the income she needed to run her aid society. *Soon, I will become as destitute as Angela,* she thought. *I will be scrambling to stay off the streets and to find respectability.* A white hot blade of fear slashed at her already shredded nerves. She tried to suppress her anger, tried to maintain her calm exterior, but her growing frustration exploded in a furious barrage of words.

"How dare you risk our income and home without talking to me first," she raged. Her brother cringed at the vehemence of her words, but she no longer felt pity for him. "You have run father's shipping company aground, and now you have threatened our very home because of your foolish need to play the socialite with your wealthy friends."

Samuel straightened at her words and his jaw twitched with anger.

Marta knew she had gone too far, but she couldn't stop herself. "At least I've tried to do something with the business," he shouted. "I've had to make real choices, not just play a Good Samaritan with a bunch of immigrants."

The words stung Marta more than she might have expected and took some of the air out of her anger. Was that all she was doing, playing? Is that how he and others saw her? "What does the bank propose?" she asked in a more subdued tone.

Samuel walked around the couch and plopped down heavily, telling her that he, too, was spent by their emotional exchange. "If we bankrupt the business and sell the house, we can meet our debt obligations. Otherwise, they will foreclose us and take the house anyway." He lowered his head and studied his feet.

Marta stood up and began pacing the room. "There must be another way. What if we raise some initial capital and arrange a payment schedule? We could use the remaining income from the trust as part of it." She stopped and looked at her brother. "Did you discuss that as an alternative?"

"Well, yes, but where would we get the initial capital?" He kept his gaze lowered and fidgeted with his hands.

Marta could see he was a bundle of nerves and realized he had been under a great deal of stress. Still, she couldn't forgive him. He had been too bull-headed and self-important for her to do that, but it did soften her anger a bit. "We have some valuable art, and I

107

have jewelry I rarely wear. And you will have to sell your club membership." Samuel's head jerked up at her declaration, but his protest died on his lips when he saw her standing over him with her arms folded. Her posture told him she would not countenance any disagreement.

"And you will have to go to work," she continued firmly. "I will also. My aid society will have to be closed." Regret tinged her voice as she announced this. All of her good work gone up in smoke. And what about work? What could they do? Samuel might get a job in an office or bank, she supposed, but what about her? She faced the same issues as Angela. Would she have to knit clothes or go to work in the mint? It didn't matter, as long as they kept their home and didn't become charity cases. They would find a way. She would have to lay out a budget, just as she had done for so many other poor families. The idea of being poor had seemed so foreign before, but now it struck her with the force of a heavy blow. *How could such a thing have happened? How could it be?*

CHAPTER ELEVEN

After Samuel left the den, Marta walked over to her father's roll-top desk, which still stood beneath the maritime clock he had always used to keep track of time. A tiny smile forced its way through her taut lips when she looked at the clock. It was, he had explained, based on a twenty-four hour cycle, not twelve, so there could never be any confusion about time when he issued a teletype to some other part of the world. Ten in the morning, he explained, was just so, but ten at night was twenty-two hundred hours. No a.m. or p.m. was needed. Marta had always liked that idea, although she never used it in her own life. Her only communications were in San Francisco or the surrounding towns, where everyone knew if it was day or night.

Samuel had said two of the ships were lost, but not the Holly Barrett. It might be a futile gesture, but she had to find out if her brother was telling her the truth. The only way to do that was to look for paperwork on the ships. Samuel normally kept the desk locked, but Marta had noticed this time the roll top was ajar. She lifted it and looked with dismay at the mounds of papers piled inside. It was evident nothing had been filed in some time. She began sorting through the documents in search of any recent correspondence or contracts involving the three ships. It didn't take long for her to find the contracts for fuel oil and cotton to be shipped from San Francisco to Hong Kong on the Holly Barrett. The sailing date was the day after tomorrow. No other clues presented themselves in the desk's chaos, but if she could find the Holly Barrett and speak to the captain, she was certain he would be able to tell her what had happened to the other two ships.

Now that Samuel had gambled their house away, such information would do little good. She could not help being curious, though, about the fate of those ships and the status of the shipments scheduled for Hong Kong. The mess she saw in the desk was emblematic of the chaos raining down on her life, but she still had to see for herself what had happened to the company her father had worked so hard to build. She put the contracts in her bag and headed for the door. She was going to pay a visit to the Holly Barrett.

Dusk had settled over the city by the time Marta took the trolley down Market Street to the Ferry Building. When she arrived, a festive scene greeted her along the water front where seamen and dock workers were gathered to celebrate the finish of another day's hard labor. Raucous voices and harsh laughter boomed from the grog shops she had recently visited in search of Missy's father. They had seemed rather sedate places at mid-day, but now they boiled with restless crowds of men who would undoubtedly drink a good portion of their day's wages before the night was done. Even though Marta was dressed in her customary trousers, it was clear she was a lady and not some whore on the stroll for a quick dollar, but that did not inhibit the men standing in the doorways. If anything, it inflamed their desires. Several called out to her with sexual innuendos that made it clear they were ready to entertain her for the night.

The unexpected and vulgar attention jangled her nerves. She did her best to ignore them and began exploring the loading docks for some sign of the Holly Barrett. Seagulls squawked nervously as she ventured along the uneven boards. The briny sea air was tainted with the rancid odor of sweating bodies that had not seen a bath in a week, if not longer. Despite the failing light, the splintered wharves still swarmed with stevedores scrambling up and down steep gangplanks. Some rolled barrels; others carried sacks on their shoulders. Pulley's swung to and fro. Men's voices barked and cursed and brayed at one another. The maze of wooden ships, blasphemous men, and unruly stacks of barrels, sacks, and crates along the docks created a giddy scene that bordered on anarchy.

Hesitantly, Marta intercepted a seaman with several days' growth on his face and crinkled skin around his eyes that was headed in the direction of the grog shops she had just passed.

"Can you tell me where to find the Holly Barrett?" she shouted above the din.

"O'er there." The man waved his hand in the general direction of the sea of masts rising beyond the Ferry Building. "Spare a man a drink?" he asked with his hand held out expectantly.

Marta knew that even if she could understand the man's directions, which seemed unlikely, she would have difficulty following them. There was too much confusion and too many ships. So, she made a quick decision. If this man really did know where the Holly Barrett was docked, it would be worth a small remuneration for his guidance. "Take me to the ship, and I will give you enough for two drinks," she shouted. She removed several coins from her bag and held them up for the seaman's inspection. He nodded and moved off at a quick gait through the confusion.

After several twists and turns on the black wharves, they arrived at a six-master schooner riding high in the water. Canvass sails were furled on booms high up each mast, while cobwebs of ropes spread out from the masts in a dizzying array of patterns and pulleys. They seemed to be tied everywhere, including to the long snout of a bow that lifted its nose in the air at a forty-five degree angle to the ship. Thicker ropes held the Holly Barrett fast to the wharf. They groaned as if the ship were straining mightily in an effort to escape its leashes.

The first thing Marta noticed was a lack of the frenzied activity she had seen elsewhere. Her instincts told her that was a bad sign. Other than a few men lifting bags of cotton into the bowels of the ship, the Holly Barrett appeared deserted. She gave the seaman his coins and approached the steep plank where half-a-dozen workers labored with their burdens.

"Is the captain on board?" she called to the nearest one.

"Ay, in his cabin." He stopped his work and wiped his brow while he stared openly at Marta. "He expecting you?"

"No, but he will see me." Marta said this with a note of defiance as she started up the gangplank. She didn't intend to get into a debate with any of these men about her presence there. The worker shrugged and went back to his business.

The plank was slippery from the sea air, but small runners had been nailed into the wood to provide footholds for the workers. Unfortunately, the runners were too far apart for someone as short as Marta and she was forced to use awkward strides to mount the roughhewn steps. The men snickered as she worked her way up the ramp. She was thankful she had worn her trousers instead of a dress.

"Where's his cabin?" she queried as she stopped to catch her breath at the top. She glanced into the hold which was less than half full of sacks and barrels.

"Back thar." One of the workers pointed to a door near the stern.

She picked her way through a tangle of crates and barrels stacked around the hold and made her way down the long, narrow deck to the rear of the ship. Marta had never been on a ship before and discovered the sensation of standing on something floating in the bay disorienting. Even though the ship was securely tied to the dock, she imagined the swell of the waves under its hull at sea and nearly lost her footing. Once she reached the door indicated by the workers, she brushed her trousers with a quick swipe of her hands and knocked.

"Come in," a voice responded. It sounded authoritative, strong.

Marta opened the door to discover a man formally dressed in a white shirt, vest, and captain's coat seated behind a desk cluttered with papers. His hair was thinning and combed in long strands across the top of his head to cover his balding crown. The loss of hair was more than compensated for by the gray bush of a beard, moustache and sideburns that covered most of his face. It was a full face, one associated with men of some girth. His black eyes flashed at being interrupted, but widened with interest when he saw Marta standing in the doorway.

"How may I help you?" he asked as he scraped his chair on the wooden floor and rose from the desk. His large frame seemed to fill the windowed alcove behind him, but Marta saw at once that while he was heavy, he wasn't fat.

The sweet perfume of un-smoked tobacco mingled with the smell of lamp oil. There was a slightly musty odor as well, one that spoke of long periods at sea when inclement weather prevented a window from being opened.

"My name is Matilda Baldwin." As much as she disliked using her full name, her instincts told her the captain was a formal man. Her eyes swept the room, taking in the navigational charts on a table to her right and the properly made bed to her left. "My family owns the shipping company."

"Yes, I know Mr. Samuel Baldwin, but I didn't think he was married." The captain's gaze was less frank than the workers' when she mounted the gangplank, but she felt as thoroughly scrutinized.

"I am his sister, not his wife." Marta chafed at the man's assumption, but held her tongue. "May I know your name, sir?"

"Captain George Phillips." He motioned to a chair beside the desk. "Please, sit down. Is your brother with you?"

"No. I have come alone . . . to get some facts straight." She shifted her weight, uncertain whether to sit or stand, but finally yielded to convention and took the offered chair.

The captain immediately resumed his seat across from her. "What facts did you have in mind?" He eyed her curiously.

"For one thing, I have noticed a great deal of activity on most of the ships, but it is largely absent here. You sail the day after tomorrow yet the cargo hold is less than half full. Is that enough to make your voyage profitable?"

The captain tugged at his beard and shifted in his chair. His bushy eyebrows furrowed into a frown. "Perhaps Mr. Baldwin should be present to discuss these matters. The shipping business is not a topic normally discussed with other family members."

The man's declaration echoed in the room. Silence followed. His tone was polite, but Marta heard the bias in his words. 'Other family members' referred to women. She stiffened her back and glared at the man. "I am half-owner of this business, but I have been excluded from the management of its operations. That ends now. I understand the company is in some financial trouble and I am here to learn what, if anything, can be done about it. If you choose not to speak with me, you will have the pleasure of discussing these matters tomorrow with my solicitor."

Another silence ensued while the captain digested her threat. She was pleased to see his dark eyes blink with a startled expression that told her she had struck home. "I will be happy to assist you in any way I can," he said at last.

"Good." Marta leaned forward and laced her fingers together on the desk. "Let's begin with my first question. Can the Holly Barrett sail profitably with such an empty hold?"

The captain sighed and shook his head. "I'm afraid it cannot." Marta heard a note of resignation in the man's voice. It twisted in her as painfully as a knife blade.

"And why is the hold so empty?"

"Many shippers fear to do business with us since we lost two of our ships."

"To pirates and storms?" Marta held her breath, fearful of what would be said next.

Even with all the hair on his face, she could read the confusion in it. His cheeks sucked in and his mouth pursed outward. "Pirates and storms? I don't understand. The ships were both sold to creditors for past due debts."

Marta exhaled the breath she had been holding. There it was, just as she had feared. Even as the walls of the company were crumbling around him, Samuel could not face her with the truth. There had been no mishaps, other than the lack of someone at the company's tiller.

"And how much longer before this ship falls into the hands of its creditors?" she asked in a subdued voice.

"I'm not privy to your company's financial obligations, Miss Baldwin, but from my years of experience in these matters, I could hazard a guess. I believe this might be its last voyage." A note of sadness crept into his voice, a tone of regret for what might have been.

Marta's earlier indignation at the man's attitude dissolved. She understood his angst. It might not be his company, but as captain, it was his ship. He would feel its loss as much as she. A dispirited feeling of defeat hung in the room. She felt its weight on her shoulders. There was no way to save the company, nor salvage any value from it. She had known that before she came, but seeing the loss first hand drove the point home with an eloquence she could not ignore.

The captain walked with her as far as the gangplank and asked one of the men to assist her in scrambling down the awkward steps. When she reached the bottom, she looked up and gave him a tight smile of regret.

He nodded in understanding.

CHAPTER TWELVE

Marta arrived at her office the next morning in a high state of anxiety. She had stared at the ceiling most of the night with a jumble of numbers cascading through her head and only dozed for an hour or two before dawn. Fingers of grey light greeted her when she finally rose from her bed. By then, she had made her decisions. She would keep the aid society open for a month, long enough to wrap up her work with the majority of the families in her files. She would ask Angela to contact the women at the Sisterhood to take the files she could not finish and she would ask them to take Angela into their fold on a paid basis. She would be worth every penny to them.

As for herself, she knew a few people through her aid society who worked with social causes like hers. She would call on them and explore the possibility of employment at a social agency. If that didn't work, there was always the mint. She had a contact there and suspected she could vault herself to the front of the application line if need be. That was not the way she liked to do things, but it was not always a kind world and she had to put herself first for a change. She would do whatever it took to save her home.

Angela's face was drawn with worry when she arrived. It took Marta a moment to realize why. She had been so caught up in her own problems, she had completely forgotten about Angela's lapse yesterday. It was obvious from the way Angela clasped her hands and fiddled with them that she had not. Marta had planned to discuss her changed circumstances with Angela that morning, but after seeing the forlorn look on Angela's face, she decided to wait until later that day or the morrow.

"Marta, about yesterday. . ." Angela hesitated, as though unsure how to proceed.

Marta raised a hand and stopped her. "Whatever happened, I'm sure it couldn't be helped. Let's not waste time worrying about it. There is much to be done today, and I am going to need your full attention. All right?" She smiled to show Angela she wasn't angry.

Relief lifted Angela's features like a theatre curtain revealing a stage. "I will do whatever you need. Just tell me."

Marta intended for them both to make house calls for awhile. That would nearly double the number of cases they could handle, enough to work through the most difficult files in the time that was left before she closed the place. It would give her satisfaction to accomplish that much. And there was still Missy to think about. She hoped and prayed Charles would have word of her soon.

Marta gave Angela three cases that she was confident her employee could handle and took four tougher ones for herself. The four she chose were all families who had recently emigrated from Europe. They had little money and limited work skills. Credit slips would be issued to each family to pick up a sack of potatoes and coal for cooking at a local warehouse where Marta kept an account, but these families needed more than a quick handout. Each either had an unemployed husband or no man in the house at all. The women needed help finding care for their children and work for themselves. Most would end up doing sewing on a piece-work basis and could not expect to bring home more than seven dollars a week. Marta would have to show them how to live on such minimal wages and how to use the few social services available to them, such as emergency care if a child became ill.

With both of them in the field, the office would have to remain closed most of the day, but that no longer mattered since Marta would not be taking any new cases. She and Angela agreed to meet back at the office no later than two, so they could review each case and prepare a new list for the following day.

* * *

An earlier threat of rain had skipped away, setting the stage for the shafts of sunlight now bursting through the clumps of clouds still lingering in the sky. To Angela, it represented a day filled with promise. Marta had not berated her for yesterday's transgression. In fact, she had given her more responsibility. Angela had been so surprised that she hadn't known what to say. She plunged into the case files with all of her energy. Whatever concerns she'd had about Marta before going to work for her had long since vanished. Marta might have been a bit abrasive in the past, but Angela had to admit she was being treated with a fair hand.

Angela had finished her second file and begun to search for the address indicated on her third and last folder when she rounded a corner and came face-to-face with the strange man she had encountered the day before. The man seemed to be all arms and legs and his style of walking was so comical, she started to smile. But the smile died on her lips when she remembered how lost she'd become the last time she saw him. The last thing she needed was to lose track of time again. She tried to look away, but the man waved his hand and before she knew it, the dancing, golden light had her in its grasp. As before, he spoke to her in a language she had never heard. The words mesmerized her nonetheless and she couldn't help but raise her face to his brilliant gaze, which was so pure she wanted to bask in it forever. When the now familiar chasm opened before her, she plunged over its side without hesitation and soared into the labyrinth below. This time, she was unafraid of the bottomless crevasse and floated in the cold air currents as if she were a bird on the wing. The air smelled of winter. The silence was so deep she wondered if she had lost her hearing.

The clip clop of an approaching horse's hooves snapped Angela awake. The first thing she saw was a faded white horse with a mangy straw-colored mane pulling a wagon of ice down the street. Next, she noticed three boys staring at her, but they quickly scattered when she raised her head and looked at the sky. Clouds covered the sun once more, and it was the clouds that bothered her. Not because of the threat of rain. The cloud bank was too thick and dark to have formed so quickly. It would have taken time for those clouds to gather in such strength, more time than she could account for. Her body trembled as she consulted her time-piece and saw to her dismay that it was after three. It had happened again! She had vanished into a dream world and time had slipped by as quietly as nuns at prayer.

Angela looked around for the strange man, but of course he was gone. Had he ever existed, except in her mind? Was she going mad? No, the golden light had been very real, as had his musical, unintelligible words. She gripped the folders Marta had entrusted to her and hurried along the uneven pavement to the office as quickly as she dared.

* * *

This time Marta was waiting for her with pursed lips and a heavy frown. She had excused yesterday's tardiness as an anomaly, but a second transgression in two days was not something she could ignore. There was too much to do and too little time for irresponsible behavior. She had hoped Angela could help her sort through as many of the cases as possible in the time she had left, but now a sliver of doubt had slipped between them.

Whatever was going on, it had left Angela in a mess. Her hair had come unhinged so that strands scudded about her face. Her breath was labored, her dress stained with perspiration. She had the appearance of a deranged person seeking absolution for unknown trespasses.

"Please let me try to explain myself." Angela managed to

squeeze the words out between the quick breaths bursting from her lungs. She had stopped inside the doorway and leaned on the back of a chair to collect herself.

Marta looked at her with concern. "Angela, I don't know what to say. It's clear you are very upset, and I want to be understanding, but I cannot countenance this continued behavior. There are things at stake you don't know about and I need to know whether or not I can count on you." Anger rose in her voice as she spoke. The words made Angela flinch as if struck by a buggy whip. Marta immediately regretted losing her patience. "What could possibly have happened to put you in such a state?" she asked more kindly.

Angela straightened her back and brushed strands of hair from her forehead before she dared to face her employer. Desperately, she searched for the words to explain herself. "This is very difficult," she began. "It's hard to believe, even for me. Twice in the past two days I've encountered a very strange looking man on the street. He has interrupted me with a flashing ring and unintelligible words. I feel myself falling and lose all sense of time. When I return to my senses, the man is gone and I'm standing just as I was before." Her face became animated as she spoke. "But that's not the worst of it. I feel as though seconds have passed, but I find I have lost hours." She looked at Marta with the pained expression of a child telling a fantastic tale and pleading to be understood.

She need not have worried. Marta's mind was already spinning with fear as she listened to Angela's bizarre story. It was *him*, the hypnotist. There could be no doubt of it. A dark shadow passed over her heart and caused her to shiver. Why was the man tormenting Angela like that? Why hadn't he taken her the way he did Missy? Marta couldn't be certain what he was up to, but she knew it had a sinister purpose that bode ill for her and Angela.

She reached out impulsively and pulled a surprised Angela into her arms. At first, she felt Angela's reserve holding her back, but she gradually yielded to Marta's awkward embrace. It was the first time they had touched since the day Angela came looking for employment. Embarrassed at her spontaneity, Marta released

Angela but kept her hands on her shoulders. "The man you saw hypnotizes people. He's the same one who kidnapped Missy." She watched Angela's face broaden with fear and quickly continued. "I don't think he intends to harm you. He would have done something by now if he did. I think he's after me."

Marta studied Angela's stricken expression and pondered what to do. It wouldn't accomplish anything to leave the poor woman in harm's way and Marta could never forgive herself if she lost another of her employees. "It might be better if you stayed home for a few days; at least until we find out what happened to Missy."

Angela's already pale face blanched whiter at the prospect of her lonely room. "Oh no, please. I really need this job." She hesitated then plunged on. "I mean, it's not just the money. I truly want to be here, to work with you. You have been a godsend for me. I won't let you down. I'll work inside if you wish." Her eyes darted over Marta's face; her expression pleaded for understanding.

"That might work," Marta replied after some hesitation. "I suppose if you keep the door locked and the blinds drawn you should be safe." She sighed. It meant more work for her in the field and fewer families she could help. Again, she remembered to tell Angela about her own dilemma, but decided the moment was too emotional. It could wait until things calmed a bit.

They closed the office for the day. Marta accompanied Angela as far as Market Street where she would be safe. They agreed to meet there tomorrow at nine and proceed to the office together. Marta watched Angela walk away, then turned and trudged towards home, a home she feared she still might lose despite her efforts.

The house was silent when she entered. She was about to go upstairs to her room when she spotted a note in Samuel's handwriting lying on the hall table. To her delight, she saw it was a telephone message from Byron and called him at once.

"Charles thinks he has a line on your girl, Missy," he announced without preamble.

What wonderful news! Marta cried out with relief. The possibility of finding Missy was the first ray of sunshine to enter her gloomy world since learning of her financial troubles and it softened her bleak mood. "When can we look for her?" she asked urgently.

"Actually, I'm waiting for Charles right now. He's making arrangements for a police raid on the establishment that's supposed to be holding her. They should be ready within the hour."

Hesitation filled the phone line between them. Marta knew what he was going to say. "Don't think to leave me behind, Byron."

"It may not be pleasant." His voice lowered with concern. "Why don't you stay there, and I'll call you the moment we know something?"

"Not on your life," she said firmly. "Missy means too much to me to just sit around and wait. I'm going with you."

He finally relented and offered to send his carriage, but Marta preferred to make her own way to Byron's house. She left at once and decided to save trolley fare by walking. There was time before Charles arrived and the late afternoon had turned mild. Besides, walking always helped clear her head, and she badly needed that. The man she now thought of as the hypnotist troubled her greatly. Even with her good luck charm, she felt the danger. He was stalking her, she was sure of it, and because he feared her charm, he was attacking her employees instead. Getting Missy back would not make him go away, of that she was certain. If anything, it might embolden him. She prayed the police would find and arrest him during the raid.

The hypnotist wasn't her only worry. She had to decide what to do about Angela when Missy returned. Given her changed financial circumstances, Marta couldn't afford to keep both women, but after today's conversation with Angela, she didn't know how she could let her go. It was a decision she might be able to put off for a few days. It was likely Missy would need some time to recover from her ordeal, and Marta would encourage her to take it.

And, of course, there was the threat from the bank, which loomed on her horizon with as much menace as the hypnotist. She needed Samuel to arrange an appointment with those tiresome men so she could present her proposed budget and buy some time.

Surely a demonstration of a good faith payment along with interest would stay their greedy hands. That meant raising cash quickly from the sale of the jewelry and the paintings. She made a mental note to contact galleries and auction houses at once. One thing that worried her was the viewpoint of the banks about making loans. Most banks, she knew, were more comfortable lending money to people who created capital through investments, such as the loan to Samuel for the shipping company. They were not as comfortable dealing with people who earned a living through wages. Yet, Marta's plan called for her and Samuel to find jobs and pay off the balance on a monthly basis. If the bank refused, its only alternative was to claim the house. Would that be in the bank's best interests? She didn't think so. Their house was large, but it wasn't a mansion like Byron's. Seizing it would not pay as handsomely as Marta's proposal. If the bank was willing to have a little patience, Marta was certain she could show them a higher return.

The thought of Byron raised her spirits. Despite all of her problems, she looked forward to seeing him again. She found herself walking briskly up the last block to his great house. By the time she arrived, she was sticky with perspiration despite the cool air, and she took a moment to collect herself before mounting the steps to the sweeping veranda. She pulled the bell beside the baronial front door and waited. By the time Henry opened it, her heart was thrumming from equal parts exertion and anticipation. He raised his eyebrows at her perspiring face and showed her into the vast entryway. As she waited to be announced, Marta tried to assess her agitation at seeing Byron again. There was no use denying it. She was completely undone by him and she didn't know what to do about it. She sighed and shook her head. There was no reason for him to look twice at her. She had no title or high social status, and thanks to Samuel's debacle, she was about to lose any hint of social standing she might have enjoyed. Given her circumstances, there was not a reed of hope that he might consider her anything more than an acquaintance.

As if to confirm her glum conclusion, Marta heard a woman's laughter floating from the drawing room, and she froze. It wasn't the kind of laughter one associated with a sister or mother. It was the raw, throaty laugh of a woman sharing an intimate moment with a man. Its effect on Marta was as chilling as a blanket of rain sweeping off the bay.

When she entered the drawing room, she saw Byron standing next to a striking woman whose full-figured body brimmed with so much sexual energy it was all Marta could do to keep from striding across the room and pulling her hair out. She was shocked by her reaction to the woman and halted inside the doorway, where she stared speechlessly at the two of them. Byron smiled, but the gesture seemed sheepish to her, as if he had been caught in a compromising position. Marta quickly returned her attention to the woman, whose full, glistening lips, short cropped, ink-black hair, and oval face exuded a sensuality that made Marta's shoulders sag. This was not a woman with whom she could compete for any man.

"Hello, Marta." Byron removed his pipe from his mouth and nodded to his guest. "Let me introduce you to one of the most original women in San Francisco, Lillie Collins. Lillie, this is the young woman I've been telling you about."

Lillie beamed a winsome smile as she stepped from behind a chair that had partially blocked Marta's view and walked towards her with the full stride of a man. It was only then that Marta realized she was wearing pants rather than a dress! Given the woman's seductive charm, Marta was surprised by her manly attire and behavior. She had never seen a society woman wearing pants in public, other than herself, of course, but she hardly pictured herself as society. She had heard stories about the Collins family that, like the other elite families in San Francisco, had amassed a fortune. Lillie's mother was trying to see her daughter properly married to someone rich and famous, but Lillie's brash behavior and infamous reputation were making that difficult. She was reputed to wash her hair in champagne, play poker with the men and attend cockfights. And she wore men's pants for most occasions.

Lillie grasped Marta's hands and squeezed them. Lillie's hands were warm, fleshy and slightly moist. Marta caught a heady fragrance that reminded her of cologne. "It is wonderful to finally meet you, Marta. Byron told me how you stood up to those men at his club. Good for you. We need more assertive women in this city." The woman's sun-splashed face sparkled with pleasure.

Marta blushed at the thought that Byron had spoken well of her. She stared at the woman with a mixture of anxiousness and interest. Lillie's clothing and manner reflected a woman who had little use for society's mores, and despite her angst that Lillie was Byron's companion, Marta couldn't help liking her. She returned the pressure of Lillie's grip despite herself. Any woman who wore pants felt like a kindred spirit.

"The pleasure is mine," she responded.

Lillie dropped one hand but held the other and guided Marta to the couch, where they settled side-by-side. "It's not easy being a woman, as I'm sure you know," Lillie continued. "Take my mother. All she can think about is getting me married off to some man with a title so she can prance around town. Never mind what I want. And heaven forbid I should decide to remain independent a while longer."

Marta was surprised at Lillie's personal revelations. They made her think about her own circumstances and caused her to wonder how things might have been if her parents still lived. Could she have pursued the charity work she so much enjoyed, for example? Not that it mattered anymore. She wasn't going to be doing that much longer, at least not through her own organization. She eyed Lillie more closely. She was at least four inches taller than Marta and squared her shoulders in a forceful manner. Yet her full lips, abundant bust line, and rhythmic hips exuded the earthy charms of a sensual woman. Her attire left little doubt about her rebellious nature. But did she mean what she said about remaining "independent," or was she just being coy in front of Byron? Not the latter, Marta decided. The woman's frank and confident manner was anything but coy.

Byron, she noted, preferred to remain standing. He crossed his arms in front of him and watched them both with the hint of a smile. What was he thinking, she wondered, and what was his relationship with this amazing woman? A fresh pang of jealousy shot through her at the idea of the two of them together, but she thrust her concern aside. It was silly of her to play such games with herself. No amount of daydreaming was going to change her undesirable circumstances. If Lillie and Byron were involved, she must congratulate them with a smile.

"By the way," he commented, "it was very sporting of you to hire Angela. How is she working out?"

"Very well," Marta replied with satisfaction. "I think she has some real initiative in her." She was tempted to tell him about her run-ins with the hypnotist but refrained herself in front of Lillie. There was no use spreading rumors north of Market Street.

"You hired Angela Cummings?" Lillie asked. "How wonderful of you. That poor lady was at a total loss after what her husband did to her. What a change of fortune. I can't imagine how she's coping."

"Yes, she was really undone by her misfortune," Byron added. "Marta, you did a great service to her."

Marta heard the pity in their voices and gritted her teeth. What would they think when they learned Samuel had lost the shipping company and that she might lose her home? She suddenly felt quite alone and "undone" as Byron had put it.

Lillie changed the subject. "I hear you have an interesting excursion planned in Chinatown, Marta. What an adventure that should be. I regret having to miss it, but I admire your courage for going there." She turned her attention to Byron. "Not even I have been there, and I have been to some unusual places," she added with the same throaty laugh Marta had heard when she arrived. Lillie stood up and walked over to Byron. "Now, I must leave." She gave him a kiss on the cheek. The playful gesture sent another sharp pang through Marta, but she stood up politely and maintained her smile. "You must give me a full report tomorrow, Byron. I shall expect all the details."

With that she returned to Marta and took her hand. "And I am very glad to have made your acquaintance, Marta," Her name had a musical quality on Lillie's tongue, and despite her jealousy,

Marta was already growing fond of her. "Perhaps I will come visit your Pacific Aid Society one day soon. I would enjoy seeing what you do there and, of course, it would be lovely to see Angela again."

She waved goodbye and strode from the room without waiting for Byron or the butler to show her out. Marta could see that she was every bit as original as Byron had said when he introduced her, and she was sorry to see her go.

CHAPTER THIRTEEN

An awkward silence ensued after Lillie's departure. Byron shifted his feet and then made himself busy striking a match to his pipe. Marta fussed with a loose thread in the cushions, uncertain what to do or say. She hadn't realized how much energy Lillie discharged into a room until she was gone. The air had crackled in her presence. Now, it seemed as deflated as a flat tire on one of those newfangled automobiles. Marta missed her already, which was a surprising reaction to someone whose hair she had wanted to yank out less than ten minutes before. Marta sensed they might become friends, but Lillie's impact was greater than that. She had made Marta feel as if they were sisters fighting a common cause. It had been a heady experience. She had even made Marta forget the nervous tension that possessed her when she was around Byron. Now that Lillie was gone, Marta's stomach was doing more flip-flops and she wished Lillie would return.

Just when the room seemed about to stifle them both, they were rescued by Henry's announcement that Charles had arrived. He bolted past Henry into the room, his blond hair flying, his blue eyes as bright as light bulbs and his rugged features dancing with anticipation. "We have found her, I'm sure of it," he announced triumphantly to the room. His gaze flicked from Marta to Byron and back again. "Good afternoon, Marta. I hadn't expected to see you here. I hope to have good news for you soon." He bowed in a courtly manner, drawing a smile from Marta.

She rose to her feet, ready to depart at once. "Byron has already told me and I am thrilled. When do we leave?"

Charles stopped and stared at her. His body twitched much as it had the first time she met him. She couldn't help thinking again about all the alcoholics she had seen in her work. How long had it been, she wondered, since he last visited his opium dens?

"Surely, you don't intend to come with us," Charles responded.

"That is her intention," Byron interrupted. "She will not be discouraged from it."

After Lillie's exhilarating conversation, Marta felt bolder than she ever had before. "Why shouldn't I join you, Charles? Missy is my good friend and I must be there to comfort her."

Charles stood in the middle of the room and ran his hand over his face in a gesture of disbelief. "It could be messy, perhaps dangerous. Entering Chinatown in daylight is one thing. It's relatively safe, then. But this time we are going in at dusk and we are invading the lair of the Chinese gangs who rule Chinatown. They won't like it." He hesitated and looked at the ceiling as if searching for divine guidance. "There could be trouble and we don't know Missy's situation. It might not be very pretty." His voice slowed before it hurried on again. "If she's there at all, of course, that is. My information is more rumor than fact," he said as he watched her absorb his words. Then he finished in a more quiet tone, "We might find nothing."

Charles sounded less hopeful than when he first burst into the room. Marta's heart missed a beat at the possibility that they might not find Missy after all. She wouldn't be deterred, however. She had to be there when they tried and she was determined to remain positive. As for the conditions surrounding Missy, Marta had already steeled herself to expect the worst. She had seen Chinatown's ugly back streets and knew it wasn't going to be pretty, as Charles had put it.

However, there was an even more compelling reason for her to go than Missy. She had something significant to offer. "There's one more thing, Charles. I'm the only one who has seen the hypnotist. If he's there, I can identify him and have him arrested."

Byron had been content to stand on the sidelines of the discussion, but now he stepped forward to signal his involvement in the decision.

"Marta has a valid point, don't you agree, Charles? I have to concur with her. It would be great luck if we could catch this man and put him away and Marta is the only one who can help us do that. Besides, we will be well protected, will we not?"

The twitching in Charles' body subsided as he came to terms with Marta's request. "You are right, of course. We will have five able-bodied policemen with us, so we should be safe enough." A tiny smile twitched at the corners of his mouth. "You are a strong-willed woman, Marta, and I admire that. By all means, join us, and let's put an end to this thing."

* * *

The Chinese called San Francisco Gum San Ta Fow, "big city in the land of the golden hills," but there was nothing golden about Chinatown at night. The soft glow of paper lanterns along the streets did little to dispel the suspicious shadows that lurked in every doorway. Paper notices peeled from blistered walls. Tiny, second-story windows glowered with the devilry of cats' eyes. The main streets had quieted considerably from the frenzied activity Marta had witnessed on her first sojourn into the Chinese quarter. When she entered the narrower passageways, it grew so dark it was as if the world had ended. In a way it had she supposed. Her world was gone, replaced by one where thieves, slave masters and hatchet men roamed the back streets. Night was the time when the tongs' hired killers generally struck. It was the time when knives flashed in the feeble light and gunshots snapped in the gloom.

She and her companions had been greeted by Captain O'Conner

and four of his officers just outside the entrance on Grant Avenue.

The Captain lifted his eyebrows at Marta's presence but said nothing. The men all sported handlebar mustaches and wore bowler hats, dark suits, and white shirts buttoned at their necks. Guns were holstered on their hips; batons were held at the ready. No one smiled or joked. It was clear by their demeanor that they were about to embark on serious business. Marta couldn't prevent a shiver of fear from creeping up her spine.

They were now slipping quietly down a particularly evil-looking labyrinth called Bartlett Alley, where smoke from chimneys and braziers mixed with the weak light of lanterns to produce an unearthly glow, and where the walls reeked of so much mold and seeping water that Marta feared they had abandoned the city altogether and stumbled into a foul-smelling swamp. She pressed her handkerchief to her nose and fought off a wave of nausea and a premonition that she was about to sink into oblivion.

Captain O'Conner had stressed the need for stealth. If they were to save Missy, they had to strike with the element of surprise. Once the tongs were alerted, the girl would disappear and their opportunity would be lost. He had also pointed out that while the tongs were careful to avoid confrontations with the police, there was no guarantee the thugs guarding the brothel would show the same restraint. In case of a fight, Marta had been told to hug the walls but to stay close so there was no chance of her being whisked away like Missy. That prospect sent another wave of nausea from her stomach to her throat, but she again fought it down. If she was going to rescue Missy, she had to keep her wits about her.

After an interminable trek along a series of odious pathways, they entered a narrow cavern where the air was as cold as the dream-induced world of the hypnotist. Marta had no sooner pulled her coat more tightly around her to ward off the chill than the captain stopped and pointed to a dusty light escaping through two curtained windows halfway down the alley. Marta held her breath and stared at the light. Instinctively, she knew they had reached their goal. The place reeked of human waste and discarded garbage. Somewhere, a door opened and water splashed in the street, surprising a cat who yowled in protest. A woman's voice cackled in response. The door slammed and all was quiet. At first, nothing seemed amiss. Then Marta spotted a figure moving through the light from the window on the left. Light flared from the doorway and quickly died as another figure emerged from the building. Their voices floated to her as they exchanged a few brief words. There were at least two men standing between Marta and the brothel where she hoped to find Missy. How many more hid in the shadows?

Captain O'Conner and his fellow officers would soon find out. They hugged the wall and slowly crept down the alley. At first, Marta hesitated to follow, but Byron gently took her arm and signaled for her to keep close to him. Charles stayed back to watch the street behind them. She had already been warned that any sound would be magnified in such a narrow space, so she placed each foot with great care and tested its firmness before committing her weight to it. In this manner, she slowly worked her way forward, all the while keeping an eye on the crouching officers ahead of her. As they got closer, the light from the windows began to illuminate them and they stopped. It was impossible to get any nearer without being spotted. Marta shivered as she watched the two men guarding the door. She had never before confronted physical danger. Her body was taut with anticipation. Her breath escaped in little puffs that quickly disappeared. The chilled air made her face tingle with the caress of a thousand fingertips. Smoke wafting past brought a whiff of meat cooking on a brazier to her nose. Every smell and image was magnified by the significance of the moment.

Without warning, all five officers stood up and rushed the two men guarding the door amid shouts and curses. Captain O'Conner and one fellow officer drew their guns, while the others raised their batons. One of the two Chinese men tried to draw a weapon, but he was knocked to the ground by a baton and lay motionless. The other guard raised his hands and stood impassively while an officer handcuffed him.

After that, things happened so fast, it was all Marta could do to keep up. She held Byron's arm as they hurried after the captain and his men. Voices shouted from inside the brothel. Yellow shafts of light burst through the doorway when two of the officers put their shoulders to the door and splintered it. A woman tried to scurry past but was seized by the arm. Captain O'Conner and two of his officers charged into the brothel with Byron and Marta plunging in after them. Inside, the scene was chaos. Women ran about screaming and shouting at the officers. Two hatchet men appeared from another room, one brandishing a gun. O'Conner fired without hesitation and the man disappeared in a heap on the floor. The gunshot boomed in the room with the force of an explosion. Marta's ears rang so violently from the sound that she became disoriented and nearly stumbled on the uneven floor. Only her grip on Byron's arm prevented her from falling. The acrid odor of burnt gunpowder mingled with the sweet aroma of perfume. It struck her as an odd combination. At last, the full reality of what had happened hit her. She had just watched O'Conner shoot a man!

The second henchman dropped to his knees when commanded to do so by one of the officers and clasped his hands behind his head

Charles appeared at Marta's side and shouted for her to go back, but she ignored him. She was not going to turn and run. Her heart hammered in her chest as she frantically searched the room for any sign of Missy or the hypnotist, but all she saw were powdered Chinese faces rushing past her. The police officers moved methodically through the room, gathering up the women and their customers and herding them to couches along the far wall.

Marta took a deep breath and followed Byron through the door where the hatchet man had appeared. She entered a hallway and saw a room where tousled sheets lay on an empty bed. The room exuded a smell of unwashed bodies. More rooms fed off the hallway. Charles joined them and they worked their way down the corridor behind one of the officers. Each room revealed a rumpled bed and small lantern, but none were occupied, the occupants having fled amidst the turmoil. Her heart sank when they entered the last room and still found no evidence of Missy. Had it been a false lead, after all? There were dozens of other brothels in

Chinatown. Missy could be in any of them.

As she stood in the middle of the last room lost in her misery, a whispery sound teased her ears. At first, she thought it was just a breath of wind escaping the foul-smelling room, but when it came again she listened more closely. The sound had a human quality to it, the kind one associated with a child whimpering. It came from beyond the wall behind her, or so it seemed. It was hard to be certain with all the commotion around her. Marta pressed her ear to the wall and listened intently. There it was again, a muffled voice crying feebly. Rushing back to the hallway, Marta looked for a door. There was none. A cabinet stood against the wall, but when she tried to move it, she found it too heavy to budge.

She was about to call for help when Byron and Charles appeared at her side. She pointed to the cabinet and the two men quickly shouldered it aside, revealing a hidden door. It was locked, but Charles shattered the thin wood with two swift kicks and stepped inside. Marta followed. Her eyes were immediately drawn to a forlorn figure bundled in a stained sheet on a bed in the far corner of the room. Light from the shattered doorway highlighted a patch of red hair peeking out from under the sheet. Marta's knees nearly buckled when she saw it.

"Oh my God, it's Missy," she cried.

Byron un-wrapped the sheet and pulled it back. Missy lay bound hand and foot with a gag in her mouth. Her glazed eyes stared into space as if she was looking at another world. Her body was so limp, Marta feared she was dead. Slowly, Missy shifted her gaze to her rescuers and tried to speak through her gag. Marta flung herself on the bed and threw her arms around her friend. "Oh, Missy, thank God we've found you." Marta shuddered and took a large gulp of air as she clung to her. Byron gently pulled Marta away so Charles could remove the gag and untie her bonds.

"It's me, Missy," Marta said as she brushed back the girl's hair with a trembling hand. "You're safe, now. We've come to take you home."

"She's been drugged," Charles observed in a quiet voice. "Most likely she doesn't even recognize us."

A cloudburst of tears welled up in Marta's eyes and cascaded down her cheeks onto Missy's where they quickly streaked her dirty face. Missy lay very still and stared at everyone, her gaze frozen and her thoughts no doubt imprisoned deep inside her mind. Her expression was so lifeless Marta feared she had lost her sanity. Then, as if by a miracle, she turned her face towards Marta's. Recognition glowed in her eyes. She blinked and managed a weak smile.

"Thank you, dear God, for returning my friend to me," Marta murmured in a quivering voice. She kissed Missy's cheeks and forehead and inhaled the musky aroma of her unwashed hair. How she loved Missy's hair!

"Come on," Byron said as he tugged Marta's arm. "Let's get her out of here before any more of the tongs' men appear." Marta wiped her face with the back of her hand and stood out of the way while Byron gathered Missy in his arms and lifted her from the bed.

They hurried back to the main room and found it subdued. Six women and eight men sat on the couch and floor in one corner staring sullenly at the police officers. Captain O'Conner was busy tying up the hatchet man who was still conscious. The man who had been shot lay unmoving on the floor, most likely dead. Marta swallowed hard at the sight of him. She had seen bodies before, but she had never witnessed a man shot to death.

Captain O'Conner stood in the middle of the room assessing things. When he saw the girl in Byron's arms, he nodded with satisfaction. "Glad to see your search was successful. Now, we better go. One of the women got away and word of our assault has most likely reached the ears of the tongs. That means more men are on their way. We should be gone before they get here, if we don't want further trouble."

The captain led the group back into the cryptic night and retraced their route up the shabby alley. There was no need to remain silent now. They hurried as quickly as they dared on the uneven pathway. As she stumbled along, Marta recalled the ugly rooms she had just seen and tried to imagine the fate of the Chinese women who worked there. How many had been kidnapped like Missy and forced into their destitute lives? What happened to them when they were no longer wanted? Marta's head pounded with the images and sounds she had witnessed. The experience had been frightening, yet she found their escape through the back alleys surprisingly exhilarating. She looked furtively about her for any sign of trouble and hurried after Byron and the other men.

They had nearly reached the end of the alleyway when shouts echoed from the direction of the brothel. She imagined hordes of figures sprinting through the shadows in pursuit of them, but she dared not look back. She ducked her head instead and increased her stride. Two of the officers turned with guns drawn to confront any pursuers while everyone else hurried around the corner. A shot barked and a bullet whizzed past the corner where they had been standing. More shots rang out as the officers returned fire. Marta's throat burned from the exertion and the tension of the chase. She considered herself in good health, but she had never pushed herself so hard before. Her breaths were becoming shorter and more explosive with each stride. To her relief, they turned another corner and the men slowed their pace to wait for the two officers to rejoin them. Heavy breathing replaced the harsh reports of gunfire as everybody tried to catch their breath. The world seemed safe again, but she knew the feeling was illusionary.

"My men have a reputation as fine marksmen," the captain announced between quick breaths. Even he was puffing from their ordeal. "I doubt the tongs' men will choose to engage us any further."

On cue, the two officers returned. "Our pursuers have turned tail and run," they reported with satisfaction.

"As I expected," the captain responded, "but let us not dally too long. The main street and entrance are just ahead."

Marta could tell by the men's quick strides and heavy sighs that they were relieved to exit Chinatown. She had now seen the mysterious quarter twice and knew there was a great divide between daylight and nightfall. The community had appeared so fascinating during her first trip, but after tonight, she knew it was a brutal place filled with nightmares and pain. She had seen the hand of misery in those wretched rooms and in Missy's dull gaze. Someone had once used the phrase "haunt of the highbinders" to describe Chinatown. It had sounded intriguing when Marta heard it. Now, the phrase filled her with images of enslaved women and ruthless men. Marta shuddered and promised herself never to return there again.

* * *

Once they had thanked the police officers for their gallant raid, Byron put Missy in the back seat of his carriage where she lay unmoving. Her glimmer of earlier recognition had slipped away behind the veil of darkness that still gripped her mind.

"It would be best to take her to my place and call a doctor," Byron said quietly. "If necessary, she can remain the night."

Charles agreed. "It may not be just the drugs that are affecting her. It's possible she's still under the hypnotist's spell, although that will wear off with time."

"How long?" Marta asked with alarm.

Charles shrugged his shoulders. "Hard to tell. I shouldn't think too long. Tomorrow, perhaps."

Marta turned her attention to Captain O'Conner. She had never heard back from the police officer who had taken her reports and she didn't want this latest incident to become lost on someone's paper-filled desk. "Captain, the man who kidnapped Missy is the hypnotist I told you about before. He's preying on young women in the tenement district where I work. I've seen him twice myself and can give you a description."

The captain removed his bowler hat and scratched the top of his head. "Charles has advised me about him, as well. You haven't heard anything about your earlier reports, I take it." It was a statement, not a question, but Marta shook her head nonetheless.

"Stop by the police station on Powell and fill out an information sheet. With a good description, I should be able to get more patrols down there for awhile. I'd like to catch this guy."

Marta nodded with satisfaction. At last, somebody was listening to her. "I'll come by tomorrow."

As the carriage departed, Marta could not help noticing the way Charles watched the weak glow of Chinatown's paper lanterns disappearing in the gathering gloom. She had no doubt the strange, oriental community was calling him back. It was the lure of the opium dens, she surmised. She wondered at their power and worried for the man.

Everyone rode in silence through the misty night to Byron's mansion, each lost in his or her thoughts. Missy lay as still as a felled log in a forest, her mind in a world Marta could not even imagine. When she thought about it, however, she realized that was not entirely true. She, too, had entered the hypnotist's world, if only briefly. She shivered when she remembered the icy void that had left her gasping for air. Was Missy in such a place? She prayed not, for it was a pernicious world filled with evil.

The doctor confirmed that Missy had been given drugs to dull her mind. Beyond that, he could not say. He wasn't familiar with the effects of hypnosis and had no opinion on the matter. He did answer one important question, however. After a brief inspection, he announced that Missy was still intact. No one had touched her during her stay in Chinatown. After the doctor had left, Charles suggested that someone should sit with Missy throughout the night, in case she snapped out of her trance and became disoriented. If that happened, it was possible she might hurt herself in an effort to escape the nightmares she had faced.

With that, Charles excused himself and disappeared into the night. Marta remembered how he had watched Chinatown fade from view a short while ago. He's going back there, she thought with dismay, back to Chinatown. She wondered how he could return to such a place after what they had just been through, but she knew the answer. Opium was a demanding mistress that could not be ignored. For those addicted to it, her siren song was irresistible. It called her lovers back with promises of a paradise that quickly turned into Hell. Marta sadly shook her head and turned her attention to Missy, who lay in a four-post bed in one of Byron's many oversized rooms.

"I will stay up with her tonight," she declared. She reached out and brushed a loose strand of Missy's hair as she spoke, causing the girl to briefly stir.

"We should take turns," Byron offered, "so we can both be sharp in the morning. If you like, you stay with her now. I will have Henry wake me at two. A room will be prepared for you just down the hall. That way, you can get some rest and still be close by if she wakes up."

Marta wanted to protest, but the tension from the evening's foray into Chinatown had sapped her strength. Byron was right. The thrill of finding Missy and escaping from the tongs had energized her, but now that the adventure was over, she was exhausted. She would need some sleep if she was going to be of any use tomorrow.

Byron relieved Marta at two as promised. Missy had flinched and trembled a few times but gave no sign of waking. Once, she mumbled a few words Marta couldn't hear. Otherwise, the room was silent.

Marta was shown to another bedroom by a maid and given a nightgown, but she was too exhausted to change and lay down on the bed fully clothed. Despite her fatigue, however, sleep didn't come easily. She tossed on the bedcovers for some time before her eyelids finally closed for good. Even in her sleep, she did not rest. Dreams of Chinese dragons assaulted her. They showered her with angry fire and rendered her body helpless until she cried out with pain. Her eyes flew open at the eerie sound of her voice, but the room was empty. By the time she heard a knock on the door announcing it was morning, she had slept less than two hours.

She opened the door and found Henry standing in the hallway looking more animated than she had ever seen him. "Mr. Wagner requests your company. I believe the young lady is awakening." The corners of his mouth inched upwards, and Marta nearly threw her arms around him. She rushed past him instead and ran down the hallway to Missy's room, where she found Byron seated beside the bed stroking Missy's hand and talking soothingly to her. Missy's eyes were open, but they flew about the room like a frightened child's upon waking from a nightmare. Marta's heart ached with so much excitement, she had to stop in the doorway and calm herself before approaching the bed.

"Missy, it's all right. You're safe now," Marta whispered as she took Missy's free hand and held it firmly.

Missy looked into Marta's eyes, and the wild expression on her face relaxed. "Is it really you, ma'am, or am I dreamin'?"

Marta looked at Byron and nearly burst into tears. "Yes, it's me. Thanks to Byron's help, we came and got you last night. Do you remember where you were?"

"Somewhere in Chinatown, but nothin' more." She pinched her freckles into a frown. "I do remember that awful man enterin' the office while I was workin' and mutterin' something to me. Nothin' much is clear after that."

Marta counted that a blessing. The less Missy remembered about her ordeal, the better off she would be. It was a night Marta would never forget, however. Her heart still raced when she thought about their dramatic raid and escape. Only one thing bothered her. There had been no sign of the hypnotist. That meant he still lurked out there ready to pounce. How long could she protect Angela and Missy from that monster? Or herself, for that matter? As satisfying as last night's rescue had been, she knew it resolved nothing. The danger was still there. Those fearsome, black eyes were waiting to strike again. Of that she was certain.

CHAPTER FOURTEEN

The next few days flew by in a flurry of work and worry. Marta went to the police station as promised and gave Captain O'Conner a detailed description of Missy's assailant. Missy wanted to get back to work at once, but Marta insisted she take time to regain her strength before returning to the office. In her absence, Angela continued to assist Marta behind a locked door. Between Missy's dramatic rescue and Angela's recent adventures, Marta still hadn't found the right time to break the news about closing her agency. She finally decided to wait until she could speak to both women together before confessing her plans.

Meanwhile, time pressed down on Marta's shoulders with the weight of a ship's anchor. She had called a buyer of luxury items and asked for a quote on the value of her jewelry and the paintings that hung in the house. The sum wasn't as much as she had hoped, but enough, she prayed, to stop the bank from taking her home for a time.

* * *

In the midst of all the turmoil, Marta received an unexpected caller. It was nearly dinner time when the front doorbell rang. Samuel wasn't home yet and for a moment she thought he had forgotten his house key. Then, she remembered the spare he kept in a flower pot on the porch and realized it couldn't be him. She opened the door to discover a young man in the costume of a livery servant holding a card on a silver tray. The bizarre scene caught Marta so much by surprise that it was all she could do to keep from laughing.

"The Baron Konrad von Reich requests the honor of calling on you in the morning," the man announced in a voice a bit too high in pitch for the formal message he was attempting to deliver. This time, Marta's lips did twitch with amusement, but she managed to maintain a serious countenance. So, Mr. Reich carried a noble title after all. She had thought as much when she met him.

"I must go to my office in the morning," she replied as she lifted the card from the tray. "May I ask what this is about?"

"I don't know, ma'am. I was just asked to deliver the card and request a meeting with you." The young man's demeanor quickly slipped from stiffly proper to something less formal. Clearly, he was not comfortable in his role as messenger to the Baron Konrad von Reich. "He requested ten o'clock. May I confirm that for him?"

"Ten is too late. I must leave before then. It would have to be no later than nine. Perhaps that is too early an hour for Mr. Reich." What was a baron, she wondered? Something like a count or a prince?

"I'll let Baron Reich know." He continued in a confiding tone. "He seemed quite keen on seeing you tomorrow. I'm sure the earlier hour will be acceptable."

"I shall expect him then." Marta closed the door and studied the card, which announced the man's name and title in an elegant script and his address as the Palace Hotel. What in the world could that insufferable man want with her? Surely it had nothing to do with a social engagement. Something to do with chess perhaps? She couldn't imagine what. As a Grand Master he was far more familiar with the game than she was and had seen all sorts of queen pawn openings, including the variation she had used on Byron. She wished she could have declined the request, but it would have been impolite to reject it. She would see it through, although she suspected the encounter with Baron Konrad von Reich would be tiresome.

Marta hadn't considered what to wear for her appointment with the Baron until she awoke the next morning. It occurred to her that social custom required that she put on a dress. She was already in a grumbling mood about having to prepare herself for such an early visitor and nearly decided to wear her normal clothing and let social custom be damned. In the end, however, she knew she must respect some degree of decorum and pulled out the same dress she had worn the day she met Mr. Reich at her brother's club. She hoped it would send a signal that she didn't consider her appointment with the Baron to be anything more than a courtesy call.

Marta had breakfasted and was reviewing a few files she had brought home from the office when the bell rang promptly at nine. There was no sign that Samuel was stirring, for which she was thankful. She didn't need her brother smirking behind her back at this odd rendezvous.

When she opened the door, Marta was nearly overwhelmed by the Baron's outrageous clothing, which included a knee-length, brocade coat, a dark vest, and ruffled, silk shirt. A top hat rose a good foot from his head, completing the costume. If the hat was meant to tame the Baron's unruly hair, it failed completely. Strands escaped in all directions with the eagerness of convicts attempting a jailbreak. The coat and ruffled shirt, she noted, did a good job of covering his oversized frame. The Baron was a man who sat too much and enjoyed a rich diet.

Marta's surprise seemed to be matched by the Baron's when he saw her standing there. His dark, brown eyes flicked past her into the house with the rush of a hummingbird's wings, then flitted back to her face where they stopped but didn't quite come to rest. He had undoubtedly expected a maid or butler and for a moment was nonplussed at what to say. He quickly regained his composure, however, and broke the momentary silence by removing his hat and giving Marta a perfunctory bow. "Miss Baldwin, it is a pleasure to see you again."

Marta suspected he wanted to kiss her hand as he had done at the club, but she kept her arms to her sides and stepped aside for the Baron to enter. "Mr. Reich, it is an honor to have you call on us." She didn't consider it an honor at all and hoped the use of the word "us" would keep the Baron at a proper distance. To her dismay, he ignored her subtlety and pressed closer to her as she led him to the drawing room.

"I was most impressed by your chess acumen the other day," he commented once he was seated on the couch. Marta sat forward in a chair opposite him in a pose that showed her uncertainty about the reason for his call. "Yet I am still puzzled by your choice of a pawn on your 42nd move. I have a keen ability to see a chess board and to replay an entire game in my head, but I have not been able to fathom that move. Surely, you saw your winning position, yet chose not to pursue it. Can you tell me why?"

Marta chafed at the Baron's inquiry. The thought of losing in front of all those men stilled galled her, especially since none of them understood what took place. She certainly didn't wish to discuss it with the pompous man seated in front of her. "I hope you have not gone to all this trouble just to ask me about a chess game," she replied with a noncommittal smile.

Von Reich shifted uncomfortably in his seat and let his eyes drift to the painting above the mantelpiece. "Not at all. Just curious. That is a lovely landscape, by the way. Who is the artist?"

Marta glanced over her shoulder. "An early work by the British artist, Turner. My father collected art. I'm afraid I do not share his interest."

An awkward silence followed her remark while the Baron frowned to himself and gathered his thoughts. "I imagine you must be wondering why I am calling on you," he offered at last.

"The question had occurred to me, yes." Marta could see that the Baron was having difficulty finding his words, but she was in no mood to help him. Her day's calendar raced through her head, and she hoped he would get to the point so that she could change into her trousers and reach the office by ten.

"Well, you see, I am rather new to all the social customs in this country, but I have been invited to a ball and hoped you might accompany me. I have met some of the men who will be there, but not the ladies. Perhaps you would be kind enough to make introductions for me. I was quite taken by you at the club," he added hastily, "and would very much enjoy your company."

Oh God, it was a social call. What could she do? The idea of attending one of those suffocating social events with Baron Konrad von Reich was more than she could bear, but how could she gracefully decline? "I'm afraid I would be sorry company for you, Mr. Reich. I do not attend those gatherings except on rare occasions. You would be much better represented by one of the daughters of the men you have met at the club."

The Baron's eyes clouded with disappointment, but he quickly regained his stride and pushed forward. "Introductions would be helpful, of course, but my main purpose in coming here is to seek your company. I believe it would be a most agreeable evening for us both if you joined me. Here is the invitation." He pulled an envelope from his coat pocket and handed it to her.

Her fingers felt the fine texture of the paper, but she did not open it. Marta's mind was buzzing with thoughts and concerns. For one thing, she had to consider the possibility that von Reich was one of those titled Europeans with no money who hoped to find a wealthy wife. In that case, she would be sorry company indeed, given her financial circumstances. There seemed little reason for him to be interested in her otherwise. She realized that by taking the envelope she was accepting his invitation and hurriedly placed it on the low table between them. She had to find some way out of her predicament without damaging either of their sensibilities.

"As I said, Mr. Reich, I do not go to these social gatherings. But if you insist upon your invitation, might I have a day or so to think about it before I reply?"

"Yes, yes, of course." The Baron rose from his seat with such haste, Marta thought he might bolt for the door, but he stood with top hat in hand and nervously turned the hat's rim while he waited for Marta to rise and show him out. To her consternation, he made no effort to retrieve the envelope. After he was gone she placed it on the mantel, unopened. As long as she didn't open the invitation, she believed she still had the right to refuse the Baron's offer.

* * *

In the meantime, Marta had more important matters to consider. The deadline was fast approaching to repay the house loan, and she saw no visible progress towards setting up a payment schedule with the bank. She had asked Samuel to arrange another meeting to negotiate such a schedule, but he had dithered. When she pressured him, he flew into a rage and stormed from the house. Normally, Marta would have been furious with her brother's behavior, but not this time. There was too much at stake to let emotions get in the way. She feared Samuel had fallen into a melancholy state of mind that prevented him from taking the steps needed to fulfill her plan.

To make matters worse, she had dropped by the house on three occasions during the day and found Samuel at home instead of looking for work. His excuse was always the same: he had no job prospects to pursue that day. So, he lay about the house in a morose mood and fled into the night after dinner. Marta couldn't imagine where he went or what he did. Without money, he couldn't gamble or drink with his friends, which left him few options. That had been her assumption, at least, until she ran into a family acquaintance that moved in Samuel's circle of acquaintances. She discreetly asked what Samuel was doing and learned he had been borrowing money from his friends so he could join them on their evening rounds. They were getting tired of giving him handouts, however, and were beginning to avoid him. Once again, Marta had to swallow her anger. It was apparent her brother had no intention of finding work and was trying to continue with his old lifestyle as if nothing had happened. She decided it was up to her to put things in motion.

In desperation, Marta called the bank and asked for Joseph

Caldwell. She was asked to wait for what seemed an hour, but was in reality less than five minutes. It was long enough, however, to put Marta on edge. She suspected Mr. Caldwell was deliberately letting her cool her heels.

"Miss Baldwin," he said when he finally answered. His voice was noncommittal, distant.

"Mr. Caldwell, I'd like to have a meeting with you about the house." She nearly stammered her words and silently derided herself for sounding so scattered. Mr. Caldwell's waiting game was working. "I have a proposal to offer that I believe will satisfy you and allow Samuel and me to keep the house."

"We would be happy to look at such a proposal, Miss Baldwin, but shouldn't I be speaking to your brother?" The man's condescending tone of voice could not be mistaken. Marta's grip on the phone tightened. Her chest heaved with indignation. It was all she could do to swallow the retort that leaped to her tongue.

"The house is equally his and mine. It would be appropriate to meet with both of us." She could hear the pique in her voice but didn't care, even though she sensed Mr. Caldwell would get pleasure from knowing he had provoked her. It was better to show a little anger, she decided, than to appear weak.

"Then, by all means, let us meet. Shall we say tomorrow at ten?"

"We will be there," Marta replied firmly.

Marta decided to talk to her brother in person about the meeting and hurried home early to catch him before he disappeared for the evening. However, when she told him about her conversation with Mr. Caldwell, he fidgeted and grew restless.

"The bank is my business, not yours. You had no right to do that." He spat the words at her as he paced around the room. "How does it make me look to have my sister making deals behind my back? Foolish, that's how. My friends will mock me if they learn of this." He ran his hand through his hair and stared at her with the wild eyes of an animal trapped in a corner.

Marta suddenly realized that her brother was not going to face their problem. He had slipped into some kind of shell that shielded him from the reality of their situation. *My God*, she thought, *if I don't do something, we are going to lose our house, and Samuel is not going to lift a finger to help.*

"Besides," he added smugly, "I have a job interview tomorrow morning." His jaw trembled with displeasure, but his expression quickly broadened into a smirk when he noted his sister's confusion at his announcement.

"That is wonderful news. May I ask who with?" Marta wanted to be pleased by the news, wanted to show support for her brother, but there was something in Samuel's fidgeting manner, the way he pulled at his ear lobe and avoided her eyes, that worried her.

"It's a loan officer's position at a bank," he replied airily as he strode with increasing importance to a chair and sat down. "So, you see, you should not be making appointments without consulting with me. You will have to postpone your little meeting." His confidence grew as he spoke. A bit of his old swagger had returned.

Marta couldn't help but note the irony of his claim and wondered what kind of loan officer someone like him would make. But more worrisome was the way his hands nervously picked at the chair's arm pads. Despite his show of arrogance, she could not shake the uneasy feeling that there was no interview, that Samuel was fabricating a story for appearances sake. Her willingness to contact the bankers directly had obviously unnerved him and claiming he had a job interview was his way of reasserting his role as man of the house.

She had intended to discuss the estimates she had received for the jewelry and paintings but changed her mind. When Samuel finally met her gaze, his wary look reminded her of a deer she and her father had once startled while walking in the woods north of the city. In that instant her decision was made. It didn't matter whether Samuel was telling the truth. She would keep the appointment the next morning. The consequences of waiting any longer would be catastrophic.

Marta tried to probe for more information about the interview, but Samuel refused to discuss the topic further and left the house without waiting for dinner. She had little appetite for preparing a meal just for herself, so she took a small glass of brandy and retreated to the drawing room to ponder the day's events. Dusk had blanketed the room in its darkening arms; she found she preferred the gloom to the glare of lights. It fit her mood perfectly. Samuel's obstinacy had torn at the few strands of hope she had left. There were too many burdens to bear. It was not just the house. She was about to lose her aid society, as well, and there was still the threat posed by the hypnotist, who lurked out there somewhere in the growing blackness. Her mind could no longer handle the pressures. Her face quickly became stained with tears. The darkening room now depressed her and she turned on the lights.

When the front doorbell rang, Marta started and quickly wiped her face. Who could be calling now she wondered as she peeked out the window? She feared the Baron had returned for his answer, but she discovered a surprising guest, one who raised a different set of concerns. For there, in all her earthy magnificence, stood Lillie Collins wearing her customary trousers and man's shirt. Marta instantly thought of Byron, and her already battered spirits sank even lower. Competing with this saucy creature's charms for any man seemed an impossible task. Not that it mattered. Her world and Byron's were about to be pushed even further apart by the prospect of her financial ruin. It was one more burden to bear, but she was determined to do it without complaint. It came as a surprise, therefore, to realize how pleased she was at that moment to see Lillie. She needed someone to talk to, and the woman spun an aura around herself that was so full of life, Marta could not help being enthralled by her. She quickly opened the door.

"I am known to act on impulse, which is what I'm doing now." Lillie studied Marta's puffed eyes and tear-smeared face. "Have I come at a bad time?"

"Yes and no. Do I look a mess?" Marta pressed her hands against both cheeks in embarrassment.

"As a matter of fact you do." Lillie eyed her critically. "Have you dined yet?"

Her question surprised Marta. She stood in the doorway uncertain what to do. It was impolite not to ask Lillie in, but she had the feeling her unexpected guest was in a hurry to move on. "No. Samuel isn't home tonight and I didn't have the energy to cook for myself," she confessed.

"Good, because we're going to dinner. My treat." Lillie pronounced this more as an ultimatum than an invitation. When Marta started to protest, Lillie took her hand and squeezed it. "No arguments. Go wash your face. I'll wait in the foyer." With that she stepped inside and stood expectantly by the hall table.

Marta rushed to the downstairs guest bathroom and did the best she could to repair the damage the tears had done to her face. She couldn't say why, but Lillie's invitation put renewed vigor in her step. Marta considered the pants outfit she was still wearing from work and wondered if she should change into a dress. The idea of two women in pants walking into a restaurant amused her, however, and she decided to go as she was.

Lillie guided her to a small Italian restaurant nearby. It was a newer establishment that Marta had never been to. *Not that I eat out much*, she thought with a sigh. Nor would she be doing much of that anytime soon. Not after the mess her brother had made of their lives.

Eyes were raised when the women entered, just as Marta had expected, but Lillie blithely ignored their stares and pointed to a corner table Marta suspected was reserved for someone else.

"We'll eat there, George," she said matter-of-factly to the maître d', who bowed and led them to the table without protest.

"You are used to getting your way, Lillie," Marta commented with admiration once they were seated.

"Hell, yes. What's the point of having all this money if we can't use it to our advantage?" She said this without umbrage, but Marta was startled by her language. Lillie Collins took some getting used to, but Marta couldn't help liking the woman's powerful independent streak.

"Of course, being rich isn't always what it's cracked up to be," Lillie continued once they had ordered their pasta dishes and were sipping glasses of wine. "Take me. Here I am enjoying my life when, bang, my mother tells me I'm to marry some Count from

England." She made a bitter lemon face that caused Marta to smile. "His family once owned castles, but he's broke now and looking for a rich wife. The man is twenty years my senior and penniless. Can you imagine? And if I refuse, my father has threatened to cut me off without a dime."

Marta immediately thought about her suspicions regarding von Reich's interest in her, but that wasn't what jarred her. It was the image of Lillie and Byron sharing that moment of intimacy when she walked into Byron's drawing room. It was the thought of the two of them sharing touches and burning lips. The dark clouds that had gathered over her head ever since meeting Lillie shifted ever so slightly and a ray of hope shined through.

"What about Byron?" she asked in a hushed voice.

Lillie cocked her head with a burst of interest that seemed to flash across the table. "Byron? What does he have to do with my dilemma?"

Marta found it difficult to meet Lillie's frank stare. Her eyes wandered over the plates and crystal which filled the small table in an array of elegant patterns and tiny prisms. "It's just that I thought . . . I assumed you two were . . . involved."

Lillie's hearty laugh filled the silence that trailed behind Marta's hesitant words and caused heads at nearby tables to turn. Marta looked up and discovered a lively smile on Lillie's face.

"I do believe you are enamored by that man," Lilly said, with much amusement.

Marta's cheeks burned with resentment. She knew it was hopeless to expect her feelings to be reciprocated, but she didn't care to be mocked about it.

Lillie saw her look of despair and reached across the table to take her hand. The warmth of Lillie's fingers was oddly comforting. No matter how much Marta tried to dislike this woman, she couldn't help wanting to be her friend.

"Marta," Lillie said softly, "I think Byron is a wonderful man, one of the finest I know, but he's only a friend. Always has been. There has never been a romantic link between us." She patted Marta's hand and released it. "You, on the other hand, would make an excellent partner for him. He's a bit of an old bachelor, but that's just because he hasn't met the right woman. I know he was very impressed with you the day you two met at his club."

Lillie's words swept away the stormy clouds above Marta's head. Lillie was not a rival! In point of fact, she was encouraging Marta to pursue her interest in Byron. Marta felt a glimmer of joy and hope spark in her heart, but it was quickly doused by the reality of her situation. She was about to face financial ruin, much like Angela. There could be no hope of "a romantic link" as Lillie had so eloquently put it. A great wall of sadness rose in her mind, but she forced herself to smile and quickly changed the subject.

"But what about you, Lillie? What are you going to do? I cannot imagine someone with a will as strong as yours agreeing to an arranged marriage."

"Oh, I refused, you can be sure of that. I told both my parents I would rather go live in the tenements than be saddled with some man who had lost half his teeth. And I meant it." She laughed again, a great hearty laugh that caused more heads to turn. "They didn't know if I was bluffing or not. They were furious with me, but in the end they backed down. Not that they cared about me. They just couldn't face the embarrassment of their daughter living among the poor."

The pasta dishes arrived, and Lillie plunged in her fork with relish. Marta watched her with fascination. There was such a magical quality to the woman. It took courage to stand up to one's parents, especially rich ones. But it was more than that. Lillie stood up to life with the same defiance as she did her parents. She had a zest for living that Marta had never encountered in anyone before. Being around her was like swimming in a whirlpool. The more Marta tried to resist the woman's charms, the more she was swept up by them.

"Which brings me to a delicate subject," Lillie commented between bites of pasta. "I hear rumors that you're having money problems." Lillie's frank remark caught Marta off guard and snapped her out of her reverie. Lillie's trials with her parents had momentarily made Marta forget her own troubles. She found

152

herself fumbling with her silverware while she regained her composure.

"Look," Lillie continued, "you don't have to be all proper with me about your situation. Wouldn't do you any good anyhow. People know the bank is putting pressure on you. Best you tell me why. I might be able to help." She stared at Marta with such a mesmerizing look, Marta immediately thought of the hypnotist. It was an unsettling association. Marta tried to deflect her companion's gaze by glancing around the room at the large potted plants and the atrium-style roof. The room was alive with the buzz of voices and the odors of shell fish smothered in linguine. It was a fairytale setting that was so peaceful, Marta never wanted to leave. She would have to, of course. The world was not as simple as a child's bedtime story. Dinner with Lillie was a wonderful respite, but tomorrow she would have to face the world and her problems.

While Marta struggled with her emotions, Lillie continued to eye her with that frank look Marta was coming to recognize as her new acquaintance's trademark. Lillie didn't pull her punches. *Well,* Marta thought, *she might as well confess her worries to someone and Lillie already felt like a person she could trust.*

"It's true, Lillie. My brother made some poor choices and borrowed money against the house. Our family business is in ruins and the bank is about to foreclose on us." She felt her eyes moisten as she spoke and looked away again.

"I knew it," Lillie exclaimed with anger. "Those damn banks are eager to lend money so long as they have their teeth in you. I've never trusted them."

Marta gave her a wry smile. "Oh, I don't think it's entirely their fault. Samuel wanted money for the business. The bank didn't force him to take it." She paused while the waiter removed the dishes and poured coffee. "Anyway, I think I have a way to save the house, but it will require a great deal of sacrifice on our parts. I'm meeting with the bank's officers to try to work things out."

"I believe you're dealing with Corchran," Lillie stated.

Marta nodded, surprised at how quickly word had spread through the community. "I'm seeing them tomorrow morning at ten."

"Don't give up hope, darlin'. Those Corchran boys bark worse than they bite." Lillie sipped her coffee, put it down, and pulled a small cigar from her pocket. Marta watched in amazement as she struck a match to it and puffed until the tip was a hot orange glow. Marta sensed the heat of shocked looks from the other tables, but Lillie puffed contentedly without giving anyone so much as a cursory glance. As before, her blatant disregard for social customs sent Marta's head spinning.

"You continue to amaze me Lilly. I have always considered myself unconventional, but compared to you, I'm no more controversial than a dog chasing its tail. Where do you find the nerve?"

Lillie smiled but didn't answer. Her expression grew serious again. "One more question," she said between puffs. "What's going to become of your Pacific Aid Society?"

Marta sat back in her chair and drew a deep breath while she tried to control the unexpected turmoil that churned inside of her. For some reason, she found it more painful to talk about her relief organization than she did the house, perhaps because she thought she could save the house but saw no hope for the agency.

"I plan to finish as many of my cases as I can by the end of the month, then shut it down." Her shoulders sagged as she admitted this. She found herself fighting back more tears. "You're the first person I've told, Lillie." She shuddered and swiped at her face with the back of her hand. "Please don't say anything until I have a chance to talk with Missy and Angela. I don't want them to hear about it from someone else."

Lillie blew a perfect smoke ring but said nothing more.

* * *

The next morning, Marta met Angela and loaned her a key to open the office, then she headed down Market Street to the Corchran Bank building located near the corner of Market and Taylor. She had bowed to social etiquette and worn a dress. The fabric chafed her skin as she walked and reminded her how much she disliked being constrained by such conventional clothing. The air was crisp and filled with the promise of springtime, and the boulevard bustled with creaking, horse drawn wagons, clanging trolleys, and sputtering automobiles. Young boys shouted the latest headlines as they waved their newspapers to passersby. A sea of bowler hats sat atop the heads of businessmen going about their errands. Women's bustles rustled along the dusty street, just like hers.

She lifted her skirt hem as she mounted the curb and entered the bank's new stone building. Once inside, a young man greeted her and directed her up a marble staircase to a second floor conference room. She had felt reasonably confident in her proposal until now, but as she mounted the broad staircase, her heart pounded with all the subtlety of a bass drum and her fingers twitched unmercifully. Without Samuel's support, she was left to face the inquisition by herself. The prospect was daunting. She steadied her nerves as best she could and stopped in front of an opaque glass door for one last look at her dress. She patted down her hair and opened the door.

The room was sedate. Heavy leather chairs surrounded a highly polished table that seemed to stretch forever down the elongated chamber. The room smelled . . . odorless. How could a room have no smell at all, she wondered? Because it was sterile, she decided. The furniture and floor had been scrubbed cleaner than a maternity ward. Paintings of the bank's founders hung importantly on the walls. Thick brown drapes covered the far windows. If Marta hadn't known better, she would have thought she was in the offices of a mortuary. In a way, she supposed she was. Life as she knew it was about to end if she couldn't convince Caldwell and Matteson to consider her proposal.

Drapes at the far end of the room were pulled back enough to cast a bright beacon of light across the end of the table. She saw three people sitting there chatting but couldn't make out their faces. When they looked towards her, however, the glare highlighted them. Marta's heart received a new jolt when she recognized Lillie seated between the two men with whom she had come to do battle.

Lillie stood up, revealing the same trousers as the day before.

"Welcome, Marta. I had a little business to take care of with these gentlemen and was about to leave, but I decided to wait to say hello first." She beamed Marta a big smile and waved her forward. The two men had risen, as well and greeted her with a politeness that bordered on deference. It was not the welcome she had expected. At their prior meeting, the men had presented themselves in a slightly threatening manner. She had anticipated similar treatment today. For a moment, she was thrown off balance.

"Lillie, this is an unexpected surprise." Marta was suddenly more nervous than she had imagined possible. It was all she could do to walk over to the group without tripping over her feet. She couldn't help wondering if Lillie's business involved hers. As much as she liked her, Marta wasn't sure how comfortable she was with the idea of Lillie discussing her situation with these men. On the other hand, Lillie had remarked yesterday that she might be able to help and, in Samuel's absence, Marta needed all the support she could muster.

Lillie gathered some papers from the table and put them in a valise. "Well, now that you have arrived, I will be on my way. Are you going to your office afterwards?"

"I plan to, yes."

"Good. I would like to drop by for a visit. See you then." With that, she shook the bankers' hands, gave Marta a wink, and left.

The room grew remarkably still in the aftermath of Lillie's departure. It was as if she had sucked all the air from the place. The only sounds were the sharp ticking of a clock in the far corner and the slight scuffling of the men's shoes on the wood floor.

"Will Mr. Baldwin be joining us?" Matteson finally queried as he gestured for Marta to sit down. His voice shattered the calm that had settled over them.

"No," she replied firmly. "He has left the details to me." She took the proffered seat and faced the men with squared shoulders and chin held high. She was a woman confronting two very conservative men. She had to show strength. "Here is my proposal." She slid several papers across the table to the men. "As you can see, it includes a substantial upfront payment from the sale of family assets. I propose a payment schedule for the balance, at a reasonable interest rate, of course."

Joseph Caldwell picked up the papers and perused them with a slight frown. His thinning hair caused a mild sheen where the skin on his head was exposed to the glaring light from the opened drapes. The fact that Caldwell took the papers first told Marta he was the senior member of the team. She estimated him to be in his fifties and at least ten years older than Matteson. Caldwell, she realized, was the one she had to convince.

Caldwell passed the papers along to Matteson and folded his hands on the table in front of him. His serious demeanor sent a chill of anxiety racing up and down Marta's spine. He said nothing while Matteson read the papers, although she was certain he had already made up his mind. From his stern expression, Marta feared the worst. She felt herself sinking into an abyss every bit as frightening as the one she had encountered when entranced by the hypnotist.

"We do not normally make loans of this kind, Miss Baldwin," Caldwell said at last. His voice was abrasive and unkind. Marta heard denial in it and her heart sank further. "However, we have been, shall we say, convinced of your integrity and the unusual nature of your position." He gave her an unyielding stare that told her he was unhappy. "I believe your numbers are optimistic, but given the circumstances, we will arrange a repayment schedule for the balance after you have delivered the promised upfront payment."

For a moment, Marta couldn't breathe. Had she heard him correctly? Had she saved her home? His words lifted her from the depths of her despair and carried her aloft on the wings of euphoria. She discovered her legs were trembling from her wild emotional swing and she had to press her knees together to quiet them. Her euphoria was quickly tempered, however, when she looked at Caldwell's set jaw. All it took was one look at his unyielding face for the reality of her situation to strike home. He didn't want to extend her the loan. He was only doing it because of Lillie! That explained his pained looks and stiff behavior. Lillie must wield considerable power to force a man like Caldwell to bend to her will. In this case, power equaled money, and it was apparent Lillie had a great deal of both.

Marta returned Caldwell's icy stare and silently thanked her new friend for saving her from this cold man. She was suddenly very glad to know Lillie, and it had nothing to do with her money. A person's world, she realized, was only as large and important as the people in it. Knowing Lillie was already expanding her horizons immeasurably.

"We will, of course, need your brother's signature on the agreement when it is ready." This was from Matteson, whom she had ignored until now. His face was not nearly so grim, but she didn't fool herself. She suspected he was just as ruthless as Caldwell.

"Deliver the papers to my house when they are ready," she replied as she rose from the table. Her knees still shook, but she was determined not to show any weakness. She would take advantage of Lillie's support and let these two men know she was in charge. "I will see that Samuel signs them."

With that she strode from the room.

CHAPTER FIFTEEN

Marta headed for her office with an overwhelming sense of relief. Thanks to Lillie's intervention, she had saved her home, at least for now. When she thought about Caldwell's hard stare, however, she knew the house was not yet safe. She had to get Samuel to sign the new loan documents. She knew he would resent the fact that she had taken action without him. She also knew Caldwell was right about her "optimistic numbers." Making the proposed payments was dependent on both her and her brother finding reasonable employment and Samuel had yet to show any sign that he was prepared to face that reality, despite his job interview claims. Caldwell might yet take her home away from her, even after Lillie's efforts.

She was pleased to see a police officer walking the street when she arrived at her office. Captain O'Conner had taken her story of the hypnotist seriously and delivered on his promise to add more patrols to the tenements. The result was that Angela had opened the window shades. Marta could see her talking with Lillie as she went about her work. Pleasant warmth spread through Marta at the sight of Lillie. Whenever Marta was around that woman, she felt better about things.

"Thank you for whatever you did back there," she declared to Lillie upon entering the office. "I never saw two men so tied up in knots." She gave her new friend such a warm embrace, Lillie's features softened to the point of blushing and Marta's smile broadened. Embarrassment was not a response she would have expected from Lillie, but she liked it. Under that tough exterior was a woman who needed the warmth of others. Marta knew they were going to be close friends.

To deflect the awkward moment, she turned her attention to Angela. "I think the added patrols will make it safe for you to work outside again. I planned to visit three families today, but why don't you go instead? The information is all here in their folders."

Angela's face shined with a happy smile that said how much she enjoyed the growing confidence Marta was showing in her. She eagerly took the documents and gathered her things. "But stay alert," Marta cautioned. "The police may have forced that awful man into hiding, but he's still out there."

"I will, I promise." She said goodbye to Lillie and hurried out the door.

"Angela thinks you walk on water," Lillie remarked.

Marta glanced out the window at Angela's retreating figure and smiled at the high praise. "It is strange. I used to disapprove of Angela. I thought she stood for everything I disliked about our city's high and mighty society. But since she faced her own crisis and came to me looking for work, I have found her to be very resilient and capable. And I've grown fond of her. I hate to think that in less than three weeks she will be unemployed again."

Lillie sat down on the edge of the table and gave Marta one of those no-nonsense looks that Marta was coming to know so well. It was a look that said the small talk was over. Lillie was all business. "That's what I came here to talk to you about. Closing this agency would be a shame. From what I hear, you do really good work. The community needs you. Those poor people need you. So here's the deal." Lillie stood up and put her hands on her hips to emphasize her words. "I've got too much income. My solicitor tells me to invest some of it in non-profit organizations like yours. I do a good deed and I save on taxes. Everybody wins."

At first, Marta was uncertain what Lillie was proposing. She'd had no experience with investments. Samuel had taken care of their finances, however badly, and told her little about them. "Are you offering to fund my agency?" she asked incredulously.

"That's exactly what I'm doing. Like I said, I gain as much as you do, and you continue helping the people who need you."

A dozen questions spun through Marta's mind. "But, I need to find a job so I can repay that loan against the house. How can I do that and keep this place open?"

"This *is* your job, darlin'. When I say fund the agency, I mean completely. You, Missy and Angela all stay. They get their wages, and you earn enough to live properly."

Marta collapsed in a chair in disbelief. Was it possible? Could she really continue to do her work there? Or was there a downside? She would be beholden to Lillie and could lose her funding on a whim. Not that she thought Lillie would do such a thing, but what if something happened to her? What then?

"It would all be in writing, of course," Lillie continued as if reading her mind. "I'm thinking a five year contract. The funding would be guaranteed from my estate." Marta opened her mouth to speak, but Lillie rolled right over her. "You give me a realistic budget that covers expenses and salaries. My solicitor can have papers ready within the week."

"Lillie. I don't know what to say," Marta replied when she finally managed to wedge her words in between Lillie's. "You are much too generous. How could I ever repay you?"

"You don't. If you did, I would just face more taxes. Look, I've already spoken to my solicitor this morning. Dropped in on him before I went to the bank. He says it's a good arrangement. Just needs to see the numbers." Lillie tapped her forehead with her fingers as if to remind herself of something. "Oh, and there's something else. I told him about your situation with the bank. He wants to see a copy of your father's will."

Marta's ears picked up. "The will? Whatever for?"

"It has something to do with the wording about managing your estate. You and your brother both share equally, right?"

Marta nodded.

"But was Samuel given power of attorney to manage the estate or did he just assume that role as the male head of the family?" Lillie's eyes gleamed with the intensity of twin stars. What could she possibly be getting at, Marta wondered?

"As far as I can recall, there was no power of attorney." Marta frowned as she tried to remember the will's details. "Simply an equal division of assets and income. Samuel was put in charge of running the shipping business, but I'm pretty sure that was all."

"Then my solicitor needs to see the will and verify that. If what you say is true, the bank may not have any claim on your house." Lillie folded her arms and looked at Marta triumphantly. "We just might lick those bastards at their own game."

Lillie's announcement hit Marta with the force of a runaway street car. She sank back further in her chair while she tried to assimilate this remarkable news. The possibility that she might be able to remove her home from harm's way was nearly too much to hope for, yet she could see the sense of what Lillie was telling her. If Samuel didn't have power of attorney, he would need her signature on any documents involving the house.

"I can have the will tomorrow morning."

"Good. Meet me at Byron's house at noon. I will have my solicitor join us there and we can decide what to do."

"Why Byron's?" Marta was delighted at the prospect of seeing him again, especially now that she knew he and Lillie were not involved, but she hesitated to share her financial burdens with him.

Lillie smiled knowingly. "Don't worry what Byron thinks. Besides, he already knows about your situation. Remember, news travels quickly in our little community of wealthy families. He also knows it was your brother that got you into this mess. I respect his insights in these matters. He has more experience than we do. I think he can help."

Marta distractedly picked up a file Angela had left on the table. Since meeting Byron, she seemed to be seeking his help at every turn. What must the man think? But, as usual, Lillie was right. Marta certainly had little experience dealing with banks or solicitors. Byron's input would be invaluable. "Tomorrow at noon, then," she said with a smile.

* * *

An opened envelope with a note inside waited for Marta on the hall table when she arrived home that evening. It had been delivered during the day while Samuel was home. He had obviously opened and read it. She was beyond being angry with her brother anymore and merely pressed her lips together in frustration as she read the message:

Dear Miss Baldwin: Since I have not heard from you, may I consider your lack of response as acceptance of my invitation? I shall do so and make arrangements to pick you up April 5th at seven.

Sincerely yours,

Baron von Reich

God, what was she going to do about that insufferable man? She had been much too preoccupied with her personal problems to even think about his silly invitation, which still rested on the mantel unopened. Now, he was making a claim on her when she had agreed to nothing of the sort. She would have to do something, but what? He had put her in a most uncomfortable circumstance. She sighed and put the note on the mantel with the invitation. She would try to think about it tomorrow, after she had dealt with the solicitor and the bank.

* * *

Marta visited the family solicitor at nine the next morning. He was a formal man. In fact, she had often used the word stuffy to describe him to friends. Not that she knew him all that well. She had only met him a few times and had always called him Mr. Adams. The office was severe in its décor, almost Spartan. Heavy, dark brown wallpaper covered the walls and stiff leather chairs faced a large mahogany desk. An antiseptic odor permeated the place that made her think of a hospital. She recalled that Mr. Adams always wore a vest over his bulging stomach, and he did so today. He reminded her of a large frog squatting behind his desk. It would have been a simple matter to ask him for his interpretation of the will, but that would bring Samuel into the discussion and she didn't want to do that until she truly understood the legal ramifications of what he had done.

When she told Mr. Adams what she wanted, he made it clear he was uncomfortable giving her the will without Samuel's permission. His condescending attitude burned Marta's cheeks. She fought back the heated words that sprang to her tongue. Not that she should have been surprised by Mr. Adams' response. She recalled how little regard he had shown for her in previous meetings, all but ignoring her and focusing his attention on her brother. She had felt like a ghost, unseen and unwanted, and had been intimidated by his rude behavior.

Now, he sat there with his protruding eyes and fleshy cheeks and made it abundantly clear he had no use for women, at least when it involved legal matters. However, Marta was not going to be intimidated this time.

"Mr. Adams, if my brother came to you with a similar request, you would hand him the will without giving it a second thought and you will do the same for me, sir. Otherwise, my brother and I will be forced to reconsider your representation." She watched the man's eyes narrow at the implication of her threat. She wanted to pick up something and throw it at him, but Marta knew it wasn't the time to show anger.

He looked away and fiddled with his vest, then slowly rose and walked to the doorway to his outer office. "Betsy, get me the Baldwin file." He returned to his chair, and they waited in silence until his secretary brought the folder. Adams removed the will and set it on his desk in front of Marta.

"I assume you will return this document forthwith. It is not something to be left lying about." He huffed his words and gave Marta a baleful stare.

She heard the underlying message. It was not a document to be left in the hands of a silly woman. She ignored the insult and put the will in her handbag. "You will have it back tomorrow." Her business finished, she rose without so much as a glance his way and walked from the room with a determined stride.

* * *

Now that Marta knew Byron was not romantically involved with Lillie, she hoped to see more of him. This knowledge nearly intimidated her as much as sitting in Mr. Adams' office. She scolded herself for acting like a star-crossed school girl, but she couldn't help it. Whenever she saw Byron, her heart fluttered and every nerve ending in her body tingled. They were tingling now as she walked up the broad expanse of Van Ness Avenue towards Byron's mansion. When she reached the long driveway, she had to take a moment to calm herself before approaching the house and ringing the bell.

She thought she detected a little more cordiality from Byron's butler when he answered the door, but given his stiff countenance, she couldn't be certain. Henry led her straight to the drawing room this time without a formal announcement. Marta smiled inwardly at this, partly because she saw it an indication of her growing familiarity with Byron. But she also guessed it was a sign that Henry was thawing a bit. She entered the room in a buoyant mood. Her eyes swept the room in search of Byron's familiar pipe-in-mouth pose and Lillie's manly attire, but her gaze fell, instead, upon the sour face of Mr. Adams! The shock of seeing her solicitor again brought her to an abrupt halt just inside the door. The cheery greeting she had prepared to voice died on her lips as her glowing mood dissipated.

"Mr. Adams," she nearly stammered, "what are you doing here?"

Byron spoke before Adams could respond. "Hello, Marta. We have only just learned that you share the same solicitor as Lillie. Quite a coincidence, don't you think?"

Marta's stomach churned as she continued to stare at the man whose insulting behavior she had endured less than thirty minutes ago.

"You can imagine my surprise," Lillie chimed in as she walked over to Marta and took her arm. "Come, sit with me. I think we have discovered some very good news."

Marta allowed herself to be guided to a nearby sofa but did not immediately sit down. Instead, she pulled the will from her bag and handed it to Mr. Adams. "I don't suppose there is any need for this," she said quietly.

"No, indeed," Adams replied with a curt smile, "seeing as how I wrote it." He gestured to the couch. "Why don't we all sit down? There are some interesting points to discuss."

Marta sat next to Lillie on the couch while the two men took chairs opposite. Now that she was over her initial shock, her mind settled and she focused on what Mr. Adams was saying. She might not be comfortable with the man, but he knew his business. She was still concerned about the recent erratic behavior of her brother, however, and decided to express her worries at once.

"Before we begin, Mr. Adams, let me say that the reason I didn't confide in you earlier was due to my brother. Samuel has not been himself lately and I feared bringing him into any discussion until I had a better idea of our prospects." Marta tried to sound firm in her explanation, but the words tumbled from her with the urgency of a sinner asking forgiveness.

"I understand, Miss Baldwin. Samuel didn't consult me in these recent decisions, and after what Lillie has told me, I agree we must step carefully." Mr. Adams did not quite smile, but his fleshy jaws relaxed and his face lost its stern expression. Marta felt the tension in her shoulders and back ease and was glad she had spoken.

"Tell her about the loan being unsecured," Lillie chimed in. Her voice blazed with triumph.

"Yes, well, the will clearly states that both siblings share equally in the estate and that neither has the right to make decisions that affect it without the concurrence of the other." Mr. Adams adjusted his glasses on his short nose and looked at Marta. "In your case, Miss Baldwin, that means you would have to agree to Samuel's negotiations with the bank and sign the contract. I take it you did neither?"

"I knew nothing about it until the bankers came to discuss foreclosure proceedings if the loan was not repaid at once. Are you saying the house is not at risk?" Marta could hardly contain herself as she spoke. Her throat was suddenly parched and her hands moved restlessly in her lap. Lillie reached over and held them. The warmth of Lillie's touch calmed her. She took a deep breath as Mr. Adams continued.

"That is precisely what I am saying. Without your agreement, the house could not be used for collateral against the business loan. Therefore, the loan is unsecured and only backed by the assets of the business. If the business has failed, the loan is forfeit."

Marta slumped back in the folds of the sofa. What wondrous news! All of her fears were banished as suddenly as smoke whisked away on the wind. Not only was her home secure, but she was no longer a charity case needing the help of others. For the first time since the shock of seeing Mr. Adams in the room, she turned her attention to Byron. His narrow face had broadened into a satisfied smile, but it was his eyes glowing with happiness at her good news that enthralled her. He might be a shy man, but his heart was kind. She wanted to get up and give the man a hug, but she wisely resisted the impulse, knowing it would embarrass them both.

Mr. Adams adjusted his glasses again, a signal that he was not finished. "There is another matter that must be addressed." He paused to make sure he had everyone's attention. "If Samuel deliberately misled the bank as to his authority, he could be prosecuted for fraud. It would depend on the understanding between him and the bank and the bank's desire to pursue the matter. From what I know about the Corchran Bank, I would say there is a very good chance they will want to exact their pound of flesh, one way or the other."

Mr. Adams' announcement cast a sobering mood over the group.

No matter how angry Marta might be at her brother, he was family. The thought of him facing a trial or time in jail was not something she wished upon him. "What can we do?" she asked.

"It is very important that we clarify things before any discussions are held with the bank regarding the loan," Mr. Adams replied. "Let me first talk with Samuel, see what he recalls. Chances are, there were no other witnesses to the meeting besides the principles. That would make it his word against theirs. If he says he did not misrepresent his position in the trust, and if he sounds convincing, there may not be much the bank can do."

Marta exhaled a sigh of relief at these encouraging words, but her heart still ached at the idea that her brother might be in some trouble. For the first time in her life, she felt pity for her sibling. He didn't mean to cause difficulties for others. He simply couldn't cope with his world. Running a business didn't suit him and it had nearly caused their ruin. As it was, their income from the estate would be reduced by the loss of the shipping business, which made Lillie's investment proposal all the more compelling. If she was going to keep both Missy and Angela, she was going to need financial help.

Mr. Adams picked up his papers and put on his hat. "I will be back in touch as soon as I have had a talk with Samuel. Good day." He nodded to Byron and Lillie and left the room without as much as a glance in Marta's direction. Irritated, she looked at Byron and saw an amused smile on his face.

"Your solicitor doesn't appear to be comfortable dealing with you," he remarked as he retrieved his pipe from his pocket.

Marta felt the heat of embarrassment rising in her cheeks and looked to Lillie for moral support. Mr. Adams attitude had always mystified her, and she had no idea what to do about it. "He was hired by my father and has always acted that way towards me. He only wants to deal with Samuel."

"If he did that to me, I'd fire him on the spot," Lillie responded. "But of course, I hired him, so my position is quite different from yours." She patted Marta's hand and rose from the couch. Marta got the message. Make the man change his manners, or get rid of him. It was something for her to consider.

Lillie turned her attention to Byron. "Before I go, tell me your plans for Eleanor's masked ball. You are going, aren't you?" The impish tone in her voice couldn't be ignored. Marta watched with fascination as Byron coughed and studied the pipe in his hand. He had grown noticeably less comfortable.

"Hadn't thought about it much." He fidgeted and avoided Lillie's bemused look.

Marta had never been invited to an Eleanor Whitman ball, but she suddenly realized it must be the ball Baron von Reich wanted her to attend. The Whitman balls were famous for their exclusivity and Eleanor ruled over the invitation list with the ruthlessness of a dowager queen. People lived and died with anxiety when it was time for the invitations to be delivered. They always came by messenger. People who received one were those she considered socially acceptable, but the list could change in an instant at her whim. As the date drew near, those who were unsure of their status fawned over her shamelessly. On delivery day, people rushed home to learn if one of the famous white, textured envelopes waited for them on their entryway table. Those who found one were ecstatic; those who did not were crestfallen to the point of despair. For many, the embarrassment of being overlooked was so great they claimed illness and stayed away from other social gatherings until the ball had passed.

Marta was dumbfounded to realize that she had one sitting on her mantel!

"You are one of the few people who can decline her ball and still be invited again, Byron, but I do think you should go." Lillie's face brightened and the pitch of her voice rose in its gaiety. "I'll bet you haven't even asked anyone. Well, in that case, I have just the person to accompany you."

Marta began to squirm with her own embarrassment. Thunderclouds of emotions stormed through her as she sat there and listened to Lillie discuss Byron's plans for the most important social event of the season. She wished it could be her, but she knew that was next to impossible. Not only was she several rungs below the social elite invited by Eleanor Whitman, if she did go it seemed it would be with the Baron. Knowing this only aggravated her discomfort making her wish she could escape the awkward moment. She couldn't do so gracefully, however. All she could do was put on a brave smile and wait until Lillie was finished.

Byron looked at Lillie with a pinched face that said he was suspicious of her intentions. He then lit his pipe and after puffing vigorously on the stem, returned his attention to Lillie, his feelings briefly hidden behind a cloud of smoke. "I don't need help finding a companion for the event, Lillie. I'm quite capable of deciding who to take, if I choose to go." He said this with a firm voice, but his narrowed eyes made it clear he was unsettled by Lillie's brash behavior.

"Oh posh. I know you too well, Byron. You will put it off until either you don't go at all, or you end up with the widow Murdoch again, who is ten years your senior and about as much fun as a dog having puppies. You are hopeless when it comes to women, and I'm going to do something about it right now." Lillie tilted her head towards Marta. "You have one of the loveliest and brightest young women in the entire damn city sitting right here in your drawing room." Lillie put her hands on her hips just as she had when she proposed investing in Marta's agency. "If you don't invite this delicious creature, I will, and you know how I can make heads turn."

Marta nearly swallowed her tongue when she heard Lillie's proposal. A bolt of heat flashed through her chest, causing her to cough and gasp for breath. Attend an Eleanor Whitman ball with Byron? Was Lillie out of her mind? It was one thing to go with the Baron; his title gave him social standing. But he was unfamiliar with San Francisco's protocol and could be forgiven for inviting Marta, who was a few rungs lower on society's social scale. Byron was another matter. No matter how highly Byron might be regarded, it would be unthinkable for him to consider her. Tongues would wag and noses would be turned to the ceiling.

She tried to object but could not find her voice. The room was filled with silence, the kind of ear-ringing silence that follows a loud explosion. She kept her eyes focused on Lillie while she fought back her nerves and tried to speak. "Lillie," she finally managed to say, "you have put Byron in a most uncomfortable position. I am complimented that you would think of me, but I am certain that Mrs. Murdoch or whomever Byron has in mind would be far more appropriate."

"Actually, I had considered the idea," Byron said in a gentle voice, "but I did not know, Marta, if you would consider such an invitation from an old bachelor like me."

Marta was so stunned by Byron's remark she thought her heart had stopped. She could not feel its beat and considered the possibility that Lillie's outrageous suggestion had caused her to have an attack of some sort. This seemed to be confirmed by the pressure building in her chest. It pressed so hard against her rib cage, she feared she would burst. It took all of her nerve to look at Byron, but when she did, she discovered a downcast look that was so sweet, it nearly swept her doubts away. The poor man was more disconcerted than she was! His expression reminded her of school dances and shy boys. But did he really mean what he said, or was he being polite so as not to embarrass her further?

Her thoughts caromed to Baron von Reich's invitation already sitting in her drawing room. Was it possible she might get two of the most sought after invitations of the year? What could she do? Byron's was the only one that mattered, but von Reich had all but commanded that she attend with him.

"Byron, I would be honored to accompany you anywhere, but I should think there are others who are more appropriate socially. I have rarely frequented your circle of friends." She tried to keep her eyes on his face as she spoke, but they slid away.

"Hell, darlin'," Lillie broke in with a beaming smile, "the only thing considered appropriate in this town is money, and you still have some of that despite your brother's follies. Not that money is a very good gauge of a person. I expect something a good deal more substantial in one's character than money if I'm going to associate with him or her."

"I agree," Byron responded eagerly. He was clearly relieved to see the topic swing away from himself. "Money is a very poor yardstick." Silence filled the room once more. Byron's face grew serious as he flicked a quick look at Lillie, before returning his gaze to Marta. "*Would* you attend the masked ball with me?"

Marta's defenses were torn asunder. The feelings that had bubbled beneath the surface since the chess match now boiled over in a flood of emotions that left her trembling with desire for this modest man.

Then, the Baron's wild hair and strange accent charged through her thoughts. The Baron had made it clear in his note that he expected her to attend with him. Declining an invitation after its acceptance was not just awkward, it bordered on scandal. Of course, Marta had not actually accepted the Baron's invitation, but he thought so, which made her situation more delicate. Marta's happy world was turning sour and there seemed to be little she could do about it.

"I would very much like to attend the ball with you Byron." She spoke so softly she was uncertain anyone could hear her. "However, I must see to a previous engagement."

Lillie gave her a quizzical look. "A previous engagement? Whatever it is, surely you can get out of it."

"I ... I don't know." Marta sank back in the cushions and fixed her gaze on the far wall. "It might be difficult."

Byron's keen expression drooped at her hesitant words. The muscles along his jaw clenched as though he were grinding his teeth. He stood up abruptly and cleared his throat. "If you have a previous commitment, you must honor it. I would not expect you to do otherwise." He fidgeted with the sleeve of his shirt and looked away.

Marta's lower lip began trembling. She knew she must look miserable. She *was* miserable. Why did that pompous ass of a Baron have to press his attentions on her like he did?

Lillie took her arm and guided her towards the door. "Come on, darlin', we've got to talk." She waved a goodbye at Byron and escorted Marta to the entryway where Henry stood ready to let them out.

"All right, tell me what's wrong," Lillie demanded as soon as they were on the street.

A trolley car clanged past them on its way up Van Ness Avenue, followed by an automobile making noises that sounded like corn

172

being popped over a fire. A dray hauling a heavy load of sacks, rumbled close enough to the curb for Marta to smell the gamey odor of the weary horse. Thunder announced an approaching storm. Such were the typical sights and sounds of San Francisco on a morning in late March. Normally they would have comforted Marta, but not today.

"Baron Konrad von Reich delivered the same invitation to me three days ago. Because I failed to say no at once, he now believes I am going to the ball with him." She inhaled a great, shivering breath. "I couldn't be more miserable than I am right now. I know I do not have the right social standing, but if Byron truly wants to take me, it is his invitation I wish to accept. Instead, if I am now faced with a horrible evening with the Baron, I would rather not go at all."

"Have you told Baron von Reich you will go with him?"

"Not in so many words. I did say I would think about it and give him a reply the next day, but between my brother and the bank and the house and my foundation, I've had too much to think about these past two days to reply. Now the Baron has taken my silence as acceptance." Marta pressed her hands to her cheeks and shook her head. "Now, Byron will ask that widow or someone else and I shall have to look at him all evening in another woman's arms." She raised her head and gazed imploringly at Lillie. "What am I going to do?"

Lillie gave Marta her no nonsense look. "*You* are going to return the Baron's invitation and inform him that you never agreed to attend with him. If he doesn't like it, he can lump it. And while you're doing that, I shall have a word with Byron about his invitation." A mischievous grin danced across Lillie's lips. "You are going to that ball with Byron."

Marta vacillated between feelings of helplessness and hope. Lillie made it all sound so simple. She supposed it was when seen through *her* eyes. It didn't seem so simple to Marta, however. Facing the Baron under such embarrassing circumstances would be terribly awkward and she didn't relish such a confrontation. She knew turning down his invitation after such a long delay would be considered impolite, but Lillie was right. She would either go to that ball with Byron or not at all. If that meant creating a social scandal, so be it. Her decision made, Marta felt as if a great weight had been lifted from her shoulders. She hugged Lillie and headed for home.

CHAPTER SIXTEEN

So many thoughts were tumbling through Marta's mind she could hardly grasp them all. She had just left Mr. Adams' office with the good news that the Corchran Bank didn't appear to have a case for fraud. A meeting had been set with the bank later that day to discuss the loan and the status of the house. Marta had asked Mr. Adams to be present then had looked him square in the eye and told him he would be dealing with her from now on and if that didn't sit well with him, he could either resign or she could fire him. Mr. Adams had sputtered and protested, but in the end he got the message and agreed to work more closely with her on the estate and other family matters. Marta chuckled to herself when she recalled the pained expression on his face and she silently thanked Lillie for giving her the courage to face him down.

Her next stop was a meeting with Baron von Reich, another man she had to face down. Every time she thought about his presumptive behavior towards her, Marta's blood boiled. That didn't make her task any easier, but it did ease any guilt feelings she had about declining his invitation. She had already penned a note asking him to visit her at home. He was due in twenty minutes which meant she had to hurry. She had observed his compulsion for promptness and didn't want to be late.

Sure enough, she barely had time to enter the house and moisten a cloth to remove the perspiration from her face before the bell rang. She opened the door and was relieved to find the Baron dressed in more typical San Francisco attire, although the sandy hair under his hat still had the appearance of wild rushes surrounding a marshland.

"I was delighted to receive your note, Miss Baldwin." He bent his thick lips into an eager smile. It was evident he anticipated her formal acceptance of his invitation. This only served to make Marta's situation all the more difficult.

She had been dreading the moment, but Lillie had coached her on how to maintain a formal manner without appearing impolite, and this calmed her. She now put Lillie's advice to practice by returning the Baron's smile with a less lively one. "Please join me in the drawing room, Baron," she said as she led him to the room where they had previously met. She indicated the same couch as before but Von Reich chose to remain standing in a stiff pose that made Marta think of someone at a military drill. He would not sit down until she did.

Marta retrieved the Baron's invitation from the mantel and took a chair facing him. Once they were both seated, she plunged into her speech before she lost her nerve. "It is very kind of you to consider me as your escort for the ball, Baron. I know you took my silence as acceptance, but that was not the case. I am afraid I must decline." There, she had said it!

The Baron's face sagged much as Byron's had when she told him she had a conflict with his request.

Guilt wheedled its way into her consciousness despite her earlier anger. Von Reich might be pompous and overbearing, but he was human. She hated seeing the disappointment on his face, which had reddened noticeably.

"I had expected brighter news," he said at last. "Why, may I ask, have you chosen to decline my offer?" His voice was terse.

Marta leaned forward in her chair and placed the invitation on the table between them. "Before I received your invitation, I was told another was forthcoming. I did not feel it proper to accept yours until I knew its outcome. I apologize for the delay, but as you can see, I was put in a delicate position. I hope you will understand." Marta stood to indicate their discussion was finished, but the Baron didn't move. She feared he was about to make a scene and forced a smile to her lips to defuse his ire.

At last, he pushed himself from the couch and brushed some imaginary lint from his trousers. "This is most irregular, Miss Baldwin." His tone of voice became disagreeable. "In my country, such a lapse in time would be considered inappropriate. I do not understand your society's customs, but perhaps such behavior is to be expected in a country as raw as this one." With that, he picked up his invitation and marched from the room without waiting for Marta to show him out.

Once the front door closed, she stood in the middle of the drawing room, fingertips to lips, and tried to sort through the guilt that still tinged her emotions. It had not been a very happy encounter, but she supposed it was the best she could expect. She sighed with relief that it was over.

* * *

Marta put aside unpleasant thoughts about the Baron as she made her way to meet Lillie at one of the most expensive dress shops on Kearny Street. She would have preferred a less exclusive establishment, but Lillie had insisted. So Marta found herself walking past the elegant shops she had ignored for so long. She still could not believe that she was going to Eleanor Whitman's famous masked ball. Not that the ball itself was so important. It was the fact that Byron had asked her! Never in her wildest daydreams would she have anticipated such a development. She owed it all to Lillie, who had spoken to Byron about Marta's circumstances with Baron von Reich and convinced him to ask her again. Goodness, what a fireball that woman was. It was all Marta could do to keep up with her.

Today was also Missy's first day back to work. Marta couldn't wait to see her, especially now that Lillie was investing in her agency and Marta could afford to keep both her and Angela employed. Better still, it gave her the resources to expand her services and help more families. That idea satisfied her immensely and she thanked the fates for introducing her to the dynamic woman who was rapidly becoming her best friend.

She did have concerns, however, the foremost being Samuel. After talking to him, Mr. Adams didn't believe her brother should face legal proceedings from his dealings with the bank, but that didn't mitigate her worries about his future. With no shipping business to run and with reduced income from the estate, he would have to do something. He had yet to indicate he had found employment. His reduced means would not allow him to carouse with his friends as he used to. What was to become of him? After the bank meeting, perhaps she could talk to Mr. Adams about him. She would never have considered doing such a thing before, but after today's confrontation she felt surprisingly more at ease with him. After all, Mr. Adams was a very capable solicitor. More important, he had Samuel's ear. Maybe he could succeed where Marta had failed.

There was one more concern that hung over Marta's head with the menace of an executioner's sword. Where, she wondered, was the hypnotist? There had been so sign of him for a week now. As much as she wanted to believe the increased police patrols were keeping him away, she doubted that was the only reason. She feared something was afoot, but she couldn't guess what it might be. One thing she knew for certain. She hadn't seen the last of the horrid man. She had to keep her wits about her and warn her girls not to become complacent.

* * *

My world is spinning out of control. Thunder pounds inside my head. My temples throb with the pain of my disgrace. The witch and her companions have snatched my grandest prize from the arms of my employers and they are screaming with rage. Their displeasure engulfs me in a roaring fire of threats that sears my vision and burns my flesh.

Their anger has poured into the streets and infected those I meet as I return to my lodgings. I notice the change at once. The local people shift their worried gazes away from me more slowly than before, but they don't concern me. To them, I am still invisible. It is the hatchet men I fear, for they no longer ignore me. Two of them are staring after me now as I pass them. Another leans against a wall and spits in the dirt while he observes my progress. They smell my weakness and bide their time. They wait for the order from their bosses to strike at me. I am no longer invisible to them.

How can I stay the hands of the tongs? They have told me to bring them a suitable replacement for the redheaded girl, but when I returned to my hunting grounds, I discovered a new danger. Police are patrolling the neighborhoods. They are like locust invading my fields and destroying my crops. They remind me of black beetles scuttling about with their guns. I dare not confront them. My charms cannot stop bullets and I cannot be arrested. In jail, I would expire in an inferno of despair.

So, I have ventured into a new area along the waterfront in hopes of locating a suitable victim, but all I have found are used women who drink to excess and spread their legs for a thin price. The tongs would not be happy with them. None would suffice as a replacement for my lost prize.

In desperation, I have ventured into the tenements once more. The sky is choked with a heavy rain that obscures the horizons and sends small rivers of water rushing down the battered streets. It is a perfect time to move about unnoticed. Those who venture out bend their heads against the wind-soaked storm and cast their eyes downward and the police are not to be seen at all. I imagine them huddled in their offices like sheep. My winter coat and hat hide me from prying eyes as I stalk the crumbling pavements seeking a victim for my bosses. To my dismay, none presents herself. The young women are huddled indoors, just like their protectors. At last, I spot a waif of not more than fifteen years crouched in a meager doorway. Her retreat offers poor protection against the onslaught of the storm. She has pulled a tattered coat around herself and peers at me with timorous eyes. She is a wretched choice to bring to my keepers, but I am desperate and lock my eyes on hers. My ring is useless in such dim light, but it isn't needed. The girl succumbs to my gaze with the ease of a hungry kitten searching for a meal.

As I suspected, the tongs are less than pleased with my meager offering. They take the girl with indifference. Still, their eyes tell me I have stayed their hand, at least for awhile. The hatchet men have slunk back into the shadows with curled lips and wait for me to falter again. The girl has brought me only a temporary reprieve. I need a far more substantial offering if I want to be invisible again.

There is only one woman who can satisfy my hunger, the witch who continues to bedevil me. She is my enemy, an abomination who I must erase from my world. Her magic still protects her and I cannot attack her employees while the police are so near. But I have other ways of striking at her, other ways of making her cry out from the depths of her soul. In the end, I shall have her, and my bosses will be pleased with me again.

* * *

"There you are," Lillie exclaimed as Marta entered the swinging glass doors of the dress shop. Lillie wore her usual dark trousers and white shirt, but her clothes couldn't conceal the woman underneath. Marta returned Lillie's welcoming hug and thanked her good fortune that this magnetic woman had no interest in Byron.

"I have found just the thing for you." Lillie held up a red satin dress with a matching mask. "Try this on."

Marta could see the dress was designed to bare her shoulders and the upper portions of her breasts. She wanted to protest her modesty but couldn't do so in the face of Lillie's glowing enthusiasm. "It's lovely," she replied instead and took the dress to the back room. As she feared, the dressing room mirror revealed more flesh than she had ever exposed before. She nearly took off the dress but when she looked more closely, she had to admit it did make her look alluring. There was a large bow in the back and the skirt billowed out with extra folds of fabric. The waist, however, was tightly drawn to show off her youthful figure. Would Byron like it, she wondered? She would have to trust Lillie's judgment. Then she looked at the price tag and nearly fainted. The dress cost more than her income for a month.

"Come, come, Marta, let me see you," Lillie beckoned from the other room. Marta sighed and calculated how she would pay for the dress. She had never purchased anything so extravagant in her life, but she supposed it would be worth it as long as Bryon found it pleasing. She hastily brushed out the creases in the skirt and returned to the front of the shop.

Lillie put her hands to her cheeks and beamed. "You are a vision. If anyone can melt Byron's old bachelor heart, it's you in that dress."

Marta's skin grew uncomfortably warm at the implication of Lillie's declaration. She hardly expected Byron to kneel down and propose to her, nor was she sure she wanted him to. She was an independent woman and uncertain what she thought about marriage. It wasn't something she had given much consideration until now. There was so much she still wanted to do. Yet, even as she protested in her mind, her body tingled at the idea of melting Bryon's heart and her own fluttered as it always did when she thought of him.

"Are you certain I'm not too bold in this dress? Will Byron find it attractive? I don't want to appear vulgar." Marta bit her lip and looked at her friend for reassurance.

"Trust me darlin'. Men are all the same. You will turn every head in the room with that dress. None of the men will consider it vulgar but some of the women might curl their lips. Don't worry, though, that will only be their jealousies peeking out from under their masks."

Lillie laughed at her own remark and turned to the sales lady. "I want you to put that dress on my account and box it up. We'll take it."

"No, Lillie," Marta protested. "I can't let you do that. *I* will pay for the dress. Please, you have done enough, and I love you for it, but this must be my responsibility."

Lillie put her hands on her hips, a sign that meant she wouldn't be denied, but when Lillie saw Marta's firm expression, she relaxed. "Oh, very well, but I have a ruby necklace and earrings that will be stunning with that dress. You must let me lend them to you; otherwise, I shall be very upset." She wagged a finger to emphasize her point.

Marta grinned at her friend's mock anger. "Agreed." She arranged for the shop to deliver the dress once payment was received and bid Lillie goodbye. She was eager to get to her office in time to greet Missy, but by the time she arrived, Missy was already waiting for her along with a young man Marta had never met. Marta embraced her friend and fought back tears. "Welcome back, Missy. We've missed you."

"It's good to be back. I was gettin' tired of doin' nothin'."

"And who is this?" Marta looked at the young man turning his cap in hand as he stood behind Missy. His build was rangy and a mop of uncombed, reddish-brown hair flopped over his forehead. He was not much more than a boy, but he stood straight and looked Marta in the eye.

Missy's smile grew timid and her eyes slid downward. "His name's Patrick. He's a friend of mine. Said he would look after me for a day or so, 'til he goes back to work."

The realization that Missy felt she needed protection gave Marta pause. Was she doing the right thing by bringing her back to work so soon? Would she be safe on the streets of the tenements? It was where she lived, and police were patrolling the area, but Marta still couldn't help worrying. Losing Missy a second time would be devastating. But, if the girl wanted to return to work badly enough to overcome her own fears, Marta must to do the same.

She looked the boy up and down. He seemed presentable, but she doubted he would provide any real resistance if the hypnotist was determined to have Missy back. Marta took a breath and smiled.

There wasn't much else she could do. "Welcome, Patrick. Thank you for being so considerate. I'm sure you will make Missy feel safer while she settles in."

The young man blushed at her kind words. He twisted his cap some more and edged towards the door. "I'll be tryin,' ma'am. For now, I'll be waitin' outside 'til Missy's ready." He said this in what was meant to be a manly voice, but the inflection was not low enough to pull it off. Marta hid her amusement at his pluck as he strode out the door.

"He's a handsome fellow, Missy," she offered with a grin. "I don't suppose his interest in you is in any way personal."

Missy's face blossomed into a deep red. She shuffled her feet. "We have been datin' a wee while. But he's a bit of a lad, if you know what I mean. Been seein' lots of girls. So, I don't take him too serious."

"Well, he must have an interest in you if he's willing to give up his free time to escort you around. I'd say you have an admirer there."

The corners of Missy's mouth lifted in a shy smile. She was obviously pleased by her mentor's comment but said nothing more about the boy. "I have looked at the folders and see a few that need attendin'. Maybe, I should start with those."

Marta looked at the folders and nodded. "They will do just fine, Missy." She took the girl's arm and gently squeezed it. "I'm glad you have Patrick along, but if you see any sign of trouble, you run to the nearest police officer and then get back here as fast as you can." Marta hugged her again and walked her to the door.

The day unfolded without incident. Marta insisted that both Missy and Angela be off the streets before she left for the bank meeting and she greeted their returns with relief. Mr. Adams was waiting for her in the lobby of the bank building, rather than in the offices upstairs. Marta interpreted that as a new sign of respect. She smiled at him as they walked up the stairs to the conference room. Mr. Adams nodded in reply. His tough exterior remained intact, but Marta saw cracks developing in his stern demeanor. She smiled inwardly but said nothing.

Once they were settled, Caldwell and Matteson joined them.

After a few pleasantries Adams got right to the point. "It appears there has been an unexpected development regarding your collateral on the shipping company's loan." He spoke smoothly, without any hint of malice. Yet, despite his unthreatening manner, his tone was severe enough to cause both bankers to shift uneasily in their chairs. Marta had to admit Mr. Adams was very good at what he did. "You see," he continued, "Miss Baldwin has equal rights to the house in question under the terms of the father's will. Young Mr. Baldwin has no power of attorney to act without his sister's consent. I am sure I do not have to tell you what that means." He slid the will across the table to the two gentlemen, who were growing more agitated by the minute. The fingers of Mr. Caldwell's free hand tapped rapidly on the table as he read the document, while Mr. Matteson's eyelids twitched involuntarily. Marta would never have guessed they could wilt so quickly under fire.

Caldwell spoke first. "Samuel Baldwin assured us he had complete authority to consummate our agreement. If he has misrepresented himself, we shall have to take legal action." Caldwell's body might have betrayed his concern, but his voice remained cold and unyielding. Marta shivered at his tone. Mr. Caldwell was also good at what he did.

"That would not seem wise," Mr. Adams responded. "You have no documentation to support such a claim, and while your bank does have considerable clout in this city, so do I. Besides, it would not be in either of our interests to let this messy situation become public. You would look a bit foolish in the role of bully, and I would have to disclose Mr. Baldwin's business transactions." Mr. Adams stared at each man in turn without blinking. "It would be to both of our advantages to settle what is left of the shipping firm and be done with it. I believe there are more assets than debts, including the money owed the other bank. I cannot promise you all of your money back, but I believe your losses can be reduced if we cooperate."

Mr. Adams retrieved the will without further comment. Silence rushed in to fill the vacuum left by his sober assessment. Caldwell and Matteson exchanged glances but said nothing. Now, it was Marta's turn to squirm in her chair. As a child, she had once watched men playing cards and marveled at their totem pole expressions as they stared at their hands. They gave no hint of what they held or intended to do. It was like that now with these men. Faces became molded. No one blinked. Marta decided she would never be any good at card games. Only chess. For some reason, she never wavered in her expression when she played chess.

"We shall consider your proposal," Caldwell said at last. His voice sliced through the room with the unexpected discharge of a thunderclap, causing Marta to flinch in her chair.

Mr. Adams never moved. "We shall expect to hear from you," was his only reply as he and Marta rose and left. "They will agree to our terms," he stated matter-of-factly as he and Marta descended the stairs. "It's in their interest to do so, and banks always do what is in their best interests."

Marta stopped at the bottom of the stairs and gave him an appreciative look. "I want to thank you for your help, Mr. Adams. Your negotiations in there were superb and I am most impressed. I do not know how much that means to you, but it means a great deal to me."

The man's dark face brightened. "I believe we shall work well together, Miss Baldwin. If I did not give you much notice before, I apologize. You have grit. I admire that. Keep your patience while I attend to the details of our negotiations. I shall see to it that your ship reaches safe harbor, if you will excuse the metaphor." With that, he tipped his hat and departed, leaving Marta aglow in his kind words.

Who would ever have predicted that I might begin to like this man, she mused?

* * *

Marta's happy thoughts scattered when she saw the beige envelope with her name written in elegant, gold letters sitting on the table in her hallway. This time the envelope remained sealed, evidence that Samuel had respected her privacy for once and hadn't opened it. Excitement seized her chest and squeezed it until she could hardly draw a breath. She knew who the invitation was from, yet she dared not open it. She plucked it from the table instead and carried it to her room, where she lay it with a shaking hand on her night stand. The conversation with Lillie about the masked ball should have prepared her for this moment, but it didn't. Somehow it had all seemed unreal, a fantasy she should not expect to be fulfilled. Even selecting that dress with Lillie earlier in the day had not released the waves of anxiety that now churned inside her. Nothing was as real as that envelope on her night stand. At last, she broke the envelope's seal and removed the invitation. It proved to be short and eloquent.

Byron Wagner requests the pleasure of
Matilda Baldwin's company to attend
the masked ball and dinner of
Mr. & Mrs. Eleanor Whitman
at their home on Saturday evening, April 5th
at eight o'clock.
Respondez, si'l vous plait

It seemed as if her life was turning a corner and she was hurtling down an uncharted road towards an unknown destination. Opening that envelope represented a commitment she had never before considered, a commitment to a man she had only recently met, yet felt she knew so well. *How presumptuous of me! It is only an invitation to a ball, not a proposal.* Yet even as she scolded herself, she thought about the shy way Byron's eyes brushed her face when Lillie suggested he escort Marta to the ball. Her heart did flip-flops all over again. Something was happening between them, she was certain of it. It had begun with the chess game and had been evolving ever since.

The die had been cast. Lillie had told Byron Marta would attend the ball with him, and despite her attack of nerves, she wanted to. There was nothing left to do but stare her fate in the eye.

186

CHAPTER SEVENTEEN

Charles had just left Byron after discussing the hypnotist's peculiar behavior towards Angela. His mind wandered as he walked along the broad boulevard called Van Ness Avenue. To his surprise, he realized he envied his good friend. The source of his jealousy surprised him even more. It was Marta. Normally, he wasn't attracted to society women. Their coy expressions, hungry laughter and perfumed moisture rising from their bodies all intimidated him. He was more at home with the prostitutes in Chinatown who stroked his body without complaint and lighted his pipe when he wanted. But there was something addictive about Marta. The blaze in her eyes, her zest for life and her spirited manner were elements he rarely saw in a woman and they stimulated him in unexpected ways. They made him want to spend time with her, touch her hair and sing her songs. Alas, it was not to be. It was obvious she preferred Byron. He could see it in the way she looked at him. There was no room for Charles in that look. Such was his lot, and he would live with it.

A trolley car clanged past him and Charles hurried to catch it. Once onboard, he returned his attention to the hypnotist and to his talk with Byron. They had both agreed there was something very odd about the way the hypnotist was acting. Twice, he had drawn Angela under his spell, only to let her go again. The more Charles thought about it, the more certain he was that the man had a deeper motive than playing catch and release with the poor woman. His behavior made no sense and didn't fit the pattern of the other missing girls. Missy was a far better example of what he suspected happened to the women he entranced. She had been spirited away to Chinatown and would have ended up a sex slave in one of the brothels run by the tongs if she had not been rescued. Just the thought of it made him so squeamish he had to swallow hard to keep from becoming ill.

The trolley jerked as it turned a corner, forcing Charles to grab a handrail to maintain his balance. What was the hypnotist up to? No matter how Charles turned it around, he couldn't fathom the man's reasoning, but he was convinced the hypnotist had something sinister in mind. Most people didn't believe that someone could be hypnotized against their will and that included Captain O'Conner and his police officers. They saw hypnotism as entertainment, something associated with magic tricks and crystal balls. But Charles knew it was possible. The evil man roaming San Francisco's streets was proof of that. He was not only very powerful, he was dangerous as well. Charles knew he would strike again but where and when were the big unknowns. And why was he toying with Angela?

Charles had nearly given up looking for answers when an idea struck him. It was an insidious thought, one that urged him forward with a new sense of urgency in his search for the hypnotist. Missy and Angela were both associated with Marta and, while the hypnotist had taken one, he had let the other go, not once but twice. Charles guessed Angela's age had something to do with it. The tongs wanted young women like Missy for their brothels and Angela was too old. Yet, the hypnotist toyed with her as one would a fish on a line. That was what led Charles to his frightening conclusion. The hypnotist had no interest in Angela and would not normally bother with her. It was Marta he was after. If it was his plan to use Angela as bait, the hypnotist's behavior did make sense in a twisted sort of way. If he managed to draw Marta into his web, he would not need to hypnotize her. He could simply overpower her; the amulet would then be useless.

Charles couldn't say for sure if that was the hypnotist's plan, but there was one thing he did know. He would not let the man threaten Marta and the only way to be sure of that was to find him before he struck again. That meant tracking him to his lair. Charles had a pretty good idea where that would be: Chinatown. Just the thought of pursuing him there made Charles jittery. No other place in the world caused him to feel as vulnerable as Chinatown for it was there that he had discovered his taste for opium. The place swarmed with opium dens. They flourished in every alleyway and backstreet. Even though he had tried for years to resist the lure of those smoke-filled haunts, he inevitably succumbed. They sang to him, just as he wanted to sing to Marta. When he heard their melody, he couldn't stay away. He did everything in his power to avoid Chinatown, but it always drew him back.

He had first discovered the dens as a young man fresh out of college who wanted to test the limits of his new freedom. He and a handful of friends, including Byron, had dared one another to enter Chinatown and plumb its mysterious depths. It was a contest of sorts, a test of wills to see who was the bravest. Charles had gathered his nerve and plunged into the maze of dingy side streets that led to Chinatown's infamous subterranean world of gambling, prostitution and drugs. No one else had the nerve to follow him so they declared him the winner. But winning the contest didn't satisfy his craving for the adventure he had unearthed there. He wanted to experience first-hand the forbidden fruits of the brothels and opium dens he had discovered and he returned on his own to explore them. It didn't take him long to become ensnared in the powerful grip of the opium drug. It transported him to places he had never imagined, places filled with fantasies and exotic images. At such times, he was master of his own kingdom. All of his fears and self-doubts were swept away. Slowly, fantasy overcame reality making it harder and harder for him to survive in the outside world. His private domain was far more seductive, far more real. It devoured him day by day. He feared one day he would be swallowed by it and disappear forever.

Charles hopped off the trolley and turned towards his mansion on Nob Hill. Sunshine poured over him with the warmth of an early spring day and caused him to perspire as he walked. It was a day to be spent outside, though, not in the dark, smoky rooms of Chinatown. Every muscle in his body twitched with desire to go there but he had to push aside his cravings if he was going to protect Marta. He had to plunge back into his netherworld and battle the demons that awaited him. This time, he was determined not to succumb to his desires, for he had a higher purpose: to probe the city's underbelly for clues to the evil that lurked there, evil in the form of the hypnotist, a mysterious man whose powers were as addictive as the drugs. He had to find and destroy the hypnotist before the man could lay his hands on Marta.

* * *

One advantage of his many visits to Chinatown was the acquaintances he had made in the local shops where he bought food and in the smoky dens where he sought his pleasures. Charles began his inquiries by stopping at the stores he had so often frequented to satisfy his hunger or slake his thirst after a bout with the pipe. At first, the merchants were hesitant to speak to him about the man he sought. Their eyes slid away from his; their shoulders hunched in denial. It was a wrinkled old woman with wisps of grey hair straying from under her cap who gave him his first scent of a trail. She told him about a strange white man who was seen from time-to-time striding in their midst, but she had no idea where he lived or what he did.

Once the ice was broken, tongues began to loosen. A short man with a protruding stomach told him the man he sought was associated with the tongs, who protected him and gave him a place to stay somewhere in the back alleys. Another chimed in with advice to stay away from the man, for he had special powers that he used to trap young women in his evil net. Still another told him the girls were taken to the brothels where they worked until they were no longer wanted. Then they disappeared.

A menacing dark fog settled over Charles as the stories unfolded. The hypnotist was real, of that there could be no doubt, and his evil lurked everywhere. Charles formed a murky image of a man who hid in the shadows and waited to pounce on his victims. He shuddered when he thought of what it must have been like for Missy and what might happen to Marta if he did not do something. But what could he do? The hypnotist's powers were obviously much stronger than his, too strong for Charles to defeat him face-to-face. Yet, he would have to try. He would have to find this evil incarnate and root him out, even if it destroyed him.

Charles was rummaging through these thoughts when a strange thing happened. Just as suddenly as people had started talking to him, they stopped. It was as if a gust of wind had swirled down the street and carried away their voices. The shopkeepers pressed their mouths shut and avoided him with sideways steps and fretful glances. Charles couldn't imagine what was wrong until he followed the gaze of a tobacco seller and saw the two hatchet men watching him from across the street. They stood with their backs to a weathered wall, each with one foot raised and braced against the rough surface, their faces partially obscured by small clouds of cigarette smoke. Charles straightened his back and tried to appear sanguine, but his insides turned to jelly. How long they had watched him, he didn't know, but he knew it was long enough to frighten the locals. His mind spun as he considered his options. Cut and run seemed the best strategy, but before he could begin his retreat, the two men uncoiled from the wall and stepped into the street with the lithe strides of hungry mountain lions on the trail of prey.

Charles' heart thrummed against his ribs as he tried to decide what to do. It was useless to run. They would be on top of him before he could reach the corner. Nor could he fight them, for they undoubtedly carried sharp knives, perhaps even guns. His only choice was to stand there and face them with his palms open in a sign of acquiescence. He was white, after all, and he knew the tongs gave their men strict orders to leave white visitors alone. Charles tried to draw a deep breath, but the fear in his chest wouldn't let him. The result was a series of shallow, gasping breaths that made him wheeze like a steam engine. The sound grated in his ears. It told him how frightened he was. The men's faces registered faint smiles that told him they recognized his fear.

"You come here for opium," the man on his right said in a sharp voice. "Your health will be better if you remember that and do not stray onto streets where you are not welcome." He spat on the pavement next to Charles. Some of his spittle sprayed on Charles' shiny, brown shoes, but he dared not protest. The other man moved closer to Charles and bumped him. Charles could smell opium in his clothes. A fellow user, he thought. Had he seen him before in one of the dens? He couldn't say. Everyone looked the same in those places. Not that it mattered. The man wasn't going to smoke a pipe with him.

"Keep your nose out of Chinatown's business," the second man hissed, "or we chop it off." He made a violent cutting motion with his hand near Charles' face. The gesture caught Charles by surprise and forced his head backwards.

With that, the two men turned and stalked back across the street, where they leaned against the wall and resumed their vigil. Charles' instincts told him to flee, but the frightening encounter had so unsettled him, all he could think about was the intoxicating bliss of the opium waiting for him just steps away. He should leave Chinatown right now, he knew, but the opium's promises urged him to stay. When he glanced at the two men still loitering across the street, he succumbed to his desire. He turned away from the street leading out of Chinatown and entered the narrow alleys with which he was so familiar. One pipe, he told himself. He would limit himself to one pipe and then go home.

His feet moved without orders. They knew the way. He could have found Blind Annie's Cellar with a sack over his head. Footsteps echoed in the alleyway. He swung his head around, fearfully expecting to find the hatchet men on his trail. To his relief, no one was there. The footsteps were his own. He tried to laugh at himself, at the heightened state of his nerves, but his mirth died on his lips. Fear followed him down that alleyway as he increased his stride. Once he turned right into the filthy alley he knew so well, Charles felt safer. He slowed his pace but walked with purpose towards the familiar door that led to Blind Annie's Cellar. It was a door, he knew, that beckoned him to his destruction.

The moment he stepped into the sultry air of the opium den, his mind grew calm. The oppressive air and stupefying smoke didn't weigh on him. On the contrary, he inhaled deeply and felt light as a cloud. He was home. Silence wafted through the room with the smoke. It was the kind of silence one associated with cemeteries at night, but the lack of sound never bothered Charles. He found it restful. He welcomed the absence of jarring voices and noisy street traffic. Only two lamps fought the gloom with their sickly light, which told him the place was nearly empty. But it was early yet. The beds would fill soon enough. A familiar figure in sandals shuffled towards him and indicated a lower bed against the wall to his left. Charles removed his shoes and placed them beside the bed. Only one pipe, he reminded himself. One pipe and then he would go. Ah, but he already knew that was impossible. One pipe led to another, then another, until his head dropped to his chest and his hands went limp. That knowledge didn't deter him, however. It was just as impossible for him to turn away as it was to limit his intake to one pipe.

The helper lit his lamp and, while Charles arranged himself on the filthy mattress, shuffled away and returned with a lighted candle and a lump of opium. Charles leaned back on his elbow and slowly worked the lump over the flame of the candle. When it was ready, he packed it into the bowl of his pipe and began to smoke contentedly. Soon, his head swooned back on the bed and his eyes lost their keen edge. Images softly blurred. Dreams interrupted his thoughts. His world slowly rotated from the threats of hatchet men to the peace of a hundred violins playing in perfect harmony. He had once again entered paradise.

* * *

A hatchet man stands at my door and I wonder what I should do. This has never happened before. I fear the tongs have lost all patience and have sent death to visit me. But how can this be? They still want what I offer and I have promised to bring them new prizes. The hatchet man has come alone, something these men rarely do. They like to travel in pairs. I take this as a promising sign and open the door.

"There is a man looking for you." The scowl on the hatchet man's face tells me he would just as soon push a knife between my ribs as deliver this message, but I ignore his rude behavior and concentrate on his eyes. This is the first time I have had a chance to study one of these brutes up close. I cannot help wondering if it would be easier to hypnotize him than one of the tong leaders. His eyes blink rapidly under my gaze. The anger in his face softens. I am pleased with this response and release his eyes before he realizes what I have done. There is no need to show my hand. It is enough to know I can control one of these men if I have to.

I understand instinctively the identity of the man who looks for me. It is the friend of the witch, the one who aided in the redheaded girl's rescue from the brothel. I feel my lips broaden into a satisfied smile. My spirits rise as I ponder my good fortune. The man has come to me! I do not have to hunt him down and risk exposing myself to the police. He is here! He thinks he is looking for me, but soon the roles of hunter and hunted will be reversed. Soon, I will hunt him.

"Where has he gone?" I ask tonelessly. I do not want this butcher to know how much I savor his information.

"Blind Annie's. He has a weakness for the dreams she sells."

This is too easy. I am almost embarrassed to take the man under such circumstances. There is no sport in it. No challenge. There is too much at stake to quibble, however. Getting rid of the man will please the tongs, who grow tired of his meddling. And it will open new doors for me in my quest to cage the witch. So, I nod to the

194

brutal man who has brought me the news and close the door. I must prepare myself. And be patient. Only the most devoted clients visit Blind Annie's. My quarry is not going anywhere for awhile. I shall wait until nighttime to go to him. By then, he will be completely under the spell of the opium. I prefer the dark for what I have in mind. I will be able to move about more easily in the dark without being seen.

* * *

There was movement in the room, new arrivals and pipes being lit, but Charles paid them no mind. They were mere shadows in his world, one filled with colors and music. The colors bent and shifted their hues in rhythm to the brilliant notes escaping from the violins and cellos hidden somewhere beyond his vision. The music and colors filled a strange room, one with circular walls but no doors or windows. In the center of the room a lone figure was dancing. A woman. The woman was Marta. She was pirouetting in time to the music. Charles saw himself enter the magical room without doors or windows and wondered how he was able to do that. Perhaps he had walked through the wall. Once in the room, he approached Marta, who had stopped to observe him. He took her hand in his and put his arm around her waist. Together, they twirled at arms length across the floor, slowly at first, then with an increasing tempo that eventually blurred the two images until they became one.

Abruptly, the music stopped and Charles stared into Marta's eyes. Her gaze was filled with such power that he hardly dared to breathe. The colors faded with the music, but not the eyes. They were as clear as ocean waves at sunrise and they bore into his with the ferocity of a hawk eyeing its prey. But how could that be? Marta's eyes were kind, soft and warm. These eyes were harsh and merciless.

It took awhile for Charles' clouded brain to realize he was not looking at Marta and that the room he had imagined was gone. He was back in Blind Annie's Cellar smoking opium and staring into the most compelling pair of eyes he had ever seen. Even in his foggy condition, he could tell that something was wrong, but the longer he stared into those incredible pupils, the less he cared. Prisms of colors burst across his field of vision, colors far more intense than the ones he had seen before. And the gravitational forces that kept him anchored to his bed seemed to weaken. He was elevating as if he were a wisp of smoke floating along on a current of air that drew him through the opened doorway and out into the night. Colors continued to explode around him as he inhaled the brisk, evening air. After the musty odors of the opium den, the air smelled as crisp as a freshly mowed lawn. Overhead, a vast universe of stars spun around his head in a dizzying array of streaking lights. What a marvelous world he had entered!

The universe shifted on some unseen axis, closing one set of images and opening another. He was walking down Kearney Street with a man at his side whose arms and legs flounced along the pavement in random patterns of motion. Luminance from the street lamps played across his companion's face in a series of shifting lights and shadows that emphasized the man's angular nose and gaunt cheek bones. Instinctively, Charles understood it was the hypnotist, but for some reason that knowledge didn't frighten him. Rather, he felt a calm settle over him that was much like the calm he experienced when smoking his opium pipe.

All of his senses had become heightened in their clarity. Horses' hooves didn't just clop along the pavement. They rang out as though calling the world to prayer. Cooking odors drifted to him from nearby restaurants with mouthwatering promises of fettuccine, fresh sea bass, sliced tomatoes, and rare prime rib. Overhead, stars fought through the glare of the street lamps in a brilliant procession of tiny suns. They no longer spun as they had before, but they winked at him as if to acknowledge some wondrous secret. He realized he had crossed a dividing line that went beyond the opium-induced visions produced by his pipe. These current images were the result of the hypnotic trance conjured by the awkward man who continued to stride along beside him with all the jerking motions of a badly managed puppet. Charles looked around and saw they were now on Market Street and headed in the direction of the Ferry Building. He knew he should run away, knew he was in danger, but the images his mind created were too mesmerizing for him to give them up. So, he walked at a steady pace as trolley cars rattled past him and autos beeped their horns. The sidewalks bustled with newsboys hawking their evening editions and couples on their way to restaurants and theaters. Around him, life moved along at its usual, frenetic pace.

It would have been easy for Charles to seek help from the passersby. All he had to do was cry out or grab the arm of someone brushing past him on the street. Surely, the hypnotist could not hypnotize them all and, once confronted by an angry mob, he would flee. But these were such wayward thoughts that Charles couldn't bring them to fruition. He was stranded on an island surrounded by protective waves that kept the real world away. He was perfectly content to follow the man beside him.

As they approached the Ferry Building, Charles was amazed to see so much activity. Horse drawn wagons vied with autos for maneuvering room in front of the grand building. People hurried through its portals to catch ferries across the bay. Nearby, grog shops were filled with stevedores and shipmen guzzling tanks of ale, while a handful of their mates still worked by lamplight on the ships tied bow to stern along the docks.

Charles sensed a light pressure on his arm and felt himself being guided past the Ferry Building, yet when he looked around, he saw the hypnotist had stopped and was too far away to have touched him. He was being steered in his mind by a force that lifted each foot and planted it in the direction of the docks. Carefully, he stepped over coiled ropes and around barrels and crates being readied for loading in the morning. Voices shouted as the workers bent to their tasks. Despite all the activity, however, he felt quite alone. When he looked behind him, he saw the hypnotist standing at the entrance to the docks watching him. He stood with his head tilted off center and stared at Charles in a manner that made him think of an orphaned child. Charles understood the message. He was to continue on his own.

He turned and walked with steady purpose towards the end of the pier. A voice called out to him, but he ignored it. His goal was only a few steps away. He hurried to reach it. When he did, he stepped off the dock without hesitation. As he fell towards the dark, beckoning waters below, he knew they would be his grave. His last image before he struck the water was the smiling face of Marta, whom he feared he had not saved. As he entered the inky blackness, he asked himself how the hypnotist could have known he couldn't swim. Then, thankfully, quickly, the cold, silvery ocean mantle enveloped him and he wondered no more.

CHAPTER EIGHTEEN

Marta hadn't been able to concentrate all day. Every time she thought about the low-cut gown Lillie had talked her into buying, a hoard of cicadas swarmed inside her stomach. More than once, she rushed to the bathroom, certain she was about to be sick. When Missy and Angela looked to her for direction, she waved vaguely at the folders on her desk and told them to choose the ones they wanted. The women soon realized Marta was not herself and divided the work between the two of them. By day's end, Marta was too frazzled to think at all and hurried home to prepare for the evening's soirée. In two hours, Byron would call for her. She had no idea how she would possibly be ready in time.

Receiving an invitation to a masked ball shouldn't have affected her this way. It was, after all, the very epitome of what she disliked about San Francisco's society. The ball was silly and frivolous, and consumed vast amounts of money that might have been used for more important agendas, such as helping the poor. Normally, she would have refused the invitation and gone about her business, but it was Byron who had asked her. The idea of attending the ball with him sent her head into a whirlwind of confusion. She still found it difficult to believe he had given her that invitation. Her doubts ran riot. Perhaps he had only done so because Lillie had bullied him. Or because he was tired of the other women in his circle of friends and wanted to be seen with someone new. Since it was a masked ball, he need not divulge her identity. Or he might just want to make tongues wag. It might all be a joke at her expense.

No, that was silly, and she knew it. Byron had made it clear he didn't have much interest in the ball. He had said it was boring to be surrounded by so many people who had no idea what to do with themselves. Conversations about problems with servants, jaunts to Europe, redecorated houses and what people wore were topics he professed to disdain as much as she did. In fact, Lillie had told Marta that if she hadn't accepted his invitation, he wouldn't have bothered to go.

That information sent a new wave of anxiety pumping through her veins. Why did he want to take her? She didn't fit in with that crowd and he knew it. Yet, despite Lillie's prodding at his house that day, his offer had been genuine. What did it mean, and why did she continue to become so unfastened whenever she saw the man or thought about him? The doubts and questions buzzed in her head as she hurried home.

When she entered the house, she heard strange grunting noises coming from upstairs. Frightened that burglars had gained entrance to the house, she crept quietly up the staircase, being careful to avoid two steps notorious for their squeaks. Hushed voices could be heard coming from one of the bedrooms, magnifying her fears. Then, a laugh pierced the muffled voices and the tension in Marta's shoulders dissolved. That distinctive laugh, high-pitched and bantering, could belong to only one person, her brother.

Marta reached the upstairs hallway and stopped outside Samuel's room. The door was ajar, providing a clear line of sight to Samuel's bed where three naked bodies, her brother's and two women's, lay sprawled across a twisted pile of covers and sheets.

The women's rouged faces and provocative poses left little doubt as to their profession. Images of Missy and the painted women at the brothel in Chinatown churned through Marta's memories and sent her head reeling. *My God,* she thought, *he has brought prostitutes into our home!*

Marta pushed the door open with enough force to bang it against the wall. All three heads swung around to find her standing in the doorway, arms folded and face boiling with anger. The satisfied grin on Samuel's face shifted to a scowl, but before he could object to her interruption, Marta spoke.

"Get these whores out of my house," she commanded as she pointed a finger at the two startled women. They quickly covered themselves with the sweaty sheets.

"This is my house too . . ." Samuel started to protest, but Marta cut him off.

"Not for whoring, it's not." The image of Missy in Chinatown flared to mind. The pain and fear Marta had seen in Missy's face were more than she could bear, and it spurred her anger. "If you want to waste your money and time on women like these instead of finding a job and building a respectable life, so be it, but don't bring them here again." She turned and stormed from the room.

Once in her own room, she allowed the emotions she had bottled up inside of her to bubble over as she collapsed on the edge of her bed with a sob. The many problems with which she had to deal the past few days -- her run-ins with the hypnotist, Missy's abduction, Samuel's irresponsible behavior, the failed business and the threatened loss of her home -- were suddenly more than she could bear. She longed for the simpler life she had known before her father died. There had been no need to assume the weight of so much responsibility then, but that had all changed. Life would never be that simple again. Her brother might continue his titular role as head of their family, but he would never shoulder the burdens. That role would fall to her. She wondered if she could handle the challenge. There was no choice, of course. If she didn't handle it, their world would fall into disrepair and ruin.

It was some time before she succeeded in bringing her emotions under control. By then, the front door had opened and closed, telling her the women were gone. She hoped that Samuel had left with them, but when she ventured back downstairs, she found him pacing in the kitchen. He glanced towards the stove, careful not to meet Marta's angry gaze.

"I thought I'd stay home for dinner," he announced as if nothing had happened. Marta smiled inwardly at his presumption that dinner would magically appear on the table. But what could she expect? She had waited on him hand and foot: cooking for him, cleaning the house, washing his clothes. That was all about to change, however, beginning with that night's dinner.

"I will be dining out tonight, brother. I'm afraid you will have to make your own arrangements." Marta kept her voice neutral, as if she were discussing the weather, not declaring a seismic shift in their relationship.

Her statement brought a look of puzzlement to Samuel's blue eyes, which finally locked onto hers. "You're not going to cook?" he asked plaintively. "What am I supposed to do? I don't have money to eat out."

Marta couldn't help glancing towards the stairs leading to the bedrooms. It was all she could do to maintain a sober face. "You seem to have money for other things. Besides, I thought you were getting a job at the bank."

Samuel pushed his fingers through his blond hair. His schoolboy gesture never ceased to annoy her. This time, however, his cheeks contracted, making him look fatigued. "I didn't have enough experience for the manager's position. They wanted me to work as a teller." His voice grew plaintive. "There's also the matter of the shipping business. It seems everyone knows that it is failing, and they blame me. Never mind the storms and pirates that wrecked our ships."

Anger flashed to the tip of Marta's tongue and she nearly lashed out at his lies. She felt her olive skin darkening with exasperation but knew nothing would be accomplished by confronting him about the ships now. She had neither the time nor the inclination to fight with her brother. She heard the tick-tock-tick-tock of the hallway clock and was seized by a sense of urgency. Byron would be there within the hour.

"Where are you going?" Samuel's query interrupted her thoughts.

"To a ball . . . with Byron Wagner." She added this last bit of information with the anticipation of surprising her brother. When his eyes blinked and widened in disbelief, she knew she had succeeded. Samuel had never seen her as anything but his younger sister, whose sole purpose for existence was to wait on him. The idea that she might be escorted to an important social event by someone like Byron didn't fit his idea of how the world worked, especially now that he no longer had much social standing.

Marta sighed. There was no point in continuing their conversation further. She withdrew a few dollars from her bag and handed them to him. "Have a good dinner with your friends, brother. We will discuss our finances later." With that, she hurried upstairs, her mind envisioning the elegant gown and the ruby necklace waiting for her in her room.

* * *

The bell on the front door rang precisely at eight. Marta had put on the red satin dress she and Lillie had picked out. She stared at her exposed shoulders and cleavage in the mirror with deep misgivings. She had never felt so naked in her life. She couldn't help but wonder if Byron would find the dress suitable. Lillie had overridden her concerns when she bought it, but her friend wasn't there to bolster her courage, now. Well, she would just have to do it herself. She hadn't spent a month's wages on that dress to lose her nerve. She straightened her back and held up the matching silk mask, which covered just enough of her face to provide some sense of anonymity. The mask made her feel better.

Still, by the time the bell announced Byron's arrival, anticipation had produced a film of perspiration on her shoulders and neck, and she had to quickly pat her skin dry with a cloth before hurrying to the foyer. She opened the door with a burst of anxious energy and stood breathing rapidly while she fought to maintain her aplomb.

Bryon had donned a wig of long, dark hair with a matching mustache and goatee that made him look quite dashing. He wore a brocade red silk jacket that complemented her dress so perfectly that Marta immediately suspected Lillie's hand in the selection of his outfit. In his right hand he held an elegantly carved mahogany staff. The ensemble was completed by a white, ruffled shirt that poured from his neck in a series of rapids over a plumb colored waistcoat.

Marta sensed Byron's eyes roaming her naked skin. She immediately felt her olive complexion darken even more than it had when she grew angry at her brother. The evening was unseasonably cool for early April and Marta could feel the nip to the air. She had brought a handsome, black shawl to cover her shoulders and she quickly put it on, immediately feeling better.

"Good evening, Miss Baldwin. It is a pity the night has cooled a bit." Neither of them had yet donned their masks. Marta could see the amused twinkle in Byron's eye. There was no mistaking his reference to the shawl now covering her shoulders and bodice, and while she was glad she wore it, his subtle compliment pleased her. It was just as Lillie had said. All men were the same, and she supposed that was not so bad.

"I must tell you I'm a nervous wreck about going to this ball," she admitted, as Byron took her arm and guided her to the closed carriage waiting on the street. She suspected more than one neighbor watched her progress from the surrounding windows, which added to her anxiety.

Bryon grasped her hand to assist her into the carriage. The touch of his skin, surprisingly warm in the chilled air, sent little jolts of pleasure tingling up her arm. "Not because of me, I hope. I assure you my intentions are entirely honorable." He said this in a lighthearted manner that told Marta he was teasing her. She smiled at his banter.

"You are the only reason I *am* going." Her bold declaration took her by surprise and she blushed some more. "I feel quite out of my element," she hastily added, "but I believe your company will steady me."

"I shall do my best. Besides, there is no reason to feel anxious. You will be the loveliest woman there, and I will be proud to escort you." The carriage's interior was beyond the reach of the street lamps, for which Marta was thankful. Her faced burned at his words. She settled back into the dark shadows to mask her emotions. A wisp of odor, a man's warmth mixed with pipe tobacco, filled the carriage as Byron settled beside her. Marta inhaled deeply. She had never sat so close to him before. The experience was both exhilarating and disquieting. She wanted to hold his hand and flee at the same time.

The driver spoke to the two horses and the carriage moved off at a steady pace. Soon, they were headed along California Street towards Nob Hill, or Snob Hill as some people called it. It wasn't Marta's first social occasion on that hill. She had attended a few events with her father as a girl. At that impressionable age, she had found all of the splendor and pomp of the social elite quite enchanting and had dreamed one day of holding afternoon teas and evening soirées at their home.

There had been a defining moment on her ninth birthday, however, when all of that changed. She had joined her father at an afternoon tea party at one of the grand estates along Van Ness Avenue. The only children in attendance were two girls over ten who treated Marta with disdain and played among themselves. Marta soon had enough of them and decided to explore the elaborate home. She wandered through a sitting room, dining room and ballroom that all seemed overwhelmingly enormous to a girl of nine. The rooms were filled with so much glitter she couldn't imagine how anyone lived there. Her home, which had always been large enough to play hide-and-seek in for hours, now seemed small and quaint.

As she moved further into the house, she heard voices and peeked into a massive kitchen decorated in blue tiles and outfitted with hundreds of pots, pans, dishes, and glassware. A large cooking stove took up one entire wall. In the middle of the room stood a great wooden table loaded with green beans, potatoes, baked breads, and freshly skinned fowl.

Marta had never seen so much food in her life, but what held her attention was the scene taking place at the door at the rear of the kitchen. Two women were talking to several grime-faced children who wore tattered clothes and hungry looks. Marta assumed the women were cooks. As she watched, the ladies piled bread and other food items into a girl's dress which she held up like an apron. The girl was no older than Marta, but her legs and arms were so thin they looked as though they would snap in a strong wind. Her red-veined eyes appeared much too big for her gaunt, narrow face.

When the women realized Marta was watching, they shooed the children away and whirled around with fearful expressions and darting eyes. Marta knew she wasn't supposed to have seen them giving the children food, but it was not their fear that haunted her later. It was the look of desperation in that girl's eyes as the food was piled in her dress. The two women begged Marta not to say anything, claiming they had only given the children some day-old bread that was to be thrown away. She knew they were lying but didn't care. For she had witnessed how good-hearted they were and how they tried to make a difference for those less fortunate than themselves.

Marta watched the children through the window as they ran around the corner of the house to a weathered wagon waiting at the delivery entrance. The children scrambled aboard, and the wagon, pulled by a horse that looked as gaunt as the girl, crept slowly from view. She assured the ladies of her silence and returned to the lawn party, where she spied the two snobbish girls seated at one of the glass tables sipping tea from china cups like perfect adults. She hadn't noticed before how plumpish they both were. They had seemed poised and elegant when she first met them, but now all Marta saw were fleshy arms and legs and self-important airs.

Marta couldn't forget the beggar girl's large eyes and starved face. She had seen poor people before, but never such a famished look. It was an image that would reshape her world. She had come to the party envious of people like those two girls. She had dreamed of gaining their friendship and hosting her own events someday. She left the party wishing she could do something for the beggar girl and her brothers. As Marta grew older, she turned away from San Francisco's money-dripping rich and focused her energies on the poorer families whose children had starvation written in their eyes.

Her brother, on the other hand, continued to find San Francisco's social life alluring and did everything he could to be included. Marta realized that the pursuit of his social dreams was partly to blame for the failure of their father's shipping company. Samuel had a need to belong but no sense of responsibility. Marta now understood that he was never going to be capable of running the company successfully. When he started to lose the money he needed to finance his social agenda, he took what he wanted from the company's coffers with no thought to their future.

* * *

The two horses labored as the carriage started the steep climb to the top of Nob Hill, but they never broke stride. An occasional automobile churned furiously past them. "Have you not considered purchasing one of those new machines?" Marta asked curiously.

"Not really. I suppose I'm too old-fashioned, but I prefer a carriage's peaceful ride to a bucking, noisome automobile."

Marta had to admit she did, as well. The clip-clop of horses' hooves on the pavement was soothing and the ride gentle. There was no doubt, however, that those infernal machines were there to stay. She wondered how long it would be before they replaced horse drawn carriages altogether.

At last, they reached the hilltop, and the Whitman estate hove into view. The house stood four stories tall. It consisted of a series of turrets and gabled rooftops, with a tower in the center that rivaled the Ferry Building's and a circular roadway leading to a two story, marble-columned entrance. A series of large lamps cast a brilliant light upon the entryway, but the remainder of the house was cloaked in shadows, giving the place a look of mystery.

Autos jousted with carriages such as Byron's for space along the wide walkway leading to the main entrance. Horses whinnied and engines whined. Dust mingled with fumes. Murmuring voices stirred the air. More than one auto bullied its way to the front as if to declare its superiority over horses and carriages. Eleanor Whitman was famous for demanding punctuality. The elegantly costumed couples poured from their vehicles and hurried up the walkway as if they feared their invitations might be revoked should they not arrive on time.

Byron's carriage finally worked its way through the long line and the coachman stepped down to open the door. Marta's nerves had calmed considerably in the carriage. Now, they swarmed around her again with the fury of angry bees. She glanced at Byron for moral support, but it was impossible to decipher any expression behind his red silk mask.

Before she had time to worry further, she found herself following several couples up the walk to the grand entryway, where a man wearing a swallow-tailed tuxedo was taking each couple's invitation and announcing the new arrivals in a trumpeting voice that overpowered the lively chatter beyond the door. He accepted Byron's invitation with a deferential nod and turned towards the grand ballroom beyond the foyer. "Mr. Byron Wagner," he boomed, "and his escort, Miss Matilda Baldwin."

Several heads turned at the announcement. Even with their masks on, Marta sensed the onlookers' eyes crawling up and down her body, assessing her. Marta observed the ladies, in turn. She was dazzled by their displays of diamond tiaras, necklaces with pearls the size of stuffed olives, and cascading earrings glistening with sapphires and other gemstones. She touched the ruby necklace Lillie had loaned her with gratitude. She might disapprove of these events, but now that she was there she felt a sudden need to be viewed as someone with a certain amount of social standing, an emotion that confounded her. Well, she sighed to herself, if men were all the same, perhaps women were, as well. And tonight she very much wanted to be seen as a woman, at least in Byron's eyes.

The room was sticky with warmth. When Byron removed Marta's shawl and handed it to a servant, more eyes wormed their way over her skin. Instinctively, she grasped Byron's arm and followed his lead into the main ballroom. She looked in amazement at the size of the room, which she calculated could easily have contained the living, dining and parlor rooms of her house. Overhead, three chandeliers made of sparkling, cut crystal blazed with light. Gold-trimmed mirrors and immense oil paintings in gilt frames hung on the walls, which were covered by floral patterns of satin wallpaper. At the far end of the room a small orchestra sent wayward notes cavorting through the perfumed air as the musicians tuned their instruments. Settees and cushioned chairs surrounded a parquet dance floor that gleamed with the shine of polished gold.

A large crowd had already arrived and splintered into smaller groups. Most stood shuffling their feet in anticipation of the evening's program, while a handful of older men and women arranged themselves on the comfortable furniture. Their conversations provided a steady buzz of voices that rose and then faded in the upper reaches of the great room. Waiters wended their way through the groups with trays of appetizers and flutes of champagne.

A voluminous woman in a white satin dress and gold trimmed mask emerged from a nearby group like a great ship putting to sea. She wore a diamond studded head band and necklace, and a brooch set with a fist-sized pearl in it. The way she walked, with her head held high and her nose turned slightly towards the ceiling, made Marta think of royalty.

"Eleanor Whitman," Byron whispered as the woman bore down on them.

Of course, Marta thought. She should have known. Eleanor Whitman was the closest thing San Francisco had to royalty. She had never met the woman, although she had heard stories of her girth. "Full-figured" did not adequately describe her. Her breasts were the size of watermelons, and her fleshy arms reminded Marta of lamb shanks. Even her cheeks, red as ripe tomatoes, were so large they looked ready to fall from the folds of her face. Yet despite her disproportionate size, the woman held the fate of every eager socialite in her hands for no other reason than the fact that her husband's railroads had made them fabulously rich. Marta marveled at the power someone could possess simply because of a husband's money.

"Byron, it is so nice to see you here this year. But where is Mrs. Murdoch?" Their hostess wore a welcoming smile, but Marta caught the chill in her greeting. The reference to the widow Murdoch was clearly meant as an insult to Marta; she had to bite her lip to keep from responding.

"Eleanor, this is Miss Baldwin. I have found her company more to my liking." Byron smiled at Marta and gave a quick wink to let her know she had his full support.

"Well, it is good of you to come." Mrs. Whitman's voice was charming, but her eyes sliced through Marta. In the flick of an eyelid she made it clear Marta's presence was only tolerated because of Byron. Yet the woman delivered her frosty message with such poise and social grace that no one watching would have been the wiser. Marta had never felt so dismissed in her life She gripped Byron's arm a little tighter.

Mrs. Whitman returned her attention to Byron. "I was just talking to Frank Bell about his new shipping company. I believe he would be interested in your point of view." She guided them towards a small group gathered near one of the settees and smoothly handed them off to Mr. Bell and the others.

Frank Bell looked overgrown and well fed. He was dressed in a pirate's costume with a three cornered hat over a red head band, a knee-length coat, opened to reveal a loose, ruffled shirt and waist sash and knee breeches tucked inside bucket topped boots. Mrs. Bell wore a dress in shades of green with leafy patterns running through it. Her mask was a composite of leaves, flowering stems and vines.

"I have just made an extraordinary purchase," Frank Bell boasted after introductions were completed. "Seems a gentleman who runs a shipping company has gotten himself into a bit of a financial mess and has had to sell off his ships. I was lucky enough to land one for thirty cents on the dollar. I have already sent it to Europe loaded with tobacco and made a very handsome profit."

Marta's stomach churned as she listened. It was likely there were other shipping firms facing financial difficulties, but she could not shake the feeling that Mr. Bell was discussing one of the two ships Samuel had lost on the auction block. She immediately thought of the Holly Barrett, which she knew faced a similar fate. "Does the company have other ships for sale?" she queried in a small voice.

Mr. Bell glanced towards Marta as if noticing her for the first time. "Not that firm, my dear, but there is another that might soon give up its last vessel." He returned his attention to Byron. "I already have my fingers on the pulse of that one. My agent thinks it has just made its last voyage. When it returns, I shall pounce at once." His fleshy cheeks shook with glee beneath his mask, and Marta had to turn away to keep from becoming ill.

Desperate for a distraction from such troubling news, she tried to focus on what Mrs. Bell was saying to the women around her. ". . . and she refuses to receive Mrs. Fitch, supposedly because of some unkind remarks made behind her back." Mrs. Bell leaned forward in a conspiratorial fashion. "But someone close to the matter claims she refuses because Mrs. Fitch is rumored to have Indian blood in her." The other women snickered at this news and shook their heads.

Marta slipped her arm from Byron's and moved away from the disagreeable group. She had always known she did not belong in this crowd, but tonight she felt her lower social position keenly. This was reinforced by the chatter she heard around her about horse shows and days at the race track. One man boasted openly about a second family he kept sequestered across the bay in the Berkeley Hills. Another pointed out a man who had only gained social prominence by hiring a society reporter to write stories about him and his wife attending social events to which they had not been invited. And two sausage-shaped women howled with laughter when a third described an acquaintance as "having a mouth so large, there was hardly room for her ears."

It seemed to Marta that the ball was merely a pretext to snipe at others, exchange insults imagined or otherwise and brag about the money being made. They wore suits from London and gowns from Paris, and most attended these parties just so they would be seen by others. They were, she decided, unpleasant people who would have slipped into oblivion long ago if not for their outrageous wealth.

And into the middle of all the swirling rumors and dragon-toothed remarks stepped the one man Marta wished to avoid above all others: the Baron Konrad von Reich. There could be no mistaking his bushy eyebrows and sandy hair, but it was his pompous behavior that truly identified him, for he matched or exceeded anyone in the room with his attitude of self-importance. At his side stood an older woman who greeted everyone with a familiarity that told Marta she was one of those who "belonged," and she could not help wondering if the woman might be the widow Murdoch.

She turned away in the hopes she might avoid the Baron, but he sniffed her out with the certainty of a bloodhound and headed towards her before she could escape. "I see you are here after all, Miss Baldwin. But no escort? Have you resorted to coming alone?"

Irony tinged his query. Or was it sarcasm? She couldn't be sure. She wanted to flee, but she was trapped by the bodies around her. The Baron's eyes slid unabashedly to her breasts, and she suddenly wished she had not removed her shawl. Her stomach churned much as it had when she heard Mr. Bell talking about buying distressed ships.

"Or, perhaps you broke our engagement for someone of higher social standing," he continued in a booming voice that carried above the surrounding conversations. Heads began to turn. The Baron gave her a spiteful look and Marta felt the heat of discomfort rising in her cheeks. It was evident the Baron wanted to embarrass her. When she tried to respond, however, no words came forth. Her mind had become as frozen as when the hypnotist had cast his spell over her. Just when she thought all was lost, Byron magically appeared at her side and she breathed a heavy sigh of relief.

"Ah, Baron, it is good to see you. And Mrs. Murdoch, you are looking lovely as always." Surprised, the Baron blinked in confusion as he looked from Marta to Byron.

Byron's comforting voice broke through the logjam of thoughts in Marta's mind, and she began to think clearly again. Now that the Baron had stopped his assault, she could turn her attention to his escort. It *was* the famous widow Lillie had mentioned! The widow smiled and nodded her head.

"Baron," Byron continued, "you already know Miss Baldwin from the club of course, but Mrs. Murdoch has not had the pleasure. Allow me to introduce Marta Baldwin to you." His use of her informal name had a wonderfully calming affect on Marta, but she still cast a wary eye at the woman some might consider her rival. The widow wore a dramatic dress that bared her long neck and shoulders and accented an ample bosom. The dress tucked in snuggly at the waist, then billowed out in a series of black-and-white ruffled rings that fell to her ankles. She might be older than Byron, but her figure was well-proportioned. Her movements had a feline quality that told Marta she would be a handful for any man. The woman did not fit the colorless image she had formed based on Lillie's comments. In fact, she looked anything but dull. Marta suspected she could hold a man's interest more easily than many of the women in the room.

"A pleasure to meet you, Mrs. Murdoch."

"And you, Miss Baldwin. I have heard such nice things about your work with the less privileged. I commend your efforts." Her smile appeared genuine, but the woman's narrow, black mask could not prevent Marta from seeing that her eyes were focused on Byron. A hot flash of jealousy nearly consumed Marta and she instinctively linked her arm through Byron's.

Thankfully, the orchestra chose that moment to strike up a lively melody, and people began to move to the middle of the dance floor. "Ah, a waltz," Byron noted with satisfaction. "It is one of the few dances I can manage. Shall we try it?" For one irrational moment, Marta feared Byron was asking the widow to dance. She sighed with relief when he took Marta's arm and led her to the parquet floor.

"Thank goodness you arrived when you did," she exclaimed. "I was at my wits end trying to think what to say."

"Lillie told me about the Baron's invitation. When I saw him arrive, I thought it might be best to find you." Byron put his free arm around her waist, and they began to circle the room to the music. His arm burned through her gown into the small of her back with the fire of molten steel, and when their bodies pressed fleetingly during a turn, the same warmth she had experienced in the carriage flowed through every pore in her body. Couples whirled past as violins breathed in her ear. Or was that Byron's breath spreading fireflies through her? All she knew for certain was that her world had been turned inside out by this man and, after dancing with him, she knew she never wanted to let the widow Murdoch near him again.

They twirled around the floor when another waltz followed. It had been some time since Marta had danced, but Byron's firm guidance erased her self-doubts. She drifted through the room like an eagle riding the air's currents higher and higher into the sky. She had never imagined it could be like this. She had dated before, even kissed on occasion, but this was different. The warmth she had felt in other men's arms had been tepid compared to the feverish heat flowing through her now. Her body ached to be touched in places she had never allowed anyone to touch before. She was ready to cast aside her inhibitions and throw herself to the gods. Without this man, she was no longer whole.

The music stopped, but Marta continued to whirl about the room in her mind. She could still feel Byron's arm pressed against her back, even though she knew he had released her. Her body trembled from the memory of his touch; her chest heaved from the pleasure of his company. It took several deep breaths before she could bring herself down from the emotional heights she had just scaled. Dazed, she looked around and saw couples forming two lines. "What is everyone doing?"

"They are preparing to dance a Cotillion, a rather athletic undertaking with a complex series of steps and turns. Not something I am much good at, I'm afraid."

"Nor me. I wouldn't know where to begin."

They fled the floor and joined the other bystanders. When the music started, it carried an urgency that reminded Marta of a military drill. The couples began a series of maneuvers she couldn't begin to understand and charged around the room in an organized frenzy. She laughed when she saw the Baron roar past in an obvious muddle, his feet tangling with Mrs. Murdoch's and his arms swinging menacingly from side to side. At last, the dance ended and everybody stood about panting and wiping their brows. The orchestra took the opportunity to put down their instruments and left the floor for a much needed break. The dancers gladly did the same.

Marta was about to suggest that they sit for awhile when Byron took her hand. "If we retrieve your shawl, I believe it would be pleasant enough for a brief stroll on the veranda."

"That sounds delightful." She nearly blurted out her words. The idea of spending some time alone with Byron appealed to her almost as much as escaping the pretentious conversations already underway again.

Byron went for the shawl and then they slipped out through the tall, side doors that opened onto the veranda. Street lamps and lighted windows flickered in the city below while stars shimmered above their heads. A crescent moon peeked over the horizon, adding a dash of charisma to the exotic setting. Even with the shawl, Marta felt the bite of the air on her skin. Instinctively, she snuggled against Byron for warmth. It was a bold move, she supposed, but she felt bold tonight.

Byron put his arm around her shoulders and for a moment the lights and stars hung motionless. Voices and laughter escaped the room behind her. An owl hooted to its mate. The fresh scent of mint and rosebuds mixed with Byron's soaped skin and that hint of pipe tobacco she had already come to love. Marta's world was tipping off center. Without Byron's strong arm to steady her, she might have tumbled down the marble steps leading to the garden below. There was steadfastness to the man that gave her strength and courage. It had begun across a chess board and flowered into something remarkable.

She was so lost in her thoughts, she was hardly aware of Byron's hand on her cheek until he gently kissed her. Marta's mind exploded in a whirling dervish of lights. Her body trembled with such a passionate heat that she feared she would be consumed by it. But Byron's warm lips did more than ignite her passion. They told her she no longer faced the world alone. They filled the void she had carried inside her since her father died. Her brother had been the only significant man in her life, but he could not provide the emotional soil she needed to complete her growth into womanhood. Byron had just done that with a single kiss. He had fulfilled her desire for happiness, and she hoped he would do so forever.

Byron started to pull away, but she stopped him and pressed her mouth to his in a long, burning kiss. All the anxieties she had harbored fled into the night. The wall of doubt she had kept erected against unreasonable expectations fell away. She closed her eyes and savored the sweet taste of pipe tobacco mixed with the sharper flavor of caviar on his lips. What a wondrous taste on her tongue! She had never experienced anything so delicious and wanted more. Crisp musical notes announced a fresh round of dancing. Marta ignored the music at first, preferring the warmth of Byron's body to the cold tongues and chilled words waiting for them inside. She clung to him a moment longer, then released him.

"Perhaps we should return to the ball." He spoke softly. His dark eyes sparkled in the light from the ballroom.

Marta nodded.

As they stepped inside, a murmur of disapproving voices and the sparkle of diamond tiaras atop shaking heads caught her attention. Someone had just arrived, but she couldn't tell who until the doorman's voice boomed: "Major Wilcox and his escort Miss Lillie Collins." Lillie had arrived at last! More heads turned as Marta strained to see her friend. Whatever Lillie had done, it was evident she was causing a sensation.

"Where is she, Byron? I cannot see her." Marta grasped his arm and rose on her toes, to no avail.

"Follow me." Byron maneuvered them through the crowd until

Marta spied her friend standing beside a uniformed military officer whose balding head fringed with gray announced that he was much older than Lillie. His pursed lips made it clear he was most uncomfortable with all the attention. But the attention had little to do with him. Marta saw at once what the crowd's fuss was about, and she gasped with laughter. Lillie had come dressed in the full regalia of a fireman, complete with knickers held up by bright, red suspenders, long, gray stockings fitted into mirror-polished black boots, a red flannel shirt, and a fire helmet. To complete her ensemble, she wore a black mask with a long nose.

Lillie began to greet acquaintances, leaving the Major standing to one side as if he were a plaything she had discarded. Despite their disapproval at her outfit, society's crème de la crème smiled and welcomed her, including Eleanor Whitman who lumbered over to her as quickly as her great frame would allow. Lillie simply had too much money and her family was far too powerful to be ignored.

As soon as things quieted a bit, Marta hurried up to her. "Lillie, what a sight you are," she exclaimed as she grasped her hands. "And arriving so late. You are much too bold."

"And look at you," Lillie cried out with delight. She held Marta at arm's length and appraised her. "I hope your escort realizes how lucky he is." She playfully tweaked Byron's nose, then turned to her own escort. "I want you to meet Major Wilcox. Major, this is Byron Wagner, one of our city's most distinguished citizens."

The two men shook hands and Lillie pulled Marta to one side. "Tell me, are you enjoying yourself, or are you miserable?" She asked this with an impish grin.

"I have never felt so happy, Lillie. I'm floating. Are my feelings ill-advised?" Marta's heart was suddenly pounding in her chest as she realized what she was asking her friend. Was the kiss they had just shared a fleeting moment of passion, or did it portend the deeper meaning she attached to it?

"Darlin,' you have that man wrapped up tighter than a boatswain's knot. You are going to see a lot more of him, I can tell you that."

Marta's eyes moistened unexpectedly, and she swallowed a shaky breath. A heady feeling of joy rippled through her. It was true, then. She cared for the man as she had no other and her affection was reciprocated. Her world *had* turned a corner and would never be the same again. She looked at Byron, who was now involved in a conversation with Major Wilcox, and smiled. Then, as she turned her attention to the Major questions began to cascade through her head. "Lillie, who is the Major and why are you with him tonight? Where is he from? How do you know him?"

Lillie made a face that reminded Marta of someone sucking on a lemon. "That's the latest man my mother wants me to marry."

Lillie's declaration caught Marta by such complete surprise, she nearly cried out in protest. "Marry? Lillie, I cannot imagine you married to anyone. Certainly not to someone old enough to be your father."

"He has great wealth, but hell, we sure don't need more of that. No, it's his status in New York society that has my mother in a tizzy. As you know, New Yorkers don't look kindly on us westerners. They think we're still fighting Indians, for God's sake." Lillie laughed at this and pushed her mask up to her forehead. "What ever possessed me to wear this thing? It's impossible to breathe. Anyway, the Major has shown a keen interest in me during his stay out here. Mother thinks he will propose. She has made it clear I am to accept."

Marta's head began to spin. "Would you do that?"

Lillie grinned. "I'm hoping he won't ask. Why do you think I wore this outrageous outfit? You should have seen his appalled expression when he called for me. I think he wants to turn tail and run back to New York as quickly as possible. I'm doing all I can to encourage him."

They both laughed. Marta knew Lillie would be a handful for any man, but if she didn't cotton to someone, life would be impossible. She was tempted to walk over to the Major and urge him to be on his way, but when she glanced towards the men, she saw a policeman talking intently to Byron. At first, she thought it was a man in costume, but then she recognized the handlebar mustache of Captain O'Connor and knew something was wrong. She saw that the man's words were having a powerful effect on Byron, who clenched his fists and raised his head as if to howl. Marta rushed over to him. "Byron, what is the matter?"

He pulled off his mask to reveal a face contorted with anguish. "It's Charles. He's dead."

Marta nearly stumbled under the weight of his words. *Dead? How could that be?* "Captain, what happened?"

He bowed slightly to her. "Drowned, madam. People say he either fell or jumped off the pier. Couldn't be sure which."

She wanted to ask him more, but it wasn't the time for questions. It was the time to console the grieving man standing before her. "I'm so sorry, Byron. I know how close you are to him." Marta realized she spoke in the present tense, as if Charles was still alive. She threw her arms around Byron and held him close. His head found her shoulder, and she could feel the silent sobs wracking him. Marta sensed how badly Byron wanted to hide his emotions from onlookers and in that moment understood what a truly private man he was. It was hard for him to display his feelings, particularly in public.

People were watching, nonetheless, whispering among themselves and speculating on what had happened.

Lillie joined them and as soon as she heard the news took command. "Where have they taken him? The morgue?"

The captain nodded.

"Then that's where we're going, right now." She turned to her escort. "Major, I trust you will find your way home. Goodnight." With that, she took Byron's and Marta's arms and marched them to the entryway. Marta barely had time to put her shawl back on before Lillie whisked them out the door and called for Byron's carriage. The captain had arrived by horse and would meet them there.

They rode in silence down the steep hill, the three of them huddled together as the carriage jostled along the uneven pavement. For some reason, Marta found the ride rougher than she had earlier in the evening. She pondered how quickly one's fortunes could turn. Charles may have been a fragile man, flawed and insecure but he had been filled with a love for life. Now he was gone, his breath snuffed out in an instant. By drowning! It seemed so implausible, yet witnesses had attested to it.

At first, Marta wondered why Lillie had insisted they go to the morgue. It seemed a gruesome prospect, but when she looked at Byron's troubled face she understood. Nothing could remove the misery he felt, but bringing some closure to Charles' life might help lessen his suffering. She took Byron's hand and felt his pain surging through his fingers, where it mingled with hers. She would gladly have taken all of Byron's pain if it would have comforted him, but that was impossible. All she could do was share his grief and hope it helped in some small measure.

Marta sat in the gloom and wondered at the dark forces that had conspired against Byron's friend. She didn't know why, but she sensed something unnatural about Charles' death. People didn't just fall off piers and drown. What was he doing there in the first place? His haunts were in Chinatown, not the Barbary Coast. *Had* he committed suicide? That seemed equally implausible. Whatever else Charles might have been, she was convinced he was not suicidal. Yet something had gone terribly wrong, and whatever the cause, she feared its origin.

CHAPTER NINETEEN

Marta had never visited the morgue, and she hoped never to do so again. Whitewashed walls and dank concrete floors reeked of disinfectants and death. Traces of blood were visible around the floor drains. Cadavers lay draped under white sheets on tables. Scalpels and tissue clamps gleamed on a metal tray. Her footsteps echoed off the sterile walls as she and her companions followed the captain down a long corridor to the main examination room. *That was where fresh bodies were brought*, she thought. *That was where they would find Charles.*

The coroner stood at a table in the center of the room waiting for them, his white examiner's coat mirroring the whitewashed walls around him. His pallid skin gave him the appearance of someone who might soon join the corpses on the surrounding tables. Marta estimated his age between fifty and sixty and wondered how long he had haunted those corridors. It seemed a terrible place to spend one's life.

The white sheet covering Charles' body had already been pulled back far enough to reveal his face, which appeared surprisingly serene. Marta had expected to see the contorted mouth of someone trying desperately to draw another breath, much as she had done when first exposed to the hypnotist's powers. But Charles looked peaceful, as one would who had simply fallen asleep and failed to wake up again.

"It is not uncommon for people to drown in the bay," the coroner offered after introductions were made. "We get at least one a month, sometimes more."

Byron reached out and touched his friend's cheek with the back of his fingers. "He feels so cold," he remarked. "And he looks at peace. Is that common also?"

The coroner adjusted his thick eyeglasses and stared at Charles. "No, I must admit that baffles me. If he had fallen in, his face should show some signs of his struggle. Even if he had jumped, there should be some hint of his desperation."

"He would never have jumped," Byron declared.

"Why not?" the captain asked.

"Because he couldn't swim," Lillie replied matter-of-factly. "And he was terrified of the water. He even refused to attend the Sutro Baths." Lillie referred to the salt water swimming tanks built near the Cliff House by the shore. Thousands of people swam and bathed there.

"That would rule out suicide," the captain concluded. "People rarely choose to end their lives in a way that terrifies them."

"I agree," Byron commented. Marta was relieved to see his composure return as he considered what might have happened to his friend. "I say that because there was nothing in his demeanor or conversation to hint at such an idea . . . suicide, I mean. I would have noticed if there were."

Captain O'Connor frowned in thought and twisted the tips of his handlebar mustache. The mustache was neatly trimmed, carefully combed, and waxed so the tips curled upward. It was apparent from his unconscious behavior that he took considerable pride in it. "That would leave two alternatives," he said at last. "Either murder, which seems unlikely since no one was seen near him on the wharf or an accident. Perhaps he went for a walk, stumbled or tripped and fell in."

"Never." Byron shook his head vehemently. "Charles wouldn't voluntarily go near the bay like that."

"Byron is right," Lillie chimed in. "There had to be some extraordinary reason for him to be there."

The captain fiddled with his mustache some more as he pondered their comments. "Something doesn't add up here, that much seems obvious. Rest assured I will investigate the matter further."

As they left the morgue, Marta considered the alternatives listed by Captain O'Connor, and Byron's and Lillie's conviction that it had not been an accident. Lillie had used the words "extraordinary reason." The phrase burrowed into Marta's mind and gnawed at her thoughts. There *was* another explanation for Charles' strange behavior, one that *did* involve an "extraordinary reason." It was a disturbing idea, so disturbing that she hesitated to mention it. She had sensed a dark force at work even before they arrived at the morgue. It had been ill-defined, but she had felt the pressure of it building behind her forehead with the persistence of an intense headache. Now that she had seen Charles' face and heard the declarations of her friends, the force took a most terrifying shape. Only the hypnotist had the power to make people do things against their will. Only the hypnotist could make Charles do what he feared most. The thought that he might have somehow influenced Charles to venture near the bay sent shock waves shuddering through her. When she stared into the darkness, she swore she saw a pair of evil eyes glowering back at her.

After Byron dropped Lillie off, Marta gripped his hand and turned to him. On the way to the ball, Marta had been thankful the carriage was dark, but now she wished there was light so she might see Byron's face. She knew her fears were only conjecture. Byron would probably think she had gone mad, but she had to tell him. There was too much at stake to keep her thoughts to herself no matter how bizarre they might seem. Marta hesitated, took a deep breath, and plunged into her story.

"In the short time I knew Charles, he became a good friend, and while I might not feel his loss as deeply as you do, I am still devastated by what happened. But I don't want you to think my emotions have undermined my ability to think straight." She tightened her grip on his hand. "I have sensed something . . . ominous ever since we learned of Charles' death, an evil force that cannot be explained by reason or logic. Now that I have seen Charles' face, I am more certain than ever that his death was unnatural."

A quiet stillness settled over the carriage as Marta struggled to find the proper words to express her thoughts. As she felt the skin on Byron's hand tighten and his fingers clench, she searched the gloom for guidance. Perhaps her mind *was* playing tricks on her. Perhaps she was just being a silly woman who confused an overly active imagination with reality. When she stared into the darkness, however, her intuition told her that what she sensed was real. Even if it was in her head, she still saw the yellow eyes that were watching her. There could be no doubt what they meant. They told her there was danger in the air.

"I cannot shake the feeling that the hypnotist played a role in this tragedy," she said at last, "and it frightens me."

Byron shifted his weight and removed his hand. The tension between them filled the carriage. "How, exactly, do you think the hypnotist was involved?" he asked in a constricted voice.

Marta didn't need to see his face to know Byron's sorrow had been pushed aside by a more robust emotion. His anger was evident. "It was what Lillie said about the need for an extraordinary reason. If Charles wasn't murdered, and if he wouldn't go near the water voluntarily, it's the only explanation left. I don't know why, Byron, but I can *feel* the hypnotist's evil in this."

"If what you say is true, I shall kill him." Byron's voice was devoid of emotion. It wasn't a threat or an attempt at bravado. It was simply a statement of fact.

Marta had no doubt that he meant what he said. But there was another fact she knew as well. Byron would be no match for the hypnotist. If Byron went after him, Byron would most likely meet a fate similar to Charles.' Marta couldn't let that happen. She had to find a way to protect him, to stay close to him until a plan was formulated to counter the threat posed by the hypnotist.

As she sat there trying to think what to do, she realized another force was at work, one nearly as disconcerting as her fears about the hypnotist. She knew daylight was the only cure for the misery they faced, and she wanted nothing more than for this tragic night to end. Yet on some deeper level, she wished the evening could go on and on, for even in tragedy she found Byron's company more than merely comforting. Sitting next to him made her head pound with a riot of emotions that had been unleashed by their kiss. She didn't want to let him go. The idea of returning to a dark house where the only thing waiting for her was a quarrelsome brother suddenly felt all wrong. She leaned back against her seat and swayed to the rhythm of the carriage while she considered her feelings. She had just waged a fierce battle to save her house from creditors but now she would give anything not to go there. There was no warmth in that house, at least not on this particular night. All the warmth she wanted was seated next to her in the form of a man who had come to mean everything to her. Despite the bone-rattling size of Byron's mansion, she was drawn to it just as surely as a moth was drawn to the warmth of a candle's flame.

Marta sucked in her breath as she tried to decide the best way to explain herself. "Byron, I have a favor to ask."

"Yes?"

"This whole episode frightens me. I know Samuel will be out to all hours and I don't relish facing my house alone after what we've been through. Would you mind if I stayed in your guest bedroom tonight? I would feel safer there than at home." It was a bold request, Marta knew, one that would be considered very forward, even by San Francisco's liberal standards. She feared she might have overstepped her bounds. She strained to see Byron's features. But the gloom persisted.

An interminable silence joined the tension in the carriage. Finally, Byron cleared his throat. "I believe we must be careful about our conduct now that we have been seen together at the ball.

You know how poisonous peoples' tongues can be in this town. I wouldn't want your reputation compromised."

Marta's heart sank. *Well spoken,* she thought, *but a declination nonetheless.*

"That said," Byron continued slowly as if measuring every word, "I find the prospect of returning to my house alone tonight just as unpleasant as you do yours." He slipped a hand over hers. The unexpected warmth filled Marta with so much desire she dared not move. "I would be honored to be your host for the remainder of this damnable night . . . as long as it is clear you have stayed in the guest room. Henry can be relied upon to stand witness to that."

"It's a good thing you have Henry," she said shyly. "Otherwise, I fear I would be at your mercy."

Byron released her hand and sat back. "You are too fine a woman for me to be tempted in that way. Not, I mean, without making an honest woman of you." He stumbled on his words and coughed.

Even in the darkness, Marta could picture him reaching for his pipe before realizing he had left it at home. She knew it was much too soon to consider making her an "honest woman," but she thrilled at the idea. Was it possible to consider spending the rest of her life with this man? He had just implied that it was. It made her head spin. Their earlier kiss continued to burn Marta's lips all the way up Van Ness Avenue to Byron's home, but the time was not right to initiate another one.

* * *

Marta spent a restless night in the guest room Henry had prepared. She tried to forget the menacing eyes that had peered at her from the coal-black shadows of the carriage. No matter what she did, she couldn't escape the deadly reach of the hypnotist. First her own encounter, then Missy kidnapped and Angela harassed. Now Charles, dead. Who would be next? Lillie? Byron? The thought of losing either of them was more than she could bear, but it was apparent the hypnotist was pursuing her friends to get at her.

Her thoughts then returned to the kiss and what it meant. It wasn't the kind of thing Byron would have done on a whim. That much she knew. It had been a declaration of something deeper, something that elicited terms like 'tempted' and 'honest woman.' Marta shivered every time she thought about the kiss and tossed about some more.

She also reached a decision during her restless night. If she thought either Lillie or Byron was in danger, she would go to Chinatown herself. Better he took her. Better she gave up her life to save theirs. Otherwise, she wouldn't be able to live with herself. If she lost Byron, life wouldn't be worth living at all.

The next morning they shared breakfast before Byron had a servant drive her home. The ashes of Charles' loss hung in the air, but so did an awkwardness about what happened the night before. Their talk was stilted and both of them fumbled with their cutlery like embarrassed school children. A serving woman brought soft-boiled eggs and toast which they ate in silence. When Marta could stand it no longer, she reached for Byron's hand. Its warmth calmed her nerves.

"If last night's kiss was a singular moment, Byron, I will understand, although I confess I hope it was not." Singular moment! Where did she come up with such words? She looked intently at Byron and searched for any sign of tension, a furrowed brow or a clenched jaw. She didn't have much experience with men, but she had been told they were often less romantic in the morning. She steeled herself for a less than enthusiastic reply.

"What a term for such a wonderful kiss," Byron replied. "Singular moment. I can hardly wait to hear how you describe the next one." His grief for Charles yielded to a small smile that melted her with relief.

There was to be a next kiss. She was nearly giddy with the thought. "You will just have to wait and see, won't you?" She patted his hand before returning to her eggs with a shy smile.

* * *

Two days later, Charles was buried and life moved on. There had been no sign of the hypnotist in the interim. The funeral was held on a drizzly day and attended by most of the important families, including Eleanor Whitman, who looked even more colossal in black than she had in white. Most of the people in attendance spent more time eyeing each other than paying their respects to Charles. It wasn't a social occasion, yet attendance was noted, along with the kinds of hats, gloves and fur coats worn by the gathering. Marta asked Missy to cover the office and brought Angela, an act of defiance that delighted Lillie. Angela stood beneath her umbrella throwing visual darts at Herbert Cummings the entire time. Herbert tried to look away, but he could feel the sting of her gaze and shielded himself behind other mourners. Lillie dressed in proper black and even yielded to social precedent by wearing a simple skirt instead of her usual trousers. Byron stood with Marta beside the casket, confirming to the world that they were now intertwined in a meaningful way. This caused clucking tongues and curious glances. Marta didn't mind. It was a sorrowful occasion, but she could not hide the pleasure she felt in Byron's company.

Ironically, they had passed a Chinese cemetery on their way. Marta had been fascinated to watch a funeral procession winding its way along twisting, narrow paths past a tumbledown collection of tombstones and markers crowded into too small a space. A fire burned haltingly in a corner of the cemetery despite the steady drizzle. Byron explained they were burning the clothes of the deceased, something about which Charles had told him. So there they were, passing one cemetery on their way to another with Charles' spirit traveling with them. For his part, Charles was buried in grand style, complete with a marble-lined vault and a massive stone slab to cover his tomb.

The funeral was a grim reminder of the evil that still stalked the streets. That reality was driven home in the form of Captain O'Connor who waited for them at the entrance to the cemetery. He doffed his hat and offered his condolences. Then he got down to business. "We've found two witnesses who saw Mr. Harwood walking down Market Street in the company of another man."

The announcement chilled Marta, even though she had expected it. "How did they describe him?" she asked.

"Tall. Angular. Walked with unsteady steps." He eyed Marta. "Sounds like the man you told us about."

It wasn't a question, but Marta nodded anyway. "But he didn't accompany Charles onto the pier?"

"No. The man stopped by the Ferry Building. Mr. Harwood went alone from there. Witnesses claim he walked right off the end of the pier without hesitation. Like he was going for a swim."

The irony of the captain's words wasn't lost on Byron, who tightened his grip on Marta's hand. "How do we find this evil-doer?" he asked.

The captain toyed with his mustache, just as he had the night of the ball. A nervous habit, Marta assumed, much like Byron with his pipe. "We have patrols out looking for him, but I'll tell you frankly, if he's hiding in Chinatown, we'll never find him. Not unless the tongs cut him loose."

"There must be some way to find him," Byron declared to Marta after the captain was gone, "and if there is, by God, I *will* find him." There was determination in his voice, which Marta found both admirable and frightening. The last thing she wanted was for Byron to confront Charles' murderer. That would be fraught with dangers she didn't want to consider.

* * *

Marta kept the aid society's doors closed until the day after the funeral and paid Missy and Angela from her dwindling funds. The police patrols had been pulled from the tenements and reassigned. Without the patrols, it was only a matter of time before the hypnotist returned. She could already feel him lurking nearby. The two women were eager to earn their keep, however, and there certainly was work to be done. So, she called them in and began a rotation schedule she hoped would keep them all safe. Only one of them was allowed to make house calls at a time and that woman wore Marta's omamori. Marta asked clients who could to come to the office, where the women worked with them behind a locked door. Marta had been so accustomed to wearing the Japanese charm, she felt lost and vulnerable without it. It was the only solution, however, that made sense. It had protected her; it should protect the others.

Marta didn't see Byron the next day. She was busy finishing the financial reports Lillie needed to invest in her foundation and Byron was trying to convince the police to continue their investigation into Charles' death. By the second day, however, it was concluded that Charles had committed suicide and the investigation was halted. This made no sense to Byron, who continued to grieve for his lost friend.

When she heard the news, Marta rushed to Byron's home but didn't find him in. Henry gave vague answers to her inquiries about where he had gone. He finally admitted he wasn't sure. All he knew for certain was that he had gone to meet Captain O'Connor. Henry fought to maintain his decorum, but Marta could see the worry lines etched in his face. Byron's behavior had become more erratic since Charles' death. The calm, self-assured man she found so attractive had been replaced by one driven by vengeance. She and Henry looked at each other, their concerns unspoken but understood. They must help each other keep Byron safe. It seemed that Charles' death was changing people, redefining relationships and forming new alliances.

Marta sensed at once that Byron and the captain were headed to Chinatown. It was the last place she wanted him to go. She took solace in the knowledge that he was with the captain, thank God for that, but it did little to quiet the fingers of fear playing cords up and down her spine. Byron was pursuing the hypnotist, the one thing she dreaded above all others, and while he was most likely safe with O'Connor, the captain couldn't accompany him forever. Like the police patrols, he would be assigned to other cases, and Byron would be left alone. Then the hypnotist would be free to strike. Her stomach churned at the thought. It took all of her strength to keep from collapsing on the sidewalk in a faint.

The only piece of good news came from Lillie, who reported that the Major had high-tailed it back to New York just as she predicted. It provided a moment of comic relief, but it did little to dampen the fears tying Marta's insides into knots. She shared

Byron's anguish and wished she could comfort him more, but Lillie thought it best to let him be. He would rejoin the world when he was ready.

* * *

The inquisitors who come looking for me are breeding like rabbits. I am currently trailing two of them down the labyrinth of alleyways that lead from the main streets of Chinatown. Smoke from a cooking fire briefly obscures my view as rats the size of tiny dogs dart past my feet. Odors of unwashed human flesh assail my nose. A young prostitute sings out to me in a pleasing voice. These smells and sounds are all familiar. They comfort me and tell me this is where I belong.

Not so the two I follow. They are foreigners to this place and are here to cause trouble. One is the police captain who raided the Stout's Alley brothel where the red-haired girl was kept. I know him by his great, black mustache. The other came in search of the man called Charles. Him, I recognize by the pipe he clenches between his teeth. They have entered my world and I want to know why.

I keep a safe distance and study the man with the pipe. Unlike Charles, this one has no vices. Prostitutes call to him but he ignores their pleas. Opium dens beckon but he walks past them with a determined stride. There is an unyielding strength in this man that bothers me. He stops passersby to ask questions about me but no one dares talk to him. Fear of the tongs silences their mouths. Even the hatchet men hide in the shadows where they can watch undetected. Only I can see their eyes floating in the darkness.

I now know the purpose of this unwelcome visit. The pipe man hopes to learn where I am. He hunts me! I find this ironic, since I am supposed to be the hunter. I hope he will ask his questions and go away, but I fear he will not. There is a resolve in his stride that was absent from his predecessor. He has the bearing of someone who does not give up easily. Why has he come to harass me? There can be only one answer. He was Charles' friend. I clench my hands at the thought of the threat he poses. It is dangerous to keep toying with these men. Unlike the families whose girls I take from the tenements, the police watch over these people. The police are their friends, and that makes them dangerous.

No doubt the eyes of the tongs have already reported the progress of these intruders and I shall have to soothe their concerns once more. I will have to be careful with this one. I cannot stage another accident or suicide. Still, if the man persists, I will have to take action, whatever the risks.

At last, they finish their questions and leave. Relief sweeps over me as I stand in the shadows watching them depart, but I know my reprieve is temporary. Their questions have gone unanswered. The pipe man will return.

Ah, but there is good news, as well. The patrols are gone, as I told the tongs they would be. I savor the moment, for I am free to roam the tenement's streets once again. I return to my hunting grounds with renewed energy, but as I stalk the rutted streets and peer around corners, I find things have changed. Those meddlesome police have warned families to keep their daughters out of sight. The result is too few victims and too many people watching for me. This is made clear when I see a girl of sixteen or so hurrying along the pavement near where I caught my last victim. This time, the girl is accompanied by a young man, perhaps an older brother, who throws spiteful looks at me as they pass. His arrogance inflames me. I want to hypnotize them both, but that is a dangerous temptation. It is better to bide my time and wait for the proper opportunity. People cannot stay hidden in their homes forever, and brothers are not always available. My luck will change.

Nor have I lost sight of my true goal, to trap the witch and imprison her. It is time to pay her and her friends a visit. When I arrive at the office they share, I see the blinds are closed and the door shut tight, but light leaks around the edges of the window. I know somebody is there. I know the witch is there. I can *feel* her presence the way a wolf senses its prey hiding in the brush. So, I return to my abandoned doorway where I can watch undetected. Once there, I settle into its quiet embrace and begin my vigil.

It is not long before the red-haired girl leaves the office and begins to walk my way. Good fortune is mine! I shall take her a second time and return her to the tongs. This time, there will be no one to nose around the brothels and opium dens in search of her. No one will come to her rescue.

I am about to step from my hiding place and snatch her, but something holds me back. I can feel a power radiating from her like rays from the sun. It is the same power used by the witch to defeat my will. Its source hangs from her neck: a charm that sparkles in the morning light! I have seen that charm before. It belongs to the witch. At last, I understand what has thwarted me. I duck back out of sight, too shocked to do more than draw an angry breath. Even from this distance, I can feel the charm's energy. It is useless to go after her, for I am powerless before that charm. My impotence makes me tremble with fury as I watch the girl turn a corner and disappear. Am I to return to the tongs empty-handed once more? Every muscle in my body aches to go after her, but I am blocked by an obstacle as solid as an oak door.

Time passes and my anger recedes. A new possibility emerges from my confused thoughts. The witch thinks to outsmart me, but her cunning may prove her undoing. By using her charm to protect another, she strips herself bare. She leaves herself as helpless as her opium-addicted friend. Now, I have the key to the door that stands in my way, and I shall soon open it.

CHAPTER TWENTY

"Lillie, I'm worried." Marta said this while the two women sipped tea at a small café near Market Street.

"About what?" Lillie asked as she set down her cup.

They had just left a meeting with their solicitor, Mr. Adams, and filed the necessary paperwork for Lillie to begin investing in Marta's Pacific Aid Society. It had been an intoxicating experience for Marta, who had never signed such a formal document before. To his credit, Mr. Adams had offered to excuse himself from the proceedings since he represented both women, but Marta respected his judgment and told him that wouldn't be necessary. The agreement was finalized and arrangements made for money to begin flowing into the foundation at the beginning of May. The timing was none too soon for Marta, whose budget was being stretched to the limit now that she had two employees and the income from the shipping business had dried up.

In fact, Marta had raised the subject of the shipping company. Lillie knew the circumstances, so there was no reason to be coy about the subject in front of her. Mr. Adams confirmed her worst fears. The Holly Barrett would have to be sold when it returned to port. The company would be closed. Marta immediately pictured the heavy, bearded man with thinning hair who captained the ship. What would happen to him, she wondered? Hopefully, he would find another commission soon. A sad depression cloaked her thoughts as she considered the fate of the company's last ship. To her mind, it had not been a particularly impressive vessel, but she had walked its deck, and that made the loss more personal. "How is Samuel dealing with the news?" she asked. "He refuses to speak with me about it."

Mr. Adams harrumphed and fiddled with the chain to his timepiece which hung across his ample stomach. Clearly, he was uncomfortable discussing Marta's brother in front of Lillie, but Marta nodded for him to proceed.

"He is not taking it well, I'm afraid. In fact, I think one could say he is ignoring the situation altogether." Was it sadness she saw in her solicitor's face? The man cared what happened to Samuel, she realized, and this gladdened her heart. Business might be unyielding, and at times cruel, but there could still be humanity in it.

"I think he might be going through some sort of emotional crisis," Mr. Adams continued hesitantly. "I have seen it before when things go wrong." He stopped and shifted his weight to a more upright position, as if he was gathering strength for what he wanted to say next. "It is possible for melancholy and despondency to set in. It can cause unhappy decisions to be made about one's life."

Marta sat back, struck by his words. Unhappy decisions? The phrase sounded almost as silly as her "singular moment" remark to Byron. Yet, she sensed peril in the words and could see that Mr. Adams was uneasy with their implications. Would Samuel consider doing something drastic? Disappearing, or worse still, taking his life? The very idea left Marta breathless. He hadn't given any indication to her that he might consider such a thing, but that didn't prevent a flurry of questions in her mind about what she should do. She would have to speak to Byron about it, see what he thought.

Byron. She seemed to be seeking his advice and counsel more and more as their relationship flowered, although little had flowered since Charles' funeral. Byron had become, not remote exactly, but less available, even when they were together. It was as if part of his mind listened to what she said, while the rest wandered off into distant realms. She knew he continued to obsess about the hypnotist. His foray with Captain O'Connor had yielded nothing. No one in Chinatown was willing to acknowledge that the hypnotist even existed, let alone tell them where the man was. Byron had wondered if their reticence was due to the presence of a police officer and discussed returning on his own. Marta had pleaded with him not to go back and he had finally relented. She had the distinct feeling, though, that he might change his mind at any moment. She had to find a way to prevent that from happening.

* * *

Marta suddenly became aware of Lillie's voice and realized she hadn't been listening. She shook her head to clear her mind. "I'm sorry. What did you say just now?"

"You said you were worried and I asked what about." Lillie stirred more sugar into her tea and stared at Marta with concern. "Does it regard your brother or Byron?"

Marta realized her mind had wandered and she hadn't answered Lillie's question. A passing automobile honked its dissonant horn and she jumped at the unexpected noise. Automobile horns always made her think of someone with a head cold blowing their nose. She hadn't become used to the abrasive sound. "Both, actually, but right now I am talking about Byron." She leaned forward anxiously. "I fear he will try to go back to Chinatown without Captain O'Connor. He thinks people might talk to him if he's alone, but that would be dangerous, particularly if the hypnotist learns he's there."

"Byron hasn't been himself the past few days," Lillie agreed, "but if he's determined to look for the hypnotist, I don't know how you can stop him." She threw her hands up in exasperation.

It was a gesture unfamiliar to Marta. She feared it signaled Lillie's resignation. Marta didn't think she had the strength to protect Byron by herself. She needed Lillie's help. "Lillie, we need to work together on this." Marta reached out and took Lillie's hands. She was always amazed at how warm and soft they were for someone who refused to wear dresses and maintained such a tough exterior. "I can't stop Byron alone, and if he pursues his obsession, I fear it will end badly. I cannot let that happen." She let go of Lillie's hands and sat back in her chair. "I will not let the hypnotist do to Byron what he did to Charles. I love him too much." Tears suddenly welled up in her eyes and she hastily withdrew a handkerchief from her pocket.

This time, it was Lillie who reached across the table and grasped Marta's hands. "Not to worry, darlin'. Byron may get a little thick-headed at times, but he's practical as well. We'll pound some sense into him. You'll see." She took the handkerchief from Marta and dabbed a wayward tear that had escaped down Marta's cheek. "And we certainly can't have you mooning around all the time. I have invested in you, now, and I always watch after my investments."

That remark teased a small smile from Marta.

"That's better," Lillie exclaimed. "Look," she continued, "I'll have a chat with him this afternoon and tell him I've invited you to join us for drinks. Be at Byron's at six. We'll straighten things out."

Marta's fears still bounced around inside her head, but she had to admit Lillie did make her feel better. If anyone could keep Byron from doing something foolhardy, it was her friend. She suddenly thought about what she had said a moment ago and opened her mouth in amazement. "Did I just confess to loving Byron?" She cringed at her bold remark.

Lillie barked a laugh that got its usual attention from the surrounding tables. "God, woman, you think the whole world doesn't already know that?" She slapped the table with her hand as she spoke, rattling the teacups. "I've just been waiting for the two of you to set a date!"

Lillie's comment elicited a broader smile from Marta. It was the first time she had confronted the idea of love directly, the first time she had used the word even in her mind, and it made her heart jump a beat. Loving Byron was the most natural emotion she had ever felt. It was as effortless as a butterfly taking wing. And now she had confessed it to her best friend, another new relationship that astonished her. Lillie had taken her by storm, just as Byron had, and she loved them both. Except for her father, she had never felt so much emotion for anyone before.

This realization caused darker thoughts to stir in the recesses of her mind. Including Missy and Angela, and, yes her brother, she had a growing family of people who were close to her, people she had to protect from the evil that continued to stalk her world. None of them could face the hypnotist and survive. Only she could, with the omamori given to her by her father. Just as fate was drawing her closer to the diabolical man who roamed the tenements and hid behind a wall of silence in Chinatown, so fate would decide her destiny.

* * *

Marta was in a somber mood when she arrived at Byron's. Henry opened the door the moment she rang and actually smiled as he let her in. She returned his pleasant greeting and followed him to the drawing room where Lillie and Byron sat with iced whiskies in their hands.

"Ah Marta, you have arrived." Byron jumped to his feet and took her hand. His hand felt cool from the glass he had been holding. It sent shivers of delight coursing up her arm. When he leaned forward to kiss her on the cheek, she boldly tilted her mouth to his lips. Oh, the fire in his kiss! It ended too quickly when Byron pulled back in surprise. She nearly buckled on the spot and took his arm. He reddened nicely and clamped his pipe in his teeth as he led her to the couch.

"Darlin', you look luscious tonight." Lillie didn't move from where she lay languidly among the cushions. Her eyes sparkled with delight, however, at the small exchange of intimacy she had just witnessed.

Marta had been very conscious of her attire and had selected an evening dress that accented her waist and breasts without revealing too much. She had also fussed with her hair and dabbed a little rosewater behind each ear. Despite her earnest mood, she wanted to portray her womanhood to Byron, and she was pleased to see from his expression that she had succeeded.

But there was also something odd about Byron's behavior and that troubled her. His eyes darted nervously about the room; his hands moved restlessly at his side. He had the look of an imprisoned animal trying to escape its cage.

"Drink?" he asked, once she was seated. A quick smile roamed his lips but failed to take root and disappeared. His smile was as restless as his hands.

"A little sherry, perhaps," Marta responded as she quietly observed him. She could see Charles' death written in the contours of his face. A sharp surge of panic stabbed her chest when she realized that Byron was not going to rest until he found the hypnotist. She could see it in his roving eyes.

He poured Marta's drink and joined her on the sofa facing Lillie. A hint of aftershave lotion imbued the air with the heady allure of perfume. Marta inhaled the scent and fought the urge to kiss him again. She shook her head and concentrated her thoughts on what they were about to discuss. She needed a clear head, not one muddled by thoughts of "singular moments."

Once they were settled, Lillie took the lead. "Let's talk about this fiend who we all agree had some hand in Charles' death." Her languid pose was gone. She now sat upright on the couch and leaned forward thoughtfully, elbows on knees. "It seems no one can find the man, yet I think we all agree he is hiding somewhere in Chinatown."

"So it would seem," Bryon agreed. "Everything that has transpired around him has taken place in or near Chinatown. And if he works for the tongs, as I suspect, then he must be living under their protection. People in Chinatown know where he is, but they are suspicious of our police. That is why I want to return without

Captain O'Connor. They might talk to me if I'm alone."

Marta took Byron's hand and gripped it. "That would be much too dangerous. Look how he mesmerized Charles, and Charles knew a great deal about hypnotism. If he were to discover you there, Byron, I shudder to think what he might do. And you would have no defense for it." She hated the pleading tone in her voice, but she couldn't help it.

"We need a strategy," Lillie added before Byron could say more. "Marta, you are the only one who has been able to resist his powers."

Marta instantly touched the amulet dangling from her neck. "Because of this charm, but even then just barely. His powers are that strong."

"Yes, but you told me you have started loaning it to Missy and Angela when they make their house calls, and so far nothing has happened. Is it possible any of us could be protected by it while in Chinatown?" Lillie raised her eyebrows to accentuate her question.

Marta sat back nonplussed. "I must admit, I hadn't imagined that." She glanced at Byron and saw an anxious look on his face. *It could be the answer,* she thought, *but what if it lost its potency in the hypnotist's lair? Or it was somehow removed?*

"That would leave you exposed, Marta. I couldn't allow that." Byron jumped up from the couch and hurried to a table across the room. "But I have come into the possession of something that I believe solves our problem." He raised an amulet similar to Marta's and waved it triumphantly in the air. "As you know, there is a small Japanese community not too far from here. I visited it and came across this charm. The shopkeeper assured me it was an omamori, just like yours." Byron's eyes shined with anticipation as he handed it to Marta.

Indeed, it was quite similar to hers, and if she held them apart, it was difficult to tell one from the other. She knew at once what Byron planned. He would wear the charm and plunge back into Chinatown. It might work, she supposed, but it was a terrible risk. There were too many unanswered questions: Byron's resistance level. The charm's effectiveness in Chinatown. Even whether this new charm would work at all. As Marta sat on the couch comparing the two amulets, she knew instantly what she must do. A current of anxiety surged through her. With luck, everybody would be protected by the two charms. If not, she had to make sure Byron was kept out of harm's way.

Lillie leaned forward to have a look.

"What do you think, Lillie?" Marta started to hand the new amulet to her. As she did so, she dropped her own on the floor, reached down and quickly switched the charms.

Lillie followed the exchange with a sardonic smile but said nothing. "It looks real enough to me," she offered after a brief inspection of the piece. "No reason to expect it wouldn't work." Lillie handed it back to Byron and turned her gaze to Marta. "It would be a relief to know you were both safe from that devil."

Marta stood up and put her arms around Byron. The warmth from his body calmed her jittery nerves. She knew she was doing the right thing. "But you must make me a promise, Byron. If you find the hypnotist, you will not try to apprehend him alone. You will get Captain O'Connor and his men."

Byron held her close and nodded. "You have my word."

Lillie offered Marta a ride home in her carriage and waited until they were settled in the cab before speaking. "I hope you know what you're doing, Marta. It's bad enough to have Byron running around looking for the hypnotist on his own, but now your situation is doubtful, as well. What if the hypnotist comes for you and that new charm doesn't work? I could lose you both. I don't think I could live with that." Lillie twisted her fingers in her hands as she spoke. It was the first time Marta had seen a nervous gesture from her sure-footed friend, and it sent a disquieting gust of doubt swirling through her.

Marta gave Lillie an impulsive hug and settled back in her seat. "I must know Byron is safe, Lillie. As soon as I saw him tonight, I knew I had to do something. He was as nervous as a bird on a wire, but he looked determined, too. His jaw was as firmly set as when I first saw him scrutinizing that chessboard. When he gets like that, nothing can dissuade him. So I took measures to protect him. As for me, the girls and I will keep out of sight until Byron has satisfied himself."

"Good," Lillie responded with satisfaction. "And if you need help, call me. I have yet to meet the man who could tame me. I doubt your evil doer would be any different."

Marta gave a quick laugh but then her expression turned serious again. "I pray it will not come to that, Lillie. Your friendship means too much for me to risk losing you to that man. He appears to know everyone with whom I associate and I assume that includes you. Please take great care until we can resolve this matter."

They squeezed each other's hands before Marta said goodnight.

Only one light burned dimly in the study when Marta entered the house. The place had a forlorn aspect about it in such light. At first, she thought no one was home, but a cough and rustling of papers told her Samuel was there. Mr. Adams' comment about her brother's fragile state of mind immediately surfaced in her thoughts. She quietly entered the study to find Samuel bent over their father's desk sorting through a stack of documents. "Brother, what are you doing?" she asked softly so as not to startle him.

He jumped anyway and tossed his head as he turned to face her. The room's deep shadows made it difficult for her to see his features, but his quick movement suggested he had been caught doing something he wished to keep private. "I thought you were gone for the evening."

His response deflected her question. Marta walked over to the desk and stared at the papers. She saw at once they pertained to the Holly Barrett. "I understand it will have to be sold," she said in a neutral tone.

"Not necessarily." He shoved his fingers through his hair as he spoke. Now that she was closer, she could see a wild look in his eyes. "It stands to make a small profit on its current run. If I can keep the ship's hold filled, there's every reason to have hope despite our recent run of bad luck."

Mr. Adams had carefully explained the effects of the crushing debt the shipping company faced. Marta knew the Holly Barrett was not sailing with anything close to a full hold. She had seen that for herself when she visited the ship's captain. But Mr. Adams' cautionary words and Samuel's unsettled behavior stayed her tongue. Little could be gained tonight by confronting her brother with the truth about the company's situation. She suspected he had come to believe his stories of pirates and storms. It was better to let him hold onto his dreams than to shatter his hopes. There would be time to face reality when the ship was sold. She lowered her head, left the room and went into the kitchen to prepare dinner.

CHAPTER TWENTY-ONE

The pipe man has returned without his police escort. I sit in a small restaurant and watch him through the window as he moves from store to store asking questions about me. I observe him stop to light his pipe while his eyes roam the shops around him. Except for a handful of local customers, the street is unusually quiet. Most shopkeepers are hidden inside their stores in hopes the intruder will pass them by. When he doesn't, they smile with their mouths but not their eyes and tell him nothing.

My eyes burn at what I see. My voices chatter ruthlessly in my head. My mind is on fire. I have done nothing to this man, yet he persists in his efforts to hunt me down. Is there no end to these would-be sleuths who think to find me? Why do they not leave me alone and go away? I know the answer, of course. He knows the witch and he was a friend of the man I took from Blind Annie's Cellar.

I pay for my meal and return to the street. My fingers itch to clutch his throat, but I must not do anything rash. I cannot have a second victim walk to his watery grave. The tongs are already edgy about the attention I am drawing. They will not send their hatchet men after me as long as my notoriety does not outweigh my value to them, but that's an alternative that becomes more possible with each new investigation. I must be rid of this man, but I must exercise caution. I need a new plan.

A wonderful idea strikes me as I follow my inquisitor, an idea that makes me smile. Why not capture him and put him on a ship sailing far away? By the time he awakes, he will be at sea and unable to return for some time. The idea delights me. I watch my quarry with new interest. I shall wait for him to grow bold enough to enter the narrow maze of alleyways where I can strike without drawing more attention to myself. Then, I will hypnotize the pipe man and send him on a long journey.

Time passes, but I wait patiently. There is no need to follow closely, so I keep my distance and tarry in merchants' doorways. Voices chatter nervously around me, but no one asks me to move on. Everyone knows I am following the white man and they watch with interest. At last, he abandons his attempts to gather information from the shop owners and wanders into the secondary lanes, as I knew he would. I have climbed to the rooftops so he cannot see me following him. I spring ahead to where I know he is going and prepare to trap him at a brothel just a block away. I watch his progress as he moves deeper into the labyrinth of broken alleyways that lead to me. He walks cautiously and keeps a keen eye on his surroundings. Slowly, he approaches my hiding place in the brothel. Just a few more steps and he will be mine.

But no, it cannot be! The witch has thwarted me again! There, dangling from a chain around the pipe man's neck is the charm that blocks my powers. She has given it to him just as she did the red-haired girl. My voices laugh at me. I nearly rush at him with my bare hands. But that would be foolish. I am no physical match for him and I would reveal my hidden world, just as he wants me to. Soon, the police would return, and this time they wouldn't leave until they found me. I must slink away like a toothless old cat and lick my wounded pride.

Or must I? If the witch has given this man her charm, then she no longer wears it. My plan sits in front of me like a dog waiting for its supper. I have nearly failed to recognize it. If she has given him the charm, she knows he is here and I can use him as bait to lure her into my web. Opportunity shines on me after all. The moment for which I have been waiting has finally arrived. I must hurry and prepare my trap.

* * *

Byron had come to the conclusion that searching any longer along the main street of Chinatown would be fruitless. It was obvious from the way the Chinese merchants retreated into their stores when he approached and shook their heads when he asked his questions that they weren't going to give him the information he sought. They knew about the hypnotist, he was certain of it, but fear prevented them from speaking. More than once, a frightened glance warned him somebody was watching, but when he turned around, he saw nothing suspicious.

It was time to change tactics. He touched the omamori hanging from his neck, clamped his pipe between his teeth and entered one of the alleyways that slinked into the fetid underworld ruled by the tongs and enforced by the hatchet men. He had hoped to avoid such a risky undertaking, but there seemed little choice. He wasn't going to leave until he had exhausted all of his options.

The narrow passages smelled of rancid water and human waste. How could anyone live in such conditions? Women called to him from doorways as he stepped gingerly over loose stones. Some of the women looked vaguely familiar. He wondered if he'd seen them when he was there with Captain O'Connor. It was impossible to be certain. They all looked pretty much the same to Byron, as did the signs announcing the myriad opium dens, brothels, and gambling establishments. His greatest concern was that each new alleyway looked like the previous one. This presented a problem for Byron. He didn't dare venture too far into the labyrinth or he would quickly become lost. Once he had penetrated a few blocks into the maze, he turned around and retraced his steps.

In this manner, he spent an hour investigating a series of

alleyways and trying to pry some tidbit of information from the residents who lived there. However, they proved as infuriatingly closed-mouthed as the merchants. Again, their uneasy eyes threw furtive glances as they shook their heads no. Again, Byron sensed danger lurking nearby. He suspected word traveled quickly in Chinatown. By now, the hypnotist probably knew he was there. Was that the danger Byron sensed? Was the hypnotist watching him? He stopped and lit his pipe to demonstrate his resolve, but his legs trembled.

After a few puffs, Byron resigned himself to his failure and started back to the main street. He had gone less than a block when he turned a corner and nearly bumped into an awkward-looking man who glared at him with the most sinister pair of eyes he had ever seen. Instinctively, Byron wanted to reach for the omamori, but his hands refused to move. His arms hung at his sides, useless. He sensed the dark power that was engulfing his mind, but when he gathered his thoughts, he found he could resist the forces trying to imprison him. It took all of his willpower, but he managed to force his gaze away from the man's beckoning eyes and hastily stepped around him. Once free, he walked as swiftly as the alley's potholes would allow towards the now familiar fish odors and discordant voices of the main street. He glanced repeatedly over his shoulder as he walked, but the alley was empty. The man had disappeared.

When Byron reached the main street, he stood hands-on-hips and breathed a sigh of relief. He had just confronted the hypnotist and escaped! A rush of pleasure swept over him as he looked down at the omamori dangling from his neck. The amulet had done its job. Yet, even as he exulted in his triumph, doubts rose in his mind and he became less certain about what had just happened. Images blurred. One moment, everything seemed real; the next, memories faded. It was like waking from a bad dream. He *had* faced an ominous presence in that hideous alley. He was certain of it. The threat had been real.

He couldn't wait to talk to Marta about it. The thought of her broadened his angular face into a smile. He started to lift his pipe to his mouth, only to discover he wasn't holding it anymore. Had he dropped it in his haste to escape the dark alley? Or had the hypnotist taken it from him? He hated losing that pipe, not just because it was a meerschaum but because it had been given to him by a Turkish ambassador and its distinctive carvings made it one-of-a-kind. Byron wanted to look for it, but he feared the forces he had just escaped. He wasn't certain he wanted to test the omamori's powers again so soon. When Byron spotted a boy with a runny nose emerging from the alleyway, he called out to him and asked if he had seen a pipe lying on the ground. The boy hurried past without so much a glance in his direction. Byron tarried awhile longer in hopes that someone else would appear, but the alleyway remained deserted. Disappointed, he finally gave up and returned to his waiting carriage. Thoughts of Marta eased his frustration over his lost pipe. He couldn't wait to see her.

* * *

Marta fussed with papers in her office but got little accomplished. She frequently rubbed the amulet hanging from her neck and wondered if it would resist the powers of the hypnotist. The Japanese merchant who sold it to Byron claimed it was an omamori and there was no reason to doubt him. It was not hers, however, and she didn't trust it enough to put either Missy or Angela at risk. She would be the one to test its powers should the need arise. However, keeping everyone inside presented a logistical nightmare. The tiny office wasn't big enough to accommodate the three of them at the same time. After several futile attempts to sort out adequate space, Marta gave up and sent both of them home for the day.

She was too distracted to work anyway. It wasn't just her concerns about the new omamori or the lack of work space. It was Byron's announcement that he intended to return to Chinatown. Even though she had switched charms with him, she couldn't help worrying about his safety. The charm appeared to have worked for Missy and Angela, but there was no way to be certain. What if it failed to protect him there? She remembered her own feelings of helplessness when confronted by the hypnotist and how close she had come to succumbing to his powers. Chinatown was his lair. It was where he went to rest, to gather himself. His powers would be strongest there. Would they be strong enough to overcome the omamori? If the hypnotist could make people do anything he wanted, even walk off the end of a pier, she supposed it was possible.

As she rummaged through her thoughts, she became aware of a light rapping sound on the door. Not so much a knock as fingers tapping. It was an odd sound. Marta stopped what she was doing and listened intently. A slight scraping noise against the door jam jarred the momentary silence. Then the light tapping came again. Marta stepped to the window and peeked through the shade. She discovered a boy of eight or nine scuffing his feet and rubbing his runny nose on his sleeve. He stood looking expectantly at the door. Marta glanced at the street but saw no sign of the hypnotist or other danger. Once she was satisfied nothing was amiss, she hurried to the door and opened it.

The boy took a surprised step backward at her sudden appearance. He wore a ragged wool cap which he quickly removed and held in his hands. One foot slid sideways, an indication that he was prepared to turn and run at the slightest provocation. His scrunched cheeks and pinched expression told Marta he was not at all comfortable with his mission and wanted to be on his way. A day's worth of dirt was smeared across his face, neck and hands. He stared at her and rubbed his nose.

"Yes?" Marta queried. "Can I help you?"

"Got a message for th' lady what works here." Edgy eyes flicked back and forth between Marta and the pavement.

The boy made her nervous. She again glanced up and down the street. Nothing seemed out of place. "I'm Miss Baldwin. This is my office."

"There's a man in Chinatown, says you should come. Says he's found th' man he's lookin' for. Wants t' show you." The boy stared expectantly at Marta.

Marta's heart thumped with equal parts hope and suspicion. Was the message from Byron? If so, why would he send such a wretched waif? "Do you know the man's name who gave you the message?"

The boy scrunched his face and scratched the back of his head. "I ain't much good at remembrin' names." Then his face brightened, and his hand dived into his pocket. He produced a pipe and handed to her. "Th' man gave me this. Say's you know 'im."

Marta turned the cream-colored pipe over in her hand and inspected it. It was clearly Byron's. She recognized the images carved in the bowl as excitement rose in her chest. It *was* Byron who had sent the boy and he had found the hypnotist! That was the message. She turned to grab her coat, but caution stayed her hand. Why would Byron trust this boy with his pipe, she wondered? He wouldn't, unless he wanted to be certain she would come. Unless the message was urgent. "Did he say he's found the hypnotist?" she asked.

His face twisted with confusion as he tried to understand what she had said. "Don't know 'bout that," he responded. "He jus' said I should get you."

She reached for her coat a second time but again hesitated. "Wait there a moment," she told the boy and closed the door. Quickly, she took the phone off the hook and got a connection to Byron Wagner's home. The phone rang three times before it was answered. She half-expected to hear Byron's voice, but heard Henry's instead. "Henry, it's Marta Baldwin. Is Byron there?"

"He went out hours ago, miss."

"Do you know where?" She held her breath.

"He said he was going to pursue his investigation in Chinatown." His voice sounded puzzled. "Is there some way I can help you?"

"No. I just received a message from him and I wanted to be certain where he was. You have answered my question. Thank you, Henry." She hung up and thought a moment longer. It seemed strange there was no note, but Byron may not have had writing paper available to him. If he was in a hurry, it would be simpler to send the boy. At last, she put on her coat and reopened the door.

The boy stood where she had left him.

"I'm ready. Take me to him."

The boy immediately turned and marched away towards Market Street.

Marta quickly locked the door and followed. People moved busily along the streets with an air of wealth and optimism that made the world seem normal. The boy ducked through the crowds, sidestepped the heavy drays hauling barrels and crates from the docks, and somehow managed to dodge between the street cars and the automobiles motoring along the street. Marta followed as quickly as she could and thanked her lucky stars that she hadn't worn a dress. She lost ground to him, anyway, and feared she would soon lose sight of him altogether. The boy suddenly slowed and waited impatiently for her to close ranks before he started off again at his maddening pace.

By the time they turned off Market Street onto Grant Avenue, Marta was puffing heavily and sweating despite the chilly April air. She signaled for the boy to stop a moment while she regained her breath. Chinatown was only a few blocks away, but their fast pace had left no time for her to consider what options she might face when she got there. Locating Byron was her first concern and she hoped he would be close by. The thought of entering Chinatown again tugged at her misgivings. The sooner she found Byron the better. But what if she encountered the hypnotist? Her hand flew to the charm hanging from her neck. She prayed it would have the power to protect her.

The sound of Chinese being spoken and shouted, smoke-laden braziers and the semi-bitter odor of pickled fish and fresh snails greeted her as she followed the boy into the mysterious streets of Chinatown. The odors and scenes seemed almost familiar to her now. She scanned the bowler hats, sallow faces and silk-braided queues for Byron's familiar face. He was nowhere to be seen.

The boy stopped abruptly and pointed to a side lane that Marta knew would quickly transform itself into a winding alley filled with unknown dangers. "Th' man says t' meet 'im there." He shuffled his feet and slid one to the side just as he had at her office. His body tensed.

Marta stared at the lane's entrance with a strong sense of foreboding. "Where exactly should I go? You must show me." She reached out to take the boy's arm but he shied away and shrugged his shoulders.

"Cain't." With that, he turned and plunged back into the jumbling crowd of Chinese.

"Wait," Marta cried out, but it was too late. The boy was gone. She looked around her with a sense of helplessness, uncertain whether to stay or to flee herself. Every fiber in her body told her to run. Every fiber urged her to follow the boy back the way she had come. Her chest banged with the force of clashing cymbals. Her head grew dizzy from the crowds swirling around her. Angrily, she bit her lower lip and pushed away the panic attack that was unnerving her. Losing her nerve would serve no purpose. She had to think clearly. The circumstances that had brought her to Chinatown still made her uneasy, but when she looked at the pipe in her hand, she knew there was no turning back.

Marta reached down with her free hand and rubbed the omamori she had switched with Byron's. Surely it would protect her. She was nearly there and Byron needed her. Knowing he was nearby gave her a burst of confidence. If he was waiting for her, she didn't want to let him down. Besides, if he *had* found where the hypnotist was hiding, he would have sent a message to Captain Connor as well. Most likely, the police were already there. That knowledge gave her strength. She waited for her heart rate to slow, returned to the side lane pointed out by the boy and stepped tentatively into the dark world that awaited her there.

It felt as though the brick and wooden walls were crowding her as she started down the lane. Second-story overhangs, grimy windows and haggard doorways closed in on her. The stench of rotting garbage that assailed her nostrils was so strong she placed a handkerchief over her nose. The broken pavement required her attention to keep from tripping or spraining an ankle. At one point an obese dowager peered at her from a recessed doorway. The woman reminded Marta of Eleanor Whitman at the masked ball. An elderly man in a loose jacket and skullcap gave her a toothless grin as he passed. Another in a bowler hat tapped on a wooden door with a peephole. Once he had been identified, a heavy bolt slid back and the door opened on a smoky room filled with card players and dice throwers. The door quickly banged shut again.

Marta swore she heard footsteps following her, but when she jerked her head around, no one was there. Where was Byron, she wondered, and why was it necessary to look for him in such a miserable place?

She had ventured further into the slimy alleys of Chinatown than she had intended but there was still no sign of Byron. She was about to give up and retrace her steps when she came upon a narrow side lane that was barricaded by a gate. A large man in silk robes guarded the entrance. Arriving couples stopped and spoke to him before entering. A waiter from a nearby restaurant carefully walked down the lane balancing a tray filled with pewter pots. The guard opened the fence wide enough to let him pass. Marta looked in and saw that the lane was brightly lit by rows of lanterns hanging from balconies. A decorated shrine surrounded by burning candles and incense stood against one wall. Musicians in brightly colored silks suddenly struck up a wild cacophony of booming drums and crashing cymbals. These were accompanied by shrill pipes and a screeching fiddle. Priests wearing vivid scarlet robes trimmed in gold and black caps topped with gold knots bowed as new guests arrived. Women in elaborate silk gowns looked down on the festivities from the overhanging balconies.

Marta was so entranced by the spectacle unfolding before her, she failed to notice the lanky figure sliding through the shadows until it was too late. A blur of motion shattered her reverie as a moist, hot hand clamped over her mouth. She tried to cry out, but the pressure from the hand gagged her. The odor of decaying fish filled her nostrils. She was pushed around a corner and half-dragged down another alley. Instinctively, she reached up to yank the hand away, but before she could do so she was grabbed by the shoulder and spun around. A bolt of fear seared her body when she found herself staring into the satanic eyes of the hypnotist. Marta knew at once that she had been lured into a trap.

Her heart pounded as she assessed the danger. She was deep inside the hypnotist's lair, Byron didn't know she was there, she was in the grip of the devil and she was alone. Marta tried to tear her gaze away from the man's demonic eyes but couldn't. Their hold was too powerful. She felt herself floating as they drew her to him. Unlike the last time she was bewitched, there was no frozen chasm waiting to claim her. Instead, a warmth spread through her body that made her skin sticky with moisture.

Just when she seemed totally lost, a remarkable thing happened. The trance-inducing eyes blinked and looked away. She was immediately released from the spell. A look of anger mixed with fear streaked across the hypnotist's angular features. His eyes fell to Marta's neck and he instinctively pulled away. The charm was working! Frantically, she grasped it in her hand and held it up for him to see. The scowl on his face told her how frustrated he was. She nearly laughed. But her triumph was short-lived. She wasn't on the streets of San Francisco, now. She was buried deep in the bowels of a netherworld where no one would come to her aid.

Marta realized this when the hypnotist reached out and snatched the charm away from her. The movement came in a flash. One moment she held it in her hand, the next, it was gone. The chain that held it was violently ripped from her neck, causing a searing pain where the metal gouged her skin. The charm disappeared.

Without the protective amulet, Marta's only hope was to avoid the hypnotist's eyes. She whirled around and started to run deeper into the twists and turns that defined the contours of the alleyway. She had never run for anything faster than a trolley car on Market Street before, but now she was running for her life. Fear gave her unexpected strength. As long as she ran, she had a chance.

She dodged garbage containers and potholes and ducked under low-hanging signs. Pounding footsteps echoed off the walls behind her. They told her the hypnotist was giving chase and that he was much too close. Thoughts flashed through Marta's mind in rapid bursts as she ran. If she could find a cross alley, it might take her back to the main street. None appeared and, even if one had, she was too lost to know which way to turn. Thankfully, it was too dark for the hypnotist to use his amber ring. He would have to focus his eyes on hers. That would give her a few seconds to defend herself, but how? She needed a weapon, something that could deliver a strong blow. Desperately, she looked for a brick or piece of wood but saw nothing. Her only hope was to keep running.

Her breathing was becoming ragged. She nearly tripped on the uneven pavement. Her lungs burned and she could feel the effects of her exertion in her legs. She dared not look back, nor did she have to. She heard the echoing footsteps pursuing her. Was it her imagination or were they getting closer?

She screamed for help as she ran, but no one came. An elderly woman in black pantaloons turned her head away as she passed. A man in soiled trousers and a badly worn jacket ignored her pleas. Light spilled out of a doorway and highlighted a young girl with rice powder on her face. One of the prostitutes, she realized as she raced past. The girl's laughter trailed her down the alleyway.

The warmth she had felt earlier became an oppressive pressure that weighed her down. She was perspiring freely, causing her clothes to rub abrasively against her skin. Her feet ached from the shoes she wore. She wished she could kick them off, but there wasn't time. Worst of all, her lungs were running out of air. Each breath she took became more painful and it took longer for her to recover. Her legs began to wobble. She moved even more slowly as the echoes of the following steps grew louder.

When the hypnotist grasped her shoulder and pulled her to a halt, it was all Marta could do to remain standing. She knew she was defeated and cursed herself for her stupidity. The bravery she had felt when she thought about her previous confrontations with the hypnotist melted away. Her eyes darted furtively about in hopes of a miracle, but there was none. She was a small animal caught in the jaws of a predator. She no longer had any doubts about her fate. There was no way for her to escape her tormentor.

She closed her eyes in one last attempt to foil him, but the hypnotist snaked his fingers around her throat and cut off the air her lungs so badly needed. Her throat burned from the pressure of his surprisingly strong hands. Her head grew heavy. A dark cloud blanketed her mind, a cloud so black no light penetrated it. She knew if she didn't remove it, she would never see daylight again. There was only one way to cast off the darkness. She had to open her eyes. When she could stand it no longer, she did so and instantly felt the power of his gaze upon her. A light radiated through her body, a warm light that transported her to a world filled with yellow and purple flowers and tiny birds that buzzed like bees. The images were so wonderful that she questioned why she had tried so hard to escape them. The pressure on her throat disappeared, allowing her to swallow a great lungful of cool air. She gasped with pleasure and swallowed more of the life-saving air. Finally, the pressure in her head subsided and she was at peace. Her body relaxed.

They began walking deeper into the labyrinth of alleys. How pleasurable it was to walk with him! Marta's feet were so light she hardly needed to touch the ground. Her delight at being with him made her giddy with happiness.

However, she couldn't help noticing the way people averted their eyes as they passed, or how they shied away from her companion. Somewhere in the deepest recesses of her mind, a warning sounded. Things were not as they seemed. The flowers and birds weren't real. The chirps and songs she heard came from the rice-powdered women they passed, not from the flower-strewn world she was seeing. But when she looked at the gangly, slightly askew strides of the man beside her, her fears scattered as quickly as mice exposed to an unexpected light. Marta no longer cared about the real world. The hypnotist had given her a far better one, a world she wanted to dwell in forever.

There was only one tiny worry that refused to let her go. It tugged at the edges of her mind with dogged determination. Where was Byron?

CHAPTER TWENTY-TWO

Byron paced his sitting room where he had last spoken to Marta and tried to decide what to do. He had expected her awhile ago and had looked forward to telling her about his experience in Chinatown, but there had been no word from her. Twice he called her office and her home, only to be greeted by endlessly ringing telephones. Each ring had hammered against his eardrum until he could stand it no longer and had hung up the phone. In desperation, he called Lillie, half expecting to find the two of them together, but the butler informed him Lillie had been gone all day and there had been no sign of Marta. Where could she be? It was uncharacteristic of her to be late.

Worry crept into his thoughts with a nagging persistence that told him something was wrong. Each time his anxiety level rose, his hand automatically reached into his coat pocket for his pipe, which was no longer there. The loss of his pipe only added to his distress. When Byron could stand it no longer, he ordered the carriage and rode to Marta's house, where Samuel greeted him at the door and told Byron he had just come in and had not seen Marta. Byron's next stop was at her office, which was firmly locked. Then he went by the police station, but Captain O'Connor was out. The officer on duty said no report of a young woman involved in a mishap had been received in the past few hours. A quick check at the main hospital elicited a similar response. Knowing she had not been harmed eased some of the tension that had been building in Byron's neck and shoulders, but it didn't soothe his underlying fears.

When he could think of nothing else, Byron ordered the carriage to Chinatown and hesitantly walked down the main street. Memories of his earlier encounter with the hypnotist were fresh enough to give him pause, but he didn't know where else to go. He approached the same merchants who had avoided him earlier and asked if they had seen a Caucasian woman about their size with black hair and an olive complexion. As before, eyes darted away and heads shook nervously no. It was clear nobody was going to help him. It didn't take long to understand why when he spotted two roughnecks leaning against a wall across the street and staring at him. The hatchet men made no attempt to approach him, but their presence sent a chilling message to the merchants and to him. He had no business there. It was time for him to go. Reluctantly, he turned and made his way out of Chinatown.

* * *

The darkness was everywhere, a thick, black darkness that refused Marta's efforts to push it away. The darkness held her arms and legs so they wouldn't move. It pressed against her tongue so she couldn't speak. It tasted rancid in her mouth and it burned her skin where it bound her. Its odor reminded her of week-old fish. She remembered that odor. Where had she smelled it? Her mind was too foggy to recall.

Dust tickled her nose causing her to sneeze. The sneeze jarred her loose from her wandering thoughts and brought her world into focus. She opened her eyes to a vague, grey light that was only strong enough to outline the shapes of things. Detail was lost, but she saw she was lying on a straw-littered floor in a small room that smelled of dank, moldy walls and unwashed bodies. She tried to sit up but couldn't. Her arms and legs were bound too tightly for her to move. Ropes, she decided. She was tied up with ropes.

Memories flashed through her mind. They burned the inside of her skull with the force of lightning bolts and sent shock waves of fear coursing through her body. She was in the lair of the hypnotist! She remembered running until her lungs burst and her legs gave out. After that, things became a blur. There had been wildflowers along the path where she walked, or was that a dream? A rice-powdered face loomed in her mind. It laughed harshly at her and floated away. Had she seen that face, or had that been a dream as well? It was difficult to separate the world that was real from the one that had so beguiled her.

The hard, wooden floor on which she lay was very real, however, as was the room. There were no flowers there, only a bleak world ruled by the hypnotist. Fresh shards of dread showered her and made her pulse quicken. What did the man want with her? What would he do? There was evil in the room. She felt its terrifying presence all around her as it seeped into her pores. She drew quick breaths through her nose and struggled with her bonds. It was useless. They would not yield to her flailing movements. All she managed to do was draw more dust into her nose. She sneezed again. It was better, she decided, to be still and save her strength.

Byron leaped into her thoughts. *Where was he? Did the hypnotist have him also? Or had he already killed him?* Marta drew a sharp breath at the thought. No, she decided. The charm would have protected him and he was too strong for the hypnotist to overpower. Besides, she realized with chagrin, the hypnotist didn't need to capture Byron. He only had to use him to draw her closer, and she had foolishly fallen for his plan. She should have known that snot-nosed little boy was part of a ploy to lure her to Chinatown. Byron wouldn't have used a boy that young. He would have found paper to write a proper note. It was her anxiety that had betrayed her, anxiousness about Byron's safety and the whereabouts of the hypnotist. In the end, her anxiety had been her weakness, one the hypnotist had exploited.

Anger welled up inside of her. Anger at her stupidity and foolish courage. She jerked at her bonds with rage but only succeeded in digging the ropes deeper into her skin where they burned with the ferocity of hot coals.

The dim, grey light slowly changed its hue to a pale blue. Details began to emerge. There was a low bed near her head. Marta could see bare feet at the end of it. *The hypnotist*, she thought with a gasp! He was sleeping right next to her. She wanted to rise up and pummel him with her fists, but she couldn't move, and besides, her fists were too small. The room held few items. A trunk for clothes. A battered table with one chair. A rusty faucet dripping into a sink whose sides were soiled with grime. A decrepit toilet. It was an ugly room, one filled with despair.

Marta heard voices outside the room. As time passed, they grew louder. Metal pans began to clatter. People were starting their day, but they were in a different world from hers. She was lost in the world of evil.

A groan swung her attention back to her captor. He was beginning to move. What should she do? Pretend to sleep or face him with defiance? Neither, she decided. She knew enough about the effects of his hypnotic spells by now to mimic them. She would act as though she was still under his control. She would greet him with a docile smile and pretend she was happy to see him. With luck, he might loosen her bonds and she could escape. Her eyes quickly searched the room for anything she could use to attack him, but she saw nothing more formidable than dirty dishes on the table. She would have to control her fears and bide her time.

The hypnotist swung his legs to the floor and stared at her. Rather than squirming or fighting the gag in her mouth, Marta lay quite still and looked him in the eye. She could see by the way he cocked his head and studied her that he was surprised. *Good*, she thought. *I have him off balance.*

He reached down and untied the gag. Marta coughed and sucked fresh air into her lungs. Oh, how wonderful it felt to be rid of that awful cloth! But she kept her elation hidden and merely turned the corners of her lips upward in a tiny smile. Suddenly, a wave of euphoria swept over her and she nearly succumbed to it. His eyes were probing hers with the precision of a surgeon. She felt their heat burning her. *He's testing me. I must not lose my equilibrium. I must stay calm and submissive.* She lay still and continued to smile.

The man stood up suddenly, revealing spindly legs and a dirty undergarment that probably hadn't been washed in weeks. Marta fought down the disgust she felt at the sight of him. Without his magical powers, he was not so fearful. He was pathetically thin. In the early morning light his face took on the aspect of an aging parrot.

While she studied him, he hastily turned away and pulled on his pants. *He's embarrassed. Women embarrass him.* It was an interesting observation, one that made her think of her brother. For all his blustering and womanizing, Marta had always harbored the suspicion that deep down, Samuel was afraid of the opposite sex although he seemed comfortable with whores. His relationships never lasted long. It also explained why he treated women, including her, with such disdain. It was possible he and the hypnotist suffered from a similar anxiety. But while Samuel was rather good-looking, this man's appearance would repel most women. That might explain his need to control the fairer sex and his obvious disregard for their feelings or well-being.

Her thoughts were interrupted when an elderly woman abruptly opened the door, bowed and entered. Her graying hair was pulled over her ears and secured at the back in a bun. She carried a tray with dishes of steaming food which she put on the table. Her movements appeared tense. She quickly gathered up the dirty plates and glasses and departed. *She's afraid of this man*, Marta thought. That wasn't a good sign. It told her not to expect any help from the Chinese she heard outside the room.

Marta couldn't see what was in the dishes but her growling stomach reminded her that she hadn't eaten since yesterday's lunch. Nor had she gone to the toilet since entering Chinatown. Both needs pressed upon her with equal urgency.

At first, the hypnotist ignored the food. He went to the sink and splashed water on his face, then pushed his fingers through his hair in a manner that Marta found remarkably similar to Samuel's behavior. The similarities between the hypnotist and her brother were disconcerting but she managed to push such thoughts aside for the moment. She had to focus all of her energy on her interaction with her captor. At last, he sat on the only chair and began to shove rice and vegetables into his mouth with chopsticks. She could see he had become quite competent with the wooden sticks. She had tried them herself one time at a Chinese restaurant without much success.

Her heart sank to think she wouldn't be fed. It took all of her willpower to keep from crying out in hunger. Something told her to remain quiet, however. As long as the hypnotist didn't speak, neither would she. So she lay on her side and watched him eat. And said nothing.

Without warning, he rose from the chair and pulled her to her feet. Deft fingers quickly untied the knot that bound her hands behind her back and retied them in front. Next, he removed the ropes from her feet so she was free to walk. To her immense relief, he led her to the toilet, turning away while she did her business. God how good it felt! She had never known such pleasure!

After she was finished, he led her to the chair and pushed her down on the hard seat. The food beckoned her with an aroma that made her taste glands salivate, but when she picked up the chopsticks with her bound hands, she found it impossible to manipulate them. She was tempted to ask him to untie her but bit her lip and remained silent. In desperation, she pushed her face into the bowl of rice and used the chopsticks to shovel the food into her mouth. In this manner, she managed to eat sufficient rice and vegetables to quiet her hunger before he pulled her away.

He led her to his straw mattress. Her heart pounded with alarm. Was he about to have his way with her? He retied her hands behind her and gently sat her down on the bed while her mind ran riot with fear. It took all of her resolve not to shout at him or try to run. He quickly bound her feet, but instead of pressing his advantage, he simply stood over her and stared. Then, he did a strange thing. He reached down and caressed her cheek with the back of his hand. His skin chafed hers and she nearly cringed at his gesture. Somehow, she found the strength to continue her charade and looked fondly at him, all the while praying that he would leave her alone.

The moment of intimacy seemed to last forever, but in reality took less than a minute. By then, the skin on Marta's cheek burned with the ferocity of a thousand splinters jabbing her. Tears filled her eyes. Her body shuddered involuntarily. When she looked away she felt his eyes searching her body for signs of her displeasure. She dared not look at him.

A loud knock at the door shattered the tense silence between them. Her captor spun around and stared at the door. The knock came again, insistent and demanding. She peeked up at him, but his attention was absorbed by the interruption. He moved with hesitation to the door and slid it open just enough to look out. An angry man's voice chattered in Chinese above the babble beyond the door. She could only catch bits of the conversation, but she heard the word tongs repeated more than once.

The hypnotist closed the door and returned to the bed. She tried to look him in the eye, but he ignored her. He pushed her down on the bed and trussed her legs up behind her so she couldn't rise. Then he again stuffed the filthy gag in her mouth. Once he was satisfied that she was securely bound, he threw on a jacket against the morning chill and departed.

Marta had no way to know the time. All she could do was watch the light brighten in the windowless room. The angry visitor and her captor's quick departure worried her. As did the references she heard to the tongs. Images of Missy in that horrid brothel roamed through her thoughts. Was that to be her fate? Was the hypnotist planning to hand her over to the men who ran the filthy place she had seen? A fresh shudder shook her. The idea of strange men's hands touching her skin nearly destroyed the calm she had managed so far to maintain.

Eventually, exhaustion overpowered her thoughts and she slept, only to be awakened by a loud bang from somewhere beyond the door. She drifted off and snapped awake again at some unfamiliar sound. Time passed. The room's brightness began to fade. A feeling of hopelessness enveloped her, a feeling that she had been abandoned. Hunger again began to worm its way back into her consciousness, along with a terrible thirst.

When the hypnotist finally opened the door, Marta greeted him with real joy. A genuine smile broadened her face. Her eyes sparkled with the relief of knowing she had not been forgotten. As before, the man cocked his head. She could see his mind working, trying to decide what to make of her greeting.

Soon, food arrived and she repeated her ritual with the chopsticks. This time, the main course was fish, which presented a challenge due to the bones, but she managed. She was also offered water, which she gulped down. A spark of hope rose in her, but it was quickly snuffed out by the prospect of that horrible brothel, which hung like a dark cloud over her horizon. If that was to be her fate, life would no longer be worth living.

The hypnotist let her do her toilet before leading her back to the bed. The room turned milky grey once more. Objects lost their shape. The voices and banging noises beyond her little world stopped the way chirping birds grow quiet when the light fades. The hypnotist left and returned again, but he didn't try to sleep. He let Marta enjoy the relative comfort of the straw bed. It was lumpy hard, but far better than the wooden floor. Her eyes grew increasingly heavy until she could no longer keep them open. She was only vaguely aware of his leaving again before sleep overtook her.

* * *

It is not yet dawn, but I roam the streets in a fury while I decide what to do. It is the tongs who anger me. They want my latest prize, but I am loath to give her to them. I have complied with their demands until now, but I want to keep this one for myself. I thought she was a witch and I wanted to destroy her. But now that I have touched her soft skin and smelled her midnight hair, I confess I am lost. Perhaps she is a sorceress after all and is bewitching me. I do not care. I must have this one. I must possess her and make her mine.

My voices laugh at me. I have never thought or cared about my victims before. They have been faceless beings whose only value was the amount of money they brought me. The tongs have already offered me more for this one than for any of my previous offerings. They sense how precious she is. I am to deliver her to them this morning. If I fail, I fear they will send their hatchet men for her. I am torn in my dilemma. If I want to keep her, I must abandon my hiding place and flee from Chinatown. But where would I go? San Francisco would not be safe. There is no other place like Chinatown where I could hide the woman from prying eyes. There are cities across the bay. Oakland and Sacramento. Perhaps I could hide with her there.

I know my ideas are impractical. It is impossible to keep someone hypnotized all of the time. Without the drugs provided by the tongs I cannot control her, not unless she wants to be with me. Her look confuses me. I see no fear in her eyes. She doesn't cringe at my touch the way others have. Even the singsong girls show little enthusiasm for my attentions. Yet, this one is different. The welcoming look on her face when I returned yesterday was something I have never seen before. It gives me hope. It makes me believe that I can outwit the tongs. My mind reels at the prospect of denying my employers and keeping her. I must find a way.

CHAPTER TWENTY-THREE

It was a terrible storm. Marta knew this from the way the deck of the Holly Barrett heaved so violently in the waves. She couldn't remember how she boarded the ship, but there she was hanging on for dear life as the swells nearly swallowed her. When the main mast snapped and crashed onto the deck beside her, she feared she wouldn't survive. Sounds of breaking hulls and frightened screams surrounded her. Another severe jolt wrenched her fingers from their grasp and she slid across the wooden deck until she banged into a wall that collapsed, pinning her so she couldn't move. They were shipwrecked, of that there could be no doubt, yet something was amiss. There was no wind, and despite the heavy seas, she was still dry. Where was all the water from the crashing waves?

Marta's eyes flew open to discover darkness surrounding her. The violent motions continued to toss her about, but she knew at once she was not on the Holly Barrett. That had been a bad dream, but waking had not ended the nightmare. It continued unabated. She was trapped under a wall of splintered wood and beams in the

266

hypnotist's room. The floor beneath her still bucked as if a horse were trying to toss her off. My God, she realized, it was an earthquake! Pain raced up and down her legs and chest. Her arms were pinned behind her by ropes. She remembered the hypnotist re-tying them behind her back after she had eaten. The weight from the collapsed ceiling and walls was so great she feared her limbs would soon be crushed. Just when she thought the shaking would never end, it settled into a rolling motion that made her think she was back on that ship at sea. Then another powerful shudder struck and the bucking began again. To Marta's relief, the renewed shaking shifted the weight and relieved some of the pressure that had been crushing her body. She was still unable to move her arms or legs, however.

With a snap of its mighty fingers, the earthquake stopped and the ground lay motionless. Dust choked the air around her, making it difficult to breathe. An odd odor that reminded her of moss-covered trees mingled with the smell of splintered wood. For a few moments, the air was eerily quiet. Then the voices started, the screams and groans and cries of agony. The pleas for help.

Marta desperately wanted to join that chorus, but with the cloth gagging her mouth, she could hardly make a sound. Frantically, she struggled against the weight on top of her, but to no avail. Her body wouldn't move. The groans and cries around her grew louder and more frantic as people began searching the ruins for loved ones. Panic seized her chest when she realized no one would even know she was there let alone where to look for her. Not Byron, not Samuel. No one but the hypnotist knew her whereabouts, but she had not heard a sound from him. She assumed he was dead in the rubble. Unless she could find some way to make herself heard, she faced the prospect of dying alone, in a shattered building in Chinatown. Her thoughts returned to Byron. She prayed he was safe. Thinking of him comforted her. He was all she had and she kept his memory close.

A sliver of early morning light fought its way through the dust and wreckage to where she lay. It revealed a jagged beam of wood near her head that had miraculously missed her. A foot further to the left and she would already be dead. She strained her neck and raised her head far enough to catch the cloth binding her mouth on a sharp point of the wood. Carefully, she worked the point under the cloth near her temple and slowly forced it upward until the cloth slid off of her head. She spit the gag from her mouth and inhaled deeply, only to cough until she nearly retched from the dust laden air assaulting her lungs. When she had recovered her breath, she cried for help. No one answered at first but then a man's voice responded in broken English.

"I hear. No see," he told her.

"Can you follow my voice?" she yelled. "Please, get me out of here."

She heard the man grappling with pieces of wood, but it sounded too far away. "I'm over here," she called. Now that the initial shock of the quake had worn off, she realized the morning was bitterly cold. It had been reasonably warm in the hypnotist's room, but the temperature of the outside air made her teeth chatter. If she didn't get out of there fast, she feared she would freeze to death. "Here," she shouted again. "I'm over here."

Wood clattered as the would-be rescuer moved more debris, but he sounded no closer than before. Then a fresh trembler struck and the ground buckled again. More dust filled the air and fresh material settled heavily on top of her. The aftershock was milder than before but it still flexed its muscles with the strength of a team of runaway horses. The grappling sound stopped. "Are you still there?" she called.

"Alle same, I get help."

"No," she pleaded. "Please don't leave me." She was greeted by silence. The man was gone. She called again, but no one came. The shrieking voices of other trapped people gnawed on her nerves until she realized there were fewer than before. Some had stopped screaming, either because they had been rescued or because they were dead. The latter thought nearly destroyed what little composure she had managed to maintain. She had been trying very hard to remain calm and positive, but the fear of dying had already crept into her thoughts. Death was not an option she was prepared to consider right now however. Escape was uppermost in her mind. Or rescue. Someone would surely come to her aid, wouldn't they? She cried out again and squirmed with a new sense of urgency, but the harder she tried to move beneath the crush of debris, the more obvious it became that she couldn't extricate herself. She needed help.

New footsteps could be heard scurrying past where she lay. Voices sounded with greater urgency. Marta called out once more, but no one responded. Was it her imagination, or were the people running faster?

Then she smelled it . . .smoke. It was faint at first, but clearly recognizable. More feet ran past where she lay. Calls grew more frantic. She didn't have to understand Chinese to know what they were saying. Fire! She was trapped in the rubble of wooden buildings and there was a fire!

* * *

Byron had finally made contact with Captain O'Connor, who promised to return to Chinatown with him in the morning to search for Marta, but that didn't prevent Byron from enduring a restless night tossing and turning in his oversized bed. The bed had always seemed too big and empty, but now it also felt lonely. Lately, he had begun to imagine Marta in bed with him as his wife, and his body had grown warm at the idea. Now that she was missing, the bed felt barren though she'd never laid her head on its pillows.

It was still dark when Byron abandoned his hopeless efforts to sleep and got up. The air was unusually chilled. He quickly threw on warm clothes, uncertain what to do. Finally, he decided to go for a walk. It was something he rarely did, but he found that the crisp air cleared his mind. By the time the first hints of daylight dusted the horizon, he had ventured all the way to Market Street so he decided to keep going. There were three more hours to kill before his rendezvous with Captain O'Connor and Byron was finding the exercise surprisingly invigorating.

Early morning sunlight was just rising from the mists of night and striking the roofs of the fourteen and fifteen floor buildings along Market Street when the buildings began dancing and swaying like palm trees caught in a storm. Before Byron could consider what was causing this magical show, the ground buckled beneath him and tossed him to the pavement. He lay stunned as the ground rose and fell to the rhythm of a head-splitting roar that sounded like a steam engine charging up the street towards him. Buildings crumbled, sending masonry raining down around him. Dust shot up in such great clouds it nearly extinguished the early morning light. Booming sounds echoed along the street accompanied by the musical shattering of glass windows. It was as if an orchestra of violins had been set in motion to answer the thunder of drums.

As the shaking slowed, Byron leaped to his feet while bricks and rocks pounded the pavement around him. He looked up and saw that the sky was filled with falling stones. Frantically, he covered his head with his hands and raced for the doorway of a nearby building that seemed to have survived the brutal onslaught of the earthquake with little damage. A man raced towards him, but before he could join Byron in the safety of the doorway, he was crushed by falling bricks. People ran in every direction, uncertain what to do or how to escape the hell pouring down on them. Byron watched in stunned silence as a great cornice from an old brick building crashed down on a man in overalls who was running with a lunch pail under his arm.

At last, the shaking stopped and the reign of terror ended. People stood in the street shivering in their night clothes in the biting cold air. All around him voices cried, prayed and called for help.

A woman whose clothes had nearly been torn from her body ran up to Byron and threw her arms around his neck. "The world has ended," she sobbed against his chest. He gently extricated himself from her grasp and looked around for help, but no one paid them any attention. The survival instinct had taken hold of some, who hurried down the street towards the Ferry Building in hopes of catching a boat and escaping across the bay. Others were already digging in the rubble looking for victims who were still alive. All Byron could think to do was to put his coat around the poor woman and help her to a curb where she could sit down. He was still dazed himself and uncertain what to do next.

The woman made him think of Marta. He started running down Market Street in the blind hope that she might appear. All he saw were scenes of destruction. In some places, the street was split open in chasms that extended in all directions. A small herd of cattle appeared from nowhere and stampeded along the street, only to disappear into one of the wide fissures. A trolley car lay on its side, its tracks ripped up and twisted as though they were uprooted trees. People wandered past him with blank stares as he continued along the broken sidewalks. He saw men, women and children crawling from the debris, some with help from volunteer rescuers. He soon ran out of breath and slowed his pace. Without his coat, the freezing air attacked him unmercifully. His exertion had initially produced warm pools of sweat under his armpits despite the brisk temperature, but these quickly turned into frosty ponds of moisture that chilled him even more. There seemed little point in continuing in this manner and he did have his own home and staff to think about. There was also the possibility that Marta would turn up there looking for him. Reluctantly, he turned and headed back towards Van Ness Avenue. Behind him, a surreal glow began to dance in the morning light, but he failed to see it.

* * *

Missy awoke to a thunderous roar and a violent rocking motion. At first, she thought someone was shaking her bed, but when she opened her eyes, she saw the ceiling vibrate violently above her head. The entire room was swaying to a nightmarish rhythm that made her head spin so forcefully she couldn't rise. Just off of her room dishes shattered on the floor and pots banged wildly into one another. Those sounds were suddenly overridden by a mighty crash that sounded as if the entire house was falling down.

The motion finally ceased and all was still. Missy lay on her back, too paralyzed by fear to move until she heard a voice crying out from beyond the kitchen. She threw back the blanket and tentatively put her bare feet on the freezing wood floor, fearful that at any moment the shaking would begin again. The air was so cold her breath formed icy puffs as she hastily threw on the clothes she had lazily draped over a chair the night before.

She had just entered the kitchen when a new trembler struck. Her heart leaped to her throat. She screamed and held onto the sink for support as the chimney crashed through the roof in the living room and cascaded in a shower of bricks and timber onto the overstuffed chairs and sofa. The door disappeared in a heap of rubble. By the time the shaking finally stopped, water was sloshing across the floor and soaking the slippers she had slid onto her feet. She retreated to her bedroom and quickly replaced the wet slippers with her shoes, then hurried down the hallway towards the other side of the house where she had heard the voice calling for help. She knew her landlady and two children slept there and she wanted to help them. Her progress was blocked, however, by the collapsed roof.

A strange odor teased Missy's nose, one she associated with the cozy warmth of a fireplace or breakfast cooking on the stove. Who would want to cook at such a time she wondered? No one, she realized. There was a fire burning somewhere and it was not in a fireplace or stove. It dawned on her that she was trapped. To get to the front door, she had to reach the other end of the hallway or go through the kitchen. Both exits were now blocked by the aftermath of the fallen chimney. She looked frantically around for some way out. Then she remembered the window in her bedroom. But the entire room was now slanted at a funny angle and the window wouldn't budge when she tried to open it. Part of the glass had cracked and splintered, but much of it remained intact. Missy picked up her small night stand and threw it through the glass with a shattering crash.

Carefully, she stepped through the opening while avoiding the jagged edges of glass still sticking out from the window frame. Shouting voices along the street greeted her as she stood on the pavement and inspected her arms and legs. As far as she could tell, she was unharmed. Her first feeling was one of exultation at gaining her freedom from the damaged house. But then she looked around at the heaps of timbers and brick that had once been the homes of her neighbors and realized just how catastrophic the demonic shaking had been. A few people had clambered from the ruins and were staggering along the street in a daze or starting to dig for loved ones. New voices joined the chorus of people trapped in the ruins.

The destroyed houses were not the worst of it, however. Just a block or two away, Missy saw smoke funneling into the sky and orange flames cavorting in the tangle of ruins that had once been factories and homes. Her pulse quickened as she hurried around the side of the house to where the other bedrooms were located. To her dismay, that entire portion of the house had collapsed. Her landlady's voice still cried out for help, but Missy had no idea where to begin digging in the upheaval she saw before her.

"I'm comin,' Mrs. Shaw," she called as she started pulling at the boards on top. They were too heavy for her to budge more than a few feet. She shivered in the cold air and wondered what to do. Her only chance was to hurry back to the street to get help. No sooner had she arrived than she saw Patrick running towards her.

"God be praised you're safe," he exclaimed as he took her in his arms. His body warmed her as she clung to him with relief.

"Mrs. Shaw and her children are trapped. You must help me."

Patrick glanced uneasily at the flames. "We haven't much time."

Missy showed him where she thought they should dig. Patrick immediately put his shoulder to the timbers. Together, they managed to shift a few lighter pieces out of the way, but the heavier beams wouldn't budge. More troubling to Missy was the fact that Mrs. Shaw had stopped crying for help and she had not heard a sound from the children. Other voices could be heard from the street, however, frantic voices filled with terror.

"Mrs. Shaw, are you still there? Can you hear me?" Frantically she pawed at the wood as the heat of the approaching fire grew steadily warmer. Fifteen minutes before, she had been freezing. Now, she was sweating profusely.

Patrick put his hand on her shoulder and gently turned her around. "We must go now." He searched her eyes for understanding but saw only grief.

"They are my friends," she sobbed. "How can I leave them?"

He held her close but didn't answer.

A wave of nausea swept over her as she felt the blast furnace heat of the approaching firestorm. Her hair was already hot to the touch. Her skin felt as though it was baking in an oven. Patrick was right. They had to flee or die. She prayed that Mrs. Shaw and the children were already dead. It was a terrible thing to wish for, but it comforted her to hope they would not suffer. She nodded to Patrick and they rushed to the street, which was now all but deserted.

"I have an uncle that lives in a town called Palo Alto," Patrick said. "I think we will be safe there until the trouble is over."

Missy stopped and turned to him. "But what about Miss Baldwin? I must go to her and see that she is all right."

He shook his head. "There'll be time for that later. Right now, we must save ourselves. There might be more tremblins and fires. Our best hope is my uncle's place."

Missy stared at the fire and tried to decide what to do. She didn't want to abandon Miss Baldwin if she needed help, but she could see that the storm unleashed by the earthquake would soon devour not only the office where they worked but everything else in its path. There was no way to stop it. A feeling of helplessness overwhelmed her as she realized there was nothing she could do. Patrick was right. They had to escape while they could. She nodded her agreement and they hurried away from the flames.

* * *

Angela had found if difficult to sleep ever since she had been forsaken and humiliated by her husband, Herbert, so it was not uncommon for her to be up and dressed by dawn. Her second floor apartment, which was comprised of two tiny rooms, never ceased to depress her. She couldn't wait to be gone from it. Thanks to Marta, she had someplace to go during the daytime. She counted the minutes each morning until it was time to head for the warmth of the Pacific Aid Society office. What a stroke of luck it had been to gain Marta's help. Without it, Angela knew she would have gone mad by now.

Her stomach rumbled at her, but she ignored it. She had eaten a sparse dinner the night before and she would have to skip breakfast for, even with Marta's support, she was having a difficult time making ends meet. Food had to be rationed until she paid a few bills. She glanced at herself in the small mirror on her night stand and saw a slightly thinner face. *The one advantage of poverty*, she thought, *was being forced to diet. Soon, she would have her schoolgirl figure back.*

The mirror suddenly flew from the stand and crashed to the floor as a wave of motion swept through the room. Angela cried out in surprise more than fear as she cart-wheeled backwards onto the floor. Her head struck a wooden chair with sufficient force to leave her momentarily dazed and uncertain about what had happened. Ceiling plaster showered her and for a second she thought it was snowing. She tried to sit up but another shock wave knocked her flat again. It was followed by a thunderous roar that seemed to fill her apartment. Something was terribly wrong.

She finally managed to roll over onto her stomach and get to her knees, but the building was twisted so badly she couldn't rise. Then the walls blew out and the floor above collapsed on her. Her last thought was about work. She was going to be late and hoped Marta wouldn't be angry with her.

* * *

I have ventured beyond the streets of Chinatown. It is nearly dawn and the city is almost noiseless. An occasional newspaper wagon clatters along the street or a milk wagon rumbles past. My thin coat offers little protection from the unusual cold that has gripped the night air but I need time to think and to clear my mind. The cold is good for that. It sharpens my dulled senses and helps me clarify what I must do. The tongs expect me to deliver my woman to them today. But once I have done so, what do I do? For the past month, my whole world has revolved around capturing her and now that I have her I don't want to give her up.

There are only two choices: hand her over to the tongs or flee with her. The latter choice is fraught with danger. If I am caught, the hatchet men will plunge their knives into me, for I could not stop them all with my powers. And fleeing is not so easy. Chinatown's streets are filled with inquiring eyes. I cannot just walk away with her. I will need a disguise for us both. The Chinaman across the alley sells old clothing. Perhaps I can hypnotize him and take garments that will help us blend into the crowd long enough to get away. Then we must make a dash for the ferry and cross the bay before the tongs realize what has happened. Once there, I must find a place for us to burrow away from prying eyes. We will be hibernating bears, only this time we will hibernate in summer rather than winter. I cannot keep her tied up, of course. That will mean keeping her close to me at all times so I can hold her under my spell. It is decided, then: *We shall flee.*

Suddenly, I stagger and reel as if the earth has slipped from under my feet! I cannot stand. I am thrown to the ground, my face pressed against the hard, gritty surface of the buckling concrete. I feel I have gone mad. Even my voices cry out in fright. I try to rise but cannot. The ground continues its sickening swaying beneath me. Houses collapse all around me. Roofs cave in, walls crumble and chimneys tumble into the wreckage that only moments before stood as buildings. I know all this without seeing it. I can tell what is happening from the sounds.

At last, the motion calms and my voices quiet. Never have I seen such fury unleashed and I shiver with dread that it will return. Cautiously, I stand up and look about. Everywhere there is chaos. It is as if a giant has stamped his feet on the surrounding houses, for they are smashed to the ground. Telegraph poles have been broken like matchsticks. They lean at strange angles, held up by tangles of wires spitting blue sparks on everyone. Wide wounds have opened in the street. Water floods from one; a deadly odor of gas sweeps from another.

The cold air reminds me of my lair. I yearn to return to its warmth. I desperately search for a familiar landmark to guide me home, but all I see is destruction surrounding me. A chorus of human cries joins the voices that have resumed their clamoring in my head. People run about shouting, not knowing what to do. Others lay trapped in the ruins, their screams pitiful and bleak. Those of us standing are sent reeling by a second great shudder in the ground. The giant still walks among the desolation. More tottering walls fall on those unfortunate enough to be standing too close. This time, I am able to keep my feet under me while I watch more buildings crumble.

I do not know how much time passed, but finally all is still. Mountains of bricks and mortar lie everywhere; legs and arms stick out of them, some still moving. Dazed bystanders move closer together and form small groups for mutual comfort. They shake their heads and nod vacantly at friends. They hug one another. As their sanity returns, they twist their heads this way and that and begin crying out for their missing husbands, wives and children. As realization sinks in, they rush forward and try to pull the living from the ruins, all the while calling the names of their lost loved ones. I watch their anguish with fascinated horror. What is it about the human mind that puts such importance on other people? On family? But am I any different than those I have been observing so contemptuously? What would I do, for instance, if it was *my* father entombed beneath those bricks? I knew the answer to that one. I would pile on more bricks and walk away, laughing.

My mind dances wildly. My voices tell me to run as far away as possible. Thoughts rush through my head like pieces of a dream. Reality strikes me then vaults away again. In the dizzying aftermath of the violence visited upon me, I have momentarily lost the balance of my existence. I have forgotten who I am or what I should do. Then, I remember the woman, who is most likely either injured or dead. She is lying in the ruins of my room. I am torn between running away and going to her. I stand there trying to decide what to do. My voices tell me to flee, yet something deep inside of me says I must find her. Unfamiliar feelings of fear, hope and despair pummel me.

Even as I stand there arguing with myself, I realize that a new abomination has reared its head beyond the nearby piles of debris and humanity, a voracious beast that leaps from place to place with silent cunning and leaves a glowing trail in its wake. It is a demon whose torch turns everything it touches into ghostly reflections of light. At first glance, the lights are a mystery. There, one flares in the morning sunlight in the direction of the wharves, then recedes again. Another radiates from the mission district with the brilliance of the sun now rising over the ruins, but it scurries from sight before those around me can be sure what they have seen. I already know. My keen senses can smell the smoke and feel the heat on my skin. I breathe the ashes that are to come and watch with fascination as spurts of flame play hide and seek in the distance.

A young man finally recognizes the beast and shouts its name: fire! Before the word dies on his lips, a fresh blaze bursts into view. And another, and another! Bright red lips lick at the kindling that was once a wealthy house or a tenement shanty. Social standing no longer matters. The flames do not distinguish between rich and poor. We are all equal before its voracious appetite. We are all its loved ones and it reaches out to embrace us.

I turn and run as fast as I dare through the rubble. My instincts have taken over and propel my feet back towards Chinatown. For I have realized what a wonderful opportunity this disaster has given me. I no longer need worry about the tongs or the long knives of the hatchet men. If they live, they will be as dazed as the others I have seen. They will see the flames and think only of self-preservation. I can escape with the woman. I can take her somewhere safe and wait out this violent storm. If she lives. If she has not been freed and run away.

My legs carry me back to the world that I called my home, but nothing remains standing. It is as if a magician has shuffled cards and thrown them into the air. The cards have landed in a heap of broken homes, shops and joss houses. Where shall I look? All the familiar sign posts are gone. The warrens of gambling hideouts, whore houses and opium dens have been buried beyond recognition. And the fire demon has come. Smoke and flames are clearly visible only blocks away.

Survivors are streaming past me carrying and dragging what they can save from the devastation. They remind me of the scurrying mice in my room. But how to find my room? If I do not hurry, it will soon be too late. I try to stop one man, then another, to ask for directions, but they hurry on with heads bowed and eyes on the ground. I look at faces and finally recognize a neighbor whose shop stood a few doors from my room. I grasp his shoulders and look him in the eyes. I want to hypnotize him and make him show me the way, but my eyes will not focus. They dart and leap like the approaching flames. Fear and desperation have destroyed my powers! My voices laugh at me until I am forced to shake my head to silence them. The man stares at me with an odd expression of sympathy and points out the jumbled lane that leads to where I want to go. Then he lowers his head and hurries on.

* * *

Marta's hope of being rescued had dwindled to a glimmer. Now, only a few voices echoed from the ruins and the smell of smoke was getting stronger. No more footsteps could be heard and no one answers when she calls. Those who remained trapped in the ruins had been abandoned, just like her. She twisted her body in a desperate effort to gain some freedom, but the rubble pressing down on her refused to budge.

Her legs were growing numb from lack of circulation and her mind was slowing down. She found it harder to concentrate on what she should do. The air was so cold she almost wished the flames would hurry closer so she could be warmed by them. That was a stupid thing to wish for! Fire meant certain death and yet she still clung to that glimmer of hope that she might be rescued. She had to keep trying to get help, even though no one answered her calls and her voice was growing weaker.

As the minutes passed and the smell of the approaching fire grew stronger, her mind slowly yielded to the reality of her situation. Her fate had become intertwined with the man who lay buried somewhere nearby. The hypnotist had met his maker and so would she. She was entombed by her fate just as he was. There was nothing to do but face it. Struggling would do no good. Suddenly, death was no longer so frightening.

When she closed her eyes, Byron appeared, and his image comforted her. How fortunate she had been to meet and fall in love with him. She remembered all those fuzzy feelings she had experienced whenever she was around him. And that powerful kiss! If she didn't survive the day, at least she would die with the knowledge of love on her lips. Marta prayed he was safe. Also Lillie, her brother, Missy, and Angela. She prayed for all of them. Her thoughts returned to Byron and that wonderful kiss. She felt it on her lips, again, and looked for his face, but it was too dark to see him. She felt the heat rising from his body, however, and that was enough.

Marta snapped her eyes awake. She had dosed off. It wasn't the warmth of Byron's body she felt but the heat of the approaching fire! The air crackled and snapped with the sounds of hungry flames devouring the wood in its path. Muffled voices were screaming somewhere beyond her prison. They were no longer cries for help but screams of agony. The voices made Marta's heart beat faster, driving fresh blood to her body and brain. *Oh God*, she thought wildly, *why was this happening?* Stop it, she scolded herself. There was no time for self-pity. She had to think clearly. Marta gathered her remaining strength and called out, once more.

"Help me. I'm trapped. Someone, please help me."

At first she heard nothing but the roar of the approaching fire and the dying screams of those already engulfed by them. Then, a scraping noise rose above the din, a clatter of feet on loose boards. Somebody was out there!

"Here," she shouted as loudly as she could. "I'm over here. God, please help me."

There it was again. The sound of feet clambering over shattered wood. The sound came closer. Boards were pushed aside. The light above her head grew brighter. Before she could call again, hands appeared and ripped at the mass of splintered wood that held her captive. The smoke was visible now, thick gray smoke that nearly choked her when she breathed. There was little time. The hands were working rapidly. She felt a shift in the weight on top of her. Suddenly, it was gone! Her legs and arms were free, and someone's arms were reaching around her and pulling her from her tomb.

She gasped with relief as the arms pulled her to her feet. A wall of flame less than a block away nearly blinded her with its fierce, orange-yellow glow and for a moment she couldn't see her rescuer. The heat from the flames pushed the cold air aside and quickly produced a film of sweat on her face and arms. They couldn't stay there much longer, but the ropes chafing her skin prevented her from moving. He swiftly untied the knots that bound her. How deftly his fingers worked. How familiar they seemed. Once her hands and feet were freed, she spun around to face her rescuer. He had moved so she could see him clearly. She found herself staring into the deep-set eyes of the hypnotist! She rubbed her painful wrists and looked at him in amazement. He was alive and had just rescued her from a horrible fate. For a heartbeat, gratefulness overcame anger; relief overwhelmed rage. She stared at his face with a mixture of happiness to be alive and fury for the terrible things he had done.

She saw by the way he tried to focus his eyes on hers that he wanted to hypnotize her, but he couldn't hold his gaze. His eyes darted across her face with the capriciousness of a restless bird. They would settle on hers and then fly off, return and then flit away again. Flashes of pleasure streaked through her body each time he succeeded in arresting his wayward gaze, but the desire to be with him quickly dissipated when he glanced away. He had been undone by the earthquake and for awhile, at least, rendered powerless. Marta's relief at being rescued subsided as anger gained the upper hand. He hadn't come for her because he was concerned about her life. He still wanted to enslave her and have her do his will. The realization made her more determined to escape.

The flames were moving rapidly towards them as they stood facing each other. The hypnotist finally managed to bring his rebellious eyes under control, but their potency remained weak. Marta refused to be deterred by his gaze. She stared into those fearful eyes defiantly, until they blinked and scurried away. Precious seconds remained for them to flee the impending firestorm, yet neither moved. The hypnotist was still trying to bend her to his will and she refused to let him do so. It was a standoff that would consume them both if they didn't end their silent confrontation. A small clock ticked in the back of Marta's head. It told her she was out of time. Her arms were already singed and her clothes heated to the point of combustion. She had to flee now or perish, yet her feet refused to move.

The impasse was broken when the hypnotist turned and took off without warning, leaping over the jagged remains of houses and shops in his bid to outrace the flames. Marta saw a lane to her left that hadn't been completely blocked and ran towards it as the hungry fire roared in her ears. She found firm footing and raced as fast as her wobbly legs would carry her away from the destruction that had once been Chinatown. A flare of light caught the corner of her eye as she ran. She looked over in time to see a fireball of flames leap forward and consume everything along the route the hypnotist had chosen. She looked for any sign of him, but the massive wall of fire obliterated her view.

By the time she had escaped the path of the flames, her lungs were bursting from the smoke she had inhaled and her body was shaking so badly she could no longer stand. She plopped down on a three-legged chair that had been abandoned by the curb and fought to catch her breath.

CHAPTER TWENTY-FOUR

Marta stumbled down Kearny Street in a daze. She was surrounded by scenes of such destruction she thought the city had gone to war. The wall of flames she had escaped was devouring everything between her and the waterfront. Clouds of black smoke buried the sun and turned day into night. The underbelly of the clouds undulated in prisms of pinks and lavenders and orange-yellows that had the appearance of theatrical lighting for a stage. Ahead of her, she saw the tall buildings of the financial district silhouetted against the smoke. Tongues of flame flickered in the upper windows, danced away, then reappeared in a deadly game of hide and seek.

At the intersection of Kearny, Geary and Third Street, the three famous newspaper buildings, the Chronicle, the Call, and the Examiner, had withstood the pounding of the shaking earth. They stood like sentinels guarding a realm that had sunk into chaos. Yet even as Marta admired their strength, yellow light flared in their broken windows and smoke curled up their sides. Soon, flames burst into view as each building succumbed to the madness going on around them.

But it wasn't just the loss of those fine structures that caught in Marta's throat. It was the columns of smoke and flames she saw south of Market Street. The entire Mission District was ablaze, which meant the tenements were being destroyed, along with her Pacific Aid Society. The world she had tried so hard to protect was gone. Poverty had been uprooted by Armageddon. Her benumbed thoughts turned to the hundreds of families she had helped . . . and to Missy who lived among them. She prayed that everyone had escaped to safety, but her own experience told her that was unlikely. The shanties in the Mission District were no different from the ones in Chinatown. Most would have collapsed in the earthquake, trapping untold numbers of residents in the rubble. She thought about the voices she had heard crying around her while she was entombed, how the voices had thinned, weakened and then disappeared as the flames approached her. It would have been the same in the tenements.

Marta said a quick prayer for Missy's safety then turned her attention to her own dilemma. The intense heat from the fires burning around her was sucking the life from the air, thrusting it into the sky with the force of a tornado. Gale-force winds tore away rooftops and sent bricks and sheet iron crashing into the streets below. One sheet banged to the concrete behind Marta with such force she screamed with fright. She wanted to run away from the inferno but discovered she could hardly maintain her balance, let alone flee. The upward thrust of the winds had created a vacuum so powerful it nearly lifted her off the ground. She fell to her hands and knees as the winds whistled about her. She began to crawl towards Grant Avenue dodging hot ashes and grit from shattered bricks that bit her hands and knees, but she forced herself forward. After half a block, the spiraling forces of the winds subsided. Tentatively, she raised herself up and found she could stand again.

Where were the firemen, she wondered? There should be trucks, hoses, men screaming orders and water shooting at the flames.

Their absence dumbfounded her. When she spotted a policeman, Marta rushed up to him. His expression was one of dazed wonderment as he stood in the middle of the street and looked around. He told her the earthquake had broken all the water mains in the city. There was no water. All the firemen could do was stand by and watch helplessly as block after block of houses, factories and offices yielded to the whims of the voracious fires. The only weapon that might check the flames was dynamite, which she heard booming in the distance, but the officer said it did no good. The streets were too narrow to arrest the flames, which nimbly leaped over the dynamited buildings and continued on their way.

When Marta reached Grant Avenue, she saw another scene that defied her powers of comprehension. Thousands of men, women, and children had poured out of the tenements with what meager belongings they could drag or carry and crossed Market Street ahead of the maelstrom. Falling ashes made their faces look like streaked window panes. Some had coats thrown over rumpled pajamas, others staggered along half dressed. Their hair disheveled, faces grimy and clothing ripped, people made their way as best they could. Marta didn't have to see her image in a mirror to know she looked just like the others.

Many of them dragged trunks and suitcases. Others pushed baby carriages or pulled children's wagons filled with clothing and valued possessions. Women carried babies in their arms and slung bundles wrapped in sheets down their backs. Marta saw one woman carrying an ironing board and iron. Another carried an empty bird cage with no bottom. Their glazed eyes and featureless faces told Marta they were as disoriented and lost as she was.

Instinctively, the crowds moved away from the advancing storm in a westerly direction. Now and again, people stopped to discard heavier items to lighten their loads. The heavy trunks were the hardest to keep moving. Men dragged them along the pavement until they were too exhausted to go any further. When they tried to sit down to rest, however, troops with bayonets urged them forward. They grudgingly rose to their feet and continued their struggle, only to collapse again in the next block.

Bands of volunteers hurried along the sidewalks urging people to move to safer ground as the inferno continued its relentless charge behind them. Some of the volunteers had been deputized and carried revolvers to discourage those who might wish to plunder the abandoned buildings. The automobiles that had seemed so fragile under ordinary circumstances now took on a heroic role as they rushed through the streets carrying bloodied and bandaged people to hospitals out of harms way. Marta nodded with grudging respect as they hurried past.

She stopped at the corner of Stockton and Sutter Street to assess what she should do. Her immediate concerns were the status of her house and the safety of those she cared most about. For the moment, Nob Hill sat serenely unaffected by the inferno burning at its feet. Most of the homes she could see were still standing. She hoped Lillie's was not in danger. Marta didn't like the path taken by the flames, however. She prayed the fire would be brought under control before it gathered the strength to charge up the hill. She had no idea how she would find Missy or Angela, but she was relieved to see there was no smoke in the direction of Pacific Heights or Van Ness Avenue. Hopefully, that meant Byron and Samuel were safe.

She decided to join the throngs of refugees headed in the direction of her home. On the way, she would stop to make sure Byron was safe and to ask about Lillie. Before she could start, however, she looked down the street and saw a scene that made her think the city had gone to war after all. The grassy park known as Union Square in front of the St. Francis Hotel was covered with army tents and filled with unfortunate families who had lost their homes. Marta was amazed at how quickly the army had responded. Then it dawned on her that several hours had passed since the earthquake. She stared at the white smoke rising from outdoor cooking fires in the square and realized she was completely disoriented. Time was spinning in circles around her. The holocaust was turning day into night.

One of the more comical sights was the mounds of shipping trunks piled around the square. They reminded Marta of children's building blocks. They looked safe for the moment, but when she looked at the wall of flames marching behind her, she couldn't help wondering how much longer those trunks and the St. Francis Hotel could hope to escape destruction.

Ashes rained down on her while she made her way along Sutter Street. As she moved farther away from the fires, sunlight began to filter through the dense smoke. She could see by the slant of the light that night was fast approaching. The capriciousness of the earthquake was evident everywhere she looked. Some buildings stood so primly on their foundations it seemed the violence had passed them by without a thought. Others had missing walls and roofs. Bricks and stones lay scattered in the streets. Telephone and telegraph poles stood broken and bent over with the same look of exhaustion as the men hauling their trunks. Electrical wires lay everywhere and had to be avoided.

The procession she had joined seemed to go on forever in an endless parade of wheelbarrows, buggies, delivery wagons and people. The trunks were fewer, she noted. Many people had yielded to the fatigue in their bodies and given them up. Despite the magnitude of their losses, Marta was fascinated by the stoic countenance of those around her. None cursed or cried at their misfortune. Some even had a ready smile. They accepted their fate and walked in silence. The one sound that punctuated the air with thundering regularity was the dynamite blasts. It was a sound that should have filled her with hope, but she heard desperation in each explosion that told her hope had fled the fires along with the refugees.

When she reached Van Ness Avenue, Marta was relieved to see the mansions mostly intact. Although some verandas had collapsed and many chimneys were either missing or twisted at odd angles above the roofs, these fine buildings had withstood the blows with far less damage than the wooden structures she had seen earlier. She turned right and hurried as quickly as her tired legs would allow up the broad avenue to Byron's home. Her heart was beating furiously by the time she arrived. She knew it wasn't entirely from her exertion. Thank God the house was still standing! She rushed to the door and knocked loudly. It was opened almost at once by Henry.

"Henry," she cried out with relief, "you're safe. Where's Byron?"

Despite the circumstances, Henry managed to maintain his decorum, but the smile on his face told Marta how glad he was to see her. "Mr. Wagner has been frantic with worry about you, Miss Baldwin. Thank goodness you are all right." He glanced down at his feet, as if to hide his embarrassment at being so forward then returned his gaze to hers. "He has been asked to serve on a Committee of Safety to help direct the affairs of the city during the emergency. They are meeting in the park opposite City Hall. Perhaps you should go there."

Marta desperately wanted so see Byron's face and feel his arms around her but she hesitated. If he was helping address the aftermath of this disaster, she didn't want to interfere. And as badly as she wanted to see him, she also wanted to find out if her home was still standing, and to check on Samuel. "If Byron is involved in disaster relief, it might be better if I don't disturb him. Can you get a message to him and tell him I'm safe?"

"I will send someone at once."

There was one other person Marta needed to know about before she started home. "And Lillie. What have you heard from her?" Her chest squeezed unexpectedly as she asked. She wasn't sure how she would cope if anything had happened to that spirited woman.

"She and her family are fine, madam. A note was delivered this morning." In spite of Henry's desire for proper decorum, Marta heard pleasure in his voice at this good news. It was hard not to like Lillie, no matter how outrageously she behaved.

"Thank you, Henry." She impulsively took his hand and held it. The flesh had the softness of a gentleman's hands. "When you see Byron, please tell him I've gone to check on my house and Samuel. I will look for him this evening."

Henry stiffened slightly at her gesture but made no move to disengage himself. His shoulders relaxed and he pressed his fingers against hers. "It is good to know you are well, miss. Mr. Wagner will be most pleased and will look forward to seeing you shortly."

Marta smiled and released his hand. Henry wasn't such an old reptile after all. But it was more than that. A remarkable camaraderie seemed to have been born out of the crisis. She had seen it in the faces of the refugees and she had felt it in Henry's fingers. People were being drawn together in new ways. Maybe some good would come from the terrible experiences they were enduring. Maybe . . . Well, there was no time to dwell on that now. She had to keep moving, even though her legs refused to listen. There would be time to sit down when she got home, if it was still there. She frowned at the thought.

As Marta joined the refugees pouring west, she realized part of the reason for her improved spirits was the demise of the hypnotist. Each time she replayed in her mind the burst of flames that consumed him, she shivered with relief. A world without the hypnotist would be a far better place, one in which she looked forward to building a new life.

The throng of refugees continued their progression along the major thoroughfares leading to Golden Gate Park and the Presidio. Those green expanses of lawns and gardens were seen by many as the last bastion of defense against the ceaseless energy of destruction that trailed after them like some mindless monster.

Dusk had settled over the city by the time Marta forced herself up the steep street near her home, yet light still dazzled the sky with the brilliance of sunlight from the conflagrations roaring down Market Street and through the neighborhoods where she had been just two hours before. The firestorm had reversed the clock, now turning night into day. She stopped to rest and to look at the holocaust, which showed no signs of slowing. Even if her house was standing, how long would it be before those insatiable flames reached and devoured it? One day? Two maybe? She could already measure the fire's progress during the past few hours and knew it wouldn't take long. The flames were moving relentlessly towards her and there was nothing to block their way.

Still, Marta's resignation couldn't prevent her from crying out with joy when she saw that her home was still standing. The chimney was gone, but good fortune had saved the roof. The chimney had fallen harmlessly into the yard, leaving the house nearly untouched. She was about to mount the steps when she saw a trooper with a rifle walking towards her.

"This your house, ma'am?" the soldier asked in a voice that was as much accusatory as it was inquisitive. He was not yet out of his teens. He held his rifle at the ready. His restlessness made him appear edgy.

Marta eyed him with caution. "Yes, I'm Matilda Baldwin. My brother, Samuel and I live here. Have you seen him?" she asked anxiously.

"He left awhile ago. Said to tell you he'd be back later tonight." The tension eased between them. The young man relaxed his grip on the rifle.

"What are you doing here?" she asked pointedly. The idea of being accosted by a boy with a rifle on her doorstep was disconcerting, even if he did wear an army uniform.

"I'm assigned to this street. We're protecting the area from looters." The young man rested the butt of his rifle on the ground and scratched the back of his neck with his free hand. "Been here since noon. Don't know for certain, but I expect I'll be here the night."

The boy sounded tired. Just like her and everyone else, she thought. The quake and the fire were taking their toll. "Would you like some coffee?" she asked.

His thin lips widened into a smile, which quickly faded. "Can't turn on the gas, ma'am. Your brother checked the house for gas leaks. Didn't smell nothing, but you can't take the chance. Only way to cook is to bring your stove out on the street."

Marta shook her head. "That will have to wait until later." She was about to offer him water until she remembered there was none. It reminded her how long it had been since she drank or ate anything. Marta told the soldier to wait and hastened into the house in search of leftovers. The kitchen looked as though a giant hand had flung pans, glasses and dishes across the room in a fit of temper. Marta foraged through the mess until she discovered a plate of chicken scattered on the floor and a container of milk that had miraculously escaped destruction. Quickly, she found two cups with broken handles and a board for cutting bread. She arranged part of the leftovers on the board and took it and a cup of milk to the soldier, who thanked her profusely. She smiled as he devoured the food and gulped down the milk. Then she turned and hurried back into the house for her own meal.

After she had satisfied her hunger and thirst, Marta wandered through the house with a sense of foreboding. She hadn't asked the soldier if it was safe to light candles, so she left the house cloaked in an eerie semi-darkness where shadows danced and flared against the backdrop of the flames slowly chewing their way through her beloved city. Even in the uneven light, she saw the fallen plaster and cracks in the walls. Items on tables had tumbled over. It was minor damage, however. The house's structure seemed to be intact, including the roof. Most of the windows were undamaged as well, which she found surprising.

Yet her home wasn't safe. Golden tongues of flame were marching towards it as relentlessly as an army across a battlefield. She had saved it from those horrible bankers, only to see it face almost certain destruction. If the flames couldn't be halted, there were practical matters to consider, such as removing the valuable paintings and jewelry. She didn't know how to save the larger paintings. Even with Samuel's help, she didn't think they could carry them down the hill to the Presidio. She sighed when she thought about the Turner landscape she loved so much. It would probably be lost.

The muffled sounds of dynamite interrupted her thoughts. The soldiers were still trying to slow the advancing flames by creating firebreaks. She noticed that there were fewer explosions than before, however. They were either running out of dynamite or giving up hope.

Marta couldn't take her solitary confinement in the house any longer. She went into her bedroom and retrieved a few pieces of jewelry with value, hiding them under her skirt. She returned to the

291

street but there was no sign of the soldier or Samuel, so she pointed herself in the direction of Van Ness Avenue again and hurried down the hill in search of Byron. This time, Henry nodded when he answered the door and led her to the drawing room.

There, lighted candles softened the sharp edges of trauma visited upon the house by the earthquake. Her eyes roamed the room and noted the extent of the damage. Fallen plaster, cracked walls, broken vases. It looked much the same as her place. She was sorry to see that the small mantle clock she had admired was now lying in a dozen pieces on the floor.

Moments later, Bryon rushed into the room and threw his arms around her, hugging her so closely she nearly gasped for air. He stood back with his hands on her shoulders and looked at her. "My God, where were you yesterday and last night? I looked everywhere . . . I feared something dreadful had happened to you. And then this . . ." He gestured at the room. His face had a ravaged look about it. His skin had a gray cast and his cheeks were drawn with worry and fatigue.

Marta's heart ached for him. If there had been any lingering doubts about his feelings for her, the look on his face banished them forever. She put her arms around him and drew him close again. He held her tightly and kissed her so fiercely she nearly fainted. The warmth of his body, the caress of his hands and the jolt of his lips on her skin engulfed her as surely as those flames would have done if the hypnotist had not rescued her.

She nearly told Byron about her kidnapping and the close call with the flames but decided this was not the time. When she thought about the hypnotist, however, the deep well of passion that was boiling within her subsided. Again and again she replayed the scene in her mind of that fireball consuming the spot where the hypnotist had been. It seemed impossible that anyone could have survived, yet when she closed her eyes, there were his, darkened by the flames but still glowering with evil. The eyes stared at her with such a relentless ferocity for a moment she feared the man was there in the room with them. She pulled back her head with a gasp.

Byron interpreted her sudden retreat as a need to regain her footing and released his hold on her waist. "I hope I wasn't too forward," he said softly.

Marta looked at the worry lines in his face and thoughts of the hypnotist vanished. She smiled and touched his cheek. "I hope you will always be that forward, Byron. It feels just right." She leaned forward and kissed him again, more slowly this time, but with the same passion.

"How is your home?" Byron asked when they finally parted. He walked her to the sofa as he spoke and sat beside her.

"In one piece, but a mess like yours." She nodded at the room.

"It may look much worse before long I'm afraid." Byron said this matter-of-factly, but Marta heard tension in his voice.

She turned and looked at him. He sat forward, his posture uncomfortably stiff. Without his pipe, his hands moved restlessly over his pants legs. He interlaced his fingers in an effort to keep them still. Marta didn't know which to inquire about first, the loss of his pipe or his comment. "What do you mean, Byron? What about your house?"

"Initial plans are being drawn to dynamite all the houses along the east side of Van Ness. All the way from Golden Gate Avenue to Pacific Avenue. That includes mine, of course." Byron's shoulders drew inwards as he spoke. It made him look quite vulnerable. Marta had a sudden urge to hold and comfort him, but fought the impulse. Byron wasn't looking for sympathy.

"Whatever for? Dynamite hasn't worked elsewhere."

"Van Ness is the widest boulevard in the entire city. By dynamiting the houses on the side of the approaching fire, a much broader firebreak can be created, one wide enough to stop the flames, or so it's hoped."

Marta looked around the room again. She couldn't say she liked the idea of living in such a big house, but she had grown fond of its architecture and grand style. "Byron, I'm devastated to hear you might lose your home."

"Well, as I told you before, I have never felt particularly attached to this place. Of course it would be quite a financial loss, but the way the fire is expanding, it's only a matter of time until it is destroyed anyway. Better to blow it up, if it helps save the homes of others."

It was true, she realized. If Van Ness Avenue did stop the advancing flames, *her* home would be saved. The irony of the situation nearly made her cry. Marta reached out and took his hand. "If destroying your home saved mine, I should feel very guilty."

Byron squeezed her hand. "If I can save your home, I shall be most pleased. But come," he stood as he spoke, "I was about to walk to Nob Hill to learn how Lillie is coping. I fear it won't be long before the fire reaches her home, as well."

* * *

Marta had lost all track of time. The dancing glow of daylight produced by the fire made it impossible to tell how quickly the hours were passing. Not that it mattered. She was much too alarmed by the day's events to think about sleeping. Her tired body rebounded at the idea of seeing Lillie.

She and Byron made their way through the rubble along California Street, where a steady stream of refugees continued to move west away from the fire. Marta estimated that their numbers had diminished since she joined them earlier. Now, they were headed back towards the very center of the maelstrom, which continued to brighten the sky with angry hues of color. The fire had become a fiery beast with a great jaw of jagged teeth, blazing arms and venomous eyes. Eyes like the hypnotist's. The wayward reflection spun inside her head and forced her thoughts inward. His eyes still haunted her causing her to wonder at their meaning. The hypnotist had died in the fire. She had seen the ball of flame explode in his path. Yet, she swore she saw his eyes in the wall of fire approaching her. It was as though they had come face-to-face again, while the fire blew its torrid breath upon them. The idea chilled her despite the inferno's heat, and she felt a wave of weariness sweep over her. There could only be one explanation for the upheaval she felt. The hypnotist still lived and was close by.

She felt his malevolent eyes upon her skin. *No you cannot*, Marta declared under her breath. She shook her head and instinctively took Byron's arm for protection. The hypnotist was dead and that was the end of it.

Byron glanced at her but said nothing. They were climbing a steep grade now and would soon stand atop Nob Hill. All was quiet there. Soldiers patrolled the streets with rifles on their shoulders. Watchmen stood in the doorways of the fine houses, ready to fend off the curious and those bent on looting the treasures locked inside. The demon fire was only blocks away and was methodically working its way towards them. Marta's heart sank when she looked at the flames. They had progressed dramatically since she fled them, and now nothing stood between them and Nob Hill.

When they reached the top of the hill, Marta saw several men transporting paintings from the Mark Hopkins Institute of Art to the Fairmont Hotel across the street. Byron queried why and was told the hotel was reputed to be fireproof. They hoped to save the institute's precious art collection.

"I doubt any building will stand up to that fire," Byron remarked to Marta as they headed for Lillie's mansion. Only a handful of people could be seen wandering about. It was tranquil on Nob Hill despite the roaring beast below. The peaceful interlude was abruptly interrupted by twin explosions echoing up the hill. "The dynamite isn't working in those narrow streets," Byron added grimly. "I do believe Van Ness will be our only chance to prevent this holocaust from sweeping all the way to the sea."

A carriage with two horses stood outside Lillie's mansion. The horses pawed nervously at the ground and snorted while servants rushed back and forth with trunks, vases, statues and paintings. The collectibles were being piled into the carriage with little forethought or organization. Horses and people alike sensed the approaching doom and were anxious to be on their way. Lillie stood in the doorway supervising everyone. She was dressed in her fireman's costume from the ball and puffing from exertion.

"Lillie," Marta called out. "Only you could keep your sense of humor at a time like this."

Lillie gave her a tight smile and rushed down the steps to embrace her. "Hell, darlin', it seemed the only appropriate thing to wear, considering our world is coming to an end." Her voice was as tight as her smile. Worry lines plowed her brow like rows of freshly planted corn. "Come inside and have some tea. We still have time before we must evacuate this place."

"I fear the flames will be here soon enough," Byron commented sadly as they walked into a vast sitting room adorned by paintings as great as those being taken from the Mark Hopkins Institute. Candles gave the room an uneven glow. A grand piano stood across the room, and tapestries graced the wall behind it. A crystal chandelier as grand as the one at the opera house hung, unlighted, from the ceiling. Everywhere, Marta saw the trappings of great wealth, soon to be reduced to ashes. It was funny in a way. The fire was destroying a great city and with it the social order that had defined it for more than a generation. Fortunes were being lost, heritage decimated and lives ruined. She had no doubt that new fortunes would be made, but would society's glittering image return? She didn't think so, at least not as before. She found it strangely sad. As much as she had disliked the ostentatious face San Francisco's society had presented to the world, it had represented a golden era that would be missed. "Where will you go?" she asked.

"Mother has gone ahead to the Hensleys. We shall join them and be your neighbors, Byron." Lillie wiped her brow and called to one of the servants. "Not that rug. Take the Persian one over there." She returned her attention to her friends. "God what a mess. I can only save a few items. Most will be destroyed, and our fortunes shall be greatly reduced. Which is good news for me, I suppose. Mother will no longer be able to afford a British Lord or French Count for me to marry." She laughed at the thought, but the laugh had a tinny sound and was too high pitched. Marta heard anguish in it and knew her friend was hiding deeper feelings of despair behind her bravado.

"I'm afraid you may not be our neighbor for long," Byron told her. "If the fire cannot be stopped, they plan to dynamite the homes on my side of Van Ness Avenue."

Lillie accepted a tray from her servant and poured the tea. "So, the rumors are true, then. I'm sorry to hear it, Byron. I have always loved your house." She looked around her. "As I have loved mine. Well, if we must keep moving, I suppose we can find sanctuary at the Presidio."

"Nonsense," Marta said as she accepted a cup from her friend. "If the fire *is* stopped at Van Ness, my house will be saved. It is not so grand, but there is plenty of room for you all. You will be welcome there for as long as you like."

Neither said a word, but their heartfelt thanks were written across their tired faces. Marta felt a rivulet of water dripping down her neck and realized she was sweating. Heat was building in the room. The roar of the pyrotechnic beast was growing louder. The night-turned-day was getting brighter.

"It's time to go," Byron remarked.

No more needed to be said. For a few, brief moments, the three had enjoyed a semblance of normalcy, but the approaching inferno would not be stayed. They put down their teacups and rose as one to face the hell awaiting them.

Flames advanced on two sides as they hurried down California Street in a caravan of servants, horses and carriage and trunks. The troops and watchmen were gone, except for a lone cavalryman silhouetted against the flickering yellow light where he sat on his horse like a statue on top of the hill. Ashes rained down on their heads. Flames sprinted up the hill to their left amidst a chorus of crackling sounds and loud thumps as chimneys collapsed and roofs caved in.

They joined the progression of remaining refugees and slowly worked their way back to Van Ness Avenue, where Byron announced himself to the soldiers patrolling the wide boulevard. Lillie promised to join Marta later and headed off with her entourage. She never once looked back at Nob Hill, but Marta did and saw a ring of fire sitting like a fiery crown on its peak.

Marta was suddenly too tired to stand and accepted Byron's offer of a bed where she could sleep. Dawn was imposing its will on the fire's colors by then and the sky was turning from rose-pinks and yellow-gold to a dingy gray. It was Thursday morning, twenty-four hours since the earthquake struck. In that time, the once proud city had become a wilderness of ravaged buildings, charred ruins and homeless people. Yet, despite the suffering and loss of human life, there was no end in sight. The fiery beast still snapped at the heels of the retreating masses. It continued to glower over its domain with the countenance of a warring king not yet satisfied with his Pyrrhic victories.

Marta lay down on the bed fully clothed and instantly slipped into a whirlwind of fiery light.

* * *

A burst of noise shook Marta from her deep slumber. She awoke to the smell of ashes and smoke and knew at once that the source of the sound was dynamite. The army was continuing its desperate effort to stem the tide of the storm blazing nearby. Only this time, the blasts were closer and louder. Fearing they had started to destroy the homes along Van Ness Avenue, she leaped from her bed and rushed down the hallway, where she was greeted by a mini-storm of activity as servants scurried back and forth with linen and containers in which they were wrapping the mansion's most precious possessions. She stepped outside and saw a new nightmare come to life. Vast billows of smoke covered the sun in a flaming rainbow of colors, just as they had the day before. But the flames seemed to have grown taller during the night and they were much closer. Not close enough to threaten the mansions yet, but they soon would be. It was only a matter of hours, now. And the dynamite she heard wouldn't stop them.

Marta hurried back inside to look for Byron. She found Henry supervising the servants much as Lillie had done the night before, but with far greater efficiency. His disheveled appearance spoke to the impending crisis more eloquently than either the clouds or the approaching wall of flames. His face was covered in sweat and grime. Shirt sleeves were rolled up. His hair was so badly mussed, it was evident neither a brush nor comb had touched it. As if to add a touch of the dramatic, dark stubble had magically appeared on his face overnight.

What shocked Marta the most, however, was the revolver Henry held in his hand. "Looters," he said in response to her inquiring expression. "Three men tried to enter the house next door a short while ago. I chased them away." He opened a small drawer in the entryway table and slid the weapon inside. "Shouldn't need it any longer, I imagine. In a few hours, the looters can have what they want."

"Where's Byron?" Marta asked anxiously as she eyed the drawer. The revolver reminded her of the young soldier brandishing his rifle outside her house. She had never been so close to firearms before.

"Master Wagner has gone to another safety committee meeting," Despite his bedraggled appearance, Henry maintained his decorum with amazing aplomb. "He thought you might want to look for your lady companions and suggested you go to Golden Gate Park. It seems that is where most of the people south of Market Street have gone to seek shelter. I expect we shall head for the Presidio."

Marta fished in her pocket for her house key and handed it to Henry. "I have already told Byron you will do no such thing. Take everything to my house and wait there. If the dynamite plan is a success, my place will be spared and you will all be welcome to stay there as long as needed. I will join you after I've had a look around Golden Gate Park."

Henry took the key with his usual politeness, but Marta couldn't help smiling when a bit of color rose beneath the day-old growth on his face. "There is food on the table, Miss Baldwin," he said softly. "Please help yourself before leaving."

At the mention of food, Marta's stomach growled. The small meal she had enjoyed at her house had hardly stemmed the tide of her hunger. She realized she was famished. She decided to visit the bathroom first, however, and gasped in surprise when she looked at herself in the mirror. Her hair sprouted like wild vines and a dusty layer of grime covered her face. Her state of disrepair was even worse than Henry's.

She wiped her face as best she could without water but didn't attempt to do anything with the hair. No one cared, anyway. There were more important things to consider than how one looked.

When she returned to the foyer, Henry had a plate of fruits and meats waiting for her. She gobbled them down with a rapaciousness that surprised her. He also offered a tall glass of freshly squeezed orange juice that tasted like liquid gold in her throat. Refreshed, she gripped his arm to show her appreciation and gave him her address before hurrying out the door.

Caravans of refugees still trudged towards the Presidio and Golden Gate Park as people continued to retreat from the advancing holocaust. A few carriages passed and an occasional automobile sputtered down the avenue. However, most people slogged along the buckled pavements like foot soldiers on a forced march. Faces were drawn; shoulders sagged; backs bent forward. Their numbers had thinned, Marta noted and they dragged fewer trunks. Guilt sidled into her conscience as she thought about the delicious food and juice she had just bolted down. Most of these stragglers had very likely not eaten in the past twenty-four hours and may not even have found drinking water.

She joined their ranks and started the long walk to the park. Her fatigued leg muscles immediately pleaded with her to stop, but she ignored the pain and pushed herself forward. Soon, she was slogging along just like the others. Sprinkled among the crowd were servants carrying household belongings and people dressed in tailored clothes. Their silk dresses and wool suits were tarnished, wrinkled and dirty. Their white shirts and faces were streaked with soot. The wealthy were fleeing the flames in less than the grand style to which they were accustomed.

Marta's sore leg muscles aggravated her as she walked, but there was a different sort of discomfort tugging at the back of her neck that bedeviled her even more. She could have sworn someone was watching her, yet when she swung her head around, no one presented himself. All she saw were the same tired faces as before. When the uneasy feeling persisted, she looked again, but saw the same sea of unfamiliar faces. Shaking her head, she faced forward and continued down the street.

CHAPTER TWENTY-FIVE

A premature dusk had descended by the time Marta reached Golden Gate Park. She guessed it was mid-afternoon, but the smoke obscuring the sun made it difficult to be certain. At the park's entrance stood a billboard twenty feet tall and a hundred feet long covered as high as people could reach with hastily written notes and business cards. Each sought a loved one and many gave locations for a rendezvous. She thought about leaving a note for Missy and Angela, but decided it was hopeless. It would take hours for anyone to read all those messages.

When she entered the park, she was greeted by scenes of chaos. People milled about looking for loved ones or someone of authority to tell them what they should do. Rows of white, military tents had been erected. They bore names such as "Camp Thankful," "Camp Glory," and "Camp Hell." Most of those arriving, however, had to get by with makeshift shelters made out of sheets, rugs and curtains. The result was a landscape that looked more like a giant quilt than a lush park. Bricks used to create cooking stoves were stacked across the lawns. Pieces of broken mirrors used for personal grooming were tied to trees. One woman was roasting a swan captured from a nearby lake. A Chinese man who wanted to start a fire in his pile of twigs asked each passerby "catchee match?" A woman with a parasol sat before a blanket spread on the lawn as if she were waiting for a Sunday picnic. There were few distinctions left between rich and poor, however. Society had been ground down to the level of the common folk by the earthquake and the fire.

Marta moved methodically through the maze of people and shelters while she looked for her friends, but it wasn't Missy's red hair or Angela's heart shaped face that caught her attention. It was an angular arm nearly lost in the blur of humanity and a long, thin leg that appeared disjointed when its owner took a step. A warning bell sounded in the back of her mind. She turned and pushed through the throng to the spot where the man had stood, but whoever she had seen was gone. She recalled the tingling sensation on her neck as she walked to the park. At the time, she would have sworn someone was watching her. She had the same feeling now. There was only one person who could affect her that way. But that was impossible. No one could have survived the inferno that enveloped the hypnotist. No one human, that is.

She told herself she was being silly, but she couldn't escape her intuition that something strange was happening. She felt a presence out there, and no matter how crazy it seemed, she feared the hypnotist still lived.

* * *

They are all gone and I have taken refuge in their house. What a fine house it is! A mansion as I have never before seen. With endless rooms and enough food for a banquet. Now that Chinatown has been destroyed, this house has become my hideaway. It is a miracle that I am here at all. I stayed too long trying to hypnotize the woman and the flames came too close. The fire's roar deafened me, yet she refused to move. What a magnificent woman she is! How fiercely determined to face me down. I was the one who finally broke away, but by then it was too late to outrun the fire. Its scalding tongue licked the backs of my legs and singed my hair as it prepared to consume me. Somehow, I stumbled into a cellar whose roof had partially collapsed, and I curled up beneath its ruins. The flames tried to reach me but only succeeded in touching my face, which is now blistered on one cheek. For awhile the heat was so intense I could not take a breath and thought my blood would boil, but the fire finally gave up its pursuit of me and moved on, letting me breathe again. I crawled out of my hole in time to see the woman run safely away from the flames. Had she kept running, I should have lost sight of her, but she stopped to catch her breath. That gave me time to slip through the ring of fire before she disappeared and to follow her.

I trailed her to the house that had been filled with furious activity earlier, but that stands empty, now. Men are busy in the street outside and police stand guard. I do not know what they are doing, but as long as they leave my sanctuary alone, I don't care. I have discovered a way into the house from the back without being noticed. So, I come and go as I wish.

The fire is creeping closer, of course. I know this by the changing smell of the ashes. They are growing warmer as they rain down from the sky. They carry the odor of burning flesh. The fire bedevils me. It weakens my powers and chases me from place to place. It is only a matter of time before I have to move again, but not until I have recaptured the woman. I followed her to the park where she nearly spied me. There was no need to stay so close. I could see she was looking for her friends and would be there awhile.

The most joyous news is that my powers are slowly returning and my near-death experience has strengthened my senses. I will have no trouble finding the woman again. She is like a delicate flower whose pollen draws me to her.

For now, I am content to prepare a room for my flower. I have cleared the fallen plaster from the bed and turned down the covers. Candles await my match. There's even a bottle of fine champagne on the night stand. It is warm, but that doesn't matter. The mood has been set nicely and once she is under my powers, she will appreciate what I have done. We shall enjoy a special night together before the fire arrives. Speaking of night, it is fast approaching. I can tell because the light from the fire grows brighter. It is time to go collect my prize.

* * *

Marta had spent a fruitless afternoon looking for Missy and Angela among the refugees crowded into the park. More army tents had been erected but not enough to accommodate all of the new arrivals. Lines were forming for everything. When people saw a new line, they rushed to join it without knowing its purpose. Food, water, bedding, it didn't matter. Every handout was gratefully accepted. Marta was aghast to see three mean-spirited, young men start a line where nothing was being offered. Soon, dozens of people stood patiently behind them. The pranksters then quietly slipped away.

At day's end, Marta gave up her search and turned with a heavy heart towards home. There had been no sign of her friends. All she could do was pray they were safe. Her mood brightened when she thought about Byron and Lillie. They should be settled into Marta's house by now. How very much she looked forward to seeing them. She wondered if Samuel was home. If so, she could imagine his surprise at the entourage of elegant people arriving on his doorstep.

She had kept a careful lookout for any more signs of the hypnotist, but had seen none. Perhaps it had only been her imagination, but she couldn't forget the odd looking arm and leg she had noticed in the crowd. She felt vulnerable as she started the long walk up Fillmore Street towards her house and wished she still had her omamori.

Most of the refugees had found a place to bed down for the night, yet the street was still busy. Several families had moved their cook stoves outside and were preparing dinner. Children ran in circles playing firemen and soldiers. An occasional trooper with a rifle wandered past. The wall of flames was still distant enough from these neighborhoods to be tolerated, if not ignored. Everyone knew by now about the plan to blow up the homes on Van Ness Avenue. There was hope in the air, at least for those fortunate enough to live west of Van Ness.

Marta's mind was filled with these thoughts as she entered a quieter block. It appeared that most of the people living there had decided to take no chances and had moved their belongings out of harm's way. Homes here stood eerily silent. No children played, no candles burned in the windows. No troopers were visible. Without the squeals of children and sidewalk chatter among neighbors, Marta could hear the crackling noises of the fire more clearly. The stillness along the street pricked her skin. She grew tense.

A sudden noise shattered the silence behind her. Marta leaped into the air with fright and whirled around. Her heart hammered in her chest as she frantically scanned the street for any sign of danger. All she saw was a large dog shoving its nose through the debris from a trashcan it had just overturned. Marta gasped at the sight and laughed a bit hysterically.

I'm a bundle of nerves, she thought as she quickened her step along the street. *I've got to get a grip on myself.* But when the silence returned, she couldn't prevent herself from searching every shadow for signs of danger. The air breathed as if it had come alive. Heavy puffs stirred the tiny hairs at the back of her neck until she swore someone was standing right behind her. She looked around nervously. It was getting late and she was very tired, but she couldn't shake the feeling that she wasn't alone.

Marta increased the pace of her walk and had nearly reached the end of the block when a hand clamped over her mouth and an arm snaked around her body. Before she could react, she felt herself being dragged from the street towards the empty houses. She smelled the now familiar stench of fish in her nostrils and knew her worst fears were being realized. How was it possible? The hypnotist should be dead. She struggled to free herself from the hard body pressed against hers, but it wouldn't yield. A muffled scream rose in her throat and died.

Once they were hidden from the street, she was spun around and forced to come face-to-face with her nightmare. She found herself staring into the baneful eyes of the hypnotist. Marta knew she must escape, but the will to run was already being sapped from her legs. She tried to look away, but his hand gripped her jaw and held it firmly. His dark pupils focused on hers with a fierce intensity. This time, the eyes did not blink or dart away. They remained strikingly clear. Her mind was already sinking into his universe and try as she might, she couldn't free herself. Marta's thoughts slowed to a crawl. Her fear vanished and the world became calm. Why was she trying to resist this man? He brought her such wonderful peace.

She saw the blisters on his cheek and remembered the fireball she thought had consumed him. Somehow, he had survived, and that filled her with joy. She couldn't imagine living in a world without the hypnotist. He motioned for her to begin walking in a new direction and she gladly obeyed.

They walked at a brisk pace along California Street until they reached Van Ness Avenue, where Marta saw men entering homes with wires and packages of dynamite. Police officers were busy keeping curious onlookers at a safe distance. Somewhere in the recesses of her brain she knew something important was about to happen, but she couldn't pull the explanation to the surface of her mind. She also knew she ought to call the policemen for help but couldn't understand why. Nothing made any sense.

One of the policemen waved them across Van Ness and they continued on their way. Once they were out of sight of the workers and officers, the hypnotist led her through a series of elegantly landscaped back yards to Byron's house. She had never seen his yard before, but she knew instinctively the house was his. She sensed his aura around the place. The hypnotist took her hand and guided her inside. He led her past the foyer, where she saw the front doors secured with wires and dynamite. More wires ran off in three directions to other parts of the house. Seeing the explosives sparked a sliver of memory. The dynamite was there for a reason and it wouldn't be long before those workers outside blew the place apart. When that happened, anyone inside would be blown apart as well and buried in the rubble. A voice in the recesses of her mind told her to flee the place, but her desire to be with the hypnotist was stronger. She turned away from the explosives and followed him.

He either had not noticed the danger or had chosen to ignore it. His full attention remained focused on Marta as he led her down a long hallway to a grand bedroom with an oversized poster bed and small couch. This was Byron's room, Marta realized. Despite her befuddled mind, she blushed to think she was in his bedroom. She could feel his presence all around her and this confused her even more. Her captor led her to the bed and lit candles while she lay down. *Why did she think of this man as her captor? Wasn't he the one she wanted to be with?* When she thought about the question, the hypnotist's face slid away and Byron's swam into view. *That* was the man she wanted. Then why was she with this man? Her mind was too clouded to answer her questions. All she could do for the moment was obey his wishes.

She lay down on her back and lifted her arms to the ropes he had prepared for her wrists. Once her arms were secured to the bedposts, he sat down beside her and opened the bottle of champagne resting on the nightstand. The cork released with a sharp pop, and frothy liquid squirted across her chest and arms. The man quickly filled two glasses. When he was done, he lifted her head and poured champagne into her mouth. Fuzzy warmth coated her throat as she swallowed and her head spun out of control. She lay back in a dizzy state of mind and watched her companion drink his champagne. He smiled at her and licked his thin lips. It wasn't a warm smile, not the kind of a smile she associated with Byron. It was cold and scaly. It reminded her of a dead fish.

He went to the bathroom and returned with a towel to wipe the spilled champagne from her dress. Rather than wiping, however, he began caressing her in circular motions that Marta found disturbingly erotic. She knew instinctively that she should resist his advances, but when his hands rubbed her breasts, her body tingled in a most pleasurable way. The fuzziness caused by the champagne disoriented her. She thought it was Byron's hands exciting her, but they didn't feel right. She couldn't make sense of her conflicted feelings, why she wanted to moan with pleasure and cringe at the same time.

Then, the room shook from a nearby explosion. The shock of the blast snapped Marta's mind back into focus. She tried to rise but couldn't. Her wrists were bound to the bed, and the hypnotist sat astride her, his hands on her breasts and his head twisted away as he tried to fathom what had just happened. *My God,* she realized, *he's assaulting me and the soldiers are dynamiting the houses.* She was about to be deflowered and blown up at the same time. Neither fate appealed to her. She had to do something fast.

The hypnotist turned back to her with eyes that darted and swooped across her face. The explosion had frightened him, just as the earthquake had before. Marta worried he would leap from the bed and rush from the room, leaving her to face almost certain death once again. Her mind raced through her options. She had to keep him there and convince him to let her go. That meant keeping her nerves under control. She forced herself to lie quietly on the bed and smile at her captor. She concentrated her gaze on his and willed him to look at her. Slowly, she calmed his wild eyes and drew them back to hers. A feeling of power rose in her as she stared at him. Somehow, their roles had become reversed. His fear had not only unraveled his ability to hypnotize her, it had tamed him to the point that she could influence him! The tension in his body relaxed and he returned her steady gaze with renewed interest. His hands began to caress her once more.

Marta could think clearly now and knew what she had to do. "You must untie me," she remarked as calmly as she could. Her voice reverberated in the room. She hadn't spoken to him since the day she accosted him on the street and drove him away from his intended victim. How many weeks ago had that been? It seemed an eternity.

Startled, he stopped his hands and stared at her in confusion.

"If you don't untie me, I can't touch you," Marta said with all the seductive charm she could muster. She feared it wouldn't be enough. It was all she could do to maintain her placid demeanor. Her smile nearly slid into a grimace. She managed to hold it in place, however, even though her lips trembled.

At last, recognition spread across the hypnotist's face. She could see the idea of her hands on him working its way down his angular features. His eyelids fluttered. His burned cheek twitched. He was more composed now, but Marta knew it was a fragile peace. She could tell by the way his arms tensed and his body coiled that he was ready to bolt out the door. She prayed another explosion wouldn't rock the house until he had freed her.

He abruptly reached for the ropes.

Marta gasped inwardly with relief as first her right hand and then her left were released from their bondage. Her ordeal was far from over, however, for he still sat astride her and waited expectantly for her to fulfill his wanton wishes. His body weighed heavily on her waist and thighs. It would be impossible for her to push him off with just her hands, and even though she had gained some control over the situation, she sensed her control of him was too fragile to risk any sudden move. She rubbed her wrists and tried to think what to do. If she didn't show him the affection she had promised, he would tie her up again. But she didn't think she could bring herself to caress him the way he wanted. Her nails dug into her palms as sweat poured from her body. Desperately, she looked about for an answer to her dilemma and found it in the champagne bottle sitting nearby on the night stand.

"Let me pour us some more champagne," she said and started to reach for the bottle. It was just beyond her grasp. To get it, she would have to turn her shoulders and stretch her arm to its limit. He frowned and warily followed her movement. His body was coiling again. Marta sensed he was about to reach out and stop her. She had to think of something to distract him. "Could you hold the glass for me? I want to pour you some." She forced her smile wider and nodded towards the two glasses beside the bottle.

Marta had heard of moments when a person's whole life hung by a thread: a hunter facing a charging rhino with time for only one shot, a boat on the verge of capsizing in a terrible storm. Marta was facing such a moment now as the hypnotist reached towards her hand. Her heart slammed against her chest and moisture stung her eyes. She forced herself to continue reaching calmly for the bottle as if it were the most natural to do, but all the while her terrified eyes following the direction of the man's hand as it moved towards hers. If he grabbed her wrist, she would know she had failed to deceive him. But he didn't! His hand deftly lifted the two glasses from the nightstand, while her fingers curled around the neck of the bottle.

He lifted the glasses expectantly, but instead of pouring, she shifted her grip until she held the bottle like a club and swung it as hard as she could at his head. Anger sparked his face and he hunched his shoulders in an attempt to duck the bottle. The result was a glancing blow that was not powerful enough to knock him senseless as she had hoped. It did succeed in toppling him off the bed onto the floor, however, and this gained her a few precious seconds of freedom. She jumped to her feet, but before she could dash out the bedroom door, two more salvos shook the house to its foundation. The shock waves sent her tumbling to the floor.

The hypnotist cried out in a mixture of anger at her assault and fear at the new explosions. He was also upended but swiftly rose to his feet on the other side of the bed. Marta's lungs felt as though they had collapsed from the power of the blasts, but she forced herself to stand. If she didn't escape now, she would soon be dead, either at the hands of the hypnotist or from the dynamite wired throughout the house. She regained her footing and raced out the door. Her mind whirled in a blur of indecision as she started down the hallway. The front door was blocked and she knew he would run her down before she could escape out the back. There was only one possibility. The moment she thought of it, she knew exactly where she was going and what she had to do. Her only fear was that the object she sought was no longer there.

A howl of frustration echoed down the hallway behind her, followed by the pounding of feet as he gave chase. Yellow, wavering arms of light from the approaching firestorm danced on the walls and cast ghostly shadows across her path. The shadows swayed seductively and lifted their arms to her. She ignored them and kept running. Another explosion boomed through the house, closer this time, close enough to make the whole house shudder and send a shower of fresh plaster cascading down on her head. Marta threw out her hands and braced herself against the wall for support as she ran.

The foyer was only steps away. She focused all of her energy on reaching it before the hypnotist overtook her. *Please be there*, she prayed as she made the final sprint for the table that stood in the entryway. She slid to a halt on the marble floor and yanked open the table drawer. There it was, nestled like a bird in a pile of papers and envelopes -- the revolver Henry had been holding earlier that day. She pulled it from the drawer and pointed it with shaking hands towards the hallway just as the hypnotist roared into the room. He came to an abrupt halt when he saw the weapon pointed at him. The light from the fire danced through the room. The acrid smell of detonated explosives gave the air a corrosive flavor. Their eyes locked, and for a moment the world stopped turning on its axis. Nothing existed in that space of time but the rage that boiled inside Marta and the furious look of betrayal on the hypnotist's face.

His eyes bore into hers as he attempted to force her into submission with his angry glare. But Marta's rage was stronger. She pulled the trigger just as a new explosion shattered the calm. The floor buckled, throwing off her aim. She had intended to shoot him in the heart, but the bullet struck his shoulder instead and spun him around. He cried out in pain and looked back at her with a hurt expression that caused her to hesitate. She blinked and aimed the gun again, but before she could pull the trigger, he darted from the room and disappeared down the hallway leading to the back yard. Marta ran after him, but by the time she reached the back of the house, he was already leaping over a hedge into the yard next door. Bushes quickly obscured her view.

She cried out in frustration and anger. Would she never be rid of that cursed man? He was about to escape but she knew he would return. She knew she would have to face him again. Then, a wondrous thing happened. The house next door disintegrated in a volcanic blast that engulfed everything in its path, including the neighboring backyard. A deafening roar nearly shattered Marta's eardrums. The percussion from the explosion knocked the wind from her lungs and sent her sprawling on her back. Her head struck the stone walkway, almost knocking her senseless.

She lay on the ground dazed and bleeding. The hypnotist had been buried by the blast, of that she was certain. The knowledge that he was finally dead filled her with satisfaction. But she feared she was about to share his fate. It was only a matter of seconds before Byron's house blew up and buried her just as the neighboring house had the hypnotist. *Run*, her brain shouted at her. *Get up and run!* But her legs were too wobbly to stand, her body too weak to respond. She felt as though she was back in Chinatown, unable to move under all those timbers.

A remarkable calm settled over her, the sort of calm she associated with the certainty of dying. She felt death's arms reaching out for her just as they had the first time she encountered the hypnotist. She lay there, her head spinning, her eyes half-blinded by the flash from the blast and tried to think what to do. Then, Byron's face drifted into the shimmering light and she realized if she died she would never see him again. What an unbearable idea! She couldn't just let herself die, not if it meant losing Byron. Marta shook her head; her will to live returned. She had to make an effort to save herself.

Somehow, she managed to raise her head and force herself into a sitting position. The world continued to spin violently around her, but she was determined not to let it stop her. She looked at the revolver in her hand. It was her only hope, but it was too heavy to lift with one hand. Slowly, she grasped it in both hands, raised it, and pulled the trigger. The gun's report echoed off the walls and pierced her bruised eardrums. The echo quickly died away. She waited a few seconds then fired again. And again. She thought she heard voices shouting from the street, but her hearing was too impaired for her to be certain. She fired once more then let the gun slip from her hands, too tired to hold it any longer.

Marta looked around at the marble fountain and neatly trimmed hedges and decided she had done all she could. Her mind was growing too numb to think anymore. *At least the world has stopped spinning,* she thought. That was something. She sat very still and waited for the blast to come.

Then voices called out to her as footsteps pounded the walkway behind her. Before she knew it, she was surrounded by men all trying to speak to her. Their voices were unintelligible, a babble of noise ringing in her ears. It didn't matter. The men's anxious faces told her she would be all right.

Then she saw the only face that *did* matter, Byron's, which beamed like a beacon among the rescuers. It was a thin face, not one that was particularly handsome, but one filled with warmth that caressed and fired her heart. His lips were moving, but his voice was as garbled as the others. She stared intently and saw he was calling her name. Her own face broadened into a weak smile and she raised her arms up to him.

Byron reached down, lifted her to her feet and pulled her into a fierce embrace. It felt so natural. She knew she would never let him go. She would hold onto him for an eternity.

AFTERWORD

The dynamite plan worked. The fire was stopped at Van Ness Avenue, although it did breech the firebreak for a few blocks between Washington Street and Pine. Wherever it crossed, it was met by frantic men who beat it back with blankets, towels, brooms and anything else they could put their hands on. It was the last stand of a band of heroes who would not give up. Exhausted, gaunt and covered in grime, they refused to yield to the snarling beast that roared at them again and again. At last, the fire lay down, as if it, too, was spent from the fury of the battle. There should have been cheers and huzzahs, but the men were too tired. Many collapsed where they had stood and gazed in wonder at their victory.

When the sun rose the next morning, three hundred thousand people were homeless. Hundreds of blocks had been obliterated and turned into a wilderness of ruins. Jack London, who witnessed it all, said the scene "is like the crater of a volcano, around which are camped tens of thousands of refugees." It was estimated that the death toll was more than three thousand people. Damage was estimated at five hundred million dollars.

Chinatown may have been destroyed, but the hand of China still reached across the Pacific Ocean in the form of the Empress Dowager, who gave an imperial decree to send one hundred thousand taels as a personal contribution to San Francisco's relief efforts. Theodore Roosevelt declined the offer.

One of the more controversial orders given the troops was to shoot looters on sight. There is no official record of how many were shot, but the mayor is purported to have warned the afternoon of the first day that "three men have already been shot down without mercy for looting." The troops began arriving less than two hours after the initial earthquake and took control of the burning city. Their disciplined presence undoubtedly helped maintain order and saved many institutions from looting.

There were many stories of bravery, but one of the most heroic involved saving the U.S. Mint. Had the building and cash reserves burned, it was feared the value of the dollar would be greatly affected. With water from a patio fountain, staffers and managers gamely fended off the fire as it roared down Market Street.

Photographs of the disastrous earthquake and its aftermath resonate as strongly today as they did a hundred years ago. It was the end of an era, a golden age that attracted European opera singers and cordon bleu chefs and was defined by elegant balls, oysters and champagne. It seemed it would never end.

But then the earth moved and nothing was ever the same again.

Bibliography

A novel is, by definition, fiction, but many times they are based on fact, and this is particularly true of historical fiction: in this case, the 1906 San Francisco earthquake and fire. I would like to acknowledge the following articles and books which provided details, facts, and insights that allowed my to describe the events that take place in The Hypnotist.

Timeline of the San Francisco Earthquake, April 18 - 23, 1906 (excerpted from Gladys Hansen's "Chronology of the Great Earthquake....")

Cosmopolitan Magazine, July 1906, "How the Army Worked to Save San Francisco" by Frederick Funston, Brig.-Gen. USA

San Francisco, Northern California Writer's Project, Hastings House

"San Francisco Yesterday, Today and Tomorrow," by The New San Francisco Magazine, May 1906

San Francisco History, "Employment of Women"

San Francisco History, "Cost of Living"

"The Story of an Eyewitness," by Jack London, Collier's, May 1906

AUTHOR'S BIOGRAPHY

Prior to becoming a novelist, Gordon Snider wrote magazine articles and two business books: Winning Marketing Strategies and How To Become A Killer Competitor. When he moved to California's Central Coast in 1999, he began writing fiction. His first novel, Sigourney's Quest, was published in February 2006, and his second, The Separatist, in August 2007. Both were published by Helm Publishing and have received enthusiastic reviews. The Hypnotist is his third novel.

Before becoming a full-time author, Gordon spent thirty years as an independent marketing consultant and taught at four universities, most recently at Cal Poly San Luis Obispo. His business background has given him considerable experience as a public speaker, and he has used that to his advantage in marketing his books. For his non-fiction Killer Competitor book, he gave seminars and lectures at conferences and conventions across the U.S. and Canada. For Sigourney's Quest, he has offered a very popular slide show and talk on Tibet to book clubs, reading groups and professional organizations, including Rotary and Kiwanis. Other marketing efforts include successful book signings at independent and chain book stores, where his "meet and greet" approach generates considerable interest and sales.

Travel was one of the industries in which he consulted. When he began doing travel photography for one of his business clients, he quickly found a following. During the 1980s and 1990s, he photographed for tour operators throughout Asia, South America, and the Himalayan countries of Tibet, Nepal, and Bhutan. It was his two photographic journeys into Tibet that inspired him to write his first novel, Sigourney's Quest.

Gordon has lived in California nearly his entire life. Home has ranged from Los Angeles to San Francisco, with stops in Santa Barbara and Pismo Beach. Currently, he and his wife enjoy walking the beaches and observing the migrating whales from their home in Pismo Beach, California. It is, he says, the perfect setting for creative writing. He speaks to book clubs and organizations.

CPSIA information can be obtained
at www.ICGtesting.com
Printed in the USA
FSHW020313160719
60053FS